Justin Jay Gladstone

&

Nitsuj Yaj Enotsdalg

ADVANCE PRAISE

A special thanks to the ninety people around the world who have read this book.

See my note on page 8 titled *A Letter from The Authors* to understand why this newest and final edition of *The Other Side I* is special and came to be.

Here are some praiseworthy things three of those ninety said about the previous edition:

Note: These reviews are shortened. You can find their full reviews on *Goodreads*.
[Search Nitsuj Yaj to find our books quickly]

Maria Ashen from **Denmark** ☆ ☆ ☆ ☆ ☆
He paints a wonderful 'Worture'. (Picture with words.)
He creates tension, excitement, and even a little danger.
He uses something I have never seen in books before, QR-codes. He paints a picture with words so wonderfully and then suddenly a code, you scan it and get a picture of what Jay imagined himself, so you can see if your imagination was close to his or completely far off. I think he did a great job showing me what he was seeing himself, instead of talking about it.

Lauren Knapper from the **UK**: ☆ ☆ ☆ ☆
I loved this book. The concept behind it was so original and so well thought out that it made the novel a fascinating read. The Other Side had so many interesting elements. It felt like it was a mystery thriller but mixed with a fantastic science fiction edge. The characters were compelling, and I was constantly intrigued to see their differences in the other universe. I can't wait to see what happens next as the story continues.

Lari from **Argentina**: ☆ ☆ ☆ ☆
This book really intrigued me! I'm usually quite picky when it comes to sci-fi because I don't always understand these kinds of worlds. At first, I didn't fully get the "rules" from the Other Side, but as the main character understood them, I started learning with him and I loved that! The plot was super original. I'd never read anything before about parallel worlds, but the idea of there being an "Other Me" out there, both excites me and also scares me.

Copyright © 2009
Illustrations copyright
All rights reserved etc.
Includes references and index.
Issued in print and electronic formats.
ISBN: 979-8-218-12127-3
Co-Story Writer: Justin Jay Gladstone
Story Director & Co-Story Writer: Nitsuj Yaj Enotsdalg
Front Book Cover Design by: Kodey Bell
Back Cover Design by: Danillo De Danno
Character Artwork: Nicole Searfoss, Vanessa Baldueza, Zoie Parshall, and Jewel Edwards

This is a work of fiction. Names, characters, businesses, places, events, and incidents are either the products of the author's imagination or used in a fictitious manner. Any resemblance to actual persons, living or dead, or actual events is purely coincidental.

All rights reserved. No part of this publication may be reproduced, distributed, or transmitted in any form or by any means, including photocopying, recording, or other electronic or mechanical methods, without the prior written permission of the publisher, except in the case of brief quotations embodied in critical reviews and certain other noncommercial uses permitted by copyright law.

For permission requests, please email the publisher:
TheOtherSidebooks@gmail.com

$\mathcal{Special\ Acknowledgements}$

To our Loving Shadow.
Thank you for the wonderful sixteen years. It was truly a blessing to give you the same happiness that you gave us. When we reunite, let's laugh at how much we used to fight for chair space while I wrote this book. Live on forever in these pages, this series, my heart, and memory.

My parents, my sister, my uncles, aunts, cousins, great uncles and aunts—thanks for believing in me.

To Maria, Davonte, Ariel, and Chris.
Thanks for inspiring me to be better and helping me avoid the practice of 'do as I say, not as I do.' This *Writing Coach* and *Marketing Advisor* program has taught me not only a lot about each of you, but a great deal about myself. I've studied and learned so much more because of my want to share my mistakes and success stories with you all. You've allowed me to humble myself and see that everyone learns differently.
Thank you all for never giving up on yourselves.
Here's to more success.

To my Patrons.
The artwork for my characters and so much more would not have been possible without your support. As of now, the Patreon program has been running for *two years*. All of you have made me feel a *little less* crazy for having listened to a voice in my mind, the one that asked if there was *another world inside the mirror*. You all helped me believe that I was right to act on that idea—to make a book series that has paved the path to the rest of my life.
Thanks to you, this dream is alive.

Lastly, thank you to those who said they'd stick around and *did*.

Books By:
Justin Jay & Nitsuj Yaj

The Other Side Series
The Other Side I
The Other Side II

A Letter from The Author(s):

You might be wondering, what is *The Other Side: Remastered?*
Well, it's all in the title. I came up with this book series when I was very young. At fourteen years old (2008), in fact. And when I did, it was initially supposed to be one book. I wrote as much as I could, from beginning to end.

And that story is what you hold in your hands now.

But of course, when writing this story, my many questions inspired new plot elements. Eventually, they spanned past the original *book* I had in mind. Suddenly there were ideas for a second book. A third. A fifth. To thirteen books that follow the same narrative.

While the narrative and the overall goal have remained the same, the execution of this story has changed.

When I started this, I had no money to my name and a low-paying job. I was literally at the bottom. But I was blessed by finding people and being found by those who would see this vision as a promise. And indeed, this story, by God's grace, has opened doors for me. I taught myself many things, such as graphic design, marketing, and other ways to improve my writing.

I made two successful fundraisers. One is ongoing, and I implore you to investigate it if you're interested in seeing this grow even more.

I published this story about *three* different times and learned a lot through each publication. The *first* time, I realized that one should not release a book without having beta readers. "One man is not a neighborhood." I was a fool not to work without others giving me their feedback. The *second* is to not release a story without being fully satisfied as the writer. The *third* is not moving forward with publication if the will is down to pressure. I'd get lots of questions, like *when is the book coming out?* I used to think people gave up on me because of the extra time I needed. Even that version was incomplete for many reasons. My impatience did not help.

But this time, things are different. When reading the last version of this book, people certainly enjoyed it, but it took them one to two months to read. That was no one's fault other than my own. I was young, a first-time author who was afraid of publishing. I was so worried about my book. I thought things like *Would this have enough description? Did I describe the environment well enough? How will I introduce this element to the story? What will my family think?* I remember going on Google and looking things up, like *How to write a scary* scene. You can see how this process would overwhelm someone. But the first thing I knew hurt my story was my learning process. I am a visual learner. Something I realized over the years as I enjoyed video games and movies alike. I also love looking at character artwork. Things from JRPGs to anime have inspired me a lot over the years.

I realized that I could not write my characters because of my lack of artwork of them. Some characters, you'll notice in the older versions, were written better than others. It was because they'd been drawn by an artist who lent me their talent and time at one point or another. But sadly, many of my other characters were not drawn. So, they were nothing but floating question marks in my head. They did not receive the same love until I was working on my second book.

But now, I own artwork for almost all sixty-plus characters in this series. And those numbers are growing by the month.

And on top of that, I had accrued (at the time) ninety ratings for The Other Side I, leaving it at a 3.75 average. That was pretty good, considering how flawed it was.

Thanks to all the opinions and reviews that went to my first book, The Other Side II was written with ease. All the flaws that my first book had were nonexistent in the second.

The biggest flaw? When they read the first book, everyone would say *Hey, I got your book! I'm* trying *to get through it.* The word *trying* stood out to me. And it only did because when people read my second book, they all said the opposite: *I can't put it down.* Not to mention, book II was always finished by readers in less than a month. I remember one person finished it in just a few days.

And then I realized.

The series had a problem.

If I were to move on and publish books in the future, how could I count on people just trusting that the series would get better after the first? What if the first was the book they gave up on?

And thus, I took a path that I thought I wouldn't take for, say, twenty years from now.

I decided to make this, *The Other Side: Remastered.*

So, you might be wondering, what's the difference?

FAQ:

Q: Will the story be different?

A: No. While my execution in *how* I tell this story will change, the continuity, the timeline, and the main events will be the same. You might notice that though the dialogue has been altered, many of the words used in the previous installments have remained the same.

Q: This book is a lot smaller. Is the page count different?

A: Yes! The original book was 608 pages. The reason why this is decreasing is because I removed a lot of scenes that I found pointless or just fluff that I wrote out of sheer nervousness.

Q: What exactly is being changed?

A: Pace. As I mentioned earlier, I was very afraid of disappointing my readers, so I wasn't sure of *how long* I should make certain scenes. As a result, some things dragged out way longer than they needed to be.

Q: Are you happy with this?

A: The word *happy* does not do the feeling justice. Believe it or not, this is *The Other Side* in its truest, most genuine form. Over the years, I have gone through a lot of struggles. Toxic relationships. Living situations. I was a slave to things that were not *God*. I was battling back and forth with addictions. Nothing extreme, just caffeine and whatnot. And so, the story was always very inconsistent because *I* was inconsistent. I recall a person once reading the books and stating that *it felt like multiple people wrote this book*. I wholeheartedly agree.

I had a lot of original ideas that I wanted in here that I scrapped because I was afraid they wouldn't be well received. Now that my current self has rejoined with my past self, they have all come to be this completed version. I love this version as much as I do the future books.

You'll notice that this book may have more expansive points to unanswered questions. You may notice that characters who were put off to the side have good reason to receive more page time here. There's so much to see. I hope you enjoy this. Thank you for your support.

Every other version of this book was what Satan took from me, and this is Jesus' gift back.

This would not be possible without our Lord and Savior, Jesus Christ. Thank you for anointing me to remaster not only my life but also this precious story.

† ᄃ:lʗ noiƚɒlɘvɘЯ †

TRIGGER WARNING:

This book will include readings and discussion around topics that may be sensitive to some readers such as: mental disorders, sexual assault, substance abuse and addiction, domestic violence, suicide, imprisonment, and physical violence.

I acknowledge that this content may be difficult to read. I also encourage you to care for your safety and well-being. Please also note that I did not write about these things as an outsider. I have plenty of personal experience. 'Experience with what?' you ask.

There's only one way to find out.

KEEP IN TOUCH WITH THE PROJECT(S)!

When you finish this story, I would love nothing more than to hear what you've thought.

Your thoughts (good or bad) will only make the series stronger. When you finish *The Other Side*, please be sure to leave us a rating and review!

(Scan this code to be brought to our Goodreads page)

RATE THE OTHER SIDE

RATE US ON AMAZON

YOU CAN ALSO SUPPORT US ON PATREON!

WHAT IS PATREON?

Patreon is a platform where people can help fund creators on a monthly or yearly basis. By making a pledge, they contribute to the creator and receive things in return!

GOALS OF *THE OTHER SIDE'S* PATREON:

1. Commission talented artists for character and background art

2. Send books to readers around the world

3. Fund creative subscription services such as Adobe, our website, and other creative platforms

4. Provide creative services (artwork & social media graphics) to Patrons in the *Writing Coach* program

AS A PATRON, YOU WILL RECEIVE:

- Acknowledgement in our Patreon posts and our published books

- Physical rewards such as: a *The Other Side* poster, t-shirts and long-sleeve shirts, hoodies, and more!

WHAT'S THIS 'CREATIVE COACHING' PROGRAM?

I offer full- and part-time writing services for individuals working on stories with hopes of publishing them. I also make graphics for advertisements, offer marketing advice, create websites, and offer consultation calls. In addition, members of the program are put into a group chat where they can collaborate and support one another.

NO AMOUNT IS TOO SMALL!
CONSIDER BECOMING A $1 PATRON FOR *THE OTHER SIDE* TODAY!

☾ TABLE OF CONTENTS ☽

"Learn how to see.

Realize that everything connects to everything else."

-Leonardo da Vinci

".esle gnihtyreve ot stcennoc gnihtyreve taht ezilaeR

.ees ot woh nraeL"

-Noelodra Ad Acniv

CRUCIAL KEYS (I)

THERE WILL BE MOMENTS WHERE YOU SEE TEXT THAT MAY SEEM ...ƎLᗡᗡBᗡƎ˥Nυ

ONLY BY HOLDING THIS BOOK TO A MIRROR, WILL YOU DECIPHER THE WORDS OF WONDER. TRY IT ON THE PAGE PRIOR TO THIS ONE...

CRUCIAL KEYS (II)

THIS BOOK FEATURES *QR CODES*! THROUGHOUT YOUR READ OF *THE OTHER SIDE*, YOU'LL COME ACROSS SEVERAL SQUARE IMAGES LIKE THE ONE SHOWN ON THE NEXT PAGE.

SCAN THE QR CODE WITH YOUR SMARTPHONE AND SEE THROUGH THE CHARACTER'S EYES.

IPHONE USERS: OPEN YOUR CAMERA AND AIM TOWARD THE PIXELATED SQUARE. A LINK WILL APPEAR AT THE TOP OF YOUR SCREEN.

ANDROID USERS: YOU MUST FIRST DOWNLOAD A QR CODE APP, THEN YOU'LL BE FREE TO SCAN.

CRUCIAL KEYS (III)

THROUGHOUT THIS READ, YOU WILL NOTICE THAT WHEN CHARACTERS ARE INTRODUCED, THEY WILL HAVE A QR CODE NEXT TO THEM.

I HAVE ORGANIZED EACH OF THE CODES IN A WAY WHERE IT SHOULDN'T INTERRUPT YOUR READING. I HAVE ALSO SET THEM UP SO THAT THEY WON'T CONTAIN SPOILERS.

IN MOMENTS WHERE THERE ARE MORE THAN FIVE CHARACTERS, I HAVE COMPILED EACH OF THEM INTO ONE BIG CODE SO THAT YOU WON'T HAVE TO SCAN OVER AND OVER. THE ONLY EXCEPTIONS ARE TO NEW CHARACTERS WHO ENTER A ROOM.

I ENCOURAGE YOU TO BOOKMARK EACH CODE SO THAT YOU CAN REMEMBER THEM LATER.

HAVE FUN!

CRUCIAL KEYS (IV)

THESE SYMBOLS WILL REPRESENT THE *PROGRESSION* OF TIME THROUGHOUT THE STORY.

THESE SYMBOLS WILL REPRESENT THE *REGRESSION* OF TIME THROUGHOUT THE STORY.

FORGOTTEN

NAMES & FACES

Genesis 1:3

☾ ☾ ☾

December 9, 2009 (Wednesday)
The Earthshine Facility ∧ Therapist's Office
7:10 a.m.

"Why must we go through this every single time you come here, Allie? I'm not going to hurt you. Not *physically,* at least. All I need you to do is tell me about that boy." This is said by a brown-skinned therapist in a white button-up t-shirt tucked into a purple business skirt. As for what her face looks like, Allie looks away to prevent more of her fear from rising. From Allie's peripheral vision, she can feel cold brown eyes covered in eyeshadow and wrinkles leering at her.

"*Allie Reincath,*" Dr. Allure Igor the therapist says firmly, glaring at the teenage girl in front of her with a maroon shirt and shoulder-length hair, "tell me about. Leon. Granttley—"

"—PLEASE DON'T SAY HIS NAME!" Allie cries out, covering her eyes, trembling.

"Ah. I must've touched a soft spot," Allure says with a grin. "You'd think *you* were a patient here for your PTSD. In which case, it can be arranged if you don't start talking…" Allure lets out a little cackle and flips the page on her clipboard.

2

Tears well up in Allie's eyes, and to this, Allure adds, "Allie dearest. I know he hurt you. I know what he did to you was horrible. What I need to know from you is whether or not he's accepted what he's done to you…"

"You know he hasn't. Otherwise, I wouldn't be here today."

"You will not have an attitude with me!" Allure blares as Allie looks down to the low carpet and away to the bookshelf on her right. "Hmph," Allure utters, "as of today, Leon is a Bishop. And he will not become a Knight so long as you, his friends, and family say he isn't meant to leave this rank. You're the last of the bunch I needed to speak with."

"I don't think he should graduate."

"And why is that?"

"Because if you asked if whether or not he…*molested me*, he wouldn't admit it. He'll again say it wasn't him or that *some voice* in his mind took over. He *really* thinks it's someone else. And until he can admit it, he shouldn't become a Knight. He should stay in this facility *forever*."

"How fortunate for Leon, then."

"*Fortunate?*" Allie questions.

"Yes. What I forgot to tell you, Allie, is that regardless of how many of the patient's friends say that he's not ready to graduate, it's the patient's word against all of yours."

"What?" Allie blurts, "But you just said—h—how does that make any sense?"

"Because so long as none of you see what's in his mind, none of you would *ever* say he's ready to graduate. Doesn't it make more sense to leave this up to us professionals?"

"Are *we all* suddenly crazy then? What's the point in even asking us?"

"That is none of your concern, Allie," Allure replies, smirking.

"What? Why bring me here then—this doesn't make any—" Allure interrupts Allie by handing over a necklace with a mirror on the front. "What's—" Allie asks.

"—You are to give this to *him* before December eleventh, do you understand?"

"You want *me* to give something to him? Dr. Igor, this isn't right. I haven't even recovered—"

"—The best type of therapy, Allie, is exposure therapy. Believe me, I would know."

To these words, Allie's face turns red. She is trembling from anger. She tries snatching the necklace from Allure who draws her hand away in time.

"Take it respectfully, Ms. Reincath."

Allie reaches out with a shaking hand, takes the necklace slowly, and asks in a quivering tone, "Can I please go?"

"Absolutely. You've fulfilled your role today."

Allie bursts outside through Allure Igor's door, covering her face as best as she can while she runs to the bathroom.

Allure stands and shakes her head, shutting her door, then looks at her clipboard. "Well, Leon, you and five others are one step closer to being a Knight…" She coos while glowering down at the picture of the brown-skinned boy on her clipboard.

SCAN TO SEE LEON

THE VOICE
IN MY MIND

Dear Aron and Nora (I)

If you are reading this, then chances are my other *and I are long gone. However, that does not mean everything we've gone through will go to waste.*

Yes, you two have read the previous chapter correctly.

What you just read between Allure and Allie is the seed of this series. Everything going forward from hereon in is the water. You'll see exactly **what** *brought* Earth *and* Heart *to their final days.*

The one writing this letter is the same person who Allure and Allie spoke so negatively of.

I am Leon J. Granttley.

With all my writing, you will see and listen to my story as I watch it unfold once again...

I can only pray you two will become the burgeoning force that saves the universe. Use what you learn throughout these books to create your destiny for all of time and space.

The lies first came from the horrible therapists in that Earthshine Facility. They diagnosed me with dissociative identity disorder. DID for short. In your time, they probably still call it split personality.

Don't worry, it's nothing to be afraid of. I have control of it now. But back then...It ran me and my life. On occasion I would switch into another person's identity—becoming someone else.

This disorder was a lot like sleepwalking. My body would be present for events that my mind could not recall. And as a result, it got me into a lot of trouble.

*Society's solution to my disorder was to force me into The Earthshine Facility. There were three ranks in this institution: **Pawns**, **Bishops**, and **Knights**; Knights being the highest.*

Unfortunately for me, there were many things that happened that I don't recall being a part of. Everyone who knew me would say otherwise. They'd say I lost my mind simply for not going with their narrative. And they were right.

But there was one thing back then that we had all wondered: What would it take to become a Knight? What did becoming a Knight mean? Would becoming a Knight mean that I could finally know the truth about this voice in my mind?

To my dismay, no one could tell me the answers to any of those questions. It was something I needed to find out for myself... it was the first of many of our mistakes to come.

Now. Come and witness the start of this tragedy with me.

From what I can see now, my story starts above the skies of a mountainous area filled with snow. A city is here. A suburban area is here. Ah yes. Of course. This is the city of Aurorae County, located in the state of Colorado. I assume that the year is 2009...

It's almost just as I remembered... This is an area flourishing with new developments... one such as the Earthshine Facility. The place that's said to reflect the sun's light onto the dim faces of its doomed people.

Despite the sun's bright light, I see a blight ruling over it. A ruler of the airs. A ruler of the darkness that shall shine above this place...

I'm watching now as crows fly over the city of Aurorae. Many are perched atop buildings, street posts, cars, and houses. There isn't a place where these crows are not. I now see black feathers falling all around this place. Almost like they're leaving a trail. And where does this trail lead back to? I wonder.

Hmm. No surprise. It all points back to the Earthshine Facility.

What is to be wrong with this city, this world, the universe, begins in this section of Aurorae. It is here that the supposed shine *within the Earthshine Facility would blind the world.*

This is the source of everything. I've been told many times by my therapist, Stefano Giro, that in time, *everything would make sense. I never believed him.*

Even now, as I watch this again, I'm still *learning. These crows fly onto the roof of a two-story, three-bedroom house. They peck at the window. Some peck at one another as a few ominous black vans drive by outside.*

Long ago, Stefano, my old therapist, asked me this time and time again.

"Do you regret having split personality disorder?"

When he asked this, a voice in my mind would laugh.

—Leon J. Granttley

☾　　☾　　☾

December 10, 2009 (Thursday)

Colorado ∧ Aurorae

Leon's Residence

6:35 a.m.

It is dark out as it is an early winter morning.

Crows caw outside Leon's frosted window. But none of their sounds awaken him. No. Leon has an even *better* alarm clock.

You're late, The Voice in Leon's mind says, *by five minutes. You don't want to miss your bus again, do you?*

Leon groggily opens his eyes while lying on his bed. He angrily stares at the white ceiling above him. This isn't the first time his *alarm clock* has awoken him, and with *his* mind, it certainly won't be the last. He brushes his teeth, places his school uniform on, blue cardigan over a simple white button-up with khaki dress pants and black dress shoes, and then…glances into his bathroom mirror. He swears that for a second, the reflection smirks at him. He shakes his head and then walks away.

Tap. Tap. Tap.

"Leon?" His sister, Amy, calls from outside the bathroom door, "Are you finished staring at yourself?"

"I'm not staring at myself. I'm just leaving," he lies, swinging open the door. The Voice in Leon's mind is deep and gruff. When it speaks, it echoes. It chuckles at his lie as he brushes past Amy, who has a hanger in hand with a purple hoodie and silver pants.

9

As Leon returns to his bedroom to retrieve his satchel, Amy screams. Leon opens the bathroom door as quickly as he can, and Amy says, "I thought," she chuckles nervously, "I thought you were playing a prank on me."

"Huh?"

"I saw your face in the mirror," she pants, catching her breath. "I just… For a second, I thought you were in the bathroom with me."

Leon shakes his head. "I guess the Earthshine Facility could use more mental patients," he says, lightly chuckling and shutting the door as Amy sarcastically says, *ha-ha.*

Many of Leon's friends say that he and Amy resemble one another. She has his face, certainly, but much longer hair running past her shoulders. She's best known for having a bright smile on her face.

Leon's parents' door is just across from his in the hallway. His father, Nero, leaves for work around three each morning. So, no snoring from him at this time unless it was the weekend. His mother, Silvia, on the other hand, is asleep to white noise.

SCAN TO SEE AMY

Hurry, Leon, The Voice in his mind says, *the bus will be out there any second.*

Leon rolls his eyes and glances out the window. *Should be fine.* He says in thought, "I think I can get myself something quick to—

And then suddenly, the roar of a school bus alarms Leon. He glances outside with wide eyes and charges out onto the driveway for it—but the bus leaves him behind. It barely gave him any time now.

Looks like you're walking to school again, The Voice says.

Leon sighs and walks up the sidewalk as The Voice laughs at him. Across the street are four familiar faces in the same school uniform. Jason, a tanned boy in red with a short buzz cut, Jacaline, a girl with white skin and blonde hair, and Deen, a boy with pale skin and long black hair covering his eyes. There is one other girl there—one who makes Leon not even want to look over in their direction. Allie Reincath. A girl whose default expression is anger.

Why don't you go walk with them? The Voice asks.

You know why, Leon thinks in response to The Voice.

I know. I just like remembering why. She hates you for what you did, you know.

Yes. I know.

Only one of these four people can call Leon his real friend. That person is Jason. As for Jacaline and Deen, they detest Leon for what he did to Allie two years ago. Deen enjoys having Leon to pick on, and Jacaline enjoys pitying him. Leon hears footsteps approaching and glances over to see that Jason, the boy with the buzz cut, is crossing the street over to him.

"Hey, buddy," Jason says, approaching Leon while Deen and Jacaline are glaring from the far distance. Allie continues facing forward, grumbling to herself.

"Hey," Leon says flatly.

"You looked like you were in your head just now. Figured I'd come by."

Leon chuckles. "I'd be lying if I said I wasn't. You guys missed the bus too?"

"Yeah." He then whispers, *"Allie got a gift for you and was trying to get us to give it to you. Lotta back and forth between us."*

"What? *She* got *me* a gift?"

"Well. It's something from the facility. But for some reason, they were making her do it. I don't get it either."

Leon can't help it, but he smiles while Jason responds firmly, "I wouldn't get too excited. She's not thinking about talking to you anytime soon, dude. After all, you still won't admit to what you did."

"Because I know I didn't do it, Jason," Leon snaps.

You sure you didn't? The Voice in Leon's mind asks. *Everyone else seems to think so.*

"Shut up!" Leon blurts while Jason stares at Leon curiously. Jacaline and Deen across the street look over at Leon. Allie does too, but only for a second.

"No," Leon says, shaking his head. "I'm sorry, I was—"

"—Responding to The Voice. I know," Jason says solemnly.

See what you did? Leon thinks angrily.

Jason clears his throat. "Mind if I ask a question?"

"Sure."

"Allie was given that gift because she was told you were graduating…that you'd be becoming a Knight soon. But. As your friend, I'm not sure if you're ready…especially after seeing that outburst."

Leon stops walking and says, "Jason, I'm getting out of that facility one way or another. I'm becoming a Knight."

"But how will you if you don't accept what you did? How can you if you're still arguing with that voice?"

12

Leon swallows. "Everyone in the facility says I should accept The Voice. But everyone on the outside says to ignore it. I have to accept that it's real and living...otherwise... I'll never move on. Somehow, they also want me to accept what I did to Allie. And I can lie to everyone but myself. I know I didn't do anything. The Voice says I did, but I remember where I was that day."Leon stares at Jason and adds, "And as far as I know, I won't graduate if I don't lie to them. If I leave that stupid facility...it'll be the best birthday gift that I can get."

"Your therapists are supposed to help you. I don't think you should *want* to leave so soon."

Leon rolls his eyes. "Jason—*you're* not the therapist in charge, okay? They put me through a lot. I'm ready for this to be done with."

Jason places his hands in his pockets. "...You're right. I'm sorry. I know it's been rough. I remember when you were a Pawn...they locked you away for a few months. We all thought you were never coming back. And then when you did come back, it was like you hadn't eaten in months."

Leon shakes his head. "I don't want to think back to those times."

I do, The Voice in Leon's mind thinks.

Mind your business, devil.

"Anyway, Leon," Jason adds, placing his hand on Leon's shoulder as the two of them stop walking, "all I'm saying is...just think about what everyone's been telling you. You have a criminal record now. Your parents know, our school knows, it's just time you accept it. I don't think you'd deserve that graduation any other way."

Leon brushes Jason's hand off and retorts by walking away.

He can hear Jason say from afar, "It's not just for *you*, Leon!"

"Thanks, but no thanks. I'll see you in school," Leon says, walking forward, leaving Jason behind who rushes back across the street to Jacaline, Deen, and Allie.

MARKS OF
THE CHOSEN

☾ ☾ ☾

December 10, 2009 (Thursday)

Colorado /\ Aurorae

Maleon High School

7:45 a.m.

The first bell rings just as Leon enters the school. He's a bit late for his first class. To his sides are the narrow green lockers that he is used to being pressed against by his bullies. Thankfully for him, none of his three bullies are anywhere to be found.

Leon creeps through the hallway, passing a boy with brown skin and brown curly hair. The curly-haired boy is shyly watching a tall white-skinned girl who is at her locker and is wearing a blue scarf with a strange symbol. Suddenly the boy with curly hair is shoved against some green lockers. He rubs his aching head as a tall, wide football player charges up to him, lifting him in the air by his collar, saying, "Well. If it ain't *Miles Lee*."

This bully is tall with dark brown skin, has short hair, and is wearing the same school uniform but with a blue cardigan. School rules declare that one must wear these cardigans with each of the buttons fastened. This bully that just shoved Miles into the locker, however, doesn't care for this rule. Neither do his two assailants.

SCAN FOR THE BULLIES

"What do you want...Etay?" strains Miles, the boy with curly hair.

"Nothing. Just wanted to say hello. Heard you were graduating tomorrow."

"Maybe?" Miles replies. "I don't know for sure!"

"You're right. Yer too damn crazy to figure that out, aren't you?"

Leon sees this and creeps away from this interaction, but a boy with a white winter hat and indigo hair tightly grabs his arm. This boy is much taller than Leon. He's shorter than Etay and stands at least 5'9. Etay stands firmly at 6'4, while Leon is merely 5'5.

"Ha. Hey Etay. Look who just tried to sneak by!" says Hades, the boy with baggy khakis, while Leon struggles to break free.

"Get off of me!"

"Hold on to you? Absolutely…" A short girl with choppy red hair snickers, holding onto Leon's other arm tightly with both of hers. She has a red electric guitar strapped to her back.

"Guys!" Leon cries out, "I'm late for English class!"

Etay hears Leon's shout and drops Miles back onto his feet, who backs away, cowers, and runs far off into the hallway. The tall girl that Miles was watching also scurries off.

"Well, well, well," Etay says, "if it ain't my second favorite Earthshine patient. Leon Granny."

"Who's the first?" Hades asks in his slow-speaking voice.

"The curly-haired freak that just ran away," Etay says flatly.

Leon glowers up toward Etay who punches him straight in the gut and then says, "That's one."

Leon wishes he could rub his stomach to ease his pain, but with Alecia and Hades tightly holding onto his arms, he cannot help his urges.

"One for…what…" Leon utters, sweat forming on his face.

"Tomorrow's your birthday, ain't it?" Etay says. "You're turning seventeen."

Alecia giggles. "And rumor has it, you're *also* graduating tomorrow."

Hades chimes in, "And that means…seventeen plus seventeen punches…"

Etay shakes his head. "Yes, Hades, I'm glad you can still add. So, thirty-four in total. You'll get your first seventeen now and the other seventeen later."

Leon looks down to the ground, accepting his fate. He tightens his stomach as best as he can, but what he doesn't expect is Etay to punch him first in the face, then kick his shin to catch him off guard. Leon cries out as a few teachers walking in the hallway chuckle in the distance.

Jason, Allie, Jacaline, and Deen also pass by as this occurs. Leon is more focused on his pain than on his *friends*.

The celebratory punches have been delivered. Leon is released by his two captors and falls onto his knees.

"Good," Etay says, dusting his fists and clothes off. "Happy pre-graduation, Granny."

"It's…Granttley… My last name is Granttley. Not. *Granny*…"

"Is that backtalk I hear?" Alecia asks with a devious smirk.

The three bullies spit on him and shove him into a set of lockers before they leave him behind. Leon rushes for the bathroom as quickly as he can to see his face. He quickly washes their saliva off his arms and neck. Thankfully, no serious bruises are on his face. But his stomach is as sore as can be. And to think. Seventeen more punches are on the way? Leon fixes his wrinkly clothes and charges straight for his English class. The day passes by swiftly as he segues through each of these classes.

☾ ☾ ☾

The sixth bell rings. Each of the students from grades eight to twelve is switching into their next class, with a four-minute window in between. Leon infuses with a tsunami of students who flood the hallway. Few are meeting with their peers and lockers, and some go directly to class. Leon tries to blend in with the students as best as possible, but Etay, Hades, and Alecia spot him like a sore thumb. Could they have found Leon so quickly because of the symbol of the Bishop on his cardigan and white button-up shirt? Miles has one too.

Etay drifts over to Leon. Hades and Alecia walk next to their leader. Etay says, "Leon Granny. I was worried I wouldn't find you again. Look. I won't be here for the next few weeks. The football team's got a league-off in a few states starting tomorrow, so I won't be around to give you your gift."

Leon swallows and speedily walks ahead. Etay doesn't give up the chase. Etay, Hades, and Alecia step straight in front of Leon, and the crowd moves around the four.

"I'm also in need of some more lunch money," Etay adds. "I hear they're serving pizza. And I want extra."

"I don't have any lunch money for you," Leon says, walking forward. "My next class is in a couple of minutes—"

Etay steps on the tip of Leon's dress shoe, ceasing his momentum, "Then you'll pay me now with the remaining punches I owe ya." Etay snatches Leon's satchel strap from his shoulder and drops it on the ground. This time, however, Etay's friends join in the ambush. Etay opens his locker, shoves Leon inside, and the three cut loose on him once again.

19

What Etay didn't tell Leon was that they *each* would give him seventeen punches. Etay draws back, glances around, and sees a hall monitor walking by. Etay glowers at the bald man and whispers, "*Guys. We got someone comin'. We gotta bounce.*"

Etay and his two friends disperse. Etay, in the distance, shouts, "Next time, bring your *other half* out to play! Hades says he's got witty remarks!"

Leon struggles to get out of the locker and sees a bald monitor with glasses staring him down with pity.

"Let me guess," the hall monitor says, "were you telling them what the voice in your head was saying again?"

"No?" Leon says with confusion, "Did you not just see what they did to me?"

"I think you might've imagined it. I'm sure it wasn't unprovoked. Because I do seem to recall you saying you'd make them suffer, before."

"That time, it wasn't me," Leon says, fully slipping out of the locker, "I...just said what I heard in my head."

"Right...do I need to contact your facility about this voice again? I just had Miles Lee taken away for his sudden outburst."

"No."

"Good. Then get to class. You have less than thirty seconds." Leon turns to run, but the monitor grabs his arm.

"What're you doing?" Leon shouts, struggling to break away from the man's firm grip.

"Twenty-five...twenty...think you can make it in less than eighteen seconds?" The bald monitor releases Leon's arm, leaving him to push forward and fall on the ground.

Leon frustratingly sighs, grabs his dusty satchel, and makes his way to the stairwell. He walks up the stairs.

You should have hit him and those bullies, The Voice in Leon's mind jeers.

You know what'd happen if I did. Then it's back to medication and basically living at the facility.

I'd take that over whatever the hell you went through just now.

Like you'd have a choice. Leon replies back in thought.

The Voice ends this mental conversation with a cackle.

Leon exits the stairwell, and his history class is merely a couple of doors away. Of all his classes, Leon hates this one the most. This is the only teacher that paid Leon any mind, and of course, with negative attention. He'd rather be ignored. Mr. Nert is his teacher, a fifty-year-old man balding from the back and front of his head. Leon pushes the creaking wooden door open, just to get his satchel caught in the door.

This would happen now, of all *times,* Leon thinks to himself as he yanks the black bag into the room.

"Ah. And as usual, we have our late Earthshine Facility patient. Your seat is reserved for you in the back," Mr. Nert says, pointing to an isolated chair all the way in the back of the room.

"Just a chair? Where's the table?" Leon asks, looking at the students with chairs attached to their small desks.

"We're out of them. Plus, you'll fall asleep with one anyway."

The students snicker at this.

Mr. Nert returns to his domain in the back of his room, meeting with his favorite snack: macadamia nuts. As he leans onto the back of his chair, he announces, "Moving forward, class—continue your read-through of *Adolf Hitler* so that we can discuss him and his story at the end of class. Afterwards, we'll focus on the dehumanization of people that came from the *Nazis*... Then during Christmas break, you'll have to write an eight-page report on *World War Two*." The students groan at this.

"I'm impressed," Mr. Nert says, glancing at Leon who's nodding in and out, even without the table to lean on, "and what kept you up at night this time? That little voice in your head?"

Leon releases a sigh as now The Voice in his mind says, *I'm sure you'd rather talk to me than him. So, I'll bother you some more.*

Leon releases a loud sigh before zoning out into yet another mental argument.

December 10, 2009 (Thursday)

Colorado /\ Aurorae

Maleon High School /\ The Main Hallway

11:36 a.m.

The seventh bell rings, dismissing everyone. The students in the classroom simultaneously rise from their blue plastic chairs. Leon waits until they all walk out so that he can avoid eye contact with them. Someone taps him on the back of his left shoulder.

"Hey, bud."

Leon faces the sound of Jason's friendly voice.

Jason asks, "How's today going for you? Anything from The Voice?"

"There's always something from him."

"You mean *it*," Jason replies coolly.

"Sure," Leon adds an eye roll.

Jason looks at Leon's torn blue cardigan, his wrinkled shirt, and says, "I'm guessing you ran into Etay today."

"What tipped you off?" Leon snaps, remembering that his friends watched and walked away.

"Sorry. I guess you're not in the talking mood."

Leon heavily sighs. "No, I'm sorry. I'm just having a bad day. Feels like the bullies have gotten even worse."

Jason adjusts his book bag. "Etay tends to get like this before graduations. It's not just you. And I don't mean that to minimize your pain."

"I know you don't."

Jason puts his hands in his pockets. "I guess it really doesn't help since the school makes you wear that symbol on your clothes."

"Nope. Just makes us easier to spot. By Everyone."

"I used to think he only picked on guys. But I saw him pick on another Earthshine patient earlier. That new girl—*Ombretta.*"

"Whoops. I got nosy," Deen says, slamming his locker and flipping his hair. He pushes Leon to the side and stands in his place while Leon veers off to his left

Deen says, "So, what am I hearing about this new girl?"

Jason shakes his head. "I was talking about how she was bullied by Etay."

"Oh," Deen says, flipping his hair again, "the chick who got home-schooled. Yeah, she's cute. But too tall for me."

"Not what we were talking about," Jason replies.

"Too weird for me either way," Deen chortles. "She's always staring at people. Surprised that they haven't taken her away yet." Deen elbows Leon. "Be careful. Your DID disorder's gonna get you in trouble again!"

"Stop it, Deen," Jason replies angrily.

What took him so long to defend you? I was beginning to worry you didn't have any friends... The Voice in Leon's mind jeers as Leon replies with a silent but annoyed expression.

Leon doesn't make eye contact with either of the two. They continue treading down the hallway with one another to the lunchroom.

The three along with of hundreds of other students arrive in the giant lunchroom. Jason sighs, staring at the sign ahead of him which says *free or reduced lunch*, a program designed for those who can't afford a meal, despite him having two jobs at sixteen years old.

Jason takes his place in line, embarrassed, and plays with his hands. Meanwhile Deen stands in the normal line despite having to return home to a trailer park. Outside of Deen's school uniform, one would glance at his wardrobe and think that he could afford luxurious outfits.

Leon takes a seat at their usual circular table. Across from him are Allie and Jacaline who both refuse to acknowledge him. Leon sets his satchel on the table then places his head atop it as if it were a pillow. While shutting his eyes, he slowly takes deep breaths to slow his heart rate. He gently drifts into a noise filled slumber both inside and outside his head.

From afar, he hears Allie's soothingly soft voice. It brings him shivers and butterflies. Being in Allie's presence is bittersweet. She is only at the table by her friends' pleading. Sitting by Leon is a trigger to her buried memories. She sneaks a few glares in Leon's direction.

Leon dozes off into darkness.

Something from his right-side crashes onto the table. Jason and Deen arrive to the table. Deen slams his fist in front of Leon's head. Leon's eyes crack open. In anger, Leon stomps his foot on the ground then lazily lifts his head upward.

"Mornin', princess," Deen grins toward Leon while he stuffs his face with a slice of pepperoni pizza. Leon turns his face away and returns to darkness.

"What, can't afford a slice of pizza?" Deen says while taking a bite.

Jason takes offense to this joke and shouts, "Knock it off, Deen! You were just complaining about your mom giving you chump change, so I don't wanna hear it."

With a mouthful of his pizza, Deen retaliates, "That's what I've got little ol' Leon here for. Am I right, sleepyhead?"

"Leave me alone, Deen. I'm not in the mood today," Leon says firmly. Jason smiles at this. Leon doesn't normally stand up for himself.

"Or what?"

Leon turns his head, and Jason's proud smile turns into a frown.

The Voice in Leon's mind whispers, *I suppose you have friends after all. You need all that you can get. Hold onto them, Leon.*

Allie, who is eavesdropping, fails in hiding her smirk from Deen's direction. From afar, Etay and his two partners in crime have their rectangular table filled with a mix of football players, soccer players, and cheerleaders. Etay is bragging about how he will score five touchdowns for tomorrow's game and how he gave Leon thirty-four punches. Some of the listeners laugh, one snorts milk out from their nose, and others give a menacing scowl toward Leon, who is completely unaware of their malevolent presence.

Allie continues her conversation with Jacaline.

Ugh. I give up. There's no way I can sleep through this noise, Leon thinks.

He opens his eyes to see that Jason is sliding over a slice of pizza. "Take mine. It's on the house."

Leon cracks a smile and grabs the warm slice to delve right in. "Thanks…" Leon intones, accidentally looking at Allie who is staring at him. She quickly faces Jacaline after the awkward gawk. Leon's head turns to the right of the floor beside him.

Jacaline waves her hands in front of Allie. "Hello?"

"Hmm? Wha?" Allie says, snapping back into focus.

Jacaline says, "I answered your question, but you never responded."

"Sorry. I was…distracted… Anyway, how did it go?"

"Oh. Well, it was awful. Jason and Deen want *you* to give him the gift," Jacaline says with a sigh.

"Me?" Allie glares at Jason and Deen who nervously wave back to her.

Allie leans closer to Jacaline and harshly whispers, *"They can't do me one favor? They seriously want* me *to give Leon that stupid amulet? After what he did?"*

"I know!" And then Jacaline whispers, *"That's what I was telling them. But you know Deen...he said you probably made the whole thing up and that you were asking for it."*

Allie rolls her eyes; her way of saying, *of course he did.*

Jacaline continues whispering, *"And then Jason said that there's probably a reason why they gave you the stupid thing."*

Allie glances down at her tuna salad. *"He's lucky he's not even in jail. I seriously can't believe those two are pushing it back onto me."*

"Right? It was tough enough just getting you to sit with us again."

"Well. You guys are all he has," Allie says coolly.

Jacaline rears her head and brushes her hair. "Please don't lump me in with those two. Let alone Deen. Leon's lucky to have *anyone* to sit near." Jacaline glances at Leon then leans even closer to Allie to whisper, *"It's almost like they're trying to get you to relive your trauma."*

Allie replies, "Or preserve it. Anyway..." She adjusts her collar then reaches into her tote bag to feel for the pendant that is cold to the touch. The silver pendant is roughly the size of her palm. She angrily stares into the mirror then opens it, revealing two halves. An analog clock is on the left, and on the right half are nine moon phases. A compass rose sits in the center of the displayed moons.

"Whoa," Jacaline's eyes pop. *"Maybe you shouldn't give him that. He'll probably think you like him again."*

"Whatever," Allie says loudly. "If he owned up to it, I might've forgiven him." Allie looks down toward the sleeping boy. "But he had the nerve to act like a tough guy during it all."

"This is what they all do, Allie. And then when we report it, we get no justice. They treat us like we're crazy... Hmm. Maybe you can push back and make someone else do it?"

"Yeah, well Dr. Igor—"

Leon hears the name *Igor,* and paranoia consumes him. He lifts his head from the table with disoriented vision. A tray full of food hurtles toward him, breaking his focus. Unfortunately for the culprit, the tray misses his head. It lands face down near Leon's feet with potato residue pouring off the sides. The clatter of the tray renders the noisy cafeteria into silence.

All eyes are on Leon, who swiftly raises from his chair and yells, "ARGH! I'VE HAD IT!"

Leon looks left toward Etay's section of the cafeteria. He sees his bullies are each glaring, but all still have their trays of food in front of them. Leon looks around to see that not one person has a missing tray. So where did it come from?

Leon's words of frustration echo throughout the cafeteria. "What do you all want from me?" No one owning up to the toss frustrates Leon. He blindly snatches Deen's tray and whips it across the cafeteria. Deen drops the crust of his pizza in shock. The tray spins like a frisbee until it hits the wall, shattering into small pieces.

"Is it because I'm not normal? Must be nice being the way you are! Must be perfect for you all!"

Allie buries her face into her arms.

Bravo Leon, The Voice says. *I didn't think you had it in you. Hahaha, maybe you* did *molest Allie after all.*

Leon falls back to his seat, defeated and weary. Jason stares around the silent cafeteria to see if the culprit is around. The perpetrator remains anonymous.

Slowly, students revive the cafeteria's usual chatter. The same tall bald monitor from earlier rushes toward Leon's table. "I'm contacting Dr. Giro."

Tears leak from Leon's eyes. He turns away from the bald man. "Please don't."

The instructor fixes his glasses. "No can do. You ignored my warning from earlier today. I'll be surprised if they still let you graduate."

Leon doesn't respond but instead thinks, *If I don't graduate...then... I'm stuck as a Bishop for another year...and then...more sessions. More torture. No! I can't go back.*

Jason faces the bald man. "Give 'em a break, Mr. Levi. Tomorrow's his birthday, *and* it's his graduation. If he gets in trouble now, he won't get to leave the facility."

The hall monitor shakes his head to Leon whose head is hanging in shame.

The bald man says, "If I help him, then *every* time there's an outburst from one of these troubled kids, I'll be forced to give them *all* a second chance. Is that what you want me to do?"

Jason argues, "If they choose to lock him in that facility again... Then he's going to be forced to repeat his junior year... It almost happened when we were freshmen."

The man points directly at Leon, saying, "You'd better get a hold of yourself and that wild behavior. It's getting out of hand again. You don't want to end up like *Miles Lee.*"

Leon's voice cracks as he says, "T—thanks, Jason," before he shyly lowers his head onto his arms.

"Don't mention it... But Leon, you really need to control your temper. I won't be able to save you every time. Have you been practicing those breathing exercises that they taught you?"

Leon turns to the side, and he sees that Jason is speaking, but his mind wanders away from Jason's advice. From afar, the monitor can tell something is still off.

Why don't you tell Jason the truth? Let him know just how crazy you really are.

☾ ☾ ☾

The Earthshine Facility is now standing proudly in front of Leon at four stories high. More than sixty rooms await patients who are desperate to cure their minds. Leon enters the courtyard and from afar can see the same therapist who had interviewed Allie two days earlier, Dr. Allure Igor. He passes a running fountain, green, luscious, and low grass to his sides. Some parts of the courtyard are covered by snow.

There are many patients in the yard—all wearing clothing with various symbols on their chests. None of them look happy. Some are drained, others are sobbing, and others…completely blank.

The automatic sliding doors open for Miles who walks out with his hands in his pockets. He lets out a heavy sigh as Allure snickers at him.

"Hello, Leon Granttley," Dr. Igor says. Miles turns around and watches the two for a split second.

"Hey, Dr. Igor…" Leon timidly reaches forward to shake her cold, bony hand. "Is Dr. Giro back by any chance?"

"I've told you already. Dr. Giro is still on vacation."

Great, Leon thinks.

☾ ☾ ☾

31

Dr. Allure Igor sits prim and proper with her hands set on her lap, her body stable and stiff. Light from outside is blotted by her curtains. While raising one of her sharp eyebrows, she glances beneath her glasses toward Leon from across her desk.

"As you know, Mr. Granttley, you're subject to graduate and become a Knight...given that you'd meet the criteria. But first, we have a few boxes we must check off." Allure grabs a manilla folder from the right of her desk and opens it.

Leon takes a deep breath.

"Now... What was that girl's name?" Allure perches the piercing pen atop her ear. "Ah. Allie Reincath, such a lovely name. How could I ever forget?" Allure holds a photo of someone's reddened neck up toward him. "Remember this?" Allure asks while Leon flinches at the sight of the photo.

"I'm not comfortable speaking about her—"

"—Leon," she growls, lowering her tone and the photo.

"I'll talk about anything else, just not her. Please," he begs before he shifts his vision to the picture frame placed face down near the therapist.

"How many times now have you told me about your childhood abuse? Now that girl's name tears you to shreds? Do I need to diagnose you with PTSD as well?"

Leon takes a deep breath. "Dr. Igor—"

32

"—Oh, what? Is this the part where you pretend you're uncomfortable with me again? Every therapist here bears the same credentials. Just like how you're like every little patient. NOW PLAY YOUR PART! You'd be wise to agree."

"What do you want me to say?"

"Watch that attitude, Mr. Granttley…that's strike one for today…"

Leon deeply exhales. "Yes. I remember the photos. I remember what she took after I…"

"Good. Now keep going!" Allure shouts, slamming her fist on the table. The shockwave knocks a book off the shelf on Leon's right. The Bishop cowers, then eludes all eye contact with Allure.

Suddenly, there are screaming and shouting sounds in the hallway. Screams from Scott, who everyone in the Earthshine Facility calls, The Screaming Man.

"Maybe we should check on him…"

"You are not going ANYWHERE until I hear from the beginning to the end, Leon Granttley. Do I make myself clear? Now as punishment, you'll start explaining how you got DID and will explain where it's gotten you today!"

Leon closes his eyes and takes one great deep breath. "From my understanding… My disorder came from the childhood abuse I endured. Particularly when my dad used to drink. I didn't really enjoy being around him or the abuse, so I separated myself from reality by forming conversations with myself. Or at least, it was who I thought it was: myself."

"Continue."

"I thought at first it was *something*. But over time, I had reason to believe that it was *someone*. I couldn't sleep at night because every time I closed my eyes, his voice was there. Mocking me in every way possible."

"What would it taunt you about?" Dr. Igor asks, not even trying to hide her grin.

Leon's eyes water. "He would make fun of my height, my hair. Even the way I acted. Every time I had something positive to think about, it would show or tell me something negative. Then one day, he told me that my only escape would be death."

Leon's mind reverts to a glimpse of this tragic memory, a younger him with much shorter hair. The younger Leon rushed to the bedroom window without hesitation. Impulse left him too rushed to unhinge the window's locks. The frustration pent up inside of him caused him to break through the window. Gravity left him falling quickly toward the grass beneath, with his head facing the ground.

Allure smirks and writes, *All it took was a couple of empty threats.*

"After that, I was told that my mom saved me. And since then…I've been watched by you guys."

Allure smiles. "And like the devil you are, years later, you ruthlessly attacked Allie."

He stands up with his fist balled. "I didn't," he says, clenching his teeth.

"Oh, and yet so quick to get defensive." Dr. Igor writes, *suicide attempt at the age of five*, then circles it and places the sharp pen back onto her right ear. "Sit down, you're not scaring anyone." She rolls her eyes. "Why do you keep running from it? Just accept what you did and move on."

Leon's forehead begins to sweat. *I hate you so much*, he thinks.

Leon sits back onto the seat. "Dr. Igor, you have to understand. I've known Allie since I was in kindergarten. Her…and Jason."

"Yes, I do remember meeting with your friend Jason not too long ago. He had much to say about you."

Leon sighs. "Jason moved one day, then it was just me and Allie. Then one day, Allie left. Out of the blue... Without any friends, I didn't know who to go to."

"Oh, I'm well aware. Your family said you wouldn't even open up to them," Dr. Igor says.

"Because I knew they wouldn't accept or understand me. So, I kept The Voice a secret. When everyone learned about The Voice, they all eventually told me to ignore it."

"So, if I understand correctly, all you had was *The Voice.*"

"Yes," Leon says, as he wipes his sweaty palms on his khaki pants and continues, "and then when I left the city to come here, I found Jason and Allie. Our reunion brought the three of us even closer." Dr. Igor tilts her head to the side with a still and blank expression.

Leon adds, "That's why it tears me apart when everyone tells me that I molested her. I care a lot about her... I could never..."

"I'll tell you why, Leon." Dr. Igor wears a paralyzing grin. "That voice in your mind. You and *IT* grew a bond while your two closest friends weren't there for you. You know what that tells me?"

Leon gulps and she continues. "*It* tells me that The Voice—that person in your head—was jealous of their return. *IT* compelled you to act on *ITS* jealousy!"

"That's not true!" Leon shouts.

Dr. Igor softens her voice, "Ah. Now we're *finally* getting somewhere." She shrugs. "Shall I read the notes that you provided Dr. Giro with months ago? It might help to convince you."

Dr. Igor reaches into Leon's folder for a few papers and peers through her glasses as she reads, *"For a while I referred to him as The Devil. It was what my parents wanted me to call him. It was because of all the negativity he would feed me. However, he didn't want to be called that. He wanted an identity, a reason to live."*

Dr. Igor's eyes quickly meet with Leon's. "Keep listening," she says as she clears her throat. *"This made me think that it couldn't have been an imaginary friend. Since normally people would create the dialogue with their imaginary friends.*

"This voice would provide me with intelligent responses—real conversations like the ones you and I are having right now. Trivial questions, bets on certain things that'd happen throughout the day, and even prompts on what actions to take."

Leon takes a slow, shaky breath.

Dr. Igor turns the page and continues reading, *"However, the more I conversed with this entity, the more he spoke about Allie. He began to act very obsessive, and—"* She pauses and shifts her focus from the files to Leon once more, then continues, *"—according to everyone here, my home, and school, I attacked her. I put her in danger. My word doesn't matter. No matter how many times I deny it, I still get penalized. So, what's the point in fighting? Might as well give up."*

Dr. Allure Igor slams the manila folder shut. "See? It had to have happened, Leon. Close friends don't randomly call assault for the fun of it. To become a *Knight* and graduate from the Earthshine Facility is to accept the unacceptable. I've lost count of how many times we've gone over this."

The office is silent, her cold words graze his skin bringing goose bumps to his arms. Aside from her exhalation of satisfaction, the only other audible sound is Scott, the screaming man in the other room. He is crying for his wife who has been deceased for nine years.

Dr. Igor smiles. "Well. It doesn't sound like you want to become a Knight so—"

"—Alright… Alright… I…I molested her…"

"Aww. See, that wasn't so hard, was it?" Dr. Igor coos, as she scribbles onto her clipboard. "And how exactly did you cope with this incident and its punishment?"

"I…used the mirror as you all instructed for therapeutic release. I talked with The Voice that echoed through it. I talked more with the one in my head too. But you know…that reminds me of something I'd been thinking about."

Dr. Igor massages her temples. "What is it now, Mr. Granttley?"

"Why should I listen to a voice that I know nothing of? Why does the voice in my head sound exactly like the one in the mirror?"

"Leon…the voice is just a figment of your imagination, silly boy. The whole point in those conversations is so that you gain a better perspective of who you really are. It was an old method once prescribed by a famous philosopher. *Socrates*, I think. Many people have reaped a plenty from this form of release. Your case is no different."

Leon squints with a puzzled look.

"Well, since you've *finally* and *truthfully* accepted that you molested Allie, I proudly welcome you to Knighthood, Leon."

Leon's eyes widen. "W—wait, what?"

Dr. Igor stands and retrieves a certificate from the second shelf in her cabinet.

"That's right," she says, "you get to graduate."

"But that didn't answer my questions. I still don't understand who or what this voice is. Why does everyone inside the facility say to listen to The Voice, while everyone outside this facility tells me to ignore it?"

"Well, Mr. Granttley. Luckily for you, Knighthood is all about finding out what the voice is. Now that you have become a Knight, you will find out what it all means, how it started, and where it comes from. You will travel through the deepest depths of your memory and heart for the true answer."

Sighing from relief, she reluctantly hands him the certificate.

"Congratulations, Leon Granttley. And if I'm not mistaken, tomorrow is your seventeenth birthday as well, no?"

Leon nods.

"Stop by tomorrow to receive your *other* gift. Dr. Giro will be expecting you."

"Alright…" Leon says, eagerly exiting her office.

"COME BACK HERE AND CLOSE THE DOOR!" Dr. Igor shouts as Leon returns immediately to fulfill her demand.

A Forgotten Moonlit Night

☾   ☾   ☾

December 10, 2009 (Thursday)

Colorado ∧ Aurorae

Keystone Circle

Leon's Home ∧ His bedroom

7:46 p.m.

China Jr. is Leon's thirteen-year-old tuxedo cat with a black goatee facing slightly to the side. She is sitting atop his shoulder, her tail wrapping gently around Leon's neck. He strokes her back as she purrs loudly. Leon lays on his bed, and she leaps atop him, then starts kneading.

After this, she jumps off to the floor. She wanders near his laundry basket which, believe it or not, is the place where her mother, China, gave birth to her and one other kitten. The other kitten was pitch black. Leon's younger self was dismayed to find that the black cat had mysteriously disappeared.

Something suddenly strikes the window. It must be a rock.

"Oh, come on, Jason. Do you have any idea how late it is?" He groans and walks over to look through the window, seeing Jason there. "Plus, I *just* got ready for bed."

Leon lazily places on a pair of boots, black skinny jeans, and his blue hoodie to counter the cool air. He exits through his front door, walks across the driveway passing his dad's white van, and meets with Jason who is standing patiently on the sidewalk. Jason is wearing a red golf cap and a polo shirt which is tucked into his khaki pants. This is his work uniform for *McDonald's.*

"Hey. I know it's late. But I'm off to work. I wanted to talk to you before tomorrow—in case I didn't get to see you."

Leon crosses his arms. "You picked a good time. I won't be at school."

Jason nods. "Oh good. That means you'll be graduating. Walk with me."

Leon shakes his head. The Voice in Leon's mind says, *I can already tell you what this will be about. Wait for it. He's gonna ask if you accepted what you did to Allie. Watch.*

"So. What's up?" Leon asks as the two walk side by side down the sidewalk.

"I'm just gonna come out and ask. Leon, wouldn't you remember hurting someone? Someone you cared about?"

Leon shakes his head, and The Voice responds, *I knew it. Have fun with this talk. Make the most of it.*

Leon replies, "Yes, I would. And I would admit it, too."

"You admitted it to the Earthshine Facility...but not to Allie herself."

"Because—"

"—you didn't do it. Right..."

Leon frustratingly groans as Jason continues, "I'm just here to appeal to your conscience. I know you're gonna graduate. But you're doing it on false pretenses. You're gonna accept something you don't deserve. And. I can't respect that. I can't respect you lying to yourself and everyone including the person YOU hurt just for your own comfort. What does that say about her feelings? Her memories?"

"I'm going home, Jason," Leon says, turning around while walking away.

"Just think about Allie! Don't you have feelings for her? Didn't you? Don't do this for me, do it for her!"

"Goodnight, Jason," Leon says as a crow flies atop a streetlight near him.

"Leon, just listen to what I have to say, and then you'll never hear from me again."

Leon stomps and turns around to face his pleading friend.

"Isn't that what DID is?" Jason asks. "Aren't patients with that disorder people who go through amnesiac states? Because... Well, it'd make perfect sense why you wouldn't remember."

"Jason, I don't have a vendetta against any of you. I really liked Allie, as a friend and..."

The Voice in Leon's mind adds, *and a lover.*

Leon shakes his head and continues, "So—I wouldn't ever touch her like that. Okay?"

Jason turns his face away. "Look, Leon, I'll be straight with you. Allie showed me the pictures...the police sorted through ten of them. Ten of them! The details are what brought you to a behavioral psychologist. If they didn't think you were fit for amnesia, you wouldn't be there. But you are. So, we all kind of have to take Allie's side." He takes a breath. "I'll ask again—Wouldn't you want the same justice?"

"Why did I even bother coming outside?"

A murder of crows now flies around the area. Many roost on top of the electrical posts and a few on the pine trees' branches. Jason walks closer to Leon and asks, "Well, where were you on that day?"

Leon turns to the side. "I don't remember. *I* say that *I* was at therapy. But THEY, as in the cops and Allie, say that I was at my house."

Jason crosses his arms. "Was your family home?"

"No."

Jason paces in small semicircles around Leon to keep his focus. "Do you remember what the weather was like? What you were wearing?"

Leon looks up toward the stars for relief. "If I knew, I would've told them. That day is just one big blur to me."

Jason crosses his arms. "It was two years ago... On *December eleventh*... And to be honest, I remember Allie saying she was giving you a chance to be her boyfriend. But Leon, I can't tell you any more than what you can tell yourself. You might not remember, but your vessel somewhere inside carries the answer. One day you'll find it... And when you do, you'll feel better."

The Voice speaks, *No matter what you've told him, time and time again your supposed best friend has told you that you've done it. Now what, Leon?*

Leon wipes the cold sweat off his forehead. "You still think I did it. I can't believe it. After everything we've been through."

Photographs of a bruised leg and arm flash through Jason's mind. He shudders, remembering the marks on Allie's neck. He ceases his momentum to face Leon. "Like I said, I'd love to say you didn't do it, but I don't want to lie to anyone. I still think you're just having trouble accepting it."

Leon thinks, *You and everyone else say the same thing.*

Jason walks over and pats his back. "Well, I've done what I can. If you won't accept it, then I won't accept you. See you, Leon. And. Happy early birthday."

With a broken heart, Leon thinks, *I thought out of all people you would trust me. It's one thing when your own family doesn't understand but this...*

The Voice chimes in, *This is priceless. He didn't even congratulate you on your graduation. I almost pity you.*

☾   ☾   ☾

<u>The Next Day</u>
<u>December 11, 2009 (Friday)</u>
<u>Colorado ∧ Aurorae</u>
<u>Leon's Home ∧ The Kitchen</u>
<u>10:11 a.m.</u>

"Leaving so soon?" Leon's father says from the kitchen, seeing Leon at the front door with his blue hoodie, black jeans, and shoes on.

Leon swallows and walks around the corner to see his dad in the kitchen, standing against the counter. He shrugs and looks away from his father. "Yeah. I figured I'd get this over with as soon as possible."

Leon's father is tall and lean. He has a maturing hairline, unlike his son. His hair is as tall and straight as his, if not slightly more. If his father were to shave his beard and mustache, the father and son would look even more alike. Especially if Leon were to gain the same forehead wrinkles and frown lines.

"I took today off so that we could celebrate your birthday," Nero says firmly in his deep voice.

The Voice in Leon's mind tempts him by saying, *Ask him if they plan on celebrating your graduation.*

No. You're full of bad ideas, Leon replies.

Aren't you curious about why there's only a birthday cake on the counter?

How do you see—oh right.

You forget. We share the same eyes. Now. Satisfy your curiosity. The Voice says.

Leon shakes his head, and his father speaks. "That little head shake you did is why we're *only* celebrating your birthday."

"What? I was just—"

"—I know what you were doing. You do that every time you speak to The Voice. Or. When it speaks to you. Leon, don't take this the wrong way but—are you sure you're fit to graduate?"

"Yes?"

"I'm not going to get in the way of your development as a person, but. If you ask me—"

Leon and his father can hear knocking on Leon's shut bedroom door upstairs.

"Leon!" Amy calls out, then says to her mother, "I don't think he's up here."

A set of footsteps trample down the stairs and find Leon and his father in the kitchen.

"Are we late to the happy birthdays?" Amy says, shyly creeping into the kitchen as her mother, Silvia, shows up behind her. The mother and daughter look very alike, but Silvia has more wrinkles.

Silvia gives Nero a quick kiss, then grabs a knife from the drawer for the cake. "What did we get in the middle of?" she asks, as everyone is now quiet.

Nero grabs his mug that says, *Worlds worst dad*, takes a sip of his black coffee, and speaks. "I was just telling Leon that…well, would you rather tell them, son?"

Leon blows air through his nostrils, "I…"

He looks at the three of them, but his mother interrupts his pause to shout, "Happy birthday!"

Amy and Nero both look at his mother with confusion written on their faces.

"What?" Leon's mother asks. "Stop looking at me like that. Today is his special day. Regardless of what he wants to do with it, it's his decision."

Amy snorts. "Still haven't accepted it, I presume."

Leon grits his teeth. "I'm out of here," he says, charging for the door as his father yells, "Leon! Don't disrespect your mother like that!"

Leon turns around at the front door and proclaims, "Thank you for the happy birthdays. You're right. It is my decision. And one day, I'm gonna find the truth and prove you all wrong! I didn't molest Allie! Okay?"

Leon and his sister have both been spanked as children. Their parents understand the art of discipline very well. Leon knows this and, despite his fear of his possible punishment, opens the door and slams it. But then…he's startled by the sight of Allie who is standing at the top of his driveway in her school uniform.

The two stare at each other. Leon can hear his father shouting in rage behind him. He's not too far off.

Leon presses forward, shouting, "Allie!"

Allie takes two steps back. She blinks, and Leon's hoodie suddenly turns red. She sees a black leather jacket over his hoodie. And then startles upon the sight of his face. A smirk forms on Leon's lips. She blinks once more, and these *new* features leave as quickly as they came.

Allie's heart pounds. "Get back! Why're you running toward me!" She takes the amulet in her pocket, throws it, and it smacks him straight in the forehead.

"Happy…birthday!" Allie cries in a sob while running away back toward her neighborhood. "Are you happy now, Dr. Igor?"

Leon rubs his forehead and lifts the mysterious amulet. "Ow…"

Leon's mother opens the door and shouts, "Leon, you're still here? You better not let your father see you! Catch!" She tosses a square shaped device into his hands. "You haven't been carrying your beeper lately. We have to keep track of you, remember?"

"Yeah. I remember."

"Okay," his mother says. "Do you want me to throw away your journals now that you're graduating?"

"No," Leon replies. "Keep the notebooks I didn't write in either. I might need them in the future."

His mother nods as Leon places the amulet around his neck, then under his blue hoodie.

Leon turns his back and starts walking toward the Earthshine Facility, but in the distance his mother yells, "Congratulations on your graduation!" This brings a smile to his face, as well as a few tears. Finally. Someone who believes him.

Man In
The Mirror

☾　　☾　　☾

L eon walks toward the automatic moving doors in the front of the facility. Sadly for him, they stay shut.

"Is it closed? No, that can't be right. Dr. Igor literally told me to come today."

Try the back entrance, The Voice says.

"Great. It's you again," Leon mutters. "Sucks that you just might be right."

I always am. Hurry up.

Leon makes his way to the back entrance of the facility. Then after pushing through the two doors, he marches for the office area, passing by the waiting room, through a long dim hallway, bringing him to the opposite side of the entrance where he had previously met Dr. Igor.

He walks down this next hallway, watching the lights dance with shadows that move along the floor and walls. Chills crawl down Leon's spine, the tiny hairs on his arms erect. He opens the fourth door on his right, cracking it slowly to find his appointed therapist.

"Why are you doing that? Come in," a thick and deep voice demands.

The door whines as Leon fully opens it. He leans in.

"Sorry. I thought that the facility was closed today."

49

Dr. Stefano Giro is a tall dark-skinned silver fox. He looks a bit different from how Leon remembers him. Instead of the blue sweater and khaki pants he normally wears, he is now wearing a dark green business suit with suns for buttons. It seems that Dr. Giro has grown weary of his beard and has instead trimmed it down to a bushy mustache. His hair is silver and neatly slicked back. His eyes are stern and focused intensely on Leon.

"Sit down," Dr. Giro says, looking toward Leon who obediently sits in the left seat. There is a glass of grapefruit juice next to him.

Stefano Giro takes a sip of his bitter drink and stares intensely at Leon, not saying a single word. Leon looks at everything but the old man.

Stefano then says, "Wait a moment… I remember you. You're that boy who thinks he's innocent…aren't you?"

"That's not true," Leon says, looking away. "I know what I did to her."

"A change of heart. How ironic. I suppose you are like the rest, then. But sadly for you, your hellish fate remains the same." The man starts reaching for his coat pockets.

"*Hellish fate?*" Leon asks, watching the old man struggle to find whatever he needs.

Hey. You had questions that none of these therapists could answer, didn't you? Hurry and ask them, The Voice says.

Leon narrows his eyes and thinks, *I do, but…how did you—*

—Hurry up and ask him, The Voice in Leon's mind urges.

"W—Wait," Leon says, "I've had a question that I've been meaning to ask for a very long time."

Dr. Giro wears a look of disgust. "You have thirty seconds...speak."

"I…I don't know what I'm getting into." Leon's brain is hit by many thoughts. He has so many questions. And now here he is, in front of the founder who brought him into this facility. The very one who groomed him to understand the little that he does now. What should he ask first? Leon's brain ponders this while his mouth blabbers.

Leon repeats, "This Knight's program, I'm not sure what I'll be doing. I wanna know about The Voice. I wanna know about everything."

Do this correctly, and I won't have to take over.

"It truly doesn't matter," Dr. Giro replies coolly.

"I'm begging you, Dr. Giro. I've been asking this for years. And no one's been able to answer these for me. I have to know."

"Which question? You've asked many."

"The one about the voice in my head. I wanna know why you kept having me talk with it. You knew it said bad things. Everyone on the outside knew that too, yet *they* suggested I should stop talking with it. I want to hear the truth from you."

The man suddenly screams out while holding his head. Startled, Leon gasps, "Are you okay?"

The man stands up from his seat and shouts even louder. "Of course!" the old man blurts, then in a lighter and smoother voice, "I've waited far too long for this day!" The man ruffles his gray hair. He ruins the combover and makes it messy.

Dr. Giro grins then sits back down. He leans his arm on the table, and a button within his sleeve clicks. Suddenly a skinny blade appears from out his sleeve. "Oops. Since when did I start carrying these?" the old man asks, examining the blade.

"Hey, get back!" Leon cries out while standing up. He grabs his chair by its handles to point its legs toward the therapist.

Dr. Giro opens his dark green amulet, reads the time, and then puts his hands behind his back. "Leon Granttley. Would you believe that out of all the patients we've had here, *you're* actually the first person to ever ask those questions?"

"What do you mean? Why wouldn't anyone else ask?" Leon asks loudly, shaking with the chair in hand.

"Because people are usually content with what society gives them. But not you. No. Because if I were to ask you what you did to that girl, you'd say that you did—nothing, correct?"

Leon says nothing but knows Dr. Giro is correct. He angrily stares up at the old man.

"You don't have to answer that. I know what you *really* think. But what I *will* say is that you have done well in treading against the grain, Leon Granttley. If you truly do not believe that you touched her—then accept that wholeheartedly. Live that *fantasy* out until your final days. But do so proudly."

Leon is frozen in place—still holding the chair so that its legs face his supposed old friend...

Dr. Giro continues, "It takes a lot of force to get people to do what you want to do. And to their demise, the poor patients have swallowed the lies we created. They'll reconstruct their own memories just to fit the narrative. But you. You're different. You, Leon, can fulfill your true purpose for me. For them. As of today, you are a Knight. And no lie shall pierce your armor."

"You're freaking me out...Dr. Giro."

"Well, consider this an unorthodox graduation! Even if you've boldly lied to our faces and told us what we wanted to hear."

Leon draws back in shock as Dr. Giro continues, "Did you think I didn't know what you've been telling your friends and family? We've spoken to each of them independently. And each of their reports conclude that you are in denial. But why does what *they* think matter? I've just complimented you on your stubbornness, haven't I?"

"Nothing you're saying is making any sense…" Leon utters, slightly lowering the chair.

Dr. Giro chuckles to himself. "At this moment in time, nothing I say will bring you relief… Ah, but in the *future*."

Suddenly, footsteps trail toward the door. The door flies open, swinging straight into Leon, sending him AND the chair into the wall. Leon falls flatly to the ground. His chest moves only for a few short breaths.

Leon's body has left a dent in the white wall. Two mysterious masked figures enter the room. These tall brutes are wearing masks with a devilish sun and moon. They are wearing dark green armor, similar colors to Dr. Giro's new suit, and have maroon-like fabric underneath the armor that represents muscle and sinew.

"It appears I've run out of time," the old man says to himself.

"Sir," one of the male guards says. "Elder Laither is set to drive. We have all the other Bishops locked and secured. Is this Bishop ready?"

"That he is."

One of the two masked figures grabs Leon's body and runs outside to the black vehicle in the parking lot.

"One day, you'll understand what I mean, Leon. In the end, it is your skepticism that we all need to move forward. *Project Earthshine* begins now." Dr. Giro says.

KNIGHT SYMBOL &...

☾　　☾　　☾

The dark, unsettling ground causes Leon's body to convulse and shake. His face and senses are numb. Through his hoodie, he feels something next to him, but he can't tell what. The way the environment is shaking…it feels as if there are bumps in the road. Of course. Leon is in a vehicle. His arms and legs are restrained by metal cuffs. Thankfully, he isn't alone. He can hear whimpers far behind him.

"It's gonna be fine, Ombretta," Miles, the boy with brown curls, whispers comfortingly to her. *"We're gonna be okay."*

"But…" Ombretta whispers back in her soft voice, *"I'm squished back here. I'm seeing shadows and…they're following this van…they took me without letting me bring my meds.* I have to go back!"

"Shh!" Miles harshly whispers. *"They'll hear you…"*

Ombretta covers her mouth, *"Sorry,"* she whispers apologetically.

How they managed to cram us both back here with three others is beyond me, Miles thinks, looking to his sides to see an unfamiliar trembling middle-aged woman, the old man named Scott—the screaming patient, and another frightened person with long hair whom he does not recognize.

"Miles!" Ombretta shouts at the sight of this supposed shadow that she sees.

"HEY! WHAT'S GOING ON BACK THERE?" a voice in front of Leon shouts. The person that yelled must be sitting in the front passenger seat. He is quite the large figure.

The only things brightening this dark drive are the blue lanterns poised out on the sides of the road. This giant figure points a flashlight right into Leon's eyes. Leon squints and turns away.

The giant points the light onto himself, shocking Leon and his fellow prisoners in the back. This figure has just revealed his face. No. This too is a mask. And it is much creepier than the ones that knocked Leon unconscious earlier. This man's mask looks like a large blue sun with two crescent moons for horns.

You can say that the spikes it has, or the rays of its sun, can even act like more horns. He has four thorns poking out from his shoulders. They seem to be bending to adjust to the height of the vehicle. These thorns—it's almost like they're living and breathing. Or is that just the motion of the vehicle?

The large figure in the front shines the light on the person at Leon's right. This isn't a prisoner. This is *also* a person wearing a mask.

"You'd better not be sleeping back there, Noire," the deep voice says, pronouncing the name, *Noo-war.*

"I'm not! I got plenty of sleep!" the whiny yet mischievous voice to the right of Leon shouts back.

"Good," the voice in the front says, "because if you do, there won't be any food for you when we get back."

"Empty threats, all of 'em. I've got all these people in here to eat," he says, slowly turning over to face Leon. "Ain't that right…"

Leon gulps, and his heart starts pounding. Is this man's smile that wide, or is this, too, his mask? It appears to be a red sun with a blue moon attached to it.

"Noire," a hoarse elder woman's voice to the left of Leon says. "We have ten minutes before we get there. Simmer down."

They arrive at an area with fewer trees where now the moon's pale light can shine freely in the area. The light shines through the windows, and Leon sees the gruesome person to his left. This woman's mask is shaped to be like a…crescent moon and Ouija board.

This mask, just like Noire's, gives Leon the creeps. Goosebumps flare on Leon's arm as she adjusts herself in her seat. Despite how old her voice sounds, her figure surprisingly reveals a young and well toned body.

"I'm just excited," Noire shouts. "We've got so many heads tonight. *And* we've got three potential *Sitio's*."

"Don't you have enough?" the woman to the left of Leon asks.

"You can never have too much," Noire adds with a pout in his voice. "Not unless you like runnin' your own errands."

A pale crescent moon shines its brilliant tint of blue light past the dark clouds, brightening the road ahead.

Leon hears rustling behind him.

"Y—your name is Miles…right?" The screaming man named Scott asks the boy with curly hair.

"*Keep it down*," Miles whispers, trying to sound polite. "*But yes. That's me.*"

"I want to get out of here. Help me."

"*I can't do that for any of us.*"

"You don't understand, *Mona's out there*. My wife. I need her back."

Miles sighs, *I shouldn't have entertained this…his wife has been dead for years.*

The woman next to Scott is shaking in place. "I'm…I'm terrified of the moonlight…yet…it's shining on us right now… And if there's birds…I'm gonna lose it…"

The unfamiliar long-haired man next to Scott whispers, *"I'm scared of people, so I don't like being here any more than you guys..."*

"I...can't stand the sunlight," the old woman says, "so thankfully only the moon's out..."

Miles whispers harshly, *"Guys, please keep your voices down..."*

Leon in the front thinks, *You really have a way of working, devil. Now, of all times, you're silent. No ideas, no taunts. Nothing. What's wrong with me... Am I asking for you to be around now? Say something!*

"Aye! KEEP IT DOWN BACK THERE!" Noire shouts.

"Jackal, calm yourself," the voice in the front booms.

"He's right," the hoarse voice to Leon's left adds, "you're smarter than them. At least sometimes I like to think so. Don't let their actions beget you."

"Don't call me Jackal!" Noire screams. "I didn't do anything wrong! I'm doing my job. You know how they get when they scream this early." He detaches his seatbelt and turns to face Miles, Ombretta, and the others in the back. "You're lucky I won't feed you to my dogs back home!"

"Jackal," the voice from the front of the van bellows, "What did *Faviané* just say?"

Noire says, "You know how *Festano* feels about negative attention. If they scream now, who knows what they'll do later." He lashes the seat with his fist. "Now all of you—shut up!"

Faviané tightens her fist. "Jackal. I hate repeating myself."

"That makes two of us," the voice in the front adds.

"Please," Ombretta in the back says, "I just want to know where we are. My anxiety is getting worse... I'm claustrophobic...and...and the shadows are all around me. I just need my medicine..." she says, clutching her blue scarf.

The driver, wearing a grinning red sun mask like Noire's, unbuckles his seatbelt and veers to the right side of the road.

"Everyone, I'm afraid Noire is right," the old man behind the mask says, setting the large black van into *park*. "*Kranfly* I could deal with a little more quiet. Will you take care of it, *Thorne*?"

"Fine," the giant in the front passenger seat says, attaching his brass knuckles with golden spikes at the end. As he steps out of the vehicle, the thorns on his shoulder stiffen and stand tall. They're now moving around like live tentacles. Now that the light is shining brighter on them, Leon can see that these are spikes with gold spearheads. They appear to be attached to Thorne's outfit, each tentacle with a mind of its own.

Thorne opens the two doors at the back of the van, and Ombretta whimpers, "Please. Let us go back to our families. None of us will say a thing."

Thorne's gigantic figure eclipses the moonlight above as he walks toward her. "End your anxiety, or *I'll* end *you*," Thorne says, glowering directly at Ombretta.

He now leans close to Scott The Screaming Man, grabbing him by the hair of his receding hairline. As Scott cries out, Thorne shouts over him, "We're almost where we need to go! Pipe down for the rest of this, got it? Nod if you agree!"

Thorne releases the old man so harshly that he falls on his back, crying aloud. How Miles wishes he can help the old man up. But not only is he restrained, Thorne has not broken his stare from any of these five. In fact, with his mask on, it feels like he is staring at everyone at once. Miles, Ombretta, and the rest of the prisoners reluctantly nod.

Laither the driver, while only breathing through his mouth, walks over to Thorne with the help of his cane which also looks like a shotgun… Is it really a cane? Hunched over, Laither limps to Thorne and says, "I just received a report from our fellow guards at the mirror. They say that the moonlight is fading in and out. We were on schedule before—but we cannot risk the clouds blocking it completely again."

Thorne backs away from the captors in the back of the van, growling. "Hmph."

He slams the doors on their faces as he and the old man make it back to their seats. The van starts moving, and Leon has an idea.

Wait. That's it. My mom gave me a beeper. If I use that, I'll be able to get her to track me! Then I'll be saved.

With Leon's arms and legs restrained, sadly he'll have to lean his elbow on the correct button to trigger the device to show his current location. The device is activated. Thankfully, it emits no sound. Though it does emit a tiny vibrating pulse. But then…

Noire turns to Leon and says, "Hey. You activate your beeper? What is that I'm feeling? Oh! Oh yeah! That's definitely a beeper!" Noire starts cackling loudly and Leon's jaw drops.

"What a classic!" Noire belts. "Hey Thorne!"

"Yes, Noire. So, I will save you an escapee's arm when we get back."

"And leg! You said an arm and a leg!" Noire cackles.

"I'm confused," Faviané says. "What bet did you two make now?"

Noire excitingly explains, "Every beeper that's turned on earns me a fresh bloody snack. Because—" Noire pushes his masked face so close to Leon's that they could kiss. Leon draws away, but Noire's creepy mask inches closer. "—fools like you think that *your parents* gave you those beepers! Those were ours to begin with! No one's comin' to save you!"

Leon swallows and looks away as Noire laughs and returns to his normal sitting position. He starts laughing so hard that his insides start to hurt. For a slight second, he removes the mask to wipe some tears away.

Leon's fight or flight instincts are triggered. He needs to get out. But how? Maybe...by kicking Noire's armored shin. Sadly for Leon, his leg restraints stop him from pulling his legs back as much as he would like. He swings his foot into Noire's shin, cringing as his toes ache from the pain.

"I'll give you one more try. *One more*," Noire says.

Thorne in the front says slowly, "Jackal...I'm warning you. Nothing. Too. Much."

"Oh. I won't, alright. One more, Granttley. I'll give you one more shot!"

Leon swallows and tries to headbutt Noire's head, but even the mask itself is hard! Leon feels a bump growing on his forehead, but he can't tell for sure because his hands are restrained.

"Time's up!" Noire shouts, palming Leon's entire head.

Faviané is humming and staring out the window until Leon's face slams into it.

"JACKAL!" Faviané shouts. "C'mon! You couldn't do that on YOUR side of the van?"

Noire ignores her, the cracks in the window, and says, "There...that'll teach you to step up to me!"

Leon's seeing stars. His head is throbbing. His vision is so blurry that he can barely tell that he's in the van. Noire pulls Leon's head once more to slam into the window until Thorne yells, "ENOUGH, Jackal."

"But!"

"No. He needs to be able to think where he's going. You know this."

I'm...I'm...going to live?

"Meh," Noire says, releasing Leon's head.

Faviané holds out her hand, and a miniature mirror appears onto her lap. She is muttering curses angrily to herself, while suddenly…the cracks in the glass disappear.

"Faviané, I heard that," Thorne at the front says. "No spirits in the van."

"Oh, as if that was an actual order. It is not my fault you don't believe in them…despite how many times they've saved you."

"Enough. They never saved me."

The mirror vanishes into thin air.

"Alright everyone," the driver says, "we have arrived."

"*Finally,*" Thorne says, as Laither steers them into a giant grassy field that is the size of a football field. There are trees surrounding each corner of this field, but unlike the rest of Aurorae County, there isn't a drop of snow.

However, there *is* snow in the trees. Many of these ominous soldier-like figures are surrounding the area. If the hostages wanted to run, this would be their only chance, for the path that Laither drives them through is the only breach in this immense rectangular shaped field.

The moon continues casting its unique baby blue light down onto the field. It glistens and shines on the green armor of this organization. The van stops to the side.

"Alright everyone," Laither says with a yawn, "we're here. Everyone wake up."

Thorne chortles. "You should retire, Laither. I don't know how you still do this."

"Eh. I like driving. It's good to be with you youngsters. Keeps me young."

Thorne the giant shrugs. "I tried." He then walks to the back of the vehicle and opens the two doors to see the frightened faces of Miles, Ombretta, Scott, and the other two sitting beside them. One by one with a pair of keys, he unlocks the restraints around their ankles. But not their hands.

"Out," Thorne says firmly, and each of the patients obeys without a single word.

Faviané unlocks Leon's ankle restraints, and then he follows her out from her side on the left. He did not want to go with Noire. Faviané and Noire stretch their legs while Thorne escorts this worried bunch to the field. Leon, Miles, Ombretta, Scott, and the other two patients follow behind Thorne. Faviané and Noire follow behind Leon and the others.

The grass feels strange beneath Leon's feet. Has he felt this texture before? Perhaps in a miniature golf course? Leon looks at the boy with curly hair and thinks, *It's him again.*

Leon looks at Ombretta with a confused look, *I think I've seen you before too...* Ombretta curiously glances at Leon while he looks away from her. Then she looks at something that is above his shoulders. Perhaps another one of the shadows that she sees?

Thorne glances up at the shining moon, looking around at a few approaching clouds. "We still have some time." He then turns to Leon and the others and says, "You all, stand where I'm standing."

Now it appears that they're each in the dead center of this grassy field. There are guards who wear armor and masks similar to Thorne's, Faviané's, and Noire's. It seems that the males have one set of armor and one type of mask while the females have another. They each have the same type of weapons—a gun with spikes at the end—and a sickle blade attached to their waists.

Since there are many of these guards, it's safe to assume that Thorne and his two teammates are the leaders of this organization. This is confirmed once one male guard meets Thorne halfway and says, "Commander Thorne."

Thorne replies, "Are you slow or just new? Where is your salute?"

The guard starts shaking and raises his left arm to the right side of his chest, using his index finger and thumb to make a *C* shape, or a crescent moon. To everyone watching, the *C* looks is backwards.

"Good. Now give me your report."

The male guard shaking in place says, "N—n—Detective Nivmar and Officer Milaw are late. But they did tell us they would be here—"

The guard stops talking once he sees two police cars show up next to Laither's van off in the distance. Laither is fast asleep in the driver's seat with his mask on. Leon and Ombretta both glance in excitement at the police cars. They're saved.

Two officers step out of the cars: one man with a jet black combover and brown skin and a woman with black hair, blonde highlights, and tanned skin. Both of their expressions are blank. The man is wearing a black leather jacket over his uniform. And he's wearing...a strange version of the American flag. So is the woman.

Leon's heart pounds in excitement, thinking, *Perfect! And now they just need to pull out their guns. Wait... Why only two officers for all these soldiers? Oh. Maybe they're decoys. Hmm. But they're not looking at the guards. Okay, wait! Why are they passing us! Hey! We need help!*

Ombretta is practically thinking the same thing as Leon. Why didn't the officers stop to help? Miles doesn't bother looking at these officers. Not even once.

"You're both late," Thorne says, pointing to the clouds in the sky.

Detective Nivmar says, "Sorry," holding the same salute as the fearful guard earlier. Officer Milaw reluctantly does the same. Nivmar continues, "We were feeding the news stations with another scapegoat."

"And what did you pick this time?" Thorne asks.

"The Loch Ness Monster. I mean. We *are* by the lake."

Thorne tilts his head, and Detective Nivmar immediately corrects himself, looking up, then away from Thorne. "I meant that respectfully."

Thorne chuckles. "I was beginning to worry that money and whitemail was losing it's worth."

Officer Milaw responds with her arms crossed. "Believe me, it's working. We don't need more fear."

Thorne laughs once more, pointing to the policewoman. "I like her."

Faviané marches forward with Noire by her side. "Thorne, we're running out of time. Noire's been summoned by Allure. He's got runaways to deal with."

"Very well," Thorne says, "then let's all move off to the side so that we can get started." Thorne briefly glances at Leon's angry face. Leon looks away as soon as he's caught staring. Faviané, Noire, and the police officers follow Thorne off the center of the field.

"Did you see the look on Granttley's face?" Thorne asks to the others. "Good thing we're not in a world where thoughts can kill." Noire cackles loudly at this. Leon, Miles, Ombretta, Scott, and the other two patients stand helplessly in the center of this field. One guard walks to the center where the Earthshine patients are and, using his arms, nudges them to the side. As for why, they don't know. But now they're organized much differently. Leon, Miles, and Ombretta are each standing on one side. On the other is Scott The Screaming Man, the woman named Lisa who claimed to hate the sun, and the man named Obi who claimed to be afraid of people.

The six of them stand, confused about their division. The only patient who appears unfazed is Miles. Leon and Ombretta are experiencing anxiety that they never have before.

"LUNAE LUX! MARCH!" Thorne shouts from the top of his lungs. And just like this, each of the masked people marches in place, rhythmically to no beat. Just the beat of their own practiced drills. Thorne commands, "Weapons out!"

A single tear rolls out of Leon's eye as he realizes what is about to happen. The pistols being aimed at them now—this is their execution. Yes. This is how it ends for them.

Leon shuts his eyes, waiting for the bullet to strike his body. He wonders what it will feel like.

A clamor shakes the ground. Everyone but the surrounding masked individuals and the police officers falls to their knees or flat on their buttocks. Is this earthquake coming from the marches of these soldiers?

In between the divided patients comes an even bigger division. The source of the rumbling. The ground itself splits and reveals darkness beneath. So, this is it. They are to fall into the pit and die. *This* is how it ends.

The ground continues to split open, and the darkness beneath is eradicated by the moonlight above. The moonlight shines so bright that the light from the pit shines upward, making nearly all the air of the entire area white. The rumbling has not stopped yet, however.

Thorne roars, "Congratulations, Leon, Scott, Obi, Lisa, Ombretta, and Miles. Accept Lord Festano's humbling welcome to *the other side*."

"What?" Leon says. "What do you mean?"

"Other side?" Scott asks. "Will she be waiting there for me?"

"No!" Noire shouts. "But this blade's been waiting for ya!" And with a tiny sickle blade, Noire carves a crescent moons shape onto Scott's forehead.

The pain makes Scott live up to his nickname. Guards from behind each of these patients appear. Three of them with leg restraints in hand for Scott, Obi, and Lisa. The other guards bring keys for Leon, Miles, and Ombretta.

The guards use the keys to unlock their restraints. In confusion, the three rub their wrists—and suddenly—Miles watches Leon get kicked forward. Leon loses his balance and falls into the bright pit below. He screams and shouts and is swallowed by the blinding light and is seen no more.

A SECOND
BIRTHDAY

☾   ☾   ☾

<u>??????? ????, ???? (???????)</u>
<u>Colorado /\ Aurorae</u>
<u>Keystone Circle</u>
<u>Leon's Home /\ His bedroom</u>
<u>??:??</u>

L eon screams, sorely jerking forward. He glances all around his bedroom. The first thing he notices is that he's sleeping on just a mattress, not his twin sized bed set. He doesn't even have a pillow. Leon looks around for his dresser. That is not here either. Not even the many posters of his favorite movies and video games. No. The wall is barren of all life and personality save for a few pictures of grungy rock, metal bands, and scribbles on the wall.

"I guess I deserve this," Leon says, looking all around the room once more. "If I were a parent, I would've taken my stuff away too." He yanks the sheet off himself and says, "But jeez, guys. A little excessive? I know I'm grounded but you took my dresser? How am I supposed to get dressed? Speaking of dressed…"

Leon looks down and notices he's wearing only a white t-shirt. He finds his blue hoodie and black skinny jeans hanging on his closet door. But something is different about the placement of this closet door. No, what's weird isn't how this closet door slides open. Nor is it the fact that now this door has a hole in it. It's the fact that it's in a different location of the room.

"They…moved me to a different room?"

He looks around his feet. "China Jr?" Leon calls out for his cat while his eyes scramble all around the wooden floor.

"I guess she's in the basement…but…what happened to my carpet? Mom always said carpets were good against the winter weather."

Leon glances out his window and sees unfamiliar houses. He runs for the window and peers outside. Not a single flake of snow can be seen anywhere. In fact, it's almost so hot that Leon is grateful for not having slept with his blue hoodie.

"Where am I? Where are the Huey's? Where are my neighbors?" Leon asks, looking around at this strange neighborhood with unfamiliar houses. His socks are off to the side of the mattress. He slips them on and finds a calendar on the ground. He lifts it but finds that he can't read it. The words are there, and certain letters like *J* and *E* are detectable. His eyes are playing tricks on him. These letters are spinning around like they're weightless flower petals blown by the wind. He rubs his eyes and tries his hand again at reading, but still nothing.

Leon drops the calendar onto the ground and the air from the calendar whooshes a few grey and black flakes onto his feet. A strange smell comes from these tiny ashen flakes. "That smells gross. Almost like…cigarettes," he says looking around. "This definitely isn't my room. This is a mistake. I think my parents kicked me out and left me somewhere else. Nothings making sense."

He walks over to the closet, and he is only mildly shocked to find that his clothes are all gone. While some can argue that Leon only likes the color blue, he can also be found in other colors like green, orange, purple, and even teal. But in this closet, nothing is found. Not a single jacket, hoodie, polo, t-shirt, v-neck, or pair of pants.

Leon looks up at the closet door where his blue hoodie is hung. "So, Mom and Dad really expect me to *just* wear this hoodie? He glances over to the mattress in disgust, taking one last look at the room.

Frustrated, he puts his pants on and the blue hoodie but rolls up the sleeves. As Leon approaches the door, he can hear loud sounds coming from outside his bedroom. He pushes his ear to the door to hear shouting.

"THAT WAS ONE FIFTY BILL'S WORTH OF WINE THAT *YOU* JUST FLUSHED!" his father shouts.

"Good! BECAUSE THEN MAYBE YOU'LL PUT OUR MONEY TO GOOD USE!" his mother replies.

"OUR MONEY? MOVE OUT THEN IF YOU DON'T LIKE IT!" his father screams.

"MAYBE I WILL!"

"Mom? Dad?" Leon asks in a worried tone.

"LET GO OF ME," Silvia cries out.

"Oh no!" Leon shouts, reaching for the doorknob. But then he realizes that something is wrong with the doorknob. It's not on the left like it normally would be. Confused once more, he reaches for the right side of the door's knob, twists, and rushes into the hallway to help his mother. But instead of turning right like he normally would, he finds nothing but a blank wall. He exclaims so loudly that it stops the fighting.

"Where are the stairs!" Leon shouts angrily.

"*Néol*? Why're you screaming like a girl?" he can hear his father yell.

"Dad," Leon mumbles. "Amy would lose her mind if she heard you say that," he chuckles lightly. "Wait. *What* did you just call me?"

"Néol?" Nero shouts. "Answer my...*hiccup*...damn question!"

"I'm fine!" Leon shouts but mutters once more about his confusion with the new name.

A few glass objects strike the ground and shatter.

"HEY!" Nero bellows.

Leon rushes to his left, now, and down the wooden stairs to see what the commotion is about. But instead, the kitchen is now on the left. Leon steps into the kitchen with now differently colored cabinets and tries to assess the situation.

"Um. You guys oka—"

And suddenly a bottle is thrown straight at his head. Leon dodges just in time as his father says, "Didn't. Didn't I tell you. To take the trash. Out last. Night?"

Leon holds his nose. "Jeez Dad," Leon says, looking at his father's bloodshot eyes, his sloppy and stitched up orange sweater, receding hairline, and pudgy face. His pants have countless holes in them.

"Um. Dad. Are you okay?"

"No," Leon's mother says, rushing into the kitchen with a broom and dustpan, sweeping up piles of glass. "He's not okay. Talk to him, *Néol*. He's spending all of our rent money on booze again."

"Oh," Nero says, "and you know...*hiccups*...what you should do? Since... Since you're the breadwinner! You should decide how we spend MY money!"

"Good idea! It might not all get blown away, then!" Leon's mother yells.

"I want you out. Tired of you," Nero mutters.

"You don't mean that," Silvia says coldly.

"You better. Hope I don't. Where would you go anyway?"

Leon's heart starts to crack. "Guys, isn't that a little harsh?"

"Wow," Leon's mother says, "I'm shocked you're getting in the middle this time." She starts to sweep up all the glass.

"Dad," Leon asks, "why are you drinking again? What about everything you did to quit?"

Silvia directs a quick glare to her husband, then Leon. "The longest your father has ever gone without a drink is two hours."

Nero walks right over and smacks Silvia right in the face. She nearly falls over. She stares at him in shock, as does Leon who then charges straight at him. But with one hand, his father pushes Leon's back straight into the kitchen counter.

"Don't you. EVER try to touch me again! *Hiccup.* Think you're a man? Protect her then!" his father shouts over Leon.

Silvia hits Nero on the head with a frying pan and shouts, "Néol! Get out!"

Fearing for what his father would do to him, Leon rushes straight for the front door. But he looks behind him to see his mother who is fearing for her life as well. She is shaking, walking away from his father who angrily stands up. Leon doesn't want to think about what can come next. He rushes back, grabs his mother's hand, and pulls her to the front door.

"I can't go! I have to stay!" his mother shouts.

"What are you talking about! We're going to Grandma's! She'll make sure you're safe there!"

"Neither of your grandmothers have their own home, you know that!"

"What?" Leon shouts back. "We just went there the other—"

"—*Néol*, you need to get out of here before he calls the cops. If you're hit too hard, you'll go back into a coma!"

"*Go back into a coma*? What are you—" Leon backs away. "A coma? What happened? For how long?"

"A few hours… Please go for your own good. Stay at your friends'. Or with your sister. Don't worry about me."

Leon's mother opens the door and pushes him straight outside, as he stumbles from being pushed so harshly.

Leon grits his teeth. He is shaking. His fists are balled so tightly it feels like his knuckles will snap any second.

"I'm really getting tired of getting pushed around like this!" He takes a few deep breaths, then raises his head with shut eyes. Once his eyes open, he expects the blue sky but instead sees a ghastly mixture of green, yellow, and turquoise. The sky is by no means clear. It is wrapped thickly with smog. So much that one would spend hours just looking for the sun.

"Okay. Let's backtrack. Apparently, I've been in a coma for a few hours. But it *looks* like it's been a few months." He looks up at the sky. "How did the sky go from blue to green? In a *few weeks* the climate changed this much? I think Mom's wrong. How could so much change in just a few hours?"

Leon turns around to see his new home, and says, "Dad wouldn't have let the grass grow this tall. All the flowers are dead. And I'm pretty sure I see cracks in the windows..." He shakes his head. "This is an entirely different house. Why are there only three bedrooms..." he says as he glances at the cracked driveway, "...and Amy's purple car isn't here. Wait. Whose red truck is that? It's so run down... Dude. Did we become bankrupt or something? Did Dad lose his job?"

Leon looks at his hands. "I became...a Knight...didn't I? Was that just a dream? What happened on my birthday?" he groans, then turns around to the new neighborhood, shoulders sinking as he skulks to the main road. "Maybe if I find Jason, he can make sense of this. If he still wants to talk. But...if this is a new neighborhood, then how can I find him?" he asks himself.

Knowing that going back into his new home is dangerous, Leon makes his way for the unknown streets. He starts staring at the yards of his neighbors around him. Or. At least what is left.

Each of these homes is barricaded by wooden blocks. Their grass is untamed and yellow. Not a single car passes through this street. He tries to read the street sign, which should say, *Echoed Intersection,* but of course, these letters like before are—

"Unreadable. Of course!" Leon shouts, stomping the ground in anger. "What am I supposed to do?" He feels something cool move on his neck, then he shifts, and then he feels something on his chest.

"What's this?" Leon says, grabbing the peculiar chain under his hoodie. "Uh." And then he remembers what happened on his birthday. Allie was in front of his own house. She threw the necklace straight at his head. And he remembers how much it hurt.

Leon feels his head. "She did that, didn't she. So then if I have this necklace… Then that means that day wasn't a lie. What happened after that?"

Leon growls and thinks, *Well, Voice? Do you have an answer for this? You've been awfully quiet, you know. Damn it. Still nothing? C'mon! This is the one time you haven't given me an idea!*

But still nothing appears in Leon's mind. Leon wanders up and down a few streets as the sun scorches him. He takes off his hoodie and places it on his shoulder. How he thirsts for both water and answers. He wanders at least within ten different neighborhoods…but each of these homes tells the same story.

All abandoned. All forgotten.

"Where is everyone?" Leon cries out to the green sky, now on his knees. "Jason. And I never thought I'd say this. But Deen. Jacaline. Allie. Where are you guys… Where is Amy? Where is anything?"

An engine's roar approaches Leon. "There you are, *Néol.*"

Leon turns around, and his eyes water at the sight of his friend in a shiny two-door red sports car. "JASON!" Leon shouts.

"Who? Whatever. Get in," Jason says.

Leon nearly trips over his two feet while running over to his friend. The friend that he thought hated him for his choice. But now, even after his graduation, has come to make amends. Jason, Leon's only friend is here, now, to save him from this nightmare.

But before Leon gets in the red car—he notices that Jason's driving from the right side of the vehicle.

"You coming in? Or what?"

Leon doesn't know what to do. Be confused? Or embrace his friend.

"Jason," Leon says desperately, rushing toward him and hugging him with one arm as Jason pushes him to the side.

"What the hell, dude?" he shouts, pushing Leon to the side. "You're gonna mess up my flannel."

Leon takes no offense to this. He lays his back on the seat and says, "Dude. I'm so happy to see you." Leon looks at the future-like interior, then pokes his head to glance at the car's exterior. "What model vehicle is this? Is this from the UK?"

Leon now notices that they're even driving on the left side of the road.

"You definitely lost your mind in the hospital. That was some coma."

Leon's face straightens. *You too with this coma thing? I'll roll with it.*

"Yeah…" Leon trails off. "I just don't know what's going on. My mom and dad are fighting. I'm in a new house. Everything's just really weird. The neighborhood's changed."

"Uh…your mom and dad fighting is old news, kid. They've always been doing that."

Leon's eyebrow raises. "Yeah? Maybe while I was in a coma, but not before then."

"I oughta back hand you for acting like this."

"What's with you?"

"What's with me? What's with you—wandering around like you lost your mind."

"Excuse me for trying to find my way around this area."

Jason grabs a cigarette from his flannel pocket and lights it, and Leon's jaw drops.

Jason puffs on the cigarette and blows the smoke straight into Leon's face, making him cough. "Why's your mom calling me, asking where you are? You know how that's gonna make you look with your girl?"

Nothing Jason says makes sense. Nothing about how Jason looks resembles anything Leon knew.

Leon pauses and takes a good look at Jason. He notices how long Jason's hair is. It's red, long, and spiky. Since when could he grow it so long? And his taste in fashion has changed. Jason always dressed conservatively— never with flashy colors or complicated patterns. But here he is in a flannel with asymmetrical tones. Even his ears are pierced.

Leon doesn't say it aloud, but he does think, *What...happened to you?*

SCAN FOR JASON

Leon faces forward in his seat. "Tell me about this coma, Jason."

"I'm not telling you crap until you call me the right name," he says, shifting the car's gears, swinging Leon forward.

"Dude!" Leon cries out at Jason's reckless driving. "Whatever you do, don't take me home!"

"I'm not. I'm taking your ass to the facility. Ever since you went there weeks ago, you've been acting different."

"What?" *Wait! That's it! The facility! They'll have all my answers!* Leon exclaims in thought. He sits back. *And if that's the case, I get to save myself all the trouble of walking. Because he knows this new neighborhood better than I do. But what did he mean by...the right name? And he's one to talk. He called me by a weird name too.*

76

☾   ☾   ☾

Colorado /\ Aurorae

The Earthshine Facility /\ The Courtyard

Time: Unknown

It was an awkward car ride for Leon. Jason just puffed away on cigarettes while driving him to the facility. He took routes that Leon had never seen before. These were routes that Leon could not have imagined would bring him here. What a godsend to have been at the right place at the right time. They passed a bunch of foreclosed houses, many shut down restaurants, and arrived in front of a long-rusted fence spanning countless acres.

Leon is used to seeing a long courtyard filled with luscious grass or snow, depending on the time of year. But now... What Leon sees is literally... The opposite.

"This place cures depression, right?" Jason asks as Leon steps out of the left side of the sports car. "Fix what you've got goin' on, then we'll talk. We need to go back out and bag us some girls."

Leon tilts his head in confusion, *The last girl I talked to was Allie, Jason.*

Jason chuckles. "Still loyal to your group of girls, I see. I feel ya. Haha. Whatever man, just call me whenever your mind's right. I'll be waiting for you." He revs the car up a few times, and Leon shouts, "Wait, Jason!"

"Not my name!" he shouts, speeding off into the distance.

Leon gives a long heavy sigh and faces the Earthshine Facility ahead of him. The building, unlike everything else Leon has seen today, looks similar. Not the same. But. Similar. But only in the aspects of its architecture. This building looks like it has been abandoned for years. Like a great fire overtook it and all its beloved paint. And then rain consumed it to bring all the rust he sees. There are also vines that have overtaken its many windows and doors, making it the graveyard it is now.

Leon places his hands in his pockets. "I forgot. Do I still have the beeper? My parents will track me down if I have it," Leon says, looking in his pocket but finds nothing. Instead, he finds something on the ground.

"A lighter?" Leon leans down to the grass and picks up a red lighter. He examines it closely and flicks the flame which burns his thumb, causing him to drop it. He picks it up and puts it in his pocket.

"Something tells me I'm gonna need this…"

Leon walks past the lifeless, rusting fountain to the front doors which are not automatic like the ones he remembers, but instead there are two doors for him to pull open. He tries yanking them a few times and dust falls down on his head.

"Kinda wish I tried the back door like yesterday," Leon says with narrowing eyes. He dusts the dust off himself and moves forward after pushing the heavy door open. It's pitch-black inside the Earthshine Facility.

He grabs the lighter from his pocket and uses its light to try and see ahead of him. He shines the tiny flame on the wooden floor ahead to see random holes in the ground. These holes vary in size. Some big. Some wide. Some gigantic.

It's best not to fall into any of them. He thinks.

He wanders forward for a bit, accidentally walking into a large cobweb, thick like a vine. Leon sees another light. Not a big one, but one shaped like a line, like it's coming from a door.

Leon swallows. "I think I hear someone's voice."

With the red lighter acting as Leon's little lantern, he wanders forward through the facility to the sound of an old man's laughter.

As Leon gets a better understanding of his surroundings, he assumes that either a fight occurred in here, or there was an earthquake that shook the place so badly that the ground uprooted—collapsing pillars, columns, desks, and countless things. Leon thinks of this hallway as the *patches of black space*. Leon follows the sound, finally able to lean against a wall. He sees writing and tries to read it. This is what he sees:

⊣ eɔstɒno Igoɩ

"Still can't tell what this says," Leon says, annoyed. Leon feels around this space and finds a doorknob. He pushes it open to find a familiar face—Stefano Giro at his desk, chomping on vanilla frosted doughnuts while on his cellphone.

"Yes, haha. Of course, Miles. Tell *Selim* I say hello. Alright. You two be safe now."

Stefano slams his flip phone shut, then nearly falls back on his chair after seeing the boy in blue staring right at him.

"Good heavens above!"

"Ah!" Leon shouts. "Sorry!"

"I just. I wasn't expecting to find you here so soon," Stefano says, standing up and dusting his face and looking at the calendar on the wall.

"Leon. Happy Birthday," he says, charging over, pulling him in tightly for a hug, "and congratulations on your graduation."

Leon's arms are stiff as the old man hugs him tightly, swinging him around, *He...he just called me...Leon...*

The old man with silver hair releases Leon, and he backs away from the old man.

"Dr. Giro. What is going on?"

Stefano tries to speak but Leon shouts, "Explain to me what's going on, now! Why did you—why are you—" Leon's eyes tear up. "What's happening to me!"

Stefano backs away, crosses his arms, leans against his desk, and listens intently as Leon vents, and his shouts echo throughout the facility.

"What happened to my family? What happened to me becoming a Knight? What's with my friends? My home? Why is everyone and YOU being so weird?!"

Leon leans against the bookshelf. "Nothing's making sense anymore... Is this another dream? Am I in another coma?"

"You're not in another coma. Nor is this a dream," Stefano says soothingly.

"How do I know? The last thing I remember is—"

"—Falling into a mirror?"

Leon's jaw drops. "Y—yeah...because of *you!* Yeah! You—well not you, but you had those weird, masked people push me into one! And then. And then ever since then...things have changed."

"And I to assume you're also having issues with reading?"

"Ye—okay. How did you know that?"

Stefano raises his finger and smiles. "I have an idea. You write down three scenarios that you think are occurring. And then we'll talk about what you've written."

"Okay."

Stefano retrieves a piece of paper and gives Leon the pen and paper so he can write.

"Now," Stefano says, "turn it over so that none of us can see it. What did you write?"

"I wrote, *future*, *dream*, and *nightmare*."

"So. What makes you believe that this is the future?"

Leon shakes his head. "You haven't changed at all..."

"It's more beneficial if you work for the answer rather than have me spoon-feed it to you. Now. Tell me about your theory on this *future*."

"Well. The easiest thing is. Wait. Can I have a doughnut?"

"I thought you'd never ask," Stefano says, grabbing one from the box and handing it to Leon with a napkin. There are seven more left.

"I'm sorry. I'm just starving. I don't know when or what I ate last," he says taking a bite. "Thanks."

"Well, you came at a good time. I just returned from *Ear*—anyway carry on..."

"Right. The future. Well. From what I remember. It was just my birthday which is in the winter. But here and today—it's the summer. Feels like it's June, if anything."

"Alright. Now tell me about the dream. Or. Nightmare, if you prefer."

Leon finishes the rest of the doughnut, and Stefano says, "Have another."

Leon giddily leans over for another with his same napkin.

"I guess it's mostly just that," Leon says. "Every bad thing you could think of happening to me is happening. Like. My dad's drinking again. And I watched him hit my mom. He never did that before. Even when I was a kid. But my mom stood there like this wasn't the first time. And. Everyone's saying that I was in a coma, which *really* makes me worry about *what else* happened when I was asleep."

"And then," Stefano grabs another doughnut, "everyone is most likely calling you by a *certain* name."

81

"Yeah," Leon nods.

"Would you look at the paper you wrote on, please?"

"Okay. What the!"

ꟻ ℲⱯᴚoⱴꞄ ,ᄅꞄⱯǝ꟒Ɔ, mɐǝꞃ, Ɔ, ᴎᴉǫʜɈmɐʅǝ

"What kind of magic—how did I—" Leon shouts.

"—Not being able to read is one of the many side effects of one's first time entering this dimension. All starts off as a foreign language you cannot decipher."

"*Dimension?*"

"Take as many doughnuts as you need, Leon. You're going to hear more than most Knights would during their first day of being *here*."

"Where is *here*? Where did *you* bring me?"

Stefano stands up with his hands behind his back, and Leon recedes, grabbing the chair once more, aiming its legs to the therapist.

"Wait. I. Déjà vu… I did this already…" Leon looks up at Stefano, "…except…you…*you had a blade out.*

Leon takes a good look at Stefano now, noticing major differences in the old man.

Stefano looks exactly how Leon remembered him. He has a wild full gray beard and mustache. Longer but curlier silver hair on his head, and he's wearing his same blue sweater and khakis. On his sweater is a certain symbol. The symbol is neither Pawn, Bishop, nor Knight, however. No. Leon's never seen this before. Leon lowers his chair and sets it back down.

"I take no offense seeing how being around me makes you apprehensive. Believe me, if I were you, I would have done the same. I've seen many people in that same seat you held, do worse. The man you saw—the one who looks like me—he brought you *here*."

"Here. You mean to this neighborhood."

"*To this galaxy.*"

Leon blinks and rubs his eyes, and Stefano places his unbitten doughnut down onto the table.

"Leon," Stefano says, sitting back down, "you're probably wondering why all these things have changed in such a short time. I tell you with relief that this is *not* the future. It is also *not* a dream."

"So, it's real."

"Yes. Where you and I once lived was a galaxy known as the Milky Way. But here in this world—things have the chance to be the opposite. The man you met was my reflection. And his name was *Festano Igor* who brought you to *The Murky Way.*"

Leon looks down at the doughnuts, then back at Stefano. "Were there drugs in those?"

Stefano bursts out laughing. "No, no. I'm serious, Leon."

"Were there drugs in mine?"

"No…"

"Okay. I think I've heard enough today," Leon says, heading for the door.

Stefano asks, "Did he have a mustache? Green jacket and pants? A deep gruff voice?"

Leon grabs the doorknob, and Stefano adds, "Did a bunch of masked individuals pick you up from the Earthshine Facility?"

He now twists the knob, and Stefano continues, "Was there a boy with curly hair?"

Leon turns around. "Yes?"

"Yes, to all? Or just yes to one?"

"All."

"That person with the mustache you saw, was my reflection."

"And the boy I saw?"

"A boy who was also a patient at the Earthshine Facility. Someone you went to school with."

"Dr. Giro, no offense, but do you hear how you sound right now?"

Stefano says nothing.

Leon continues, "A world that reflects ours? A multiverse? Don't you think the future makes more sense than anything you just said? We're six months ahead of our own time, Dr. Giro."

"Do you have a better explanation as to why everyone has called you a different name?"

"What, *Neol* or whatever?"

Stefano grabs the same piece of paper and starts writing.

"I can't read, remember?"

"Oh, right," Stefano chuckles. "Alright then. Try and use the letters in your own name, and see if it matches what they've been calling you."

"Alright," Leon sits back down and talks aloud while writing, "*Noel?* No. *Lone?* That's dumb. *Ne—*" He pauses. And suddenly everything comes together. His mother, his father, and his own best friend have called him by the name—Néol.

"It's...true...they have called me that."

Stefano smiles, then grabs a photo from his wallet showing a picture of himself and the same man who Leon mistook for him.

"Is this the same man you saw?" Stefano asks, pointing to the angry doppelgänger next to him.

"Unbelievable..." Leon utters.

SCAN FOR STEFANO | FESTANO

"If one thought created the universe, then who was the first to think? It is this thought which gives birth to the idea—that someone out there, somebody unknown to us, pondered… *What if there was a world that reflected ours?* That question, I believe, is what made this place… Or perhaps, even planet Earth."

After this explanation, Stefano lets Leon digest what he can.

"Can I have another doughnut?" Leon asks, but this time in a sad tone.

"Absolutely." Stefano hands him a brand-new doughnut with even a new napkin.

"I guess I have one question," Leon says, taking a small bite.

Stefano nods.

"Earlier, you said I wasn't supposed to be here so soon. What did you mean by that?"

"Oh. Well. Hmm. I'll try to explain it without overwhelming you. But. It's obvious, now, that you've been brought against your will, correct?"

Leon nods.

"Well. Normally when people are brought to this world, they normally don't come and find me until a few days have passed. Sometimes a few weeks. I've had some show up even after months. But. *Normally.* I would visit them in their new homes to try and break them into this new situation—and gently. You on the other hand, Leon, showed up maybe not what—a few hours after your *switch*?"

"Well, everyone here has been saying I was in a coma, so are you sure it's not been a couple months?"

"Well, your switch took place on December eleventh. And. Today is June twelfth."

Leon narrows his eyes. "But yet, we're not in the future?"

Stefano shakes his head. "No. But we *are* six months ahead of our own time."

"What?"

"You see, that is what I meant when I said I try to wean people onto these concepts slowly… Of course it's going to be hard for you. You lived one way, knew your own concepts for so long that naturally all of this would overwhelm you. But yes. We are twelve hours ahead of time, and we are also six months ahead."

Leon swallows. "You're right. This *is* a lot to take in."

"Well, you've always been a person who liked having the answers right away. Which. Isn't necessarily a bad thing."

"But also, isn't always good. Because. You're right. Sometimes I can be impatient."

"But. You should see this as a benefit. You didn't wait for things to come to you. You fought. And I think that makes you special."

Leon fights a smile and asks, "So, why are *you* here? Did your reflection switch you too?"

"Well, I'm around to serve as everyone's guide. So. When a Knight is switched here from Planet Earth, it is my job to walk them through everything. Otherwise—they'll be vulnerable to the dangers of knowing nothing."

"Like with me not being able to read."

Stefano nods. "And there's much worse than that. But. I digress. For people who've been switched to this world, *I* normally reach out to them. I would visit them in their new homes, tell them about this place, the rules, what to expect, etc."

"Why do that for them, though?"

"To arm themselves with knowledge, with the hope that they will fight my reflection back."

Leon yawns. "Sorry. It's not you. I'm just. Wow. This was a lot."

"But you kept up. I'm impressed."

"So. What now? If I'm in this reflecting world, how do I get home?"

"Well…that's not really easy for me to answer."

"Oh?"

"We must first speak about *your* reflection, Leon. The boy named *Néol Yelltnarg.*"

Leon trembles at his name but continues listening.

"That boy was the supposed devil-voice in your mind. Has been. Always was. He had a life and under my reflection's suggestion, switched you here to *Planet Heart*, for his gain."

"But why? Why go through all of that? What do I have that he doesn't?"

"I apologize ahead of time," Stefano says, looking at the clock on his rust colored amulet, "but I'm short for speaking. I must be on my way. I'm visiting someone named *Ombretta* to see how she's dealing with all of this. After her, I'll be traveling to visit a few others who are also in your situation."

"So, am I supposed to just go back to Neol's house? I'm gonna be honest, I don't really feel comfortable being there. My—I mean…his dad and I…well we almost fought. And while I'd like to try and protect my—I mean…"

"Don't worry, you'll get used to it."

Leon nods. "I'd like to protect my—I mean. His mom. But. I'd also like to prevent any more conflicts."

"Hmm." Stefano starts packing a few things into his briefcase. "There's an option for people in your situation. Two, but *one* of those options isn't available to you right now. Your one option is to stay *here* at the *Heartshine Facility.* At least for fifteen days."

"*Fifteen?*"

"Yes. Stay here for fifteen days so that you can learn all that you need to about this world—as it takes fifteen days to be able to read and decipher words. But. Here at least, you'll be safe. You'll be safe from Néol's unruly family, and you'll be safe from anyone else that would figure out your *true* identity."

"No offense, Dr. Giro, but this place is a trash heap."

"Not all of it," Stefano says with his briefcase in hand. "Come. I will show you to a room I made specifically for people in your shoes."

And so, Leon follows Stefano outside the room. Stefano leads, turning on the lights inside as they both head up a broken staircase to the third floor. Stefano on occasion warns him about which of the steps are the faultiest.

Stefano brings Leon to an all-white room with a twin bed, a desk, and a stack of booklets titled, *Equilibrium & Chaos*. Leon walks over to the desk and grabs one of them. It is a book with what looks like two churches. Or. Two towers. The side on the left has doves perched atop a tall tower, and a murder of crows perched atop the tower on the right.

"You're welcome to keep one of those. I made them for people who are switched here."

Leon places it down onto the bed. "Thanks," he says in a sad tone.

"Inside that dresser over there are packs of granola bars, unsalted peanuts, and bottles of water. I stuffed all that I could in there."

SEE THE BOOKLET

"Dr. Giro, after these fifteen days, how do I get home? Why was I brought here in the first place? I know you mentioned my reflection, but I feel like there's more."

"There's a lot more. So much that I cannot explain in a day. What I suggest for now, though, is that you look through that booklet. I know you can't read but look at the pictures. Let them be your visual aid."

"Yes, but. How. Can. I. Get home. You're not answering that."

Stefano takes a long sigh. "I don't know how to say this, Leon, but… You won't be able to go home. Not for a long time."

Leon's heart shatters. "So if he switched me here, we can't switch back?"

"You can…but the forces behind why you both switched are more nefarious than you could imagine. It's a miracle you came here in one piece. Many people are not as fortunate as you. And believe me. I acknowledge the pain you're feeling. Leon, my suggestion is that for now you stay in this facility, avoid bringing attention to yourself, and *do not* go wandering around outside. You make yourself a target for them and they'll destroy you."

Leon plops onto the bed. "I don't believe this."

"I'm sorry," Stefano says, turning away. "I know this isn't what you wanted to hear. But I promise. You will find your purpose in this. This isn't an ending but can be a positive beginning. I'm late. I have to go, but I *will* be here for you during these fifteen days. At least. I'll try my best to be. Goodbye, Leon. Be safe," Stefano says, shutting the door to the white room.

"Yeah. You too."

Leon glances at the booklet. He sits on his bed and opens it to the first page. He can't read it, but here is what it shows:

REFLECTION PRINCIPLE #1

INTO
THE MIRROR

☾ ☾ ☾

<u>Day 1:</u>

Leon awakens on the twin bed while flat on his stomach. He opens his eyes and sees something dark. Someone. Or. *Something* tall looking down on him.

I can't move! Why can't I—Oh no. Is this sleep paralysis? No. What the... What's it... doing with its hands? Leon thinks in panic. *Get away from me!*

His heart pounds like a speeding train, but thankfully, the being does nothing but stand as they watch each other curiously.

Of all times, Leon cries out in thought. *I'm stuck. Just like how I'm stuck here in this stupid world.* The creature pushes its face close to Leon's and then...

He awakens, gasping for air.

"What. Was. That?" Leon says, looking all around him and the white room.

He shakes his head. "I don't wanna see that again. That was weird."

Suddenly there's knocking at the door.

"Dr. Giro?"

The therapist opens the door. "Good evening, Leon," Stefano says.

"*Evening*? Just how long was I asleep?"

"Well, you've probably been exhausted with all you've been through. But. I just got here. So, perhaps all day."

"You're probably right. Not like I can tell what time it is anyway."

Stefano grabs his rust colored amulet from his pocket. "Well, it is eight fifty-five pm. I should also tell you that your very own amulet can tell the time too. Along with other things."

"Good to know. I'll try to remember that in fourteen days," Leon says as they both laugh.

Stefano asks, "Would you rather us speak in here? Or downstairs?"

"Um," Leon thinks for a second about his recent encounter with that shadow being. "Downstairs is good."

Leon follows Stefano out of the room and down the broken stairs.

"So, how was your rest?"

Leon thinks about how to answer this question. Should he admit that he was crying almost all night?

"It was pretty good."

"That's good to hear. Most people when they're switched here experience extreme depression. Adjusting here tends to take a toll on the mind."

They step into the office and take their seats. Leon at the patient's side, of course, and Stefano in the therapist's seat.

"I bet," Leon says, "I mean... You grow up your whole life knowing and loving one family. Then you just come here to be with the exact opposite of that."

"And it goes beyond that. It ties you to jobs and friends and circumstances, too. But before we start, I wanted to show you what I wrote for Néol's family so that they wouldn't suspect anything..."

Remembering that Leon cannot read, Stefano reads from a paper on his desk out loud:

I'm writing to keep you informed about your son, Néol Yelltnarg, and his progress here in the Heartshine Facility. We will unfortunately have to keep him here for fifteen days due to his extended suspension at Noelam High School.

To combat this behavior, I've taken it upon myself to sentence him to a juvenile penitentiary where he will be scared out of this negative influence. If you have any questions, you may call my secretary at this extension.

Ext 1964.

Sincerely,

Festano Igor.

Putting the paper down, Stefano continues, "That will buy you some time here, so that they don't go out looking for you."

"I appreciate that."

"Absolutely. So, Leon. Let's start with the basics of this dimension. We will start from the simplest of things, with *what* brought you here. Your disorder."

"My disorder?"

"Yes. Do you believe in it still?"

Leon doesn't respond.

"Maybe that's not the right question."

"No, it's just... I mean, yesterday you said The Voice was my reflection all along, right? It's just weird to imagine how that's possible. I mean, I heard him speak to me before. I remember even worrying that they were my *own* thoughts. But he would literally *speak* to me. And now you telling me this...makes me feel less crazy."

"Yes. Your disorder was never real to begin with. But. He is a living and breathing person. He has his own DNA, his own blood, his own heart, life, thoughts, and feelings. And in many of these things, you two are the opposite."

Stefano grabs the booklet titled *Equilibrium & Chaos* from his desk. "Like I mentioned earlier, I made this booklet for people like yourself who were switched over. These contain the rules that can teach you everything you need to know about this dimension and more. And yes, the pictures were drawn by yours truly." He opens it and points the first page to Leon and recites, "*Reflection Principle Number One. One cannot exist without an other. If you exist, then surely other forms of you will as well.*"

"So that's what those two people represent," Leon says, looking at the pages that Stefano is holding in front of him.

"Yes!" Stefano exclaims. "And for everything that exists…there is an *other*. Néol is your other. Your reflection."

"So, I don't have DID. But. Instead, a reflection. Wait a minute!"

"Yes?"

"If. If my disorder's fake—then—is *he* the one who sexually assaulted Allie?" Leon grits his teeth and stands up. "Oh, if it's because of him—then he's the reason for all of this! He ruined my life!"

Stefano nods. "Sort of makes you wonder why he would switch with you, hm? Because now he's just switched himself over into that world with *your* problems."

"What is he doing there?" Leon grits his teeth. "I have to know!"

"Patience, Leon."

Leon sits back in his seat. "Sorry. This is good news. Because now I know who to blame for all of this."

"Well…the truth is Néol isn't *truly* the one to blame. He's been manipulated, just like you. Just like all of those patients."

"What?"

Stefano's phone rings. "One second." He picks it up. "Yes? Okay. Please stop yelling, *Elliot*. I will be right there. And please tell *Lovyam* to be patient."

Stefano slams the phone shut. "I'm sorry, Leon. I have to go."

"But you were just about to tell me about who I should blame!"

"My reflection. He trapped you here because of a lie he sold to the people on both planets. If you give me time, I will explain things to you. Hopefully tomorrow." Stefano grabs his briefcase and rushes out the room without saying goodbye to Leon.

$$\mathbb{C} \qquad \mathbb{C} \qquad \mathbb{C}$$

<u>Day 2:</u>

Leon is laying on his back. He opens his eyes widely to see a shadow this time floating directly above him. His lips are sealed. He cannot scream. His arms and legs are frozen. He can't wiggle his fingers or toes. All he can do is stare at this thing. Whatever it is.

I can't even roll out of bed! He cries out in thought, *Stefano! Somebody, help me!*

Suddenly, the crown of Leon's head starts to vibrate. He can feel a buzzing sensation digging into him as these words crawl through his ears,

"time is relentless. No matter how great the intake of wisdom,

No one can chance the page for a second chance at fate.

What's done is set in stone for life.

Time's essence is comprised of lessons wrought of pain and baggage.

One doesn't simply snap into maturity.

It takes time, with the nature presented to us.

Our mindset chooses the connotation of our memories.

I felt the breadth of that lesson shortly after my 17th birthday.

Woe to me for there is so much that I wish to tell you...

And yet somehow even though you stand in front of me,

you are too far, too distant to listen."

Leon cries out, "Gah!" He swings forward on his bed, looking around at every corner of the room. "What was that?" He rubs his head. "And what was that feeling... Felt like someone was drilling into my head. That really hurt...and...what was it saying to me?"

Leon lets out a wide yawn and stretches.

"Oh?" Leon says, looking onto the desk nearby him. "A new pair of jeans. And. A new hoodie!" He rushes over. "This one has two black sleeves…and the body's blue. Dr. Giro must've gotten this for me."

Next to these clothes is a white t-shirt, a pair of socks, and boxer briefs.

"He didn't have to do that for me…" Leon says, and then suddenly…

But he did. Didn't he?

Neol! Leon shouts in thought.

And he did it specifically so that you could stay there. Which you will do.

No! When I find a way there, I'm gonna come there and—

—I wouldn't get carried away. You'll never come back to this world. Later.

Neol! Leon shouts out in thought, but his cry falls onto his reflection's deaf mind's ear.

"So. It's true then. He's in my world. Living my life," Leon grins. "But Neol, what if I told you that someone's helping me find a way back? Bet you didn't expect that," he smirks.

Leon slips his new clothes on, rushes downstairs, and is disappointed. He's disappointed to find that Stefano is not in the office like he had hoped. Saddened, Leon walks up the stairs and sits on the twin bed. "But. I'm stuck here. And I only have one way to learn anything… I need to know more about this world. So that…I can get home. And bring *you* back here."

Leon spends the rest of the day laying down and staring at the ceiling. Eventually, he tries his hand at reading once more. Sadly, the words and few numbers across the pages are still scattered. He passes out with the booklet on his face, drool dripping down the side of his cheek.

☾   ☾   ☾

Leon awakens and finds Stefano right at the door with a box of doughnuts. The label is facing Leon. He cannot read it, but it says:

Ascendin' Donuts.

"Huh?" Leon tilts his head in confusion. "Where'd you get that?"

"One of the only places on this planet that I'd get food from," he chuckles. "I'm sorry I wasn't able to stay for long yesterday. Did the clothes fit alright?"

"Yeah," Leon says, sitting up. "Thanks for that."

"Good," Stefano says with a smile.

"So, um. Neol spoke to me yesterday."

"Really. Hmm. I'm very surprised that he contacted you. Reflections normally tend to vanish after they've stolen one's identity."

"Not mine. He was taunting me just as he has before."

"Hmm. What did he say?"

Leon looks to the side of the bed where his hoodie is. "It's not important."

Stefano slowly nods.

"But. I do have questions about this world," Leon says, still looking away. *But I can't let him know why,* Leon adds in thought.

"Very well," Stefano says as he sits on the ground, pretzel style, and Leon joins him.

"On another day," Stefano says, "I will tell you all about the universe. But for now, you should know more about," as Stefano holds up the box of doughnuts, "how certain things and ideas came to exist. To do that, you must on a smaller scale understand where in the world we are."

Leon nods.

"The reflection of the USA is the ASU. Short for, *America's States United*. You'll find that our currency known as USDs are no good here. They pay with ASUs here. While *our* country ended the Cold War with Russia in 1991, ASU is still in a Cold War with Russia's reflection, *Aussir*. As a result, this country is still undergoing its *Great Depression*. I believe here, though...they call it the *Extreme Depression*. Lastly...America on Earth is a place that is often feared because of its many resources, but *here*, this country is bullied because of its lack thereof. Notice a trend?"

"Hmm. Yeah, actually. So not *everything* is the opposite, but *some* things are."

"Exactly. That's how the *multiverse* works. Not *everything* needs to be reflected here. But. What one world chooses, the other world may reject. Sometimes they both may agree on something, others they may not. Think of the multiverse as an infinite place of *multiple outcomes*."

Leon crosses his arms. "I see...when I saw my friend earlier. Or. Neol's friend, he was driving on the left side of the road. And his driver's seat was on the right, too. I thought he got the car from the UK or something."

Stefano shakes his head. "I wish I knew that earlier."

"Knew what?"

"That you'd seen one of his friends. It can be quite dangerous."

"Is it forbidden? I thought I was supposed to live his life?"

"It's not forbidden… But the organization we're up against…what they want most is for you to not cause a scene when living here. You must be very docile and submissive to this world's society. But what happens more often than not, is someone innocent like you would meet friends and family of the reflection, and well… The personalities or conflicts would clash so much—that the results are all sorts of fights. I've seen an abusive husband be switched here to abuse an innocent woman."

Stefano continues, "I've seen a wife who cheated on her husband on Earth just come here to try and do the same. I'll spare you the details on the domestic abuse that came after, but…let's just say the police came to them and things got ugly very quickly. That said, Leon, you shouldn't bring any attention to yourself."

"Okay. So, I just have to know Neol's friends and family ahead of time, and then I can adapt."

"I suppose we should focus on the friends of Néol, then. Let's just assume that they're reflections of *your* main group of friends. Who do you want to start with?" Stefano asks, reaching on the corner of his desk for a blank sheet of paper and pencil.

"Sort of generous for you to call them friends, but… We can start with Jason."

"Alright," Stefano says, writing the name *Jason* down. Stefano then draws a dash next to Jason's name, then writes *Jonas* next to it."

"Jonas?" Leon says aloud. "How'd you figure it out so quickly?"

Stefano chuckles. "When you do this for as long as I have, it becomes easy. Alright. So, tell me about Jason. Through him, we'll learn a little more about Jonas."

Leon gives a quizzical look and holds his chin.

Stefano adds, "Doesn't have to be anything special. Here, how about this. Is he kind? Yes, or no?"

"Very kind. And. Honest, too." *So honest that he admitted he never believed me with the Allie incident.*

"Hmm," Stefano says. "Alright. Is he a…giving person?"

"Jason? Oh yeah. He actually has two jobs. He's doing it to help his family. I think he has four brothers and two sisters, too."

"Wow. And he's doing this all while being in high school? When does he sleep?"

"I ask him that question all the time."

"Well, I hate to disappoint you, Leon. But this isn't sounding good so far."

"What? Why? I just told you that he's kind and helpful."

"Agreed. And while those things are good for you who is friends with Jason, it's bad for you who wants to be friends with *Jonas*. You just indirectly told me that Jonas is selfish and mean to people."

"What? How could you prejudge him so quickly? People aren't that black and white. Would *you* like it if I said that about you?"

Stefano turns to the side. He's heard this argument time and time again. It's taking all his power not to roll his eyes here as Leon rambles on.

"Leon. I'm telling you this from experience. I've met *many* reflections. While I'm not saying that *all* reflections are evil, I *am* saying that opposites do tend to exist. It's rare that they *don't* match that stereotype."

"Yeah, but at this point, you're just saying he's a ruthless manipulator."

"I didn't say that."

"I'm just saying, I think they could change."

"Don't you think you're just projecting?"

Leon pauses.

"I don't mean this to be rude, Leon. I know that you've been prejudged most of your life. But I don't want you to misunderstand. You can go forth and meet Jonas and the rest that Néol knows if you'd like. I won't stop you. But I can't guarantee that you two would get along. So, I will advise this. There will be many things that you weren't present for. For the sake of your discretion, agree to disagree. You cannot argue with what you were not present for, so why bother? You must assume that they are correct."

Leon sighs, "Alright... But you know. Maybe I can help him not be manipulative if he is."

"It's not your matter to deal with, Leon. He's not your friend. He's Néol's. The quicker you accept this harsh truth, the easier it will be for you to flow here. For your sake, I suggest not interacting with him at all."

Leon shakes his head and looks away.

"When you're able to read, look over that book with the *Reflection Principles*. It'll tell you the same thing I'm telling you now."

"That's stupid. And this organization just wants us to be okay with this?"

"Supposedly. That's my hunch. I don't know what the *Lunae Lux* truly wants. But I *have* noticed that they pounce on people who act out."

"So, we're all eventually going down, you're saying?"

"Yes. I expect that if nothing's done."

"So, what can we do?"

Stefano pauses.

"Dr. Giro?" Leon asks, noticing that the old man is looking away.

"That. I'm still working on. You see. The enemy can read my mind. Like how Néol can read yours."

"Wait, *what*? He can read my thoughts?"

"Yes."

"And I'm guessing that's how he always knew what to say."

"But you can read his too."

"I can? I've never heard his thoughts."

Stefano thinks, *I suppose Néol learned how to block him off, then.*

Leon straightens his legs and lays onto his back. "There's so much to this. If Néol knows all this stuff, then it's no wonder he pulled this off."

Stefano looks at his amulet's clock. "Yes. But you will catch up to him, don't worry."

"Wait—before you go."

"I know. You're eager to learn more about my reflection, right?"

Leon nods.

"Tomorrow. I promise," Stefano says. "I'll try to bring you some shorts or something so you don't always have to wear jeans. How're you doing on food?"

"Umm…" Leon runs over to the drawer, pulls it out, and sees three more granola bars. "Not too good. Weird request, but… You think you can bring me some cereal? Or eggs? It's been a while since I had something warm…"

"Hmm. I can work on that. I can't promise warm food considering there isn't a stove or microwave that I can bring. But that might mean I'll have to skip out on tomorrow."

"Yeah, that's fine. I'll remind you of where we left off, though."

Stefano stands up. "Very well. You have a blessed night, Leon."

MAP OF PLANET HEART

☾　　☾　　☾

<u>Day 4:</u>

Leon sneaks into the office. He finds a few things that grab his attention. Videotapes with titles of course that he can't read, many files, and what he assumes is a map of the entire county.

This of course, too, is a map he can't understand. But based on its size, he assumes that it is for the county he's in now. He folds this map and places it into his pocket. He sees a bunch of manilla folders behind the desk.

"If this is a therapist's office…then I wonder if one of Néol's files is in here…"

But he knows he wouldn't be able to find it just yet since he can't read.

He eats the last of his granola bars and deals with a starving stomach for most of the day. Leon tries to fight this dizzying headache with sleep.

ℂ   ℂ   ℂ

Day 5:

Leon wakes up with an even worse hunger headache. He looks around the white bedroom to find no one. Nothing but the desk and the dresser. But at his door there is a shopping bag.

And...a small bag of doughnuts poking upward. Leon charges right out of bed and digs into the bag. He tears open the first plastic wrapper not even knowing what it is and bites the bar. It's sweet. It must be a cereal bar. He consumes the sugary snack like a ravenous beast. He repeats this with a protein bar and then drinks an entire bottle of water.

"So wholesome..." he says in a relieved yet exasperated tone. He looks inside this shopping bag and sees a note. It reads:

Leon, I'm sorry I broke my promise. There were a few emergencies that I had to look after. I imagine you might have eaten your way to the bottom of these snacks to find this here note. Readables, enjoy. Also. There's a pair of basketball shorts here for you, as promised. I will see you when I can.

"Thanks, Dr. Giro," Leon says while smiling and shaking his head. "You forget. I can't read."

☾　　☾　　☾

Leon is disappointed to yet again not find Stefano. No note and no gifts this time around, either. Most of this day he paces around the room, wondering what could have happened.

Was it this mysterious organization that captured Stefano? But how could Leon avoid them when he knew nothing of them? Now, he has even more questions. Out of boredom, Leon tries to leave this white room to see what else may be upstairs aside from the bathroom. But everything is sealed off. Everything except the mural which says:

"Hell is…real?" Leon asks aloud, staring at a mural that seems to have been draw in blood. The mural is certainly one he's seen before—or so he thinks. The mural shows a moon with sharp eyes and what looks to be a sun trapped in its jaws. The sun has shut eyes.

Leon sees something dark move out the corner of his eye, along with a few footsteps. "Who's there?" He hears no answer and shouts, "Screw this!" He runs back to his bedroom—the white room. From this point forward, he chooses to stay inside his room, except for when he must use the restroom. Because of this new fear of something or someone stalking him, going to the bathroom becomes a chore.

☾ ☾ ☾

<u>Day 7:</u>

Leon lies awake on his bed, tossing his amulet up and down. Up. And down. Up and down. He does this repeatedly until it falls flat on his mouth.

"Damn it," he says, rubbing his lips. "This thing's heavier than I thought…"

He sits up. Despite being bored, he's afraid to explore this facility alone. After all, he has seen shadows moving around him quite a few times with no explanation. Knowing that Stefano isn't here, however, Leon decides to break one of his rules and sneaks outside. He opens the front door and wanders out onto the dead grass within the courtyard. "I won't go too far…"

He sees something black hide behind the fountain. "Alright! That does it," he says, creeping for whatever or whoever this *thing* is. Leon creeps to the side of the fountain but is dismayed to find…writing?

When the
man in the mirror gives us permission, we will seize the boy of envy.
The man
in the mirror saved us from those who hated us for how we looked. The
color of our skin was our curse. But the man in the mirror saved us.
We peacefully await his death
and rebirth. Once he returns, we can enact the final part of his plan.
We will find the boy of envy, give him the journal,
and finally become the main participants in this long drama.
Lord, we exist for you. We would
be nothing without you. You are everything, and we are nothing.
And to this you will say to us: I am everything, you are nothing.

108

Most who find these words will make no sense of them. But let those who have eyes see. Let those who read it hear. Let those who wonder think.

(.-ƎE-.)

The man in the mirror has two minds.
Two thoughts.
Two wills.
Two consciousnesses.

"I don't know what any of this says...but it feels like something led me here—"

Something sharp taps Leon's shoulders. Both shoulders. Alarmed with a racing heart, he looks all around him as the Heartshine Facility's door shuts behind him.

"Stefano?" Leon cries. "Don't lock me out! I'm sorry! I was just bored!" He rushes back to the front doors. He pulls and pulls and is shocked that the doors weren't locked. He rushes in, heads straight up to the white bedroom, mumbling, "Someone's playing a trick on me...or...I don't know. This place is weird. I've gotta leave." He rubs his shoulders. "Maybe I'm losing my mind...but... I don't have DID. I can't. It was all made up. I don't know why it was made up, but... Stefano says it was. But maybe...do I have schizophrenia, then? What do I really have?" Leon shakes his head and rubs his shoulders. "I know what I felt. That was real."

☾   ☾   ☾

<u>Day 8:</u>

Leon is running outside the front doors of the facility with the map he stole from the office in hand. He knows he can't read the writing. He does his best, anyway, to try and read the geography of the map and match it to his current setting.

This works until Stefano catches him red handed in the middle of the courtyard. Leon does the walk of shame back to the facility with Stefano right behind him.

"I wasn't trying to go home!" Leon shouts, now sitting on the bed, his voice echoing in the white room.

Stefano crosses his arms and stands at the door in silence.

"I wasn't!"

"Leon…not only was I not born yesterday, but I also have dealt with plenty of other former Knights who tried the exact same thing as you."

"So what?" Leon asks. "So what if I'm trying to go home?"

"Which home? To Néol's? Or yours on Earth?"

"To Neol's."

"Leon. Lying won't help. I'm trying to protect you."

"By keeping me hostage in here? Something's in here, Dr. Giro! There's blood on the walls. And one of the doors shut by itself. I think even once the sink turned on without me in there. I can't be in here *by myself* every day," yells Leon in frustration.

"Well, would you rather be with *his* family?"

"Anything is better at this point. I'm bored out of my mind. And I'm sure my reflection's having a great time."

Stefano nods. *And you just gave yourself away. Now I know what you really want.*

"Leon…" Stefano says, "…did you know that if you leave this world *before* the fifteen days are finished, that they would reset?"

"They would?" Leon shouts while Stefano rubs his nose and looks away.

"Well," Leon adds, "it shouldn't be a problem if I make it home."

"And if they brought you back by force?

"Just show me how to get home. I *need* to leave. I left my family behind on a bad note. Allie needs the truth. I've got a lot to clear up with my name!"

"There is no home to get back to!"

Leon swallows, glaring at Stefano who takes a deep breath and gently says, "Leon. Your life from the moment you became a patient at that facility was destined for change. You may *never* see them again. And you might not even graduate high school. What you knew on Earth is gone forever. And. Others there will experience the same and worse. And if not now, in time they will."

"Why? Why can't I just switch him back here?"

"Even if you switched Néol back here—you would have to answer to the *Lunae Lux*! *They're* who brought you here."

"Why? Tell me why they did this."

Stefano points to the floor. "Join me on the ground."

And so, they sit across from one another, pretzel style.

Stefano gives a heavy sigh. "It all started…with the idea of helping people. And believe it or not. The idea of doing that didn't come from me. It came. From my reflection, *Festano Igor*. The idea was for both of us to start facilities that could help people in *both* of our worlds. The Earthshine Facility was created by me, and The Heartshine Facility was his creation. Both facilities had the same goal: heal those with traumatic issues, mental disabilities and so on. Over the years, we became even better at our practices and spread our knowledge to other therapists. We would recruit new talent, expand our resources, and our buildings underwent expansions. In time, we even tried to bring mistreated people out of mental asylums. We brought them into ours so that they could be healed from the wrong that society had put them through."

"So, you two were friends?" Leon asks.

"Brothers, even. So I thought."

"Well. This was a better start than I thought it'd be. Everything in the end was made to help others."

Stefano shakes his head. "Indeed. Ideally, both facilities on paper were meant to heal people but—look around. You said you saw blood on these walls. And having been a patient yourself, can you say for sure that that's the facility's intent?"

"That's true. But wow. With how strict you are about switching around to different worlds, I never would've guessed that you two did the same thing."

"I pose these rules for you and everyone else's safety. To not only prevent someone else like him from rising. But also. To protect you, your friends, and families."

Leon turns away for a second and then asks, "So if this Festano guy is so bad, then how was he the one who came up with the idea to help people?"

"Someone very close to my other suffered from an unfortunate fate. And that person's shortcoming connected us both. I felt bad for Festano. I really did. He was broken by the loss. And out of remorse and understanding of why we had connected, I thought of something that could repay him for the loss he had suffered. Rather. Both of our losses."

Leon nods. "And thus. The facilities were born."

"Indeed. Again, everything on paper seemed well. But in time, instead of being sympathetic to those individuals or their minds, the faculty of these facilities and society would shun them. The mentally ill would even be used for benefits in finances or sympathy. The hope of healing these patients was a fallacy cast by Festano. But the worst part is…since *I* was the founder on Earth, he used his similar appearance to tarnish my name. He made everyone think that *I* was kidnapping these patients. Torturing and murdering them. That *I* was responsible for all the bad in that facility. I became a wanted figure. And I've been on the run since. I can't show my face on Earth. And here on Heart, I'm wanted by Festano himself."

"I'm sorry to hear that. I didn't know. It explains so much…why he was there on the night of my graduation. I truly thought he was you. I figured you'd just shaved your beard and got a new wardrobe. The only *real* difference was your voice. Maybe even the way you spoke."

Stefano laughs uncomfortably. "You won't be the last."

"But what about the people on this planet? Were they also lied to?"

"Well, I was under the impression that both facilities would cure the same things. But later, I found out that The Heartshine Facility was more focused on…curing depression. I can't really say it was too much of a lie…"

"Huh? *Just* depression? While yours was focused on—"

"—A multitude of disorders. Precisely. And we continued expanding. Probably still are today. Here on Heart, people would claim that they were depressed and then would sign up at the facility to be cured."

Leon's eyes widen. Stefano continues, "All I know is that these are the people who would steal an Earthling's identity at some point. They can enroll or *be* enrolled as early as five years old."

"*Five?*"

Leon thinks, *How old was Néol when he enrolled? Or did someone enroll him?*

"Wait," Leon says aloud, "but isn't *this* the Heartshine Facility? How are people enrolling if this has been shut down for years?"

"My thoughts exactly. I don't know what happened to this particular facility. But this being inactive doesn't mean Festano wouldn't build another elsewhere."

Leon shakes his head. "Okay. Okay. Back to the Earthshine Facility. Because no one has been able to answer this. What are the ranks, and what do they really mean?"

"Brace yourself for this," Stefano says, chortling a bit.

I'm ready. It's finally time I know the truth... because things changed ever since I became a Knight...

"It's as you know. Everyone starts off as a Pawn. This is a position for new patients that have most recently been traumatized from a certain situation. With whatever occurred with them, this label normally has programs that would make people desperate to grow."

"Could you say that differently? That was a lot to take in."

"Think of it this way. It's like what happens to people in the army. When their heads are shaved and they resemble the other recruits, their identities are broken. And what comes next is their resurrection. While in the army, the weak are those who give up in bootcamp, and to the facility, *all* who are enrolled are weak. And to exit this facility, you *must* be strong."

Leon nods in agreement, and Stefano continues, "Pawns in their final stage not only acknowledge their disorder, but they see themselves as a fault being trapped in existence."

"Hmm. Sounds accurate…"

"Should I continue?"

"Yup. I'm keeping up."

"Good. As you recall, Bishops endure interviews, lie detector tests, and more to see *where* they are in their progress to *healing*. And beyond that, they can even belong to subcategories based on their faults and tendencies."

"What do you mean by faults? Isn't everyone faulted?"

"On paper…but in the facility's case, they're referring to OCDs and phobias. Consider yourself unlucky if you have those…"

"Why?"

"You'll never be seen again is all I can say. I've personally known Bishops who had cleaning OCDs or sometimes phobias of water, and during their graduations, they would vanish. Not to be seen here on Heart or. The *other* place I'll tell you about shortly."

Leon is silent. He continues listening.

Stefano continues, "Bishops would be told by society that they should ignore The Voice because of it being *fake*. But in the facility itself, the therapists would tell them to continue speaking to it because it's *real*. They would gaslight patients back and forth into thinking that either-or was possible."

"Sounds about right…"

"But as for society, Leon. Well, you tell me. How did they treat you for having DID?"

"Like I was crazy. If I did so much as raise my voice, sometimes people would cower. And not because I was intimidating. It was like I was…unpredictable."

115

"And thus, we move toward *the lie*. The lie that gave you that disorder."

"You mean…"

"Yes…I know *you* didn't harm Allie. I knew it from the beginning just like with everyone else. You've been framed. As for your reflection and why he framed you, I can only assume that there's *something* that you have that he doesn't."

Maybe…a family? Leon thinks, *After all, I didn't see his sister. And his parents were fighting…*

Stefano continues, "But with Festano who manipulated your reflection and because of all of what happened, you're here."

"But. Why? I still don't get it! All that trouble. All those years of being locked away, bullied, and starved—just to come to this world? You're telling me that this is the fate for everyone in that facility?"

"I wish. But no. We'd have a much better chance of retaliating if everyone did. No. What he's doing to the other population of Knights is what makes him…" Stefano trails off and starts trembling. He breaks all eye contact with Leon, staring at the white walls.

"Stefano, what did he do?"

"He traps them in a place called *Hell*."

And with these words, Leon recalls the blood drawn mural that he saw on the wall which said: *Hell is real.*

Stefano's words come out shakily. "Those people, Leon, are people who've lost all their freedom. They have the will to fight back but can't. They have no choice but to rely on those who know nothing of their whereabouts."

"Oh…" Leon says.

"Knights like *you* who've been switched over are their only true hope at being rescued. And. That organization I've been telling you about…They're his army. Festano Igor commands an army known as the *Lunae Lux*. And they will stop at nothing to perpetuate this nightmare. Even if it means wiping *you* and your *other* out."

Leon looks down, *So if I switch back in secret…I'll have to be careful—*

Stefano shocks Leon by tightly grabbing both of his shoulders, "Leon. You must be wary of those who wear the faces of demonic suns and moons! They're leaders. The ones who have the most distinct masks are also the ones who change them the most. So sadly, I can't tell you what they currently look like."

"Stefano, are you always on the move because of your reflection? It's because he can read your mind. Isn't it?"

"Yes," Stefano says as he releases Leon's shoulders.

"And without you. There really isn't any hope. Is there? Because only you'd know as much as him, really. Only *you* could go around teaching all the Knights what we should truly know."

"Well, I do my best to not get caught. Aside from helping everyone, I make sure I tell no one where I go or why. Just as I change my behaviors to keep them off beat, they change their masks to weed out familiarity."

Stefano glances into his rusted amulet's clock. "And speaking of which, I almost lost track of time," he says in a panicked tone, standing up.

"Wait! Stefano!" Leon says, watching him grab the doorknob. But then he thinks, *If I ask him too soon…it'll make him suspicious…*

"Nevermind," Leon says.

Stefano pushes the door open and without facing Leon, says, "Next time, I will teach you what you need to know about returning to Earth."

Leon's jaw drops as Stefano leaves the room.

Day 9

Leon awakens on his bed.

No! Not again! he cries out, staring up toward the creature clothed in black with red eyes. It is doing nothing but standing there, staring at Leon as he tries his absolute hardest to move his mouth. He tries moving his arms, his legs, but of course, like before, he has no such strength. Instinct drives Leon to want to say a few prayers he had learned from his childhood, but even trying to think them aloud does him no good. Somehow, his mind is sealed from certain thoughts.

The shadow being takes a step closer. Just like before, it has one palm open and the other hand moving over it frequently.

Stay away from me!

"Perhaps not today...perhaps not even when you first see Her...but it will be when it is time to fix all."

What? Leon thinks in response to the creature's gibberish. A sharp dagger starts stabbing into the crown of Leon's head. Leon cries out, but his shouts do not reach the room. His shouts echo only in his head.

Is this shadowy creature getting some sort of delight from this? Countless sharp spear-like tentacles appear from behind Leon, piercing his back countless times. But there is no blood, no visible wound from this strange ambush.

The shadowy creature shakes his head. It says, "To the under side I go. Back"

And suddenly, he awakens.

"Why…why does that keep happening to me?" Leon wonders aloud, rubbing his head, then his back.

"I haven't had sleep paralysis this badly since I was a kid…I'd better not tell Dr. Giro. He might make me stay here longer than I need to."

☾   ☾   ☾

Day 10

The next day, both Leon and Stefano are sitting in the office.

"Alright, Leon. Today's the day I show you how to travel to Earth, as promised. Now. Did you bring your amulet?"

"I did," Leon says, holding it up proudly.

"Good. Make sure you always have it with you. As I mentioned before, it has many tools within it.

Leon curiously looks at the amulet. "It does? Looks like a regular mirror and watch to me."

"Its clock is certainly handy because, as you know, both worlds are twelve hours apart. So, keeping track of time is especially important. But. If you open it—"

Stefano opens his amulet to show Leon an example, and Leon exclaims, "It can do that?!"

SCAN FOR LEON'S AMULET

Stefano smiles and nods. "Do you see the nine moons?"

"A whole bunch. Hmm. Almost like they're all the moon phases?"

Stefano nods again. "Now pay *close attention*," he says firmly as he points to his open amulet. "When you stare into the center of this amulet, you will see a transparent pointer. I'm sure you know how to use a compass, so all you need to know, is this. Earth is on the *east*. Heart is on the *west*. Now tell me what I just said."

"Um," Leon raises an eyebrow. "Earth is on the east? And. Heart is on the west?"

"Yes. So…" Stefano grabs a piece of paper and uses a pencil to draw. He draws two circles and then a line from the right circle to the left. "You and I are here on the left within Heart. To arrive in Planet Earth, we must find a mirror that is facing the direction of east. Néol, in this case, would need to use a mirror to travel in a westerly direction."

"Oh. I see. But what happens if we travel in any other direction?"

"It can potentially spell life or death. Any other direction would take you to an unknown world. And…we don't know what else is out there. Maybe another daring soul knows, but I can surely tell you—Earth and Heart are all I know," he says, then scratches his nose.

Interesting… Leon thinks.

"It truly makes me wonder, though," Stefano says, scratching his beard. "Which of these two worlds came first? And. What would happen if we ventured astray toward uncharted areas? What would happen if we were to travel straight in one direction?"

"I wonder how all of this came to exist…" Leon says. "My life before this was just Aurorae County. Never thought about space, let alone the universe."

"Most people tend to see what's in front of them…but I believe that the universe is infinite, and it's because of *one person,* whose thought gave birth to planets with inhabitants such as you and me. The people within those planets continued to create and push among the galaxies' boundless fabric."

Leon yawns, and Stefano says, "Well, you're probably exhausted from all of this. So, I suppose I could teach you how to leave another day—"

"—I'm up for it now!"

Stefano smirks and chuckles. "Very well." He grabs another piece of paper and writes the numbers one through ten.

"First Leon, I'll have to torture you with a lot of information. A lot of what I say may not make sense, but the more you know, the better."

"I'm ready," Leon says with a determined look. *Why did I lie? My eyes are already heavy. C'mon. Focus...*

"Wait," Leon says, "I have an idea. If you're going to explain something complicated, can you use simpler terms?"

"You're right," Stefano says. "They normally say that if you can't explain something in three different ways, then you truly don't understand."

Stefano draws a dot next to the number one. "This is the *Zeroth* dimension. This is also known as nothingness. You can say that this is completely useless because we cannot detect it."

Leon nods.

Stefano crosses out numbers one and two. But on the third, he draws a cube using dotted lines to show all ends of its interior. He then draws a spiral intending it to represent a galaxy.

"The *Third* Dimension. Space. Outer. Space. This is what can be found with the use of numbers." Leon yawns and Stefano narrows his eyes. "I know this seems boring, but you *need* to know this."

"Fine, fine," Leon says, wiping his eyes. "I'm ready."

"Alright. The *Fourth* Dimension. This is space time. This is where you, me, and everyone else who exists resides. This is *any* world that someone resides in."

"So, Planet Earth and Planet Heart. They'd be the fourth dimension?"

"Correct. Now this is where things can get confusing."

"Uh-oh."

"The *Fifth* Dimension. This is determined by imagination. Remember what I was saying earlier about the multiverse and how it is full of alternate possibilities? This dimension is basically us being aware of how every universe has its own timeline. The people you met—Néol's mother and father. And even Jonas. They're all a part of *his* life, taking part in their own story, while reflecting your friends."

"Oh. That's not so bad," Leon says, folding his arms.

"The *Sixth* Dimension. This is the act of life taking the form of a star. Let's say I did not come to the facility today, and you instead decided to stay in bed and sleep. Just that thought alone created an alternate world."

"What? You thought of it, and now it exists?"

"We can't know this for sure—" Stefano says, rubbing his nose and looking away, "—but... Yes. Remember the quote—*If one thought created the universe, who was the first to think*? Take that quote literally, and you can do *anything*."

"Could I live as the person in that world?"

"No. You can only be who you are now."

"Hmm. That makes sense. I guess everyone would end up living everywhere if that were the case."

"Precisely. We're almost there. We have four more to go over. Alright. The *Seventh* Dimension. This is the plane that allows us to glance at every dimension. And perhaps, if we were God himself, we too could use this dimension to see *everything*."

"How do you know about it if we can't get there?"

"I can't comment on that. I can say, though, that people think of this realm as a telescope to all life. Imagine the universe as a zoo for God to peer into."

"Huh. Just says how tiny we truly are."

"Three more to go. Want to take a break?" Stefano asks.

"Nah. I'm keeping up."

"Good. Next is the *Eighth Dimension*. This one gives us access to all universal histories, also known as infinity. We can compare everything without taking all into account. The *Ninth* Dimension is similar to the last two, but it again would pertain to God's knowledge. Only he could be omniscient to know what's here."

"Well, what is there?"

"Everything. All the history that exists is here. Everything that is anything is accessible for him here. Perhaps the same can be said for anything that wishes to come close."

Leon yawns once more. "Sorry. I'm not bored."

Stefano chuckles, "And we have arrived at the final dimension. The *Tenth*. This is where we end. This is the pinnacle of our imagination; there is no way possible to continue, unless…" He trails off.

Leon unfolds his arms. "Unless?"

"Unless, if one such as you, and me, were to arrive to—" Underneath the number ten Stefano writes *The Eleventh Dimension,* "—a world reflecting the Fourth Dimension. This is where you and I have traveled to the opposite…*the Other Side.* A world that serves as our mirror. Names, ethnicities, genders, sexes, events, morals—truly anything that exists can be reflected here."

"Huh." *He still hasn't given me the answer.* Leon sits up. "So, wait. What happens when I walk through the mirror? Let's say it's facing east toward Earth. What happens after that? Which of these eleven dimensions would I go to?"

"You would arrive at the Eleventh Dimension." Stefano flips the same paper over to its blank side and draws a bridge with doors on both sides. "Once you walk through the mirror, you would appear out of one of these doors. And all you need to do is walk forward. So long as you used the compass correctly, you'll arrive at your destination."

"But then, why did I need to know all about these other ten dimensions?"

"Believe it or not, the knowledge of each of those will come in handy, one day," Stefano says, glancing at his amulet. "But you did well, Leon."

"That's almost too easy." *And now…I can go home. I just need to find a mirror.*

"But. There's a catch."

"Huh?"

"Do you remember what the moon looked like on the night of your shift?"

Leon shakes his head.

"Well. Think carefully about that. When you have your answer, tell me it when we meet next."

Damn it. He knew what he was doing. He probably already knows that I want to go back home, Leon thinks.

C   C   C

<u>Day 11:</u>

Stefano knocks on Leon's bedroom door. "Leon, is this a good time?"

"Yeah."

Stefano creaks open the door to see balls of paper all over the floor. As he steps inside, Leon is on his bed, crushing a piece of paper and adds it to his scattered collection around the room. He groans, "I can't remember what phase it was. I can barely remember that night as it is."

Stefano laughs and says, "What phase do you *think* it was?"

"I don't know the names. So. This one," Leon says, facing the paper toward Stefano. "I think it's a half moon."

"Close...sort of."

"I give up, then," Leon says.

"Let's talk a bit about the origin behind the name, *Earthshine*."

Leon sits on the bed and crosses his arms. Stefano, this time, leans against the wall. "Our answers are made most apparent to us when we look backwards. Everything is connected to a single moment. All emotions, actions, and words have origin. The same goes for everything you've seen. For instance, you call this place the Heartshine Facility, and the patients from *our* world address the facilitators as Earthshine Guards. I want you to ask yourself why it is that you call them that."

"I never heard of the word *Earthshine* until I started attending that facility. I called them Earthshine Guards because that's what the other Pawns called them. I just thought it was normal," he says with a shrug.

"Well. The Guards cannot be called Earthshine Guards without Earth or its Facility to house them. The facility couldn't exist without a creator. And a creator is nothing without an idea. The solar systems follow the same pattern. Without the sun, no planets would ever know life. Without the moon, we could never know of tides. With no sunlight to grace the moon, we would never know Earthshine. And without Earthshine, one could never come to this reflected planet. This is the law of Luna, motion, and light."

Leon sits forward curiously on his bed. "So then, what is this *Earthshine*? Is it based off something?"

"Yes. As the moon rotates around Earth, sunlight touches its surface in different angles. Depending on how the light strikes the moon is what gives us the nine phases that we have now. You've already seen through pop culture and folklore how the full, half, and crescent moon are used quite frequently. But of all these moon phases, there is *one* that captures light from not only the sun but the planets as well. Some people refer to this phase as *Planetshine*. But for our home planet's namesake, Earthshine is more apt."

"I didn't know the moon could reflect light. I always thought it was just a floating rock."

"Leon, the moon *is* a mirror. But because of the event's rarity, it's often very difficult to notice. Some note that this *Earthshine* is brighter than a full moon and to many others even brighter than the sun. Identifying it is a challenge because of the clouds that shroud the light's path."

"So, you've seen this yourself?"

"I have. Quite a few times when I used to rely on it."

"Relied on it? What would you need it for?"

Stefano takes his left hand's forefinger and thumb to make a *C* shape. "The moon you saw looked mostly like this."

"You're right. I actually saw the Earthshine Guards use that symbol as a salute." Leon's eyes glow, and he reaches for his necklace to open the locket. "So that's why the moon phases are on here. It's so we can track down the crescent moon."

Stefano grins. "Very good, Leon. Now are there any other burning questions that you'd like to ask?"

"Plenty. So, I can use this *Planetshine* phase to get home?"

"Well, *Heartshine* is your key to getting back home. However, like I said, you're more likely to find a crescent moon than you are this special moon phase. Crescent moons appear about once a month which makes Planetshine…very rare."

"Oh. Well, that's useless then."

"For now, it may seem that way. How you will get home is based on everything you've taken from me during these sessions." The doctor walks out into the hallway and says, "When the time comes, commit all that you know and have heard to memory. You'll find your answer in that sanctuary."

On the *twelfth* day, Stefano did not show up. This became a problem for Leon because not only was he alone, he also had no money or ASUs to purchase food. Leon was stranded, hungry, and alone. It didn't help that he woke up while it was dark. Now, even his sense of time is ruined. He awoke with sleep paralysis a few more times. But thankfully, this time nothing spoke to him. However, he did feel like he was being watched. This made him   afraid   of   falling   asleep   for   a   bit.

On the *thirteenth* day, he thought about Néol and what he was up to on Earth. He couldn't read Néol's mind as Stefano had suggested, and without a voice in his mind to keep him company, Leon experienced true loneliness. This was the one time he wished to have The Voice near.

He wished that he would have done things differently with his family—that even if they believed he did what he did to Allie, that at least they were kind enough to fund him and his *healing* at the Earthshine Facility. As corrupt as the place was, they still had the intent to help.

Out of boredom, he made his way to Festano's old office, searched through the manilla folders, not by name but by the headshots inside each. He saw many faces. Only two were familiar, but only because they could have been reflections of people he'd seen.

Like the boy named Miles, for example. Except in his picture, he had straight hair. He found Néol's headshot and was surprised at how much the two resembled one another. Néol had a scar on the right side of his chin. And his eyes seemed much more tired.

His chin was pointier than Leon's, but their hairstyles were the same. Néol's default expression seemed to be anger, like Allie's. The photo was in black and white, so Leon couldn't tell what colors he was wearing. But he could see a hoodie, so that wasn't far off from his own fashion.

"I need to know more about you, Neol. Because right now, I'm stabbing in the dark with the little I know." Leon has brought the folder back to his bedroom. "The second I'm able to read again is when I'll learn everything. I'll know just who you really are and what you're doing in my name."

On the *fourteenth* day, Leon did not get an ounce of sleep. The stack of papers within the manilla folder were thick, and it made him wonder what the files spoke of. Were they about good things? Or bad things?

He spent another part of this day rehearsing every horrible scenario. Leon, at another part of this day, imagined himself finally meeting his reflection and wondered what their encounter would be like.

Would the two stare each other down and then burst out laughing at the ridiculousness of the situation? Would they meet and then fight to the death? Or would Leon plead to be switched back and sway his other to agree? It is the final scenario which scares Leon the most.

If Néol is who Stefano says he is, then what would he do if he encountered Allie? His family? His friends? Those at his school? These thoughts convert every minute into hours for Leon. And the boy ends up almost never sleeping again.

☾　　☾　　☾

<u>Day 15:</u>

Leon holds the amulet's clock to his face, then throws it by his feet on the mattress. "I've had it with this stupid place. I'm losing my mind. I have no food. And I can't read. I never realized how much I'd miss doing something THAT simple," he wearily says while lying down with another hunger headache consuming him. It's a strain just for him to keep his eyes open.

Leon narrows his eyes then gets his feet off the bed. Like a zombie, he makes his way to the bathroom. He stares into the mirror, waving his hands frantically. "You gonna show yourself again, Neol? Hmm? Are you happy? You like living my life? Stealing my crap?" He punches the mirror, slightly bruising his fist. Frustrated that Néol not only won't reply to him, but that he also isn't taking the bait. He hopes to see *something*. Movement in the mirror. A taunt. Something to show that all of this isn't some lie. Below him is the sink. He twists the right knob first and burns his hands in the running water.

"Damn it!" he shouts. "I forgot," he says, finishing his sentence in a mocking tone, "*everything here's the opposite.* So, hot water comes out if I twist the right knob, now. Blah blah blah!" He shuts off the sink, then cools his hand off with the towel nearby.

"I'm done with this place," Leon says before grumbling a few swears under his breath.

Leon makes his way down the broken staircase, nearly tripping down the stairs over his two feet. With the red lighter, he illuminates the dark hallway and pushes the front two doors open to see a dark sky with green undertones.

He reaches under his hoodie for his amulet and stares at the clock's moving hands. The numbers, to his dismay, are still unreadable...or at least...so they seem. Leon watches the clock's hands in shock as they point to numbers that finally make sense to him.

Leon's heart pounds like a jackhammer as he dashes up the stairs to find the manilla folder that belonged to Néol. He only has one thing in mind—to read. "I can read! It's three pm? Wow. I must've been able to read the whole time!"

He throws the folder onto the bed and scatters the documents all over it. "What to read first... Oh. This one has his profile." He turns to the second page.

REFLECTION PRINCIPLE #2

"*Néol Yelltnarg. 5'6, brown skin*—yeah, yeah. He looks like me. What about his personality? Hmm...*he voluntarily enrolled at the Heartshine Facility at five. Enrolled here at the Heartshine Facility because of depression and frustration from child abuse.*"

Leon continues, "*Prior to becoming a Pupa, he was suspended from school several times due to numerous assaults on*—fellow students?" Leon swallows and keeps reading, his heart racing with his scanning eyes. "*Had the police called on him for mercilessly beating his father bare handed...*his father? How? His dad pushed me into that counter like it was nothing... What's with this guy?"

Leon places the packet down, then grabs another piece of paper. "This one's a police report. *Caught joyriding with Jonas Aicrag.* Yep. Definitely sounds like Jason's reflection."

Leon grabs a different piece of paper from the bed, and this one makes him yell, "*SHOPLIFTING?*"

Leon throws the paper onto the bed, slips his hoodie on, his jeans, and shoes. He speeds down the broken stairs. "This guy's gonna ruin my life. If he did all this stuff here, then what's he gonna do on Earth? Screw what Stefano said. I'm getting out of here. I've gotta get back."

Leon barges into the room with a sign that reads, *Festano Igor's Office.* At another moment, he might've been grateful to read. But now, he's too anxious and desperate to leave. He grabs the phone on the wall, holds it to his ear, and hears a dial tone. He's relieved to hear that the phone works.

"They've gotta have some kind of database with phone numbers in here..." he mutters, holding his chin. He scans all the books on the bookshelf until his eyes find a giant book titled *The Blue Pages.* Curious, he opens the book and cycles through all the last names until he finds *Aicrag.* He knows this is Jonas's last name since the documents lying around his bed confirm it. It is the reflection of *Garcia.*

Leon calls about eighteen different people with the last name Aicrag, embarrassing himself more than the last as he awkwardly asks for Jonas. None of these people took these calls politely, some even cursing him out. But on the nineteenth call...

"*Hello?*" a woman on the line says.

"Hi, is there someone named Jonas there?"

"*Jonas!*" the woman shouts.

Leon's jaw drops.

"*What!*" Leon can hear someone shout on the other end.

"*It's for you! Come pick it up!*"

After a bit of rustling on the phone, Leon mutters a plea, "Please don't be how Stefano said you were..."

"*Hello?*" Jonas says very crankily.

"Hey! Jonas," Leon shouts very abruptly. "Can you come pick me up from the facility?"

"*They're finally letting you out, huh? Hey wait. Aren't you at the penitentiary?*"

I forgot about that! Leon panics in thought. *Stay calm, Leon, you've got this.*

"Yeah, I uh. I got dropped off here. Left some documents that I had to come pick up."

"*Look Néol,*" he cackles, "*I dunno why you're explaining yourself to me. I asked one thing.*"

Leon holds the phone away from his ear and says nothing. He takes a deep breath and then asks, "So…can you get me?"

"*Yeah, I guess. We gonna go out? Eden's buying me food, I can get 'em to cover you, too. Matter a fact, I'll bring him, and then we can jump him together! Hahaha!*"

Wait. What? Leon thinks, *umm…Eden…is that…Deen's reflection?*

"*Yo, Néol, you still here?*"

"Uh. Yeah."

"*Alright, so I'm gonna pick Eden up, and then we'll come pick you up.*"

Jonas hangs up the phone before Leon can thank him.

Leon hangs the phone up and says, "What did I just sign up for? No. No way. I'm not actually gonna beat Eden up! No way. I just need a ride home…that's all."

☾ ☾ ☾

Before stepping out of the facility, Leon throws Néol's lighter onto the floor.

"Won't be needing that anymore. Goodbye, Heartshine Facility." He then steps outside.

Leon is waiting outside of the Heartshine Facility with everything Stefano gave him: his hoodie, the booklet of principles, the map of the area, his basketball shorts, and his knowledge of this reflecting world. A black two-door sports car honks as it nearly runs into Leon who jumps away just in time.

"What the?" Leon says, jumping out of the car's path. "The Lunae Lux?... But I didn't do anything wrong...did I?"

The right door on the drivers side opens, and out comes Jonas who is cackling, "That was priceless! Shoulda seen your face!"

Leon takes a deep breath. A boy with very pale skin, a white button-up, red hair, and glasses comes out of the passenger door with his hands up.

"I'm sorry, I'm so sorry, Néol," the boy says in a very nasally voice. "I tried to tell him to stop. I really did. I'm sorry."

So, this must be Eden. Already I see a difference between you and Deen. Deen would never apologize. Not for a million dollars, as much as he'd need it.

Jonas walks right over and kicks Eden in the shin saying, "Yeah, but he didn't convince me well enough, so I'd say you owe 'em two, Néol." Eden leans down and whimpers as he rubs his shin.

Leon swallows, *If I don't do this... I'll be lost wandering around... but if I do... no. I have to do this. I have to get home.*

Leon recalls all the times when Deen would trip him during their warmup jogs in gym class, all the times he'd take his baseball cap and throw it somewhere far like a frisbee. Leon takes every horrible moment from Eden's reflection and channels it all into this one. Solid. Kick to Eden's shin.

Eden falls to his knees, lying on his sides as he tries to ease the pain from his legs. The only thing equal to Eden's pain, is the pain in Leon's heart.

Why... why did I do that... Leon thinks, putting his hands to his head.

Jonas laughs even louder. "Amazing! He didn't hold back this time."

Eden cries out a bit more as Leon looks away in shame.

"Alright, run it off you drama king. We gotta take *this one* home," Jonas says, pointing to Leon with his thumb before getting back into his seat. Leon hesitantly walks toward the two-door vehicle.

Eden finishes rubbing his wounded shin and says, "You...you can take my seat."

"Was never yours to begin with," Jonas says coolly.

"Thanks," Leon utters, avoiding Eden's sorrowful eyes. Eden presses a button behind the passenger seat to make it lean forward so that he can get into the back seat.

Leon sits in the passenger seat, and Jonas starts driving. Leon notices that he and Eden are the only ones who clipped their seatbelts in.

What did I get myself into, Leon thinks with his heart pounding. *If Neol puts Eden through that kind of thing all the time, then—*

"—Yo, Néol," Jonas interrupts Leon's thought.

"Huh?"

"I'm taking you home, right?"

"Yeah."

"You comin' out after you get changed or nah? I know a fun arcade nearby. Lots of chicks. And Eden there in the back brought extra dimes."

"I... I have to go home."

"Lame," Jonas says, glowering toward a cop car in a parking lot. Jonas passes the cop, and the police officer suddenly follows.

Leon gulps, "Uh. Jonas? You have your license, right?"

"No? The hell's with you and all these questions? And why's my license matter, huh? So, what if it was suspended?"

"*Suspended?*" Leon shouts.

"You had no problem joyridin' with me a few weeks ago. I don't see the problem now."

Leon shuts his eyes and slouches on the seat, *So this is how I die. I'll really go to a penitentiary at this point.*

The cop suddenly passes them by and drives ahead.

"You need a cigarette," Jonas says, annoyed. "You've been stressed out."

Oh, come on, Jonas! How much does my other do?

"Peasant, fetch me my cigs!" Jonas commands Eden while glaring at him through the rearview mirror.

Eden in the back swiftly retrieves them from his shirt pocket and obediently hands the box to Jonas, who grabs himself one tobacco stick and then one for Leon.

"Here's one on me," Jonas says, lighting his and then Leon's before handing it off to him.

Leon thinks, *Is there any way to pretend that I'm smoking?*

"I forget," Leon says. "You know, because of the coma. How do you inhale again—"

"—Bro, just puff on the damn thing!"

Leon shakes his head…he stares at the cigarette…places it on his lips and inhales what tastes like tar, bitter smoke, and all things that make him cough his lungs out. His eyes tear up as he hacks. It feels like all the air in the world vanished. Jonas looks at Leon with pity. He pulls over to the side of the road and unlocks the door,

"Dude, I'm gonna kick your ass if you throw up in here. Open the door if you need to! I *just* got this car detailed!"

Eden tilts his head. For some reason he doubts that Jonas can beat Néol up.

Leon wipes his mouth. "I don't…" he coughs once more, "have to throw up, but I do feel sick…can we roll down the window for the rest of the way."

Eden taps Jonas' arm. "Hey, you know that makes sense. He's been locked away. Maybe his tolerance built up."

Leon fights a smile. *Eden, you're not that bad after all.*

"Hmph," Jonas says. "I guess that makes sense. No problem. Just need to get you smoking again, then."

Leon nods in agreement with Eden and Jonas, and Jonas rolls down the window to throw his cigarette out.

"You can throw yours out too," Jonas says. "If you killed my buzz, I already know *yours* is gone."

I want to say sorry, Leon thinks, *but something tells me Neol wouldn't say that either.*

Leon rolls down his window and throws his cigarette outside. It's silent in the car for a bit.

Eden asks, "Hey, can we play some tunes? I heard *Fall In Girl* just put out a new song."

Jonas ignores Eden and says, "Fifteen days and you haven't gotten back to normal. Ya know, Néol, you've changed after that coma. Feel like I lost my only friend. Now I feel like I've got just *this one* in the back."

"That's not true," Eden says, somehow not minding that he was insulted yet again. "You've got *Ellia and Anjelica.*"

"Ellia's not my friend. I'm tryna... I'm tryna...nevermind. And Anjelica just keeps her nose in her books. At least Néol here liked to take risks..."

There's a brief pause. Jonas narrows his eyes, looking at Leon at every available chance. "But the more I look at ya, the less I think you've been hit by a car."

Leon rears his head, *hit by a car?*...

"Yeah...now that I think about it...how'd you come out without any scratches?" Leon avoids eye contact by turning to the side and slumping his shoulders.

"Jonas," Leon replies without looking at him. "What're you talking about? If I got hit by a car, I wouldn't be here, don't you think?"

"That's what I'd like to think, along with the others, and yet... Here you are, sitting right next to me. You're walking just fine. Only thing that's messed up is your damn brain."

Leon doesn't say anything. But Jonas adds, "You know what *I* think? I don't think there ever was a coma. I think you staged that car accident. And to get out of killing that person, you staged the whole coma."

What is this guy talking about. No. What is Neol capable of? Killing someone? Now I'm starting to get just what Stefano meant. If Neol did all this—and hung out with this kind of crowd—then who am I to try and hang out with them? They'll spot me as I'll stand out like a sore thumb. Just look at all the tests I've already failed... If he sees through me...then the rest may too. So, am I just supposed to be a hermit?

Leon doesn't reply. He's stuck in even more of his thoughts.

"Dog got your tongue?" Jonas shouts. "I must be on the money, then."

Eden in the back snickers at how, for once, *Néol* has no witty comeback.

Suddenly, Stefano's words come to Leon's mind. *"There will be many things that you weren't present for. For the sake of your discretion, agree to disagree. You cannot argue with what you were not present for, so why bother? You must assume that they are correct."*

Leon then thinks of what Néol would say. Leon tries to remember how Néol would speak to him whenever it was time to taunt him. Leon had *already* kicked Eden's shin and inhaled on a cigarette. What harm can imitating him do?

"It's a miracle what time can do for one," Leon says, trying to make his voice deeper. "I guess I heal quickly."

Is that how he'd say it? Maybe my voice could've been deeper.

"Hmm. I still don't buy it," Jonas says. "I think somethin's up."

Leon glares at Jonas and tries once more to speak like his reflection. "Do you hear yourself right now?"

Leon disconnects his seat belt. "I got in a car accident to kill myself and then get in a coma? I was in a fake coma and I forgot your name? I killed someone, so I staged this whole thing? Which is it, Jonas? Huh? Make up your mind. I think you're just mad because I'm another person you can't control. Or. You're just mad because you're paranoid."

"Eden!" Jonas shouts almost immediately. "Where did the car crash take place?"

Eden fixes his glasses. "Two streets away from here, actually."

Jonas smirks. "Yup. Glass was spread everywhere. And the guy in the pickup truck died before the authorities showed up. And guess who had to go back and make sure *Ellia* didn't have a heart attack? Me! Then you were gone for like fifteen days. Right after that, you saw me, forgot who I even am, and then you got punished by those creeps at the Facility."

Leon thinks, *I don't know how I'm gonna pretend to be a part of something I'm not, Dr. Giro. I'm just gonna fight the narrative. It's what I know best.*

"Jonas," Leon says, "if there was an accident, did I leave it with any scratches or bruises?"

"You are in denial," Jonas says, glaring at Leon—but something catches his eye. Or, rather, something missing catches his eye.

"No freaking way." Jonas suddenly brakes and pulls over to the side of the road.

"What?" Leon asks.

"Turn your head."

"Why?..." Leon says, dropping his fake persona.

"I need to see something."

Leon hesitates but slowly turns his head, showing Jonas the right side of his face.

"Aha!" Jonas shouts.

"What?"

"That scar. How the hell did it vanish? The one your cat *Shadow* gave to you."

I give up. Not even ten minutes in this car and it's like I'm in therapy again. I can't have a single conversation without being interrogated.

"I don't remember."

Jonas chuckles to himself, he lunges over Leon's waist and swings open the door, "And I don't remember you being welcome in here!"

Leon stares at Jonas with sorrow, every plea he can think of comes to mind, but nothing comes as quickly as Jonas who reaches even further to push Leon out.

"Go on!" Jonas says. "You in the back! Help me get 'em out otherwise I'm taking it out on you!"

Leon tries to hold on with all his might, using his arms to grab onto the seat, but the two working together are too strong. Leon is also sleep and food deprived. So, this doesn't help with his energy.

"Guys, please!" Leon cries out.

"Néol, pleading? Disgusting!" Jonas cries out as Leon slides out and falls on his bottom.

Jonas glowers at Eden through the rearview mirror. "You come up and take his spot. At this point *you're* more worthy." Eden eagerly starts inching for the passenger seat.

Leon gets up, and before he can get back in, Eden slams the door.

"Guys!" Leon shouts, pounding the passenger window with his fists. "I need to get home!" Leon's definition of *home* at this point is twofold. Did he mean he wanted to go back to Earth? Or back to Néol's?

Jonas rolls down the window, and Leon speed walks to the driver's side as Jonas says, "Maybe this walk will help jog your memory."

"I don't remember *anything*!" Leon shouts. "Happy now? The coma made me forget!"

"Too late. But hey. Lucky you. We're by *Ellia's* street. But chances are, you don't even remember her!"

Jonas rolls up the window and shuts Leon out. He speeds off, leaving Néol's reflection in the dust.

Leon can only stand and stare as the only reflections—his only chances of getting home—drive off in the distance.

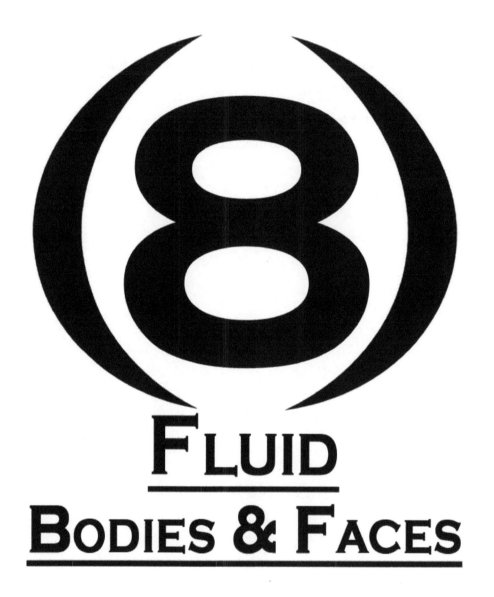

FLUID
BODIES & FACES

☾ ☾ ☾

Everywhere Leon goes, a storm follows. So far, this metaphorical storm has traveled with him from Earth all the way to Heart. Sadly for him, a literal downpour of rain comes down on him, soaking his hair, clothes, and shoes.

No one can tell the difference between the falling rain and his dripping tears. He wipes both forms of water away when he can. The clock on Leon's amulet tells him that he's knocked on countless doors asking for someone named Ellia for almost five hours. No one is kind to him upon his entry. Many slam the door in his face.

One muscular man pushed him out all the way onto the street and another startled him by threatening to bring out their gun, refusing to buy whatever products Leon wanted to sell.

Then there was the old woman who pulled a hunting knife on him. He ran as quickly as he could from her. Leon then had a different idea. He had forgotten that he had a map with him.

He checks off all the areas he knows he visited and then proceeds to newer parts of this neighborhood for his target, Ellia. Ellia is Allie's reflection, and at this point, his only hope for getting home. But what if she too is the same as Jonas, Néol's family, and literally everyone he has met? Dr. Giro was kind to him, but perhaps it was only because they once shared the same planet.

Leon walks over to a cul-de-sac and is surprised when he finds names on their mailboxes. The rain starts to subside.

"Allie…Reincath…" Leon mutters while staring at the last names. "If I'm lucky…then…" His eyes glow, he finds a reversed arrangement of the last name, Reincath. He finds a black mailbox with the label *Hactneir*.

"That's gotta be her. *Please*, God, let it be her…" Leon utters, walking up the driveway to the two-story and three-bedroom home.

This yard is one of the first he has seen with a clean appearance. Well, in terms of the trimmed green grass at least. There are nearby garden gnomes that are all tipped over. Looks like they may have been for a while. But regardless, it's still better than how most of these places were kept.

Hmm. Allie always lived with her grandmother. I wonder if that'll be the same here.

Leon passes the dark green truck in the driveway, rings the doorbell, and a short elderly bald man answers the door. He has lots of wrinkles on his face. The most defined ones are the ones under his eyes and his frown circles. Leon thinks, *Well that's new. I don't think I've ever met Allie's grandfather.*

The old man lifts his cane and sticks it through the doorway, jabbing at Leon's chest.

"You know you're not welcome back here, Néol."

Leon narrows his eyes. *Oh great. What did he do here, now? I suppose acting like Neol won't help me here. Chances are he'd be rude. I'll just be myself here.*

"Hey, good evening Mr. Hactneir. I was just wondering if Ellia was here. Wanted to uh…drop something off."

"Hmph. You gonna drop off the replacement for my window screen?"

Leon swallows, "Uh. Yes. And I'm sorry for what I did to your screen."

"Hmph. You've got ten minutes, and then I want you out. I don't want you both sneaking out the window again, you hear?"

Leon nods. The old man moves to the side as Leon steps into the home with mostly wooden furniture.

"Ten. Minutes," the old man repeats as he limps away with his cane, sitting back on his rocking chair in the living room.

"Got it," Leon says firmly, then points up the stairs with a quizzical look. "Uh…she's upstairs, right?"

"You forget where you've been sneaking out of? Hmph. You must've hit your head on the way out of my window."

Leon rolls his eyes and walks up the stairs, *Another day on this planet, and another amnesia joke.* He makes it to the top of the stairs and sees a set of photos on the wall. Judging by the drastically diverse climates in the photos, Leon assumes that these are all from vacations in the past. There's one photo with Ellia's grandfather, another man, and a woman with long black hair past her buttocks. This long-haired woman looks like Allie.

Hmm, Leon thinks. *This photo was taken recently. Is that Ellia's mother? No way…she's holding hands with some guy… I guess Allie must've lied when she said her parents were dead. One cannot exist without another. Huh. Well. Here they are in the flesh, I guess.* Leon glares at the old man in the photo and walks away.

Ahead of Leon is a shut door, presumably Ellia's. But Leon's attention is caught by a piece of paper pinned to the wall with a thumb tack. The sketchbook paper shows a black cat with a white triangle crest on its chest. All of this was drawn with a black ink pen. There isn't a line out of place. The drawing can be mistaken for a real photo. The cat is looking up and to the right at something. Leon studies the drawing for a long second, then sees the name, *Shadow,* in the corner.

"Didn't Jonas…say something about a cat named Shadow scratching Neol? Was it Ellia's?"

Leon shakes his head, then hesitates with his hand over the doorknob. He thinks about everything Dr. Giro has said lately. He thinks about how the therapist was correct about what would happen with Jonas. But. There is one thing that Leon knows about both reflections and Allie. It's that Allie hates him with all her soul. So, what then would this encounter bring?

Much to Leon's surprise before he can even open the door, someone comes flying out of it and right into his arms. His heartbeat ceases as she wraps her arms around him. He doesn't even get to see what she looks like. Not until she draws her head away from his chest with her lips puckered.

"What?" Leon nearly shouts as she backs away.

"I'm sorry—I. I heard my grandfather yell. I knew he was talking to you…I should've at least said hi before I—" as she runs back into him for a second hug. "But it's just been so long. I was so worried about you."

Leon's heart is pounding out of his chest. He wonders if Ellia can feel this.

"Néol?"

"Uh…" Leon reluctantly holds her back. "Hey. It's. Been a while." *I have no idea how Neol would've said that! Was he even the romantic type? Ugh!*

"How's your head feeling after the accident?" she asks. "I heard you hit it pretty bad."

With all his might, Leon resists rolling his eyes at this repeated question and says, "It's been better. But. I'm glad to see you again, *Allie,*" and the two stare at each other with the strangest looks—Leon looking at her like a deer in headlights.

"*Allie?*" Ellia says back.

"I—not Allie! I meant—Ellia. Ellia is your name." *Already off to a good start. Nice job, Leon!* He shouts in thought.

In Leon's defense, the only thing he saw of her before she charged into him was her hair. But just the top half. While Allie's hair barely touches her shoulders, Ellia's is in a braid that droops down past hers. Allie can always be seen in maroon, but here, Ellia seems to like blue. The color of her walls say so.

"Hey!" The old man shouts from downstairs. "Time is up! Out, Néol!"

Ellia giggles, "You know, I'm surprised he let you in after what happened last time." She pulls his hand and drags him to her window. "This time, I've got a safer way for us to get out."

"You...want us to jump out?" Leon asks.

"Of course. How else can we sneak to the lake together?"

149

Hearing Ellia say the word *together* makes him feel warm inside. Leon glances out of the window to see two mattresses stacked on top of one another. "Oh…okay. Alright. I'll jump first, then."

Ellia giggles, "Works for me. Then I can get my sketchbook. Can't go anywhere without that." Leon smiles and thinks, *Just like Allie with her camera.*

He lifts his feet onto the windowsill, takes a deep breath, and slides through the window onto the mattress, buttocks first. He stands up and looks up at her window. Ellia's grandfather can be heard shouting for Néol in the backround. The grandfather can even be heard shouting about how Ellia had better not leap out the window yet again. Too late. With her tote bag in hand, Ellia falls out the window the same way Leon did. She grabs his hand again, guiding him into her grass-filled backyard. A few crows perch atop trees and watch her guide Leon deep in the backyard, past a set of trees that lead into the woods.

Now that they're in the woods, Ellia releases Leon's hand. They're just a few yards away from the edge of the lake. They're walking on a path of dirt leading them to where they can see the lake farther ahead.

"I bet you missed the lake," Ellia coos. "Our secret spot."

"The lake? Yeah. It's been a while." Leon swallows nervously. *I guess Néol likes the lake, too.*

"How's your body feeling?" she asks.

Leon laughs and says, "Well, I jumped out of your window, didn't I? So, I'm doing pretty good," and she joins him in laughter, hiding her reddening face.

"You sure your grandfather won't be upset with us doing that?"

"Are you sure you actually care about that?"

Oops, Leon thinks then says, "Good point."

"You know," Ellia says, "you sound a little different."

Here it comes, Leon thinks.

"They probably didn't give you cigarettes in there, did they?"

"Nope," Leon says as he tries to look upset. "The holding cells allowed for no smoking whatsoever."

"Hmm. But you smell like it."

"I was just with Jonas and Eden."

"Oh. Hmm. Did you and Jonas fight again?"

"Yeah."

"He's been trying to get with me ever since you got in that accident. Not to start drama, but... It made me uncomfortable. Aren't you two supposed to be best friends?"

"Supposedly. But *knowing Jonas*, it doesn't surprise me." Leon now shoves his hands in his pockets, thinking about how his reflection, Jason, would never do such a thing.

They finally arrive at the lake. Ahead of them is a pier which is pointing to the sun floating higher within the green sky. There are ducks looking for food in the fresh blue water. Leon follows Ellia's lead. He assumes that she has a certain routine with Néol, so naturally, he follows along. First, she sits at the pier then calls him over. He's shaking more than ever. The last time he was this physically close with a girl was with...Allie. And that was years ago.

Ellia leans on his shoulder. The warm feeling inside him returns. It's been so long since he could just sit this peacefully with anyone. It's been even longer since Leon last had warm thoughts like these in his imagination. Leon blinks—and Ellia's baby blue shirt becomes maroon. Her hair suddenly is much shorter. Her eyes even change from blue to red. The two lean closely together and—

"—I'm sorry," Leon says, standing and backing away. He blinks again, and Ellia is Ellia once more.

"No, I am…" Ellia says, playing with her braid, standing up and walking away. She stops fidgeting with her hair after a while but keeps her back facing him.

"What? Why're you sorry?" Leon replies.

"It's your first day back. And I suppose I'm just doing what I wish I'd done before your accident…"

Leon swallows.

"Néol," Ellia says, walking forward to him, "I…I like you. A lot. I've liked you for years. Since we were kids. You never made fun of my art. You always protected me. And you're always so insightful, and you make me feel so—"

"—I'm not…Neol."

Ellia rears her head, and this time covers her reddening face.

Leon looks in the other direction and mutters, "Dr. Giro was right. I can't live up to being *him,* so why try." He walks away and sits back down at the pier.

Suddenly from behind, Ellia wraps her arms around his neck and kisses it. "I don't care what the amnesia did to you. You're still Néol to me."

Leon looks down. "No, Ellia. I'm *not* Neol."

"Néol, the doctors said you would go through this. It's up to me to remind you of who you are."

I can't just tell her where I'm really from…she'd never believe me. I'll have to make something up. But out of everyone here. It hurts to lie to her.

"I'm his…long-lost brother," Leon says, standing up to meet her as she also straightens up.

"Long lost…" Her voice trails off. Ellia takes a few steps away but then grabs the sketchbook from her tote bag and flips through the pages. She flips and flips until she finds one page with a drawing of a boy who looks exactly like Leon. But the main differences are the dark scar on the right side of his chin, his more rugged and tired face, but—even something as subtle as this—his lighter skin tone. He's only slightly lighter than Leon.

Perhaps it's from the fact that there is less sunlight here on Planet Heart. Ellia has included all of these details within her sketchbook then looks up at Leon. She sees someone *like* Néol, but there is a difference in Leon's softer features, a slightly rounder face, and even less spiky hair than his reflection.

"I can see it," Ellia's voice cracks, "but I don't get it. So is Néol— *dead…?*"

"No," Leon says, gently grabbing her shoulders. "I promise you he's not. He's just…not *here* right now."

Her hands fall to her sides. "I don't think I understand. Why are *you* here then? You're saying you're his long-lost brother. But why switch with him?"

I can't tell her the whole thing… I can't.

Leon releases her and looks away. "He…wanted to see what it was like to have a family, I guess. I really couldn't tell you. He never even told *me*. I just woke up here." He sits back down at the pier and sighs.

Ellia sits next to him, and the two stare off into the sparkling blue water. She leans close to him. "You know," Ellia says, "I had a feeling something was off."

Leon laughs, "No way. You practically threw yourself at me!"

Ellia shoves Leon, and they share a laugh. "I thought you were him. But I felt it was too good to be true," she says.

"What do you mean?"

"I think my feelings…I mean—" she stammers, "I mean. I think. I don't think he feels the same way. So, when you leaned in…"

Leon nods. "Oh…did you ever tell him how you felt?"

"It's like I said. I waited. I waited to the side and hoped he'd come around. And then when the accident happened, I thought it was too late. That's why I was so excited when I saw you. I was stupid enough to think something changed…"

"That easy to tell, huh?"

"Yeah. I remember thinking that he got shorter!" She bursts out laughing, and Leon narrows his eyes with a straight mouth.

"Oh, I'm teasing N—. Wait. What *is* your name then?"

"I'm Leon," he smiles. "Leon Granttley." He holds his hand out to shake hers. "And you're…Ellia Hactneir?"

She shakes his hand in return. "I am. And I'm impressed. You're one of the first people to ever say my last name correctly."

A murder of crows flies by. A few of them roost on the trees. Some of them are cawing, while others are silent.

Ellia scribbles onto her sketchpad, and almost in an instant, she starts drawing.

Leon asks, "Wait. Are you—"

"—Yup. I'm drawing you."

"Wh—why?"

"I'm terrible with names. But I *never* forget a face." She looks up and stares at Leon's chin. "You know, the missing scar's the first thing I noticed. But I thought, hey. Maybe this hospital's budget increased, and they bought a scar removal machine."

She draws Leon almost completely the way he looks now. Leon watches as Ellia now draws herself sitting next to him on this pier. Then. She pauses.

"Something wrong?" Leon asks, trying to meet her blue eyes.

Ellia writes *Leon* underneath his illustration. She tilts her head. "That's...so cool..." She then writes Néol's name next to his. Ellia adds, "You and Néol's parents... I feel like they knew each other."

"They don't know each other."

"But you guys have the same letters in your name! And you said your last name is Granttley, right?"

Leon swallows, "Yeah..."

She writes his last name next to his first and then draws lines to connect the letters.

"What? How..."

Ellia then looks at Leon with wonder. She then says, "Okay, I'll try mine now."

Leon's eyes gape, *Oh crap! She's gonna figure it out!*

"Let's see..." Ellia writes her own name, and after a few seconds of silence from them both, she asks, "Um. What was that name you called me earlier?"

"Uh," Leon looks away.

"*Allie?!*" she shouts and stands up. "Then I have a long-lost sister too? No way... That's so exciting! I always wanted a sister!"

Leon stands and meets her. "Wait. Ellia. I lied—"

"—Néol? Ellia?" a girl's voice says.

Leon and Ellia turn around to see a blonde girl in a shawl mixed with red. She's wearing black jeans and has shoes with an insignia that looks familiar to Leon.

"*Anjelica?*" Ellia says in shock, now turning red.

Leon, Ellia, and Anjelica each walk toward one another.

"I can see why you forgot about our study night," Anjelica says, looking at Leon. "Look at who's fresh outta jail."

Leon puts on his Néol persona once more and says, "Feels good to be free."

Ellia starts giggling, turning red once more.

"Aw, well I'm glad you two are catching up." Anjelica grabs Ellia's hand. "But don't forget...we've got a history exam tomorrow..." she mutters, dragging her away.

"Wait," Ellia says, breaking free, "I need my bag."

"Oh, right. How would we study without that."

Leon chuckles, remembering how once Jacaline wrote someone a check for five hundred dollars to take her finals. Interesting how now Anjelica would do all it would take to study. Even dragging Ellia away from an intimate moment.

Ellia slips the bag onto her shoulders. "So, will I see you later?"

"Well, where are you guys gonna study?"

"We'll study at my place," Ellia says. "Maybe you can come over later tonight? I feel like we have more to talk about."

Leon looks away. "I...um. Because of the *prison stuff*, my parents aren't letting me stay home. So. I don't really have anywhere to go."

Anjelica fixes her glasses. "Well, no one said you had to leave. But you just can't disturb us."

Ellia winks. "You can come with us, *Néol*."

Leon smiles and places his hands in his pockets.

Anjelica and Ellia scurry just a few inches farther from Leon. It seems they want to whisper about something. What they don't know is that Leon can still hear.

"*So did you tell him?*" Anjelica asks, cracking a few twigs with her steps.

"Kinda...and then you showed up..."

"Oh! Well. You guys can talk all night. But it looks like it went well..."

Leon smiles and shakes his head. *What am I getting myself into...* He looks up to the green sky and its yellow clouds. *You know, it's kinda nice. Not being bothered by The Voice...having some time with... Wait. Can I even call them my friends? They still think I'm Neol.*

Ellia and Anjelica cease their whispers and speak at a normal volume.

Anjelica says, "Heads down. Your grandfather's pretty upset."

"You went there?"

"I didn't know where you were. I thought we were going to meet at your place like we planned."

"I know...I just... I didn't expect..." Ellia turns around and smiles at Leon who nervously waves.

"I wasn't expecting him," Ellia continues. "We kinda just...snuck here. So, great. I've got a lecture coming to me, then."

Leon catches up to them. "Hey, I've got a question. Sorry. Couldn't help but eavesdrop. But. If your grandfather's upset, how am I gonna get in?"

Anjelica raises an eyebrow. "You hit your head pretty hard, didn't you."

Leon narrows his eyes at Anjelica.

Ellia grabs his hand. Their fingers interlace, and to this, his heart pounds. "I'll remind you," she says. "So. These woods will take us to my backyard. You're gonna come through the back sliding door. My grandfather likes to sit on the rocking chair on the front porch to wait for me, so you'll have all the time you need to sneak through the back. Sound like a plan?"

Leon nods. "Alright. We've gotta do this right, though. If the cops show up—"

"—you worry too much *Le*—" Ellia pauses, turns red, and looks away from him to the dirt path leading them back to her backyard.

During the last few minutes of this walk, Ellia does not release Leon's hands. She reviews her sneaky plan to Leon as they approach her backyard. Once they arrive, the girls split off and walk to the front of the yard.

Leon remembers the plan. Wait by Ellia's back door until he hears the door latch click. Then when that happens, he'll have to slide the door open and make his way back up to her room.

Leon hears the latch click, and suddenly a cane pokes through the doorway. "You think I was born yesterday, Néol Yelltnarg? I know all about your darn schemes!"

Leon backs away, and the grandfather shouts, "I've got *119* on *swift dial!* You'd better get out right now or else—"

Leon lifts both of his hands up. "Mr. Hactneir—I'm sorry for popping your screen door out. I was just trying to—"

"—No lip from you! I know all about you. I saw you and your friend joyriding the other day—nearly hit me on the road. I don't wanna see you here again. NOW GO!"

Leon grits his teeth and runs away back to the woods where he and the girls came from. He sees a bunch of crows waiting for him. They surprisingly don't fly away when he approaches them. He turns back around and watches Ellia's house from afar.

"Well, Ellia. I guess I've gotta go now—huh?"

Leon sees Ellia at a window above the back door. It looks like she's trying to say something… But Leon's too far away to decipher her code. She holds up her hands to say, *Wait.* Thankfully, this hand gesture is the same in both Earth and Heart. She retrieves her sketchpad and writes, *TWO HOURS.*

"Oh…" Leon says, looking at his moon amulet's clock. "I think she means come back in two hours. Got it," he smiles. "I was gonna say… I didn't know where I was gonna go."

Leon yawns then sits against a tree trunk in the woods and shuts his eyes. Without knowing it, he falls asleep.

So, a voice in Leon's mind says. *I see you've met Ellia.*

Leon doesn't respond. He's too far gone within slumber.

I wonder how you'd feel about me meeting Allie again...

Leon opens his eyes, *What did you just say?*

That woke you up. So, what's going on with you and Ellia?

Why're you worried about it? Didn't you want this?

I'll ask you a better question, Other. Are you talking to her to spite me? Or is it because you're replacing Allie with her?

What?

It's one or two of those answers.

Leave me alone, Leon thinks.

"He's so annoying," Leon says, reaching under his hoodie for his amulet's clock. "Alright. It's basically been two hours. I'm going back."

Leon stands up and stretches to find at least ten crows in front of his path.

"Why are you all just…" Leon swallows, "…staring at me?" He tries passing them. And weirdly enough, these birds leap out of the way and continue staring at him as he wanders off toward Ellia's backyard.

"Is she gonna give me a sign this time? Or…" Leon stretches, looking up toward the same window from before.

Ellia shocks Leon by running straight out into the yard. "Hey. I'm sorry about earlier."

"Are you sure it's okay being out here like this?"

"Of course. He's asleep now. But come in with me now. We'll talk about why he hates you, er…Néol, later."

"Haha, alright."

Leon follows Ellia back toward the front of the house. She sneakily guides him up the stairs as they hear the snores of her grandfather downstairs. She slowly shuts the door, and Leon steps into her room.

Now that there are no sudden movements to catch him off guard, Leon actually has time to observe this bedroom. Ellia has pictures of people that she has drawn all over the wall. They're all very neat and organized. There's one section of drawings that are all in black ink, others look like they've been digitally drawn, and even a few with just crayons. Then, Leon sees something he's never seen before: Ellia's desk, which is one that is combined with her bed. Literally. Her desk is underneath her bed which is high above.

"Wow. That's so cool," Leon says, looking at the loft-inspired bed.

"Well, how else was an only child going to have a bunk bed?"

"Good point," Leon chuckles. "So. About your grandfather..."

"Right..." Ellia says. "My grandfather would never walk up these stairs in his life. Plus, I can hear him snoring. So, you'll be safe with me."

"But how long can I stay here?"

"First, can you explain *everything* to me? Before we were so *rudely* interrupted by Anjelica," she says jokingly. "You were going to say something. Something you lied about."

Leon turns away. "Right."

"Be honest with me, Leon. Tell me what you're going through. I'm not going to judge you. I don't think you'd lie about needing somewhere to stay. I literally saw you sleep in the woods. You're crazy," she ends with a laugh.

"You really believe that I'm not Neol. Don't you?"

"Well, yes. I think the biggest giveaway is that you don't even say his name correctly."

"Wha...?"

"Yes! His name is *Nay-ole*. The *e* in his name has an accent. It's a *Chrenf* name."

"A what name?"

"There's a country named—anyway. My point is you're pronouncing his name wrong."

"Oh…hm. So, it's *Né-ol*. Got it."

"See, that wasn't so bad. But yeah, and now after talking to you more, I know you're not him. And... I like that."

Her words combined with the feeling in Leon's chest leave him speechless. "I'm glad you trust me. So. I'll tell you everything."

Ellia dims the light, climbs the ladder up to her bed, and waits for Leon to join her. She leans against the wall.

"Well. Where to begin," Leon says, looking up at the ceiling and noticing that Ellia had once glued glow-in-the-dark stars to her ceiling.

"I'm from a world that reflects yours. While yours is called Heart, mine is called Earth. And on that planet is someone that reflects you. Her name is Allie. *Allie Reincath*."

"Oh," Ellia says, but with a sad voice.

"Hm?"

"Was she your…you know, girlfriend?"

"Oh. No. She…she hates me."

"*You*? Why, what did you do to her?" Ellia asks with a playful angry look.

"Nothing. To be honest, this is how Néol gets tied in. Two years ago, Allie was…sexually assaulted. Now because of this, *I* have a criminal record. Everyone I know thinks that I did it to her. That I'm the one who turned against my friend. When the truth is, the person that did it is…Néol."

"What?"

"I'm sorry, Ellia. But Néol did something to her. I wasn't even with her that day. *I* was at the Earthshine Facility. I truly don't remember what they had me do all day. But I *know* I wasn't home. Yet, that's where this all started. Néol did what he did to her in my own home. Despite me being asleep, Allie somehow got photographs of her bruises, turned them in to the police, and then got me arrested. It was court case after court case until they finally decided that I was too young to go to jail. I had just turned fifteen at the time... So, we all know I wouldn't have survived. But in return for not being put in juvenile detention, I was enrolled at a place called the *Earthshine Facility*."

"Oh my gosh..."

"It gets worse. They said that because I didn't remember doing what I did to Allie that I had DID—short for Dissociative Identity Disorder. Because, guess what? If someone says you did something that you don't remember, you're a clear candidate for the disorder."

"That's so stupid."

"I've been saying that for two years. But no one believes me. None of my friends or family. Maybe just my mom, if anything."

"I believe you."

They stare at each other for a moment, and then Ellia looks away.

"I know Néol more than I know you. And while it hurts to think he'd steal someone's will like that, I wouldn't put it past him. I know he's been through a lot, but I can't help but think of why he'd do it."

Leon sighs, "Yeah, that's what I've been trying to figure out. I spoke to someone who has a hunch on why. But it's still not making sense. Why touch Allie? Was it all to get me here? What do I have that he'd want so bad?"

Ellia looks at Leon, and he says, "I mean, look at you. You like him so much. What would he gain from everyone that hates *me*? I have maybe one friend. That's it."

"That's true," she says, staring into Leon's brown eyes as he stares back at her. "Sorry, I didn't mean that as an insult." She bashfully turns away. "So, what happened after you got here?"

"I woke up in Néol's bed. I saw his family fight, and then…Jeez. It all happened so quickly. I got kicked out of his home shortly after, too. Then, I wandered around the streets and got picked up by Jonas. Then. I stayed at that weird Heartshine Facility for fifteen days."

"The Heartshine Facility? I think Néol used to go there… I thought it was shut down for all the murders," Ellia states.

"I guess that explains the blood on the wall."

"It was just a rumor, but you confirmed it."

"Do you know why he went there?" Leon asks.

"Not really. Néol never told me anything."

"I wonder why you'd like him, then." Leon says.

"He's just…very mysterious. And sometimes I get jealous because of all the girls that try and go after him." Leon chuckles at this, and Ellia adds, "I know. I know it's stupid. Really stupid. Anjelica tells me all the time. But he protected me a lot. I used to get picked on for drawing in class, and sometimes he'd stop my bullies from trying to take my sketchbook. I tried keeping him around since." Ellia shakes her head and leans on Leon's shoulder. "But saying this out loud…makes me see how stupid I was. I liked someone that didn't even care about me. You know?"

"I know just what you mean," Leon says, putting his arm around her.

"Can I ask you something?"

Leon nods.

"If my name reflects Allie's, then... Are our personalities the same? Or are those also the opposite?"

"Hmm. No, I'd say your personalities are a lot different. Like you're a lot giddier. And I don't think I've ever seen Allie smile, even when we were kids. But I think anger's just her default expression."

"Hmm. Well, you know, I have another question. Well, more something I've been wondering since you're from an opposite world. But. You seem to be more in tune with your emotions. You've held me. We almost kis—and... You know, I just. I guess I was just wondering if I'm feeling the way I do because of Allie's hatred."

"Oh. I see what you mean. You wanna know if you feel like this because she hates me. I'm gonna be honest, I don't know if emotions work like that. But I could be wrong."

"I guess I just wanna know if what I'm feeling is real. Because I wouldn't say I like you. I think it's too soon. But I know for a fact that I like *being* around you. And talking to you is really fun. I feel like I can be myself."

"You know?" Leon smiles. "Me too. You know, I never thought of it like that. But Allie and I *never* had the chance to be like this. We never got to because the day we were supposed to meet, all that stuff I told you about happened. I was gonna tell her that I liked her."

"Aw."

"Yeah. But she's way past forgiveness at this point. I think the only thing I want to do now is just tell her the truth. She's probably suffering from PTSD and doesn't even know it. Every time she sees me—" Leon sits up straight. "Crap. Every time she sees Néol—she's gonna think—"

"—Leon, it's okay. What can I do to help?"

"I don't know."

"How did you get here? There has to be something."

164

"I…"

Ellia shakes her head. "I regret even asking that. I don't want you to go."

"I don't want to go either. I just. I know I have to set things right with him."

"I think you will," Ellia says with her tone becoming sour.

"What's wrong?"

"Nothing." She looks away but continues holding onto his arms.

"Hey," Leon says firmly. "When I go back home, I'm not gonna forget you. And. There's always a way for me to come back."

"Thanks, Leon."

"So," Leon says, now leaning his head back on the wall, "what did Néol do to make your grandfather hate him?"

"My grandfather always says he was a young man once and that he knows Néol's type. Since the first day they met, Néol walked in with his shoes on, didn't shake his hand or anything. He left a bad taste in his mouth. Then recently, he went joyriding with Jonas, and that didn't go well."

"Yeah. He mentioned that to me earlier. He said that *I* almost hit him."

"I'm sure it wasn't on purpose. I know what happened with Néol and Allie is really bad. But I know him. He had to have a reason. He's very calculating. Everything he does has a purpose."

"Calculating. Wait. I just realized something." Leon takes out his amulet and looks at the nine moon phases on it. He notices that the crescent shaped phase is glowing bright red.

"Ellia," Leon says, shaking a bit, "I think I'll be able to go home tonight."

"What?" Ellia tries to hide the sadness in her voice.

"Yeah! If I'm right, tonight might be the only night of Heartshine. It says so on my amulet. Do you have a mirror?"

Ellia tilts her head to the side. "Do you have to go tonight?"

Leon climbs down the bed and calls her to meet him by the window. She raises the blinds for him, and he points to the red moon, glowing so bright that it pierces even the clouds.

"Wow…" Ellia says in awe.

Leon holds her hand. "They call this crescent moon phase *Heartshine*. And if the light from the moon touches a mirror, a person like me can walk through it and go to *The Other Side*."

"I see…" Ellia releases his hand. "So you *do* have to go."

Leon watches her walk away. "I have to. My family. Allie. They all need to know the truth. And I have to expose Néol and bring him back here."

"I almost don't even think *I* want him back here."

"It's not up to us, Ellia."

"Then who is it up to? You were so nice to me—sure he defended me, but you actually talked to me. We connected. Most other guys are like Jonas. They just ask you simple stupid things like what your favorite color is. But you—"

"—I know. I feel a connection too. But. Who says I never have to come back? We can meet again. But if I don't go back now—"

"—Things will get worse. Okay. I'll get you a mirror."

She steps into her closet and retrieves a long vertical mirror as Leon says, "We might need to bring this outside for the moon light to touch it."

"Okay. My grandfather's a heavy sleeper, but we should still toetip outside."

Ellia is reluctant to but lifts the mirror out into the backyard for Leon. He isn't too far behind her.

"Ellia, you okay?"

"Mm-hmm," she says as the two arrive right in the middle of the yard. The red moonlight from above lights the area up, exposing the tears in her eyes.

"Hey, Ellia. Don't lie to me. You're not okay."

Ellia cracks a smile. "Guess it takes one to know one, hm?"

Leon chuckles and wipes her tears away. "I suppose. After all. I did pretend I was Néol. Didn't I?"

"I like you as you."

"And that's why you shouldn't worry. I can always come back."

Ellia smiles. "Pinky promise?"

"People on this planet do that too? Okay. I pinky promise."

Their pinky fingers lock. Then Leon holds his amulet to see what direction they're standing in. He leans the mirror on a ground well, then adjusts the mirror so it faces east, just as Stefano had previously instructed. The light touches the mirror and nearly blinds them both. The mirror glistens with a red glow, leaving Leon feeling warm inside. Ellia grabs Leon's hand before he can walk closer to it.

"Hey, Leon?"

"Hm?"

"How can I…meet Allie?"

"Well, I can tell you what Néol did with me. Try saying her name in your mind. You never know. Maybe she'll say something back."

"Really? You mean even you and Néol share thoughts?"

Leon nods.

"Wow. Then maybe…one day we can all switch. And. Maybe we can all spend time together."

"Maybe," Leon says, looking down. "After everything Néol did, I really doubt we could get along. Just hearing all the horrible stories makes me not want to meet him."

"That's fair. Well, as long as I can see you then. And maybe Allie too?"

"We can try. Do me a favor, though? I've never done this, so could you wait outside just in case?"

"Of course."

Leon holds up a hand to wave goodbye, but then instead he rushes toward her to give her one final hug. "Thank you, Ellia. For believing me. For everything."

"Don't forget me. And even when Néol comes back, I'll remember you."

Leon can feel a few of her tears on his hoodie's sleeve. They stand and hug for a little while longer until she hesitantly releases him and says, "Alright...you should go."

"Right. Well, goodbye, Ellia..."

Ellia smiles. "See you on the other side."

Reflection Principle #6

☾   ☾   ☾

Leon steps out onto a crystal path full of many colors. This rainbow-like path looks as if it's made of glass. Leon is standing in a special blanket of the galaxy where he can see countless stars and comets. Clouds even. A black hole. Things that Leon never thought he would get to see in person. Above him is the same Heartshine moon that led him here. The only thing that is different about this red moon is that the light doesn't seem so bright out here in this vast darkness.

He turns around to see a crystal gateway made of the same material as the bridge. He sees a sun and moon with faces. These murals scribed in gold both wear expressions of anger. The two are glaring at each other with murderous rage.

"So, this is the Eleventh Dimension…it's beautiful." Leon looks all the way down the crystal path to see another gateway. "I'd better hurry. If it's nighttime on Heart, then it's daytime on Earth. He could be in school as we speak. I'd hate to see what'd happen if he met with Etay."

Leon dashes all the way down the bridge to the gateway. He hesitates, stretches his hands through the watery like portal, and a hand grabs him!

"What the—" Astonished, Leon tries to retreat, but this hand pushes him onto his back on the bridge.

"What just—"

169

"—Surprise," a boy looking very much like Leon says, appearing through the mirror.

"Néol?!" Leon shouts in shock, crawling backwards while looking up at his reflection. Someone he was not expecting to be here. Leon quickly takes in the black scar on Néol's chin that everyone had referred to. He sees his lighter skin, the cold look of disgust that Leon couldn't wear even if he tried. The tired eyes. The chiseled chin. It was all there just as Leon had imagined.

Néol is wearing a black leather coat over his red hoodie with his very own amulet hanging down his chest. His amulet, however, is not as smooth as Leon's. His looks more gothic, spikier than Leon's could ever be. He has a chain on the side of his black skinny jeans. These jeans have many holes. Leon crawls back as far as he can go and stands up once he notices that Néol is simply just standing and staring.

SCAN FOR NÉOL

Leon glares at Néol. "How did you know I'd be here!"

Néol snickers at Leon, watching him stand to meet his eye. "Leon, I've been listening to your thoughts this whole time," Néol says, reaching into his pocket for a cigarette. He lights it and inhales.

Leon's heart is pounding. Here and now, he's finally been able to not only see but hear the voice of the old devil in his mind. The Voice that caused everything between him, Allie, and the Earth-based society which judged him. All the frustration, the headaches, the hunger that Leon endured has built up to here. Now, not only can he return home, but he can finally have the answers he wanted.

"Néol—did you do *anything* else to my family or friends while you were there?" Leon asks firmly.

"Wouldn't you like to know? All that matters is that you need to go back to where you belong."

"Stay back, Néol," Leon growls as he plants his feet onto the crystal ground. "I don't want to have to fight you!"

"Yes, you do. You've been waiting for this, probably your whole life."

Leon braces his feet, looking below at the dark and colorful abyss that will consume either reflection if they take the wrong step. Leon knows he cannot kill his reflection because of what it will do to him. But fight, perhaps. Leon's never fought anyone in his life.

"You know," Néol says, "us being opposites totally works to my advantage." Néol walks toward his reflection. "And do you know why?" Néol rolls his leather sleeves upward. "It's because I'm not a pacifist like you."

Leon puts one foot forward and balls his fists. He swallows as his reflection gets even closer. Leon grins. "You don't know that."

Where's every human's weak spot? The stomach. Of course, Leon thinks, then charges straight for his reflection. Néol puffs on the cigarette, throws it off the bridge, then elbows Leon straight in the face. Leon's still standing but is now holding his cheek. *Then I'll just kick your shin!*

Néol smirks, catching Leon's swinging foot. "You forget. I can read your mind," he says to Leon, not breaking eye contact. He pushes Leon's foot away. "Try again," he says firmly.

Leon backs away, not knowing what to do. He can't think. Néol will just read his thoughts. But there's one thing Leon hears from his reflection.

I'm in your mind, Néol says, making his voice echo throughout Leon's so loudly that he instinctively covers his ears. Néol punches Leon in the stomach, and he falls to his knees, spitting on the bridge.

"Give up?" Néol asks as Leon angrily grabs onto Néol's leg, trying to pull him down. Néol shakes his head and kicks Leon in the face, then kicks his stomach more times than Leon can count. Leon lays on his back now, his dizzy eyes staring up to the galaxy while he nods in and out.

Néol grabs Leon's arm and drags him across the bridge into the portal leading back to Planet Heart and throws Leon onto Ellia's grass. "HEY!" Néol shouts to the crows surrounding Ellia. "Shoo! I'm taking care of it." The crows fly up and away into the trees. But they're still watching…

"Néol?" Ellia shouts, surprised but then sees Leon who's laying down, practically lifeless on the ground. "What happened!" Ellia shouts. "What did you do to him?"

Néol gets right into her face. "I thought I told you to make him want to stay."

Ellia's heart drops. "Things changed, Néol! All you told me was that *someone else* was coming here! I didn't know what it meant until now."

Néol turns his back. "Well, you clearly like him so I don't see what would've been so hard about keeping him here."

Ellia says nothing. Leon looks up and in pain whispers, "*Ellia…is…that…true?*"

Néol crosses his arms while smirking. He walks away from her saying, "Tell him, Ellia. Tell him the truth."

Ellia grits her teeth. "It's true…Néol told me a few weeks before June eleventh that he'd be leaving. He never said why. Or where he was going. But he said that this *person* would be here…and that I should do whatever I could to make him happy." She glares at Néol. "But I didn't believe him. I thought, for once, he said something that didn't make sense."

Ellia rushes down to Leon's aid, wiping the blood from his swollen cheeks and squinting eyes,

"When we met, I thought about Néol's request. To make you happy so that you would want to stay. But the more I got to know you, the less it became about doing his favor and more about me just getting to know you."

I see... Leon thinks. *So you would've believed me all along.*

Ellia continues, glaring at Leon's reflection under the red moon's light. "But the hardest thing for me, Leon, was knowing you were from that world. Because when you said *set things right* earlier, I knew what it meant. It wasn't about either of your reflections. It was about...doing what we thought was right..."

Néol crouches and stares right back at Ellia. "Hate to say it, Ellia, but this world's already been connected. You would've found out about Earth someday or another. The *normal* you knew is gone and dead. Everyone's eventually gonna switch. You included. Like it or not."

"But why, Néol? What's so bad about our world that you'd want to leave?" she asks.

Néol stands and turns his back on them both. "A lot of reasons. This world is dying. I hate the people here. And from what I know about Earth, there's a lot more there."

"You...you hate me too?" Ellia says, choking up.

"You're the exception."

"Just put everything back to normal."

Néol shakes his head. "I'm too far gone to turn back now, Ellia. What's done is done. If I don't keep this up, then I too will get in trouble. And by default, so will he. And you."

"Ellia!" her grandfather from the back door screams at the top of his lungs. "I'm calling the cops! I've had it with you and that boy!"

Both Leon's and Néol's hearts race. The two reflections think, *If the cops come here...then.* And the two stare each other down. Néol looks above and sees a collection of clouds coming to cover the moon in its Heartshine phase.

"I'm outta here," Néol says, slipping through the mirror and completely vanishing. And just like that, the clouds cover the moon, ceasing Heartshine. The moon returns to its normal white sheen.

"Leon…" Ellia says, rubbing his hair.

"Ellia," Leon strains, "I can't…get arrested. If I do, then… I'll be in big trouble. Can I…go back with you?"

Ellia starts sobbing and shakes her head, disagreeing. "I can't. My grandfather called the cops. I don't know if I can sneak you in again."

Suddenly, blue and red lights flare in Ellia's driveway. Two officers walk into the backyard, guns out.

"Well, if it isn't Leon Granttley," the one officer says.

Leon narrows his injured eyes toward the towering man. He's seen this man before—him and the female officer behind.

Leon recognizes these officers because they are the same ones who appeared to the Lunae Lux on the night of his birthday. His graduation. His switch. They're the same officers that refused to help Leon and the rest of the graduation patients…all because they're collaborating with the Lunae Lux.

"You can call me, Detective Nivmar," one officer says, glowering down at Leon, "and this is my partner, Officer Milaw."

Leon and Ellia don't say a word.

Detective Nivmar puts his gun away, and so does Milaw. Nivmar says, "We've been watching you for quite some time. We know all about what Stefano has told you *to do* and what *not* to do."

Leon gasps, "What? How?"

"That's not up to me to tell you. But what *I am* here to do, is bring you in. You have a meeting with the Lunae Lux."

Leon shuts his eyes, *And now this is how I die. It's all caught up to me. You were right, Dr. Giro. I'm going to Hell, now. This is how it happens. And I dragged Ellia into it, too. Wait. Ellia!*

"You can take me in," Leon says solemnly, opening his eyes, "but please leave her out of this."

"Oh, she's in more trouble with her grandfather than anyone else. But. With her knowledge of the other world, given time, she'll become useful later."

Ellia wears a look of disgust at the officer's last sentence.

Milaw rolls her eyes. "C'mon, young lady. We've gotta take you inside."

Ellia looks down at Leon who's in her lap, she whispers, *"Will I...see you again?"*

"I'll come find you. I marked this place on the map."

The Detective laughs. "Don't make promises you can't keep. Now, let's go."

Milaw escorts Ellia back into the house where her grandfather thanks the officers and then slams the door. While in handcuffs, Leon is being escorted to a police car, or at least he thinks he is. Behind this police car is a black limo.

"This is where you'll be going," Nivmar says, shoving Leon forward to the center of the limo. The door opens for him, and a strange wind sucks all the air out from around him. Ellia watches from her living room window as a strange force lifts Leon off his feet and pulls him into the limo.

175

BLACK FEATHERS
FLOCK TOGETHER

June 29, 2009 (Monday)

Planet Heart

Odaroloc ∧ Eroaura

Mada's Circle

7:33 a.m.

"Come take a seat, Leon Granttley. Or should I say, Néol Yelltnarg?" Allure Igor says, lying on her side in the corner of a long seat that seems to wrap around the interior of this limo. He is shocked to hear that Allure is inside. But his mind has much to worry about.

Leon is standing at the door of this limo, still wondering what wind pushed him inside the vehicle. To his right is the driver far ahead. But to his left are the people he has an appointment with.

Faviané, the strange woman with the voice of an old woman but the figure of a young adult, is to Allure s right. Her ouija board themed mask faces Leon, and it startles him.

On the floor of this limo and in front of Allure s feet are two strange creatures with stitch marks where their eyes should be. These creatures could be mistaken for walking skeletons with thin layers of flesh. One creature is paler than snow, the other is darker than a moonless night. One seems to be filing her fingernails.

Oh, take a seat already," Allure says forcefully. If we wanted to hurt you, I d have ordered it already."

Leon swallows and sits down on the leather seat. A pair of handcuffs literally float in front of him. A strange purple smog seems to be surrounding them.

"Hold your arms out," Faviané says with her hands sitting on her lap.

Leon obeys, holds his arms out, and the handcuffs snag onto his wrists.

"Good. So you *do* know how to listen," Allure says, then you ll make our job much easier. Tell me. What were you doing recently? Why do you think we ve brought you in here?"

Leon looks down at the floor of the limo and answers only one of her questions, For...meeting with Néol s friends."

"I thought Stefano made himself clear when he said you *could* meet with those that Néol knows?"

Leon looks right into Allure s dark eyes. He wants to shout, *How do you know that*? But he knows her quick temper from all his times of seeing her on Earth. Outside of the facility and here at the mercy of this limo's darkness, what else would she do?

"He did say that," Leon admits.

"Right," Allure says, then shouts, LAITHER! Set the coordinates for Néol Yelltnarg s address!"

"Yes, ma am!" Laither, the old guard shouts back."

Leon s worry slightly eases, *I m leaving here alive?*

"Leon," Allure says, you re not in trouble for speaking to the people Néol knew. You re in trouble for sharing the secret with them, preemptively. You see. When a Knight like yourself is brought over to this planet, we,— the Lunae Lux—have it so that they live the miserable lives of the reflection. That is the agreement we made with your *other* long ago."

Allure continues, However, our contract states that *we* must subdue the reflection by making sure that they don t leave this planet. In short, we don t care about what you feel while you re here. The more misery, the better."

"But...why?" Leon asks, throwing caution to the wind.

"Because the misery you feel transforms into delight for your reflection. The despair from missing your family. Your friends. Your home. The pain of feeling even *more* out of place with people you don t know. I know your reflection isn t the best with showing his emotions. But I promise you, it all works for his benefit. He chose this instead of where you *could have* gone."

"He chose this instead of Hell?"

"Is it a surprise that he did?"

"A little...but I guess I want to know why he didn t pick the worst option..." Leon says.

"Most Heartlings refrain from picking Hell because of the risks involved. If a person goes there and loses all hope—well, you tell me. What did *you* feel when you were alone, hungry, and tired? You stopped wanting to live, didn t you?"

"No? I still wanted to fight."

Allure coos, Then maybe you would ve done just fine in Hell. Then again, most people *say* they would fight to the end. But throughout the years, I ve seen people start off strong until their worries eat them alive. Eventually, they lose the will to live which puts the reflection at risk and consequently, our whole program."

"All I want to know is what this is for. Why go through all this— gaslight myself and Allie just to bring me here today?"

Suddenly that eyeless being lunges, stretching its deformed hands toward Leon s face. The demon and Leon could have kissed by being this close. Its…surprisingly human-like teeth fail in biting his nose off.

While there is nothing in her hand, Faviané's recedes. It looks like she just pulled something backwards. Whatever this invisible thing in her hand is, it succeeds in drawing this pale, bald, and eyeless beast back toward Allure, who slaps it in the face and shouts, Are you insane? Behave now!" The creature cries out in fear, shaking near her feet.

"To answer your question, Leon," Allure says, wiping the creatures purple drool from her hands, "why we ve done all of this is *kranfly* none of your business. Not even your reflection knows the deeper reasons. But the *only* reason why you ve been spared from going to Hell *today*, is because Néol has succeeded in bringing us more patients to the Heartshine Facility. This is your first and final warning. After this, your next punishment is never seeing the sky of this or any world ever again!"

The limo comes to a stop, and Laither shouts, We re here, Mistress! Permission for a smoke-break?"

"Granted! But make it quick. I m hungry. And I want Earth s food! Not the crap here," Allure shouts, then softens her voice. "Are we clear, Mr. Granttley?"

"Yeah…but just to double check. So, I m allowed to see Néol s friends and family…?"

"Correct…" Allure says as Faviané nods as well.

Leon continues, But I m *not* allowed to talk to anyone about the reflecting worlds?"

"Indeed. The damage is already done with that Ellia girl. So I don t care if you see her. And since she knows about this now, I know we can influence her to enroll in the facility later. But while you mention it. You were caught trying to transport yourself back to Planet Earth. That won t be allowed, either. *This* is your new home, Leon. If Néol is caught back on this planet, or if you are caught roaming around Earth, BOTH of you will be sent to Hell! Get the spirits to open the door, Faviané."

And just like that, the limo door Leon entered from opens. Leon is flung straight out of the limo and right onto his chest. He can t lift himself up. Not with his handcuffs on. Faviané with her strange ouija board mask steps out and crouches next to Leon.

"I almost forgot to remove your cuffs. My apologies." Faviané says a few whispers, and suddenly the same purple smog floats around Leon s wrists, disarming the handcuffs which fall to the ground. The handcuffs then float back into the limo.

"To answer the question you asked Detective Nivmar earlier, Leon."

Leon turns to the side to look at her mask as she speaks.

"Have you ever wondered why you ve been seeing a murder of crows lately?"

Leon is frozen in place. He wants to nod but cannot. But the answer is *yes*. He s been seeing them for as long as he can remember. Since his talk with Jason on December ninth, since…no. It has been longer than that. Leon s been seeing the crows for years.

I ll take your silence as a yes." Faviané lets out a creepy giggle. You may have thought that a bad omen was upon you, hm?"

Leon hangs his head down in shame.

"If you don t want to meet with us again, you should know that we re always watching… All that is living isn t always real… Remember that the next time you see a crow fly by… For the murder is never unavailing."

Purple smog suddenly surrounds Faviané, and just like that—she s gone into thin air. Leon, though, can hear her cackling with Allure inside the limo. The limo speeds off into the distance.

"I can t believe that s what those crows were… I was never safe. They all looked so real, too," Leon says to himself, rubbing his aching face, his pained stomach, and bruised arms while standing to stare at the house he rejected—Néol s very own home. He walks to the front door of his reflection's home. But before his fists can pound on the wood of that door, he pulls his hand back, looking down at the ground.

"If I step inside…I basically accept the fact that I m stuck here. That I have no way of *ever* getting back home…"

"Well said."

Leon turns around slightly to see the boy with curly hair; the one he d been seeing in school, the Earthshine Facility, and even on the very night of their switch.

Miles?" Leon says in shock.

"Good to see you still remember me!" With his thumb, Miles points to a teal two-door sports car behind him. Come, take a ride with me."

"*You* have a car?"

"My reflection *Selim* has a car. Two actually," Miles says, correcting himself. " C mon. We ve gotta talk." Miles leads Leon toward the vehicle. And Leon rejoices for finally not having to walk once more. However, Leon accidentally walks to the right side of the car.

Miles lets out a faint smile. Passenger door's on the other side."

Oh. Whoops," Leon laughs nervously.

Don t worry. It took me a while to get used to it too." Miles gets into the car from the right, and Leon rotates around to the correct seat as Miles starts the vehicle.

A voice within Miles mind whispers. As it talks, it sounds like it s directly in his left ear. It says, *Now remember, Miles…don t be too hard on him. His confidence is already quite low…*

Correct… another voice says, this one sounding like it is coming from his right ear. *The last thing you ll want to do is anger him.*

Miles clenches his jaw. *Leave me alone, you two.*

Another voice chimes in and shouts, *Judging by the yapping of those voices, you ve picked Leon up!*

I have, Miles replies within his mind.

Nice! How s he lookin ? this voice that sounds similar to Miles asks.

Pretty bad. But hey. I m about to speak to him. So I ll need to focus.

Alrighty! I ll leave ya to it. You ve got this, Other!

Thanks, Selim. I ll keep in touch, Miles thinks, ending this mental conversation as he drives forward, looking at the crows perching atop the streetlights. Leon sees this too.

Great. Back to being watched," Leon says in a choppy breath.

If it makes you feel better, they never stopped."

Leon gazes at the crows as they watch him, saying nothing.

So," Miles says, looking at the fresh bruise on Leon s cheek. What happened? You didn t look like this when we got here."

Leon explains the entire situation to Miles. He starts all the way back from when he first arrived on Heart, all the way until his recent encounter with the Lunae Lux. During this, Miles takes turns into random streets. It seems he has no real destination. He is just doing this to buy time in the car.

I m going to be frank with you, Leon. I think you had this coming. Stefano warned you from the start."

I *just* wanted to see my family."

I know you did. *Everyone* here does. All the other Knights want to."

Leon rests his chin on his fist. Wanna not minimize my issue? I still want to see mine. I left on a bad note."

Leon, I m here just to make sure you learn from your mistake. So that hopefully you make the right choice the next time around."

Do this by crashing the car. Kill him, a voice in Miles' mind jeers.

"And what's the *right* choice? Avoiding an inter-dimensional relationship?"

Miles shakes his head. "No one cares about who you date, Leon. My reflection's in a... Oh wait. You remember Ombretta, right? My other's dating her."

"You're kidding!"

I wish. Miles thinks then says, "So no, there's no rule against it. You can talk to Ellia all you want."

"Well, I guess there's some good news then. I thought it'd be forbidden or something."

"We're all learning about this just as much as you are. Stefano, regardless of how much *he* knows, is still learning. He only *just* put together that booklet for us all. The booklet of Reflection Principles."

"I see. So, wait, you brought up your reflection. Are you two close?"

"Like brothers."

"Hmm. Just like Stefano and Festano used to be. Can you trust him?"

"Absolutely. Our story's a little complicated, but I'll tell you on another day. It's quite long. All you need to know, though, is that *you* can trust him."

Leon holds his chin. "So I can trust *your* reflection, but what about Néol? Why's *he* siding with the Lunae Lux? And if you got switched here like me, why's yours friends with you?"

"I guess if I'm gonna put it shortly, Selim enrolled into the Heartshine Facility for the same reason as Néol. But then he met Stefano, who then put him into contact with me. Then Stefano met with us in secret and let us know about all these things and more before they happened."

"Explains why you were the only calm one during our switch."

Miles nods. "You're observant. To be honest, I was only calm because Stefano prepped me for the whole thing. I just stayed quiet and submissive to avoid getting on their bad side."

"Smart. But you're actually okay with being here? I'm surprised you'd willingly give Earth up for this place."

"Well…" Miles replies. "We thought that I could rendezvous with the other *Neo Knights* here on Heart, while Selim could complete assignments with my other good friend on Earth."

Miles steers the wheel with one hand, then tugs on his curl with the other, and Leon says, "Miles. Help me get back home."

"No."

"Just for a little bit."

"No, Leon."

"C'mon! I *just* need to tell them that I'm okay!"

"Leon! Did you *not* learn from your lesson just now? How hardheaded are you?"

"Very! And you should be, too!"

The Voice jeers to Miles, *If you are too condescending, you will scare him away.*

Miles heeds The Voice's advice and softens his tone. "Leon, when Stefano told you about how to return to Earth, it was for a different reason entirely. For *emergencies*. Not for returning at your convenience."

"As if any of this was convenient."

"You're not one to talk. Stefano has the hardest job out of everyone. Trying to appease *our* personal needs while also trying to protect us. Some people resent him for it."

"Well, I wouldn't know that. He was gone before I could even say goodbye."

"Probably because he was off on the run again. You know, from the Lunae Lux that *just* gave you your warning?"

"Honestly, it just feels like I've been kidnapped, and everyone's been coaxing me into staying at this dumb dying world. I feel like no one cares about where *I* want to go."

Miles turns on his hazard lights, then pulls over to the left side of the road to give Leon his full attention. "*Coaxing?*" He looms closer to Leon. "Do you even understand the gravity of this situation? Your family and friends are in danger, Leon. Everyone on both of these planets are in trouble! You think going back home will solve your problems? Your idea of a solution is like cleaning up a mess during a tornado!"

Miles pivots back to his window to scan around for crows. "Count your blessings... Because you're the lucky half of the population." He turns back to look at Leon, who is looking out the window. "Look at me, Leon."

Leon starts tapping his foot and faces Miles.

Miles continues, "The other half of the *Knight's* population is sentenced to Hell. They don't get this kind of freedom... All they have is torture. And there are hundreds. Tens of thousands of people are trapped underneath *some* planet's crust—and you define these petty problems as turmoil? Don't be so selfish. Your troubles do NOT stop the worlds from spinning."

Miles shifts the car back onto the road. A brief silence overtakes them.

Miles sighs and speaks once more. "We all want to go home. But we can't... Not yet... So, if you can't find it within yourself to make it about other people, then I suggest making it about your personal redemption... Or, by the case of your anger...*vengeance*. You can direct your reckless indignation toward Festano and the Lunae Lux."

The two are quiet all the way until they arrive back at Néol's residence. Miles parks the car. Leon rests his chin on his fist, his foot stops tapping.

Leon draws in a long breath. "Miles...can you tell me more about this...Hell?"

Miles plucks at the cuff of his orange dress shirt. "I'll make you a deal, Leon," he says as he unlocks the door for Leon. "If you trust me enough, then let me treat you to this wonderful café."

"Where? How will I get there?"

"It's called the *Libri Café*. And I'll pick you up. My friends and I meet there all the time."

"I'm a little hesitant, not gonna lie. I'm not the best with people."

"I can imagine," Miles replies. "You've only ever had one friend. But now you've got Stefano, Ellia, and me."

Leon smiles and looks away.

Miles adds, "I know you'll find ways to relate to them." Leon looks Miles directly in the eye, trying to detect promise.

"Trust me on this."

"Alright," Leon says, stepping outside.

Miles glances at his watch. "Try to get some sleep. Your eyes look really tired. I'll get you around two p.m. on Wednesday."

Leon waves. "So, two days from now? Sounds good. See you then."

10

ANOTHER

SIDE

℃   ℃   ℃

I t is dark as it is an early winter morning. Later than normal in terms of when Leon would normally get up for school. Crows caw outside Leon's window. But none of their sounds awaken Néol. No. He has an even better alarm clock. The feelings of Leon's pain force a smile on Néol's face as his cold and tired eyes open.

This is a smile that no one other than his cat, Shadow, who is laying on his chest, has seen. Shadow is the same size as China Jr. Shadow is an all-black cat with a white crest on her chest and another patch of white on her belly.

"Hello, my little *Shadow*," Néol says gruffly, petting her. Scratching behind her ears and rubbing beneath her chin with his fingers. She purrs and leaps off him onto the ground to groom herself. She crawls under the bed, growling at China Jr. who is also under this bed but is hiding in fear. The two hiss at one another but proceed to eat from their separate food bowls. Néol kicks the blanket off of himself, stands, and stretches.

When Néol first entered Leon's room, it was filled with Leon's favorite video games, like *Fantasy Final Seven*, *A Kingdom's Heart*, and the *Legend of Link*. There were posters of his favorite movies and even some rock bands. But now? Néol has posters of bands that he favors taped to the wall.

Ones such as *Woe is You*, *Of Rodents and Women*, and even *The Word Death*. The musicians in these band photos each come from Planet Heart. As one could expect from any metal or grunge band, they wear almost all black, have long or spiky hair, spiky bracelets, shoes, and some even wear black makeup.

Néol walks to the closet and glowers at Leon's school uniform. "I'm not wearing this crap again. Makes me feel like a damn nerd." He instead places his usual clothes on. Black skinny jeans with holes in them, his red hoodie, and his black coat over it. He also puts on some boots and clips in two black stud earrings. He walks outside the room, shutting the door behind him, then heads off to the bathroom. On his way there, he sees Amy. Néol speeds into the bathroom before she can and closes the door on her.

"Um, excuse me?" Amy says, after knocking a few times.

"I'll be out in a few."

"Gonna stare at yourself in the mirror again?"

Néol smirks into the mirror. "No need to." He combs his hair with his hands then blinks—suddenly seeing a boy in a blue hoodie smile at him. Néol blinks again then shakes his head. "Hmph. He's probably in the bathroom right now. That's all."

And Néol is correct. Right now, on Planet Heart, Leon is in Néol's bathroom, cleaning and treating his wounds from his recent skirmish with rubbing alcohol and ointment.

Néol finishes with the bathroom.

"Hey," Amy says from outside, "you're gonna miss the bus again if you take any longer."

"Not taking it," Néol replies coolly, opening the door, brushing past her.

Amy grabs Néol's arm quickly and sniffs him. "You reek...you smell like tobacco."

Néol shrugs her arm off. "Why do you think?" he asks, leaving her behind and rushes down the stairs.

Amy raises an eyebrow and says, "Teenagers are so moody."

Néol walks out the front door and onto the sidewalk. He sees the school bus out in front of him. Somehow, he's not completely late. The bus driver and the students inside are shocked to watch Néol wave them off. The bus leaves him behind, and once the dust clears, he can see Leon's friends: Jason, Deen, Jacaline, and...Allie.

Jason and the three who are walking across the street are following their usual routine—talking about all things related to school and drama in their houses. Allie glances over once at Néol. Then twice. She stops in place, and her mouth drops. Néol seems to be paying this no mind.

"Hey, Allie. You okay?" Jacaline asks.

"That's...what...he was wearing that night," Allie says, pointing in fear at who she thinks is Leon.

Jason grits his teeth and glares at Néol. "Seriously?"

"It's like he's *trying* to trigger you," Deen says, rolling his cardigan sleeves up. "That's below even me."

"I'm gonna go talk to him," Jason says.

"No, you've had your chance," Deen says, handing Jason his book bag.

"What're you gonna say to him?"

"I'm just gonna talk to 'em. He just graduated and look at what he's doing. Now, keep my bag warm. I'll be back."

Deen rushes across the street to Néol. "Leon, what the hell's with you?" He then slaps his hand on Néol's shoulder. "You see what you're doing to Allie?"

"No," Néol says, standing still. "But *you tell me* since you've had the nerve to run over here."

"Oh… I see. Graduated and now you're a little cocky?" Deen tries to grab Néol's hood to pull over his head, but Néol firmly grabs Deen's wrist until Deen cries out for him to let go.

"Leon, knock it off!" Deen shouts.

"You mean knock your wrist out of place?"

"What?"

Néol twists Deen's arm until he has no choice but to get on his knees. Néol releases his wrist then crouches next to Deen, looking down at him. Jason, Jacaline, and Allie are watching this with open mouths and wide eyes.

"Now," Néol says with a blank expression. "Say what you were saying to me again?" He asks, holding Deen's ear.

Deen rubs his wrist. "I…I was just telling you that you were freaking Allie out!"

"And then you tried to touch me. That's where you messed up." Néol glances over to Allie's direction and sees her shaking, then he looks back to Deen. "What I choose to wear has nothing to do with what she *thinks* happened to her. Now. Go back to your friends," he says, passing Deen and walking forward.

Deen sits there for a moment, still rubbing his wrists. Jacaline starts rubbing Allie's shoulders to ease her worries. She even gives Allie her own winter jacket just to stop her from shivering from the awakened trauma. But Allie is frozen. This cold look that Néol seems to naturally wear—is *exactly* what she told her grandmother, friends, and Allure about. This was the side of *Leon* that she feared. To her, this is Leon's split personality.

"Jason," Jacaline says in a pushy tone, "go check on Deen!"

"R—right!" Jason says, watching Néol walk farther ahead.

Néol shakes his head and thinks, *This kid took so much crap from people, that it looks like I'm gonna have a lot of cleaning up to do.*

Néol finally arrives at Maleon High School. He pushes open the doors to see the hallway filled with students. Ahead of him is a boy wearing school uniform but with suspenders and books in his hands. This boy has a face like Miles', but their hair texture is the opposite. While Miles has curly hair, this boy's hair is straight and combed backwards.

Selim sees a girl with black hair and glasses. He walks over to her while waving.

"I'm Jordan," the girl says to the boy.

"And I'm *Miles*—" The boy pauses, looking directly at Néol for a second and grins. "Anyway, yeah, I'm Miles. So what class are you off to?" Selim asks, watching Néol closely. But to *Miles'* surprise, someone tall taps his shoulders. Selim nervously turns around to see a fist fly toward his face. His reflexes save his pretty face just in time as he ducks.

"Phew!" Selim exclaims. "Dude, you almost hit me there."

Towering over Selim and the girl, Etay closes in on him. "You have any idea who you're talking to, Miles?"

"Uh, yeah! A really cute girl? Why?"

"Yeah. *My* really cute girl!" Etay blares, cracking his large knuckles. Both Alecia and Hades appear behind *Miles* to grab his arms, restraining him the same way they did with Leon and all the other Earthshine patients.

Selim cries out as Etay punches him in the stomach. The force from this last punch breaks Alecia and Hades's grip. Selim falls to his knees.

"Ow…" Selim utters. "Okay… I won't talk to this one…"

Etay picks Selim up by his straight hair as the bell rings. He whispers, *"You and your straight hair are dead after this class."*

SCAN FOR SELIM

A locker slams beside Etay's ear, and he looks over. "Aye bro? You slam that locker that loud again and—Leon Granny! It's been a while! I know you missed me!" Etay releases Selim's hair, and Selim falls hard on his buttocks.

Néol shakes his head.

"How's it feel to finally graduate?" Etay asks, getting close to Néol's face. "You owe me *at least* nineteen days of lunch money…"

Selim looks up as Etay, Alecia, and Hades surround Néol like he's their prey.

"Look at this," Hades says, circling around Néol. "He's not even wearing school uniform."

"I like it," Alecia jeers. "Means he finally brought out that crazier half you wanted, Etay."

Etay turns and points to Jordan who is still staring in shock. "I'm gonna talk to you later about this!" And Jordan runs down the hallway as quickly as she can.

"Hey," Etay says, leaning down and close to Néol's face. "You hear me, Granny? You haven't answered me yet."

Néol grins right in Etay's face and slams his forehead into Etay's nose. "The better question is," Néol says, not even rubbing his head, "did you feel that?"

Uh. Miles? It's your old pal, Selim. I uh. I wish you could see this. But Néol just hit Etay!

He what?

Yes! I'm literally about to watch them fight!

Where are the hall monitors? This is not good…

I don't know!

Well, get one! The less trouble Leon gets in, the better!

And with this, Selim dashes out into the hallway, passing the crowding students as they curiously watch.

"Bro, you just hit my damn nose!" Etay cries. "I think you broke it—and I'm now gonna break you!"

Néol swiftly kicks Etay in the groin, now bringing the giant quarterback to his knees. Néol then grips his head, pokes one thumb in his eye, and slams his head straight into the locker, making a loud clang. Etay falls back onto the ground in shock. Blood drooling from his nose, his eye leaking tears, his once smooth face cut and gashed from Néol's surprise attack.

Allie, Jason, Deen, and Jacaline open the school doors and become witnesses to the aftermath.

Néol glowers at Hades who is shaking in place. Néol walks right up to him and pulls his winter hat down past his eyes, then knees him straight in the chest, making him gasp for air.

Jason's jaw drops. He tries to run to Néol, but Deen stops him. "Let go of me, Deen!"

"Jason...that's his other half...there's no getting through to him..." Deen releases Jason and looks at Allie. "I'm sorry I doubted you, Allie. That kids a psycho. I believe you now." In response, Allie shakes her head and looks away.

"Took it to happen to you first. You're pathetic," Jacaline says.

Hades pushes his hat upward so he can see and crawls away to Etay who is still in shock from the pain.

Néol walks toward Alecia whose back presses against the locker. "Burn this into your memory," Néol says. "If their brains are too damaged to remember, then you'd better. Otherwise. Next time will be worse. Got it?"

Alecia nods obediently. "We're sorry L-Leon. And. Congratu—"

"—Shut up. Just clean 'em up," Néol says, leaving the three behind.

Ahead of him is Selim with the bald hall monitor who then calls the janitor with his radio and says, "Hank, you're gonna need a mop! Two actually!"

Néol walks up to the monitor.

"Alright," Néol says. "What's the next step, bald man?"

"What is wrong with you, Leon? What's the story here?"

"Ask *Miles* who's standing next to you. They went after him, then myself, so I taught them a lesson."

"You…did that?" the monitor asks, looking back at Néol whose response is a smirk.

The bald monitor stands there in shock. He rushes to Etay's aid. Etay and the two bullies watch Néol as he walks toward Leon's first class.

Néol has made quite a name for himself while being here on Earth. During most of his classes, he would sleep and spend time alone. Sometimes he would sneak out to smoke a few cigarettes in the bathroom. The smell would leak out into the hallway, but no one ever knew who to blame. And when the suspicion did fall on his shoulders, the students knew better than to say anything. After all, they had seen what had happened to Etay, the star quarterback.

Néol doesn't tolerate any nonsense from Leon's teachers. Mr. Nert, the history teacher who had originally made Leon his emotional punching bag, was made into a fool by Néol. The class was a witness to many amusing events. Some where Néol would spit in Mr. Nert's coffee whenever he would step outside. Sometimes Néol would write obscenities on the chalkboard. Mr. Nert would never know who to guess. Naturally, he would blame who he thought was Leon, but never had any proof.

Then there was the final straw that killed Mr. Nert's pride. Néol poured a bottle of super glue all over his chair. And for the entire day, Mr. Nert walked around with a chair attached to his buttocks.

Néol specifically planned this because he knew Mr. Nert was also coaching the football team after school, so going home for a change of clothes wasn't an option. While Mr. Nert couldn't prove that Néol was doing what he did, he did cause the teacher to leave him alone.

During lunch in the cafeteria, Allie and her friends are shocked to see that *Leon* chooses a table all by himself to sit at. Néol is completely content with his three slices of pepperoni pizza. He eats by himself, sneaks to the bathroom to smoke on occasion, and then sleeps when he can. But to his dismay, since he is more of an introvert, a girl shows up to the table. She's an attractive brunette with green eyes. Néol raises his head from his arms, rubbing his sleepy eyes.

"Hi, I didn't mean to wake you up."

Néol smirks. "Yes, you did. Otherwise, you wouldn't be here."

The girl blushes and plays with her hair. "I just wanted to say that my friend thinks you're cute."

Néol looks off into the distance and sees a group full of attractive cheerleaders. These seven girls each see him look over and turn away as quickly as possible.

"Hmm. Depends on which one."

"She's the only one with the cardigan on."

"I'll think about it after my nap."

"Okay. Well, here's her number," the brunette says, sliding over a small piece of paper.

Néol chuckles, crumbling the paper and putting it in his pocket. "Awfully bold of her. But gotcha. I'm gonna rest now." The girl giggles and returns to her table as she and her friends continue chatting.

Jason and Deen are glowering over, jealously.

Deen hits Jason's arm. "Dude, he pulled that number without even trying!" Jacaline rolls her eyes and tries to keep speaking to Allie who is doing nothing but staring at her empty food tray. Did she ever get food?

From afar, Selim is chewing on a slice of pizza. Next to him are also a few girls. There's one other boy here, but this person is silent. It seems like he's not as bold as he thought he was. He eventually gets up and leaves Selim and the girls behind.

"Yeah, so as I was sayin'," Selim says, putting his arm around one girl who blushes. "I'd love to take you in my sports car sometime."

"Okay, sure. After volleyball practice, then?"

"Sounds goo—" But before Selim can finish his sentence, he sees the bald monitor waking Néol up and then bringing him outside the cafeteria with him.

Oh no… He's in trouble, Selim thinks as he watches Néol smirk while following behind the monitor.

An hour passes. Outside of the school is Amy, Leon's sister, in her purple car. Néol is walking toward her with a straight face.

"Suspended?" Amy cries out. "Seriously? Mom and Dad are so pissed!"

"Had to stand up to my bullies. What can I say?"

Amy lectures on how *Leon* could have prevented a fight by being the bigger person and walking away. Néol ignores this entire speech by smirking and looking out the window.

Amy adds, "I seriously don't think you should have graduated from that facility. Well. Mom and Dad are out right now, but they said no TV, no allowance, and—"

—Néol phases out Amy's words, rests his chin on his fist, and thinks, *And just like that, no more school for me.*

11

Meeting Ground

☾ ☾ ☾

Miles cautiously drives through the dense and misty fog with Leon who is asleep in the passenger seat. While Miles' drive on the road is smooth and peaceful, the two voices that always have something to say join him. They say things like, *You braked too hard just now.* Or, *You're driving too slow! Speed up!*

Because of these two voices, Miles is never truly alone. And sometimes with Selim being preoccupied with other tasks, he must deal with these two voices throughout the day. They are partially the reason why his eyes always have bags. He is the king of overthinking.

Miles huffs in relief for finally arriving at a giant parking lot. He parks, and the ceasing of the car's motion awakens Leon who yawns very loudly.

"Good evening," Miles says, detaching his seatbelt as Leon does the same.

"Hmm. Yeah. Good evening," Leon yawns and stretches while looking around. "Pretty big parking lot for a café, huh?"

"Oh. I was actually in the middle of explaining earlier…then I realized you were fast asleep."

Leon rubs his eyes. "Sorry about that. I thought that nap I took earlier would've helped. I've been sleeping nonstop."

201

"You needed the rest. It's alright." The two exit the teal sports car, and Leon follows Miles toward the building.

"So, this is *really* called the *Libri Convention Center*," Miles says. "It's a meeting ground for people on Planet Heart for many reasons. Say you were a business owner, and you wanted to rent an auditorium or conference room, this would be the place to do it at."

Leon nods as they pass a few more rows of cars and get closer to the large three-story building.

Miles adds, "Companies like coming here to give out free samples of their products. They'll also sell them or might just come to network. As long as you've got a charming personality, it can all work out here."

"Oh, okay," Leon says. "So it's a multipurpose facility?"

"Exactly. And they have a café where they serve food and coffee. They also have a huge restaurant inside. So, sometimes businesses will meet for meals either *before* or *after* their big meetings."

They arrive at the building, and Miles pushes open one of the two doors for himself and Leon.

"I typically meet with my friends here because the crows can't follow us into buildings. And they've got no right to. It's a public place where we'll still be living as our reflections."

"Oh...that makes sense. Well, now I feel a bit more at ease."

"Doesn't hurt to be too safe when you can, though," Miles adds.

Miles leads Leon forward. The purple lighting in this lobby is dim. A greeter is to their right, waving at people who are entering and leaving. To their left is a coffee shop named *Planetbucks* with barstools for people to sit on. It seems that even here, the smell of coffee is the same. There are even tables where some people are working on their laptops. Others are writing on sheets of paper. Leon follows Miles forward. They push through a door and walk into a wide hallway with various kinds of paintings and portraits on the wall.

"Wait," Leon says. "Can we look at some of these? Some of them look kinda familiar."

"Sure. I didn't take you as the type to appreciate art."

"Not normally, but... I want to see what art from this world looks like."

There are numerous styles of painting spanning Baroque, Gothic, Surrealist, Abstract, and tons more. Leon curiously stares at a large portrait showing a frowning man wearing white garb with black hair hanging down to his chin. Below, the drawing's name reads *Anom Asil*.

Leon gasps, "No way... This is the reflection of the *Mona Lisa*..."

Miles turns away from the painting in front of him to the sound of Leon's astonishment. "Yup, you've got it. We have the same painting on Earth but drawn differently." Miles moves closer to whisper, *"Here, it's assumed that Noelodra Ad Icniv envisioned herself as a man."* Miles' eyes veer over a few inches away. "If you think that's cool, then check this one out."

Leon follows him as he points to a painting grafted in oil, crayon, and pastel.

"You've had to have seen something similar," Miles suggests while he scratches his chin, "but where, I wonder?" Miles leers over to Leon as he ponders.

"Hmm... It looks really familiar. And...creepy."

The painting is slightly different from Leon's memory. He recalls a bald man under an orange and red sky. The sky here is illustrated as dense scribbles of blue and black. The water is now orange and red. The woman shown here is wearing a baleful murderous expression toward the world. Underneath the painting is the creator's name along with text to explain the artist's inspiration.

"I was running along the road from two enemies – the moon was setting – suddenly the sky turned black – I paused, amazed and enlivened, and stood in front of the border – there was sweat and fears of darkness above the black-indigo ravine and the city – my enemies crept upward, and I stood there trembling with woe – I sensed a perpetual silence passing through all."

Miles says, "This drawing is called *The Silence of Nature*. The artist's name here is *Draved Numch*. She's from the country reflecting *Norway*...So here on Planet Heart, it would be called *Yawnor*."

"I wish I had a camera. I'd show Ellia—I mean...my family on Earth some of these... But, wow. This world has so many reflecting things."

Miles ignores the first part of Leon's sentence regarding Ellia and says, "I prefer to see Planet Heart as a parallel with *alternate* outcomes. Saying this place is *just* an alternate isn't fair. We really don't know which world was created first. We just know of its presence. That's all. I think it's good to pay respect to one's origin when it's known." Miles points ahead of them. "And speaking of origin...I think there may be something else you'll find interest in." Miles waves Leon over to his direction.

The doors behind them swing open as human traffic swarms into the hallway. Leon follows Miles' tactic, sticking to the wall like glue to shimmy across to the next three artifacts.

Miles points to an artifact trapped behind glass. It is a golden aged piece of paper with cursive written in reverse. The drawing on beige paper has schematics showing a circle in the shape of a crescent.

"To you," Miles says, "this world is an alteration of our very own world... But this painting might say otherwise. It can imply that either both worlds were created at once, or... That Planet Heart came before ours. It's one or the other. Recognize that moon phase?" Miles asks as he points to the worn paper.

Here's what Leon sees:

Leon says, "Yeah. It's Planetshine...or...Heartshine in this planet's case. So, this Noel guy's the one who discovered it? Er... She?" he corrects himself.

SEE WHAT LEON SEES

"I wouldn't say discovered it... But *Leonardo* and *Noelodra* definitely put the phenomenon on the map. Earthshine came from *Leonardo*, and Heartshine came from *Noelodra*. They *originally* believed that light came from the moon's atmosphere and ocean."

Miles continues, "Their years of studying light and shadow led them to that conclusion. Thousands of trips to the moon in today's time tell us otherwise... But in the 1500s, that belief was spread throughout the worlds. As wrong as they were, they were still onto something. If the two of them were immortal, they would've lived to have seen that Planetshine is the gateway to where you and I are today."

Suddenly a vibration sounds from Miles' pocket. "One sec, I'm getting a call." He reaches into his pocket to open his flip phone.

"Miles speaking..." He places one hand in his pocket and turns to the side. "Yes, yes... I'm just showing Leon some art..." His palm covers his face. "*Caleb*, we're basically right outside... Yes, you can start ordering food for yourself."

Leon continues to stare at the drawing while Miles mouths off to the person named Caleb on the line.

So, you're how we all know about Planetshine, Leon thinks, looking at the name *Noelodra Ad Icniv.*

Miles slams his phone then releases a deep sigh. "Ugh. We'd better hurry. Caleb's apparently *super hungry.*" He shoves the phone into his pocket. "Anyway, ready to go? We can always talk more about this."

"Definitely. Because now, I have lots of questions…" Leon says as he moves next to Miles.

"Well, glad to know you appreciate art. Selim finds this all very boring… I have two other friends who also appreciate art, but they're always too busy. The glass is half full, I guess."

Leon folds his arms. "I wanna know how people came to learn about Planetshine… And which world did first. That'll explain how any of this came to be… It could probably even explain Festano's issue with our world."

"Who knows? But I don't think there's any point in looking in the past. Sometimes, everything you need is right in front of you." The two of them arrive at the end of the hallway, and Miles pushes the two-way doors, holding one for Leon.

Leon says, "It doesn't hurt to wonder, though. I mean, think about it. What if Leonardo discovered it but then sold the idea? Or… What if someone read his notes and then…" The two continue ahead into a dining room, the smell of seafood tickles Leon's nose. The enticing aroma ceases all his thoughts. They continue walking through the hallway passing a couple of chefs with black suits and hats.

"I know that smell from anywhere… That's lobster…" Leon moans as drool nearly slips from his mouth. He wishes that Stefano gave him money to spend.

"Gross. You like seafood? And here I thought we could be friends," Miles says, chuckling. "But I suppose if there's any guilty pleasure I have," Miles turns to face Leon with tears flooding his eyes, "it's *French toast*. Here, though, it's called *Chrenf toast*. And I would literally die for it…"

Leon sticks his tongue out in disgust. "Meh, really? I hate the smell of cinnamon."

"Keep these things to yourself, Leon," Miles laughs. "*Toni*, who you'll meet, will force-feed you things you never tried if you say that kinda stuff."

Leon gulps.

"Alright," Miles says, "we normally meet in the center of the tables over there." But suddenly, *something* grabs Miles' left bicep. He spins in a circle while trying to get a glimpse of the perpetrator. Leon steps a few inches backwards as Miles struggles with finding the mysterious force. The wind from the impetus blows their clothing and hair.

"Was that you, Leon?" Miles says while catching his breath.

Leon scratches his head. "I felt a wind too, but I'm way over here. You almost hit me when you spun around like that, though…"

"Something grabbed me…" Miles says in a shaky voice while dusting his sleeves off.

Leon notices a tall girl walk her way to Miles. She grabs his left arm and says, "Oh, how I've missed you and your biceps, Selim…"

Miles flatly replies, "*Ombretta*, I'm not Selim."

"I brought a surprise for you…" She places a narrow can of pineapple juice in his left hand.

"I'm not Selim. It's me, Miles," Miles says, handing the can back to her.

"Oh! I…I thought maybe he used a different conditioner again or something…" the girl with the tiny mole under her left eye says. "Ah, I'm sorry! You and Selim look so—"

Miles plasters a smile on his face as he looks up to the girl. "I know, Ombretta. We look almost identical. Next time just look at our hair first. He perms his so it can be straight. You can't miss it."

"Ugh, you'd think I'd know this by now... You and I literally went to school together... I'm sorry, Miles! I feel so embarrassed! Tell him I said hey, okay? He hasn't called me in a while." The tall girl turns to Leon with her finger pointing at his face. "You look familiar, too...have we met before?"

"N—no... Not that I t—think..."

Miles wraps his arm around Leon's shoulder. "You'll have to excuse my friend. Leon gets nervous around girls, isn't that right?"

Miles, come on! Leon thinks as he glares. *That's not true.* He shrugs Miles off who chuckles nervously.

Ombretta giggles. "Well, you two look busy, so I'll let you both go. See you at the Estates later?"

"Maybe," Miles says. "Depends on how long I'm here tonight."

Ombretta nods. "Okay."

"I'll tell Selim that you were looking for him," Miles says dismissively. He waves her away. The tall girl with the blue scarf nods then runs back over to the bar with her friends.

"Oh, so that's Ombretta," Leon says. "She was the girl that was homeschooled, right?"

"Yes, she was. She was also with us on the night of the switch. You'll get to talk to her more later. Give me a sec," Miles says while he shuts his eyes.

Miles calls out to his other in thought. *Hey, Selim. Your girlfriend, Ombretta...was looking for you.*

Which one?

I just said, Ombretta...

Oh really? What'd she say? Guess I really am unforgettable.

I'd rather not get into that now. Just figured I'd let you know.

What's with that tone?

It's nothing.

Miles, I'm telling you. Let me find someone for you.

Enough, Selim. Just give her a call soon.

Oh, fine. I'll talk to ya later. But believe me when I say I sense jealousy...

"Alright, I'm ready," Miles says aloud, sighing, leading Leon through a crowd, then through a sea of filled circular tables. They cut to the center to where Miles sees five familiar faces from afar. As they walk, Leon gazes at the golden chandeliers hanging above them. They're each emitting a warm purple light.

"About time!" yells a bearded man wearing a reversed red baseball cap. He scratches a few breadcrumbs out of his chinstrap beard and adds, "You guys were looking at art for that long? I had two appetizers to hold me off."

Here is everyone at the table:

Miles finds himself an empty seat, looks at the capped man, and says, "I'm glad *you* at least got to eat, Caleb. What about everyone else here?"

SEE ALL SITTING AT THE TABLE

"They wanted to wait for you," Caleb pouts.

"Gee. How kind of them," Miles says flatly.

Leon shyly finds himself an empty seat next to a boy his age with red hair. A short and plump woman with long black hair as dark as the Earth's night sky shouts to Miles, "Miles Lee! How dare you waltz in here without giving me a hug!"

Miles sighs then walks over to Toni to hug her. She wears a wide grin, hugging him back. "Sorry, Toni," Miles says.

"And is this your friend?" Toni asks, as she releases Miles.

"Yes, he is," Miles says, sitting back down.

Toni shouts, "And you're gonna just let this poor boy sit down without introducing all of us? We could be serial killers for all he knows."

There's a boy next to Toni who has long black hair just like hers. He's been eyeing Miles down ever since he hugged Toni. This envious boy suddenly shocks Toni, hugging her tightly, refusing to let her go. Toni hugs this long-haired boy back.

Miles sighs and takes a deep breath. He stands and says, "Everyone, this is Leon Granttley."

"My dear," Toni says, "you are most certainly *not* in your twenties like the rest of us... How old were you when you were enrolled?"

The eyes of all these staring people give Leon no chance to breathe. A part of him wants to curse at Miles for bringing him on the spot to a bunch of people he doesn't know. While slightly shaking, he replies, "I'm s-seventeen. I was put on watch at six, then officially enrolled when I was fifteen."

Everyone at the table gasps. The boy with red hair next to Leon reaches his hand out and says, "I feel like you're also an introvert. So, let's team up against everyone here. We'll start with Miles."

Leon chuckles and shakes the boy's bony hand. "I like this plan. What's your name?"

"Scudero. Rob Scudero," replies the boy with pale skin and blue eyes.

"Unbelievable..." a woman with long brown hair says, looking at Toni, "...they just get younger and younger nowadays."

Caleb chimes back in, "Agreed, *Ellen*. I wouldn't be surprised if they started bringing in preschoolers."

Toni shakes her head in response. "Well, Scudero, I suppose you're no longer the baby of the group. You *just* turned eighteen, after all. That just leaves Miles and Leon."

"Am *I* the baby of the group?" says the long-haired boy next to Toni, poking her shoulder over and over.

"No *Tenny*, you're not the baby of the group. But you're still precious to me either way."

Because of her comment, Tenny looks like he could fly to the moon. He seems rather attached to Toni... Literally. He starts leaning on her shoulder after this short remark. Toni doesn't seem bothered by this, though. In fact, it seems like she welcomes it.

"Good evening, everyone," a tall waiter says to the group. "Just so you all know, the orders you placed were slightly delayed. But we should be back on track within the next ten minutes."

"Excellent," Caleb says, "because your boy is ready for seconds and thirds."

"Excuse me, sir," Miles calls to the waiter who rushes over. Miles whispers, *"Were you able to get my...you know, beverage?"*

"Oh dear," the waiter says. "Yes. Right away, Mr. *Selim*, I will fetch you the finest glass of warm milk that I can find."

Caleb bursts out laughing. "Oh yeah! Can't forget his precious warm milk!"

Miles gives a heavy sigh, and Caleb adds, "Hey waiter, don't forget his widdle bib, too! Bwahahaha!" The waiter tries to be professional by hiding his laugh.

"Alright, Caleb..." Miles growls. "Just try not to have your crumbs fly on our guest today, okay?" He then looks at Leon who's trying his hardest not to laugh. "It's okay, you can laugh. I like having warm milk with my Chrenf toast."

"That's so weird, right Toni?" Tenny says, tapping her once more.

"Yes, Tenny," Toni says. "That *is* very weird. But Miles was always a little weird. We all are," she says, taking a sip of her glass of *Nurse Salt* soda.

"Wait," Leon says, watching the waiter leave. "I actually didn't get to order,"

"Oh, it's okay sweetie," Toni says. "We knew Miles' order because he always gets the same thing. But for you, we ordered you a margherita pizza. Is that okay?"

"That's *more* than okay. I love pizza."

Toni smiles. "We're going to get along just fine."

Tenny wears an angry look toward Leon. But Leon doesn't notice.

Toni adds, "I ordered more appetizers for us since Caleb decided to eat everything!"

"I'm *not* sorry," Caleb replies. "I love garlic bread sticks."

"Yes, and so do we, Caleb," Toni snaps. "So don't eat them all this time."

"Yeah! Don't eat them all!" Tenny adds right after Toni.

Leon nervously raises his hand, and Miles mouths, *No don't,* to Leon because he can guess what he's about to say.

Leon says, "I, uh. I never had those before."

"Sweetie, you're killing me. Well, I'm sure Miles told you already…"

"Yeah…that I'll be forced to eat them…"

Ellen lets out a slight laugh along with Scudero and says, "He learns quickly."

You know, Leon thinks, *normally I'd be a lot more uncomfortable … But these people. It's hard to believe that they were part of the Earthshine Facility. They're actually treating me like I'm human. And they seem… happy.*

"So, Leon," says Caleb, "what's *your* disorder?"

"CALEB!" everyone but Leon at the table shouts, Toni and Ellen being the loudest.

Leon lets out a laugh. "It's alright…but I'll tell you guys what mine is if you all tell me yours."

Everyone, especially Miles, wears a look of relief.

"Deal," Caleb says, leaning forward on the table.

"Mine *used* to be DID," Leon explains.

"Wait," Caleb responds, "like Dissociative Identity Disorder? No way!"

Ellen speaks, "And you said, *used to*?"

"Well, yeah…" Leon says. "I know it was a lie from Festano. So, I don't think of it as a disorder anymore." Miles smiles after hearing these words.

"Honestly," Caleb replies, "I never met anyone with DID—er, anyone who used to have it. I would've asked if you were *Leon* or *someone else*. But I guess that question's pointless now."

"Still would've been a good question," Leon replies. "I used to think that the voice in my mind *really was* my alternate personality. Sometimes he would suggest that I did certain things, and if I felt like it was right, or if I was weak enough…I'd do them."

Caleb shakes his head. "Well, I'm glad that you made it past yours. I know mine's a lie, but I still live by it. Ask anyone here. I've, uh… Got an eating disorder."

Toni interjects with a smirk. "He likes to binge eat."

"Toni!" Caleb shouts.

"Aww. Well, it was fine when you put Leon on the spot, so consider it karma." Tenny high-fives Toni for this.

"Hmph. Well, I'm taking everyone down with me!" Caleb glances at Ellen who is shaking. "Ellen next to me suffers from anxiety."

"Caleb!" Ellen's face flushes. "Come on. Let me speak for myself." Caleb snickers, and Ellen looks at Leon with red cheeks. "Yes, I suffer from anxiety." She holds her hands up. "As if you couldn't tell from my shaking hands, already. I was worrying about how you would've taken Caleb's little gesture. I thought it would scare you away."

"Oh," Leon responds with his hands up. "I'm not offended at all. Believe me, I've been through worse. And that was nothing. In fact, it's kinda nice talking to you all about it like this."

"Well," Caleb replies, "I'm an open book. So, if you have any questions, throw 'em at me." Leon nods in response.

Scudero taps Leon and whispers, "*I haven't told the others in detail, but I have a sleepwalking disorder.*"

Leon whispers back, "*What? No way.*"

Scudero continues whispering, "*Yeah, like one time I actually drove my dad's car out onto the road. It was crazy. My eyes were shut and everything. No one was hurt...but it sure bit me in the butt later.*"

Leon replies, "*Remind me to hide my keys from you—haha. I'm kidding, I'm kidding. I don't even have a car.*" And to this, Scudero laughs with Leon.

"I suppose it's my turn now," Miles says, looking at Leon. "I've been diagnosed with schizophrenia. I'll typically hear two voices throughout the day."

You mean, like right now? one of those voices say in Miles' mind.

Miles shakes his head and refocuses. "And...they like to disrupt me throughout...really anything. But if it's a bad day where I'm stressed or if I lose a lot of sleep, I'll *actually* see things. My reflection, Selim, has been helping me get over this, though. Just sucks. I know it's not real—but I've been dealing with it for so long."

"Ah, that's alright, buddy," Caleb says, patting Miles on the shoulder. "Means you're messed up just like the rest of us."

"Yeah. Thanks Caleb," Miles says with narrowing eyes as everyone shares a laugh. Leon notices that Tenny hasn't spoken about his disorder. But he drops this as he assumes that Tenny may not be comfortable with sharing yet.

"I suppose that just leaves me," Toni says, reaching into her pocket for a strange black device. She slides it across the round table to Leon. "See those three buttons?" Toni asks.

Leon nods, also acknowledging a strange symbol on the back of the lighter.

"So, that lighter can ignite three different colored flames. I use those flames to keep track of the mood I'm in. It helps me keep track of my emotions. The yellow one at the bottom represents me when I'm my most calm. The second button emits an orange flame. I save that one for when I'm excited about or even paranoid about something. And then there's the third button for the blue flame…"

Ellen clenches her jaw. "One I'm grateful to have barely seen."

"Darling," Toni coos, "I wish I could say the same. Nifty though, isn't it, Leon?"

Leon nods with a smile.

"Now, fork it over before that flame turns blue!"

Alarmed, Leon slides the lighter right back over without a single word. Toni, Ellen, and Tenny chuckle at this.

"But yes," Toni says, "I'm a pyromaniac. They classified me as this when *I*, or my reflection *Iont*, set my house on fire. I'll never forget it. She tried locking me in my own house as everything went ablaze. She ran before the cops came and said that I should *enjoy the fire*. Well. My boyfriend at the time returned to what was left of our home and blamed me. And who could *I* point the finger at? No one. What made matters worse, was that I used to be a pyrotechnician. So, I was the perfect suspect."

Leon shakes his head. "I'm sorry that happened...it's crazy how they dig so deep to use something you love against you. And all of you look like really nice people. It makes me sick that any of you had to go through anything."

"That means a lot, Leon," Ellen replies, her brown eyes locking onto him. "And what did Festano do with you?"

Caleb playfully shouts, "Oh, so it's okay if *you* ask about his personal life?"

Ellen yells back, "Everything's already out on the table so—yes!"
Caleb and Ellen share a laugh.

Leon explains his story to everyone, and they listen intently. He explains everything, starting from how he originally wanted to speak to Allie about his feelings for her, to how Néol's interference turned that all into the incident with her being sexually assaulted.

"That's terrible," Ellen replies.

"Yeah," Leon says, looking away. "And now I just want to return home to tell her the truth. I can't imagine what she's been going through...but now that I know it's a lie. I have to."

Toni chimes in, "You'll make it home *someday*, Leon. And then you can tell her everything." Tenny nods in agreement, and Leon smiles.

"Well," Caleb says, "I'll tell you right now. That won't happen without the help of your reflection, Néol."

"Wait, why do I need him?" Leon asks.

"Hold on," Caleb says, his nostrils flaring to the smell of the garlic bread sticks, "food's here."

Miles grins, *And so is my glass of warm milk.* Selim laughs at this thought.

The waiter delivers a few baskets of breadsticks, placing them in the center of the table. He brings everyone their choice of food. Miles, his precious Chrenf toast, *éplam syrup*, and of course, his glass of warm milk. Everyone tries holding in their laugh, but Caleb bursts out laughing as Miles makes himself a milk mustache.

"So anyway," Caleb says, biting into a breadstick as Leon reluctantly follows, "you'll need your reflection's help if you ever wanna get back. Because according to the sixth Reflection Principle, you need the help of your reflection to switch between planets without Planetshine."

Reflection Principle #6

"Wait, seriously? I need his actual help?"

"Well," Caleb stuffs his mouth more and swallows. "Not *literally.* But you two *do* need to have a connection for it to work. If not, you'll be like most of the Neo Knights here."

I didn't know that was a thing. Then again, I just skimmed through that booklet, Leon thinks. "Great. So, more obstacles are in the way of getting home," he pouts.

"Leon," Miles says, "you mean you still want to—"

"—Oh no, focus on your food," a soft voice says as a small tanned hand clamps onto Miles' shoulder. "I'll take care of this."

"*Aepis?*" Miles says, looking at his amulet's watch. "I thought you weren't showing up."

Leon looks in Miles' direction to see a boy with long hair, teal ear gauges, and a teal septum ring. He is wearing a short dark red hoodie that is exposing his belly button. His pants are decorated with moons and belt straps all around. His shoes have gaping crescent moons with their mouths facing upward.

Huh, Leon thinks, *I thought that was a girl. Secondly, I would've thought he works for the Lunae Lux, seeing the way he's dressed.*

Aepis walks over to Leon, holding his hand out. "And you're the runaway I've heard so much about. I'm Aepis," he says in his soft voice.

Leon clears his throat and reluctantly shakes the boy's bony hand. "Leon," he says, then scoffs in his mind, *Runaway?*

"Well, Aepis," Miles says, glowering at Leon, "to catch you up to speed, Leon was talking about wanting to go home...*again...*"

Leon rolls his eyes, and Aepis nods.

Way to sell me out, Miles, Leon thinks.

Miles continues, "And the timing couldn't be any better for you to show up. Because earlier he asked me about Hell, and I figured—since you're the only person to escape, that you could share your story with him."

Leon blurts, "You've actually been to—"

"—Yes," Aepis responds quickly, "lived there. Not *been to.*" Aepis rolls up his sleeves, exposing his tanned skin with slashes, scars, and bruises of all shapes and sizes. Some of these wounds have healed more than others. Other wounds trail past his elbows. Leon and a few others flinch at the sight. Toni covers Tenny's eyes. Ellen looks away. And Caleb tries to just focus on his food.

Aepis rolls his sleeves down and says, "I could show you my legs, too. But I know it'd spoil Caleb's appetite. So. I'll spare you."

The words, *Thank God,* are written on Caleb's face as he keeps his eyes on his tomato soup.

"Is it really as bad as they say it is? What is it?" Leon asks.

Aepis giggles and wanders over to Leon. Everyone watches as Aepis stands over him. Leon nervously turns around. "What are you doing? Why're you standing behind me like that?"

"Seeing something," Aepis replies smirkingly, his skinny fingers tapping on his chin. He shouts, "Oh no! That person over there needs a doctor!"

With these words, everyone, including Leon, looks away to the tables around but sees no one needing help.

Suddenly, Leon and his chair are falling backwards. Aepis catches Leon with his foot before he and the chair meet the ground. With his leg, he lifts Leon back so that he can sit at the table.

"Why'd you do that?" Leon shouts. "Put me back up, dude!"

"I wanted to see how quickly you'd lose your temper. And since you seem heated, I have my answer."

"What do you mean? Can you get away from me now?"

Aepis lets out a loud cackle, "*Everyone* in Hell starts off strong. In the face of life—all living things are resilient. But *everyone* has a tolerance for pain. A breaking point. I've seen some of the strongest men and women *down there* break down in fury and frustration. And Leon…you snapped when I made you fall backwards. You probably would have attacked me if I didn't catch you."

"Yeah, because you—"

"—I didn't ask for the reason."

Leon grits his teeth, and Miles sees this.

"My point here, Leon, is that if I pissed you off *that* quickly, then why would you bother questioning the luck you have?"

"I'm getting tired of this," Leon shouts, standing up. "I said this to Miles already, and I'll say it to you. Stop minimizing my pain. I miss my friends. I miss my family."

"Aww. You mean you miss them too?" Aepis points to all the others at the table. "Look around you, Leon. You think that *they* don't miss their families? Look beyond this table, at all these other people. Some of them are also Knights like yourself who've been switched over. You think they don't miss their lovers? Their children? Their brothers? Their sisters?"

"Then I guess I'm a little selfish," Leon says, sitting down.

Aepis smirks at this then sighs, "Let's think smaller, then. Since you *clearly* don't care about people."

"I was being sarcastic."

Aepis ignores him. "Leon. And the rest of you can answer this. I won't use any riddles this time, I promise. If one reflection dies, the other follows, correct?"

Everyone nods.

"Right," Aepis continues, "but what would happen if we could *reflect* an emotion?"

Caleb answers, "Well. Simply put, if pleasure exists, then its opposite is sorrow."

"Very good, Caleb," Aepis says condescendingly. "I wish every correct answer would get you one strand of hair back."

"What!" Caleb shouts back, trying not to think about his receding hairline under his red cap.

"That said, Leon," Aepis says, "you desire pity. You want sympathy. But did you ever imagine the things this would bring to your reflection?"

"Yes. I have thought about that."

"Hmm. But these are just *petty* emotions. Now imagine being restrained in a place where there's nothing but intense heat. No water. No family. No friends. You're practically naked! And worst of all. There is no one that can hear your screams. *No one!*" Aepis shouts, slamming his tiny fist on the table. And this shocks everyone, mostly Leon.

"To make matters worse…" Aepis continues, tears welling in his eyes, "they have these demented Lunae Lux soldiers. Bastards crazy enough to be in this crater with you that will torture you. Like devils, they know your physical and mental weaknesses. And they torture you based on them. They know everything about you. So, Leon. Your mother. Your father. Your sister. Your three little friends… That girl, Ellia. And her reflection…*Allie*."

"Wait, how do you know about—"

"—You know what they'd do to you down there? They'd make you relive your worst situations. Over and over and over and over! Then there are maggots that crawl on you—and no matter how many you think you kill—there's another to replace it!"

Aepis continues, "You'd cry for it to end, but you'd never get that! And that's the worst part! It makes you cry for death, but death won't come! Why? Because then they tease you with a bit of water. A little life. A little hope. And that could come from your reflection up in Earth who *may* or *may not have* experienced a bit of displeasure. Just that moment of joy is enough to keep you going…maybe for a few hours. But when people finally get sick of waiting to be saved…let's just leave it at them no longer being with us living folk."

Leon looks down. Aepis smirks, wiping the tears from his eyes and adds, "*How could we be free if their dying breath were to become ours?* That is something Festano Igor wonders all the time. Because he knows that Hell is a halfhearted cure to those seeking happiness. He knows that if Earthlings end their lives, it will create sadness for the Heartlings that he swore to save. And then. Their family in turn will be miserable. But people will do anything for temporary satisfaction. Won't they? And you know this. Because here you are on Planet Heart—begging to see your family for even just a few minutes. When you know you'll want to go back, again, and again."

"Alright. I get it," Leon says, looking down and away from everyone who watches him. "I am lucky. I suppose we all are...it's like Stefano said. Even though bad came to us, we're taking it to try and use it for something good...because at least we *can* fight."

"Yes, Leon," Aepis says. "If you can't return home *now*, you *can* return once you've played your part here. With *us*."

"Fine. What can I do to help, then?"

Miles interjects, "Well, Leon, why I brought you here today was to ask you if you'd like to join us. Stefano named our organization the *Neo Knights*. We're all the Knights that were taken from Planet Earth against our will and—what you see here today is the resistance."

"How do I join, then?" Leon asks. He sounds somewhat annoyed.

"I believe my job here is done," Aepis says, smirking at Leon who returns a glare. "Until next time, everyone. Oh wait," Aepis says, walking behind Caleb, knocking his baseball cap off his head, exposing his receding hairline, then says, "Alright, now I can go."

"Aepis," Toni shouts. "You get your butt back here and give me a hug."

"Of course, Toni. How could I forget," Aepis says, wrapping his skinny arm around her neck as she embraces it. Aepis makes his way to Ellen as well for a quick hug and then away past all the tables, completely vanishing into the crowd.

"Sorry if that was intense for you," Scudero says to Leon.

"Yeah," Caleb says, picking his red cap up, "he's *really* good at upsetting people."

REFLECTION PRINCIPLE 3.2

"But he was telling the truth," Ellen says.

Miles chimes in, "And to answer your question, Leon, to join is simple. You have to make a connection with your reflection."

"A connection?" Leon asks. "Do you know who my reflection is? I can tell you all about him."

Everyone but Leon shares a laugh.

"Believe me," Toni says, "we all thought the same thing. You don't need to be buddy-buddy with your reflection. You just need to make a pact."

"A pact for what?"

"To switch from world to world," Toni replies. "So long as it's verbal, it'll work. It can take place in your minds, too."

"I don't think he'll be up for that…"

Caleb says encouragingly, "Well, no one said you have to make a *real* bond."

"Right," Ellen says. "You can forge a bond with him. That's what we all did. Everyone, except Miles."

Leon shakes his head, disagreeing. "I'd rather not forge a bond. No offense to you guys, but it sounds fake. And I've grown up being fake to enough people… I'd rather us be friends…even though I know that's not possible."

Miles grins. "Well, Leon, if you did manage to make a real bond, you two would become a *hybrid*. Like Selim and me. It's what you call two reflections that work for the same goals."

"I like that better, but I still don't think it's possible. I know it's a rule, but is there any reason why I have to forge a bond with him to join?"

"Well," Miles replies, "to be blunt, you'd sort of be useless to yourself and our organization if you can't switch back and forth between worlds. We may have points in time where we'll have to escape danger by running into a mirror. And what good is it if we just left you behind because you needed a moon phase to warp?"

"That's fair." Leon gives a long sigh. "Great. So now I've gotta become friends with Néol..." A symbol on Ellen's earrings catches Leon's attention. "Wait a second," Leon says, noticing Scudero has this same symbol on his shirt.

Caleb turns his cap around, pointing and saying, "I've got it too!" Miles chuckles and lifts his arm and points to the symbol on his sleeve's cuff. Toni lifts her lighter, facing the symbol to Leon. Tenny feels left out, not having one of his own. So, he holds onto Toni's arm.

It is a sigil with two circles. Both circles are divided by a wavy line in the center. Both circles take their own identity: one shaded in its entirety, the other with an open hole. Surrounding the sigil itself are many rays of light molded into the shapes of two crescent moons.

"This is the *Equilibrium Sigil*," Miles says. "The Neo Knight's emblem. It represents the dream of equality for both sides. A symbol of both worlds acknowledging and respecting each other. Stefano repurposed the original symbols of the Pawn, Bishop, and Knight symbols."

"Say I do join..." Leon says wearily. "How do I know I won't be followed by the Lunae Lux?"

"Oh, you'll still be followed," Caleb laughs. "But with us, you'll have a surplus of protection."

Leon's eyes gape. "Wait, are you all trained fighters?"

They each have a laugh, and Ellen says, "No, we aren't. But we *do* have Neo Knights that are specially trained to fight."

Miles butts in. "Sorry to cut you off, Ellen." Ellen nods approvingly and Miles says, "Leon, you honestly won't have anything to worry about as long as you follow the rules Allure gave to you. *Everything* we do is in secret. And *when* you join, we'll fill you in on all the coming adventures."

Toni chimes in, "But what's most important is that you know you're not alone."

Caleb nearly jumps out of his seat. "And did we mention that Stefano purchased a set of condominiums for us all to stay in?"

Leon's eyes widen. The words, *He did?* are written on his face.

"Yup!" Caleb whispers to Leon's lack of words, "*And it's a place that's uncharted. You can't even look it up on Elgoog.*"

"El…goog?..." Leon asks.

Scudero taps Leon and whispers, "*It's Planet Heart's backwards version of the search engine.*"

"*Ohh. Thanks,*" Leon whispers back.

Miles glances at his amulet's clock and his empty plate and says, "Well, it's getting late. I should probably take you back to Néol's home. But first. I want to give you this." Miles grabs an orange cellular device from his pocket and slides it across the table to Leon. There's a charger wrapped around it.

"A cellphone?" Leon says with excitement in his voice.

"Eh," Miles says. "They call it a *reacher* here. They base it off the phrase, *How can I reach you?*"

225

Leon glances at Caleb who shrugs and says, "Don't look at me. I didn't name it."

Miles laughs and continues, "So, Leon, what do you think? Will you forge a bond with Néol?"

"I definitely wanna join. I've been lonely up until recently, and tonight, with the exception of Aepis earlier, made my night."

"Good," Miles smiles. "Then through that reacher, I'll give you a call and give you tips on how to forge a bond."

"No thanks," Leon says, smiling back. "I'll try it my own way first. If I fail, then I'll contact you."

Miles nods. "I'll respect your decision. Everyone here already has their phone number in there. That phone can text and call. But it has a lot of trouble working on Earth because the satellites are too far off. So…it's really just for communicating with us here on Heart. Though if you're lucky, you might come across a reflecting satellite tower."

"Works for me." Leon stands up and waves goodbye to everyone.

Toni shouts, "Leon! I know you don't plan on leaving here without giving me a hug!"

After these goodbyes, Leon and Miles depart. Toni covers everyone's payments with her reflection's credit card. Caleb asks for extra boxes for the leftover breadsticks which Ellen tries to talk him out of. Scudero and Tenny have a good laugh from this. Leon and Miles step into the teal car and make their way back to Néol's house. Toni and the others gather in their van and drive off to this *secret* condominium space that Stefano purchased for each of them.

SEE LEON'S REACHER

12

THE CHILD WHO SMILED

☾   ☾   ☾

Miles is speeding on the highway back to Néol's neighborhood. However, to Miles' surprise, Leon asks if he can be dropped off at Ellia's house instead. Shortly after making this request, Leon passes out in the passenger seat. Throughout this drive, Miles enjoys the brief freedom from those two pesky voices.

And then Selim chimes in.

Dude, Selim says within Miles' mind, *I've got some crap to tell you later.*

You can't tell me now?

I'm a little busy with Éphraim. But. Let's catch up in the Eleventh Dimension later. It's about Néol.

Great. Something I should tell Leon?

Eh. Not unless you want him to sneak home again.

Great, Miles replies in thought.

Anyway, I figured I'd let ya know. I'll talk to ya.

I hate when you tease me like that. But sure. I'll talk to you later, Selim.

Twenty minutes later, Miles parks the teal car just outside of Ellia's cul-de-sac. Before Leon steps out, Miles says, "I'll keep my phone handy in case you need me." Once Leon grins at this, Miles blares, "But I'm *not* your taxi driver. I just mean for emergencies."

229

"Okay... And. Thanks for introducing me to your friends today. I needed that."

"Of course. But they're not just my friends anymore. They're yours now, too."

Leon smiles at these words.

"Remember," Miles says sternly, "contact me if you need help with befriending Néol. I'll give you three days since we're short on time. If you fail within that time, I'll initiate *my* plan."

"Deal," Leon says, exiting the car. He then watches Miles drive off. Leon sneakily makes his way into the cul-de-sac. All the streetlights are on. But lucky for him, none of Ellia's neighbors are home. He assumes this by the absence of cars in their driveways. And each of the lights in the houses is off.

However, he does see a dark green truck in Ellia's driveway. He steers clear of her house's windows, treading slowly into her backyard by the trees at the side of her house. He finds a small rock nearby, and just like how Jason did to him in the past, he throws a rock to her windowsill.

Nothing yet.

Leon jokes to himself, "I need a bigger rock." He spots a boulder bigger than himself and says, "That'll do."

He chuckles at his joke, then leans down for another small rock to throw. But just before he can, he looks up to see Ellia's blushing face. She whispers, "*I'm glad you're okay!*"

"*Same!*" he whispers back. "*Come with me to the lake!*"

"*I'm grounded,*" she pouts, leaning her chin on her fist.

"*So?*" Leon smirks. "*Sneak out.*"

"*But they're no mattresses.*"

"*I'll catch you.*" Ellia quietly laughs at this, and Leon adds, "*It'll just be for a bit.*"

"Oh, alright... He's probably taking a nap anyway. Wait by the woods for me."

Leon crosses through her backyard and makes his way for the woods. He stands beside the giant tree he fell asleep at. Ellia finds him, of course, with her tote bag. She runs into his arms, and time almost freezes as the two hold each other.

"You're okay... I was so worried," Ellia says with relief as the two walk side by side down the dirt and woodsy path.

"It's been a crazy day and a half...to say the least," Leon says, "but you first. What happened with you?"

"Well, my grandfather grounded me."

"For how long?"

"He didn't give me a date. He was more upset with Néol than anything else. It's so annoying. He *always* ends our talks with *I was young, once.*"

Leon laughs. "Well, that's a relief."

"What about you? Where did the police take you?"

"Well...they actually brought me into a limo..."

As they push farther throughout the woodsy path, Leon explains all that happened between him and Allure Igor. He fills her in by whispering everything that occurred at the Libri Café.

"Wow. Sounds like a whole week got packed into a day," she replies.

"Right?" Leon says as they get closer to the pier at the lake. "It was humbling to say the least, though."

"So that means you'll be staying for longer?"

"Kinda," Leon says as the two of them look around for crows but thankfully see none. Regardless, Leon chooses the volume of his next words wisely as they sit at the pier.

Leon whispers, "*I have to befriend Néol. And no one knows how long that could take…otherwise I really would be stuck here without that moon phase. I guess I just got lucky the other night.*"

"I owe you an apology…regarding…what Néol was talking about the other day."

Leon faces forward toward the moon on the horizon and says nothing.

Ellia sighs and speaks. "A few weeks before June eleventh, Néol brought me out here. Around that tree, actually," she says, pointing to a large tree trunk. "He carved a certain date on the tree. He told me that on that date, there was gonna be an accident…and that he would be leaving. He then added that *someone new* would take his place. He said this person's voice would sound different. That this person would carry himself differently and would even look similar. I didn't believe him. Not one bit."

"Why didn't you believe him?" Leon asks.

Ellia looks at Leon. "Because it made no sense. And when I asked for more info, he gave me *one* solid instruction."

Leon looks forward. "And that was to keep me happy here."

Ellia looks down after he says this. She then grabs Leon's hand, causing him to look at her. "But I promise you, Leon, that even when we first met, that intention *never* crossed my mind. While I did meet you thinking that you were Néol, you opened up to me. And showed me more than all the tiny fragments he's shown me throughout the years. So, I can tell you this confidently—I like being around you. Because you're *you*. I like that even when you're afraid of showing who you really are—you try it anyway."

Leon doesn't face her. Instead, he looks down and asks, "Ellia, be honest with me…do you like being around me because you're replacing who Néol was with me?"

"You know…I wondered the same thing, too. But when I was around him that night, and he told me that he was too far gone…I honestly lost some respect for him. Because here *you* are, Leon, trying to do everything in your power to fix things. And all I heard from *him* was that he messed up and he won't try to fix it."

Leon is silent.

"Are you mad?" she asks nervously.

"No, and I'm sorry I asked that. It wasn't even originally my question. Néol asked me that…he asked me when I was asleep in your backyard."

Ellia smirks. "See, that's why you're not supposed to sleep out in the wild, lunatic." They share a laugh together and stare into each other's eyes for a bit. Leon breaks the silence and says, "Well, thanks, Ellia. I needed that. I've been betrayed and lied to so much in my life. I just needed to know if this was real."

"Maybe it's not. It could just be a dream, like you originally thought it was."

"I don't think I'd want that."

"Me neither," Ellia agrees.

"But you know since everyone keeps mentioning it. Can you tell me about this coma? Because I don't remember being around for any accident."

Ellia puts her hand to her chin. "Well. Jonas called me, saying that you crashed in a stolen vehicle right by his home. When the police found you, they saw—"

"—WAIT!" Leon shouts. "Sorry I didn't mean to cut you off. I remembered something. I remember the flashing police lights. I *was* there. But I don't remember crashing…"

That's because, says Néol from within Leon's mind, *I dragged you there after your switch.*

"You what?" Leon shouts, standing up.

"Leon?..." Ellia utters, startled from Leon's shout.

Néol doesn't respond after this. He vanishes as quickly as his voice came. Leon shakes his head then looks back at her. "Sorry, Ellia. I think Néol just gave me my answer." He sits back down. "Here's what I understand. It sounds like there *was* an accident. *But*, I wasn't there BEFORE the accident happened."

"Oh?"

Leon nods. "Yup. In my mind, Néol just said that he dragged me there after my transfer. The last thing that I remember from that night was…being kicked forward into this pit. I fell into this glowing mirror and then…I was laying on my chest…Yeah…that's right. And then Néol leaned down to me and said, '*It's about time I take what's mine, for good.*'"

Ellia continues, "And then you woke up here…in the crashed car."

"Yup. They must've placed me in that car right after it crashed. And I guess since I was unconscious, they brought me to the hospital where I slept for a few hours. Just to come back into my bed… All of it was to gaslight me into thinking I *really was* in a coma. But in reality—"

"—You'd be around people and situations you wouldn't understand. So of course it seemed like amnesia."

"This makes so much sense now…" Leon says, holding his hand up to high-five Ellia. Their hands meet, and then Ellia sees a few crows fly atop the treetops. She taps Leon's chest and points to them.

"Yep. Those are our watchers," Leon confirms.

"They're so creepy…there's like three of them watching you… Oh. And ew! There's a few by the water over there. Are their eyes supposed to be that red?"

Leon shakes his head. "Figures."

"Are you sure we'll be okay?"

"Well, they know you know about the reflecting world. So, the damage is done. We just can't tell anyone else about it. Like Jonas, Anjelica, or Eden."

"So, just between us? I can live with that."

Leon places his hand on his chin and whispers, "*And now we're back to the main problem. I'm trying to figure out what I can do to befriend Néol.*"

"Hmm." Ellia grabs her sketchbook from her tote bag. "Well, maybe we just need to think about why he *really* left."

After she says this, she starts drawing Néol in black ink. She draws him in a star formation, then draws three lines and connects them to him.

Leon holds his chin. "I remember seeing in his profile that he went through child abuse...and that somehow he enrolled in the Heartshine Facility at five."

"I wouldn't put it past him. He was always the most mature out of all of us. So maybe. This has been building up for a long time."

Leon thinks, *Explains his violent side...*

"His family has to be one," Leon says with certainty as she writes *family* on the first line.

"Family can *definitely* be one," Ellia says. "His parents fought nonstop. And they've been threatening each other with divorce for years. He's never opened up about it, but I'm sure it hurt to see."

"If watching them fight hurt me, then it definitely hurt him."

"Hmm..." Ellia says with her hand on her chin.

"Oh!" Leon shouts. "You know, I didn't see his sister there."

"*May?* She actually moved out to the city a few months ago. I spoke to her privately about it before. She couldn't stand her dad. And she was trying to persuade her mom to come with her."

"Were Néol and his sister close?"

"*Very*. I think they both confided in each other when their father would abuse them. I've seen them laugh it off together."

Leon narrows his eyes. "Write his sister down. I think we're getting closer."

The two sit for about fifteen more minutes and throw more and more ideas at each other, but nothing else sticks.

"So," Ellia says, "I'd chalk this up to his parents fighting and his sister leaving." She takes a close look at the crows, then whispers, "*Leon—I think what you should do is try to put his family back together.*"

"*What?*" he whispers back.

"*No, see me out.*"

"*See you out?*"

"*I guess you guys don't say that in your world. Anyway. Look— you're the one that has to pretend you're Néol, right? So, then you should be the one to talk them back into getting along again.*"

"*Ellia, I like the idea but—*"

"*—You're more in touch with your emotions than Néol is, Leon. It has to be you.*"

Leon looks down. "*But what if I make things worse?*"

"*We don't know what could happen. But. You want to tell everyone in Earth the truth, someday, don't you?*"

"*You're right. I'll find a way to get them together, then.*"

Ellia looks around and says in a normal voice, "We should probably get back. My grandfather might try to check on me."

Leon nods. "I'll walk you back."

"Duh, where else would you go?" she asks playfully as he laughs with her. They start making their way back to her house through the woods.

"It's really dark," Ellia says, reaching for Leon's hand.

"Oh, you know, I forgot Miles gave me this…"

"A reacher? No way. My grandfather won't get me one. Can it text, too?"

"I think Miles said it could." Leon faces his reacher's bright screen to quell the darkness in front of them.

"I'll try to get one too, and then we can text each other. But for now, I'll give you my house phone number. Then you won't have to break my window with rocks."

They talk for a bit more, arriving at the outskirts of her backyard.

"Alright, I'll let you walk back from here," Leon says with Ellia smiling back.

"I'm gonna try to do extra chores tomorrow," then she whispers, *"because if I can get ungrounded, then I can help you get to his sister in the city."*

"What?" Leon whispers. *"You think I'm going there?"*

"Yes!" she whispers back harshly. *"Did you really think calling them would be good enough? They need to see your face. Like how I like seeing yours."*

Leon rolls his eyes with a smile. "Alright, alright. I'll see how things go at Néol's house tonight. I'll see you later, Ellia."

After one final hug, the two split off. Ellia to her backdoor to find her grandfather who is still asleep, and Leon who calls Miles during his walk back to Néol's house with the help of his map.

"Hey, what's up, Leon? Need a ride?" Miles says.

Leon looks around for crows, then whispers into the phone, *"So here's the plan. I'm gonna bring his family back together. I think that might bring him back."*

"Admirable, but most reflections try that, Leon."

"Well, this time's gonna be different."

"Keep me posted. Have a safe walk home."

13

MIRRORED
SIBLINGS

"Darn it," Leon says, trying to twist the locked doorknob. He trails around the backyard to find that the sliding door's glass is almost nonexistent. Shards of glass are all that's left on all the corners of the door's frame. A piece of glass is hanging down. He taps it so that it falls, shattering on the ground. This, however, does not awaken the slumbering, snoring man in the living room, Néol's father.

Leon remembers Stefano saying that Néol's father's name was *Oren*. Leon steps in through the backdoor to find Oren passed out on the living room floor. He keeps his shoes on.

Leon finds Oren wearing the same exact attire as he was when Leon first saw him. But these clothes look even worse. There are more holes, more missing buttons, and stains from liquids all over. Most likely those liquids were alcohol.

Disgusted, Leon looks around to see that the entire living room is in disarray. The TV is broken. The glass belonging to portraits are shattered. The same tale can be told about the kitchen. The kitchen table's legs are broken. Dishes are piled in the sink. Some have fallen out of the sink and are on the ground. He sees what looks like tiny pieces of rice on the ground… But since when can rice crawl?

"Are those...maggots?" Leon says, putting his hand to his mouth. "Dude...when's the last time this place was cleaned? Oh, I can't with this smell. I'm gonna puke... I gotta get outta here," Leon says, running away from the mass of crawling larvae on the floor. He rushes up the wooden stairs to Néol's parents' room, finding no bed. No TV stand. Nothing. If there was anything in the room, it's gone now.

Leon enters the walk-in closet to find nothing but just a few clothes of Oren's. And even these clothes are beaten up. Despite them being on hangers, Leon doubts they are even clean. Leon accidentally steps on a few empty beer cans and bottles.

"I guess Néol's mom really is gone. Great." Leon steps forward, bumping into the belly of Oren who drunkenly stares down at him.

"Néol...where were you...where's your mother..."

Leon gulps, backing away farther into the walk-in closet. "I don't know, I just got back."

"Liar...you were with her...—" Oren hiccups. "You helped her move all this crap out, didn't you..."

"What? I was at the penitentiary."

Oren stumbles over to Leon, clumsily grabs his neck and pushes him into the closet's wall. "You've always been a liar!"

Oren grabs Leon's arms and pushes him to a different wall. He trips Leon onto the ground. Then Oren gets atop Leon and grabs his neck with both hands.

Desperate, Leon feels around for *anything* that he can strike Néol's father with. Oren's weight is slowly squeezing the air out of Leon's lungs. And with Oren strangling his neck, he slowly loses air.

Leon grabs something cold and skinny. It's a bottle! He swings the bottle to Oren's head. But he's too slow. Oren catches Leon's hand.

He's gonna crush me... Néol...how did you beat someone this heavy...

I was resourceful, Néol responds.

The drunken man leans closer to Leon's face, grinning a devilish grin. Leon shuts his eyes from the horrifying sight and swings his head straight into Oren's eye, making the man cry out.

With the pain distracting Oren, Leon swings the empty bottle to the back of Oren's head. The drunken man rolls off Leon. Leon leans over Oren, punching his jaw a few times shouting, "This is why they all left you behind, Oren!"

The drunken man shouts, "OFF OF ME!" And pushes Leon down onto his buttocks. Leon stands up quickly, glaring at Oren who pushes Leon to the side. The drunken man stumbles out toward the bathroom nearby. Leon follows him.

"You made me bleed..." Oren says angrily. "You...you think you're a man now?" he utters, teeth gnashing. "I want you out of here...by the time...I get back..."

Both the father and the reflecting son glare at one another. Leon watches Oren walk down the wooden steps, slowly, as he clumsily hangs onto the rail for his life. Leon's body and hands are shaking. His legs are frozen solid.

That's...exactly what my *dad was like...*

Leon walks to Néol's room with wide eyes. He's in shock. He shuts the door and sits on the floor, against the wall. He covers his face in his hands.

Dad said that he drank to celebrate his new job at transit authority... and Mom always added that after that first bottle of champagne, he had trouble stopping. It turned into him saying he'd only drink on the weekends. Then he included Fridays. Then Mondays to get past the beginning of the week. It went downhill from there. If it wasn't for my mom telling him how much it hurt Amy and me, he would've kept doing it. Leon raises his hands from his eyes, then grabs the Reflection Principle booklet from his pocket. "I know I saw something in here talking about addictions..."

Leon punches the ground after reading this principle. "Did the act of my dad giving up alcohol become the reason why yours won't stop?"

Reflection Principle #7

To this, Leon stands, throwing the booklet to the side. "How am I going to fix your family *and* mine? It's either one or the other at this point... What should I do... No." He grits his teeth. "I have to get home. They need the truth. I'm gonna fix the damage Festano and Néol did."

Leon's reacher starts to vibrate.

"Hey, Ellia."

"Hey! Guess what. So, I did some extra chores, and I'm ungrounded."

"Nice."

"I thought you'd be happier about that. Are you okay? You sound out of breath."

"Ellia, I just fought his father."

"Oh no. Are you okay? Where is he now? I hope he doesn't call the cops again..."

Leon shakes his head, fighting back tears as his voice quivers. "I'm fine. I just realized—"

Suddenly the front door downstairs opens and slams.

Leon looks out of Néol's window to see Oren stumbling out to his red truck outside. "Uh…" Leon utters to the phone.

"*Leon?*" Ellia says with worry.

"I'm watching him—he's getting into the car? No! He's too drunk!"

"*Go Leon! Stop him!*"

Leon puts the phone down. At this same time, Oren starts the truck and drives off. He reverses out the driveway—past the street—into an abandoned front yard and into the house itself.

"How'd that get there…" Oren utters drunkenly. "Whatever…" he says, shifting the vehicle into *drive*. Leon rushes out the front door to see Oren driving off to a street away. Leon runs as fast as he can—but the drunken man passes an intersection and…

"NO!" Leon shouts, watching Oren's red truck being slammed by an even bigger truck. An eighteen-wheeler carries it a few yards away.

Leon falls to his knees. He waits there in the middle of the road knowing *exactly* what this will mean for his father. How much time will Nero have? Minutes? Seconds? He sees a crow land beside him and peck his arm. He gets up and runs as quickly as he can to the phone he left upstairs.

Leon turns his back on this gruesome scene and walks back into Néol's house. "And I never even got to tell you that I'm sorry… I never got to tell you the truth…" he sobs while his head pulsates. He walks past the open door and cries out, his pained voice echoing throughout the walls of the barren and ruined house.

"Now I get it, Néol. Now I get it… You were trying to leave this behind. You didn't want to see them destroy themselves…because of your father's drinking…because of *my* father's lack of it… I did this to you…it was *my joy* that did this to you!"

REFLECTION PRINCIPLE #8

He sobs into his hands, alone at the foot of his stairs…And above him is only one family photo which has not been touched by Oren's drunken rage. He sees a younger Oren, Néol's mother Aivlis, May, and Néol. The four are standing together in front of a red background. Néol is a child in this photo. And surprisingly has a smile on his face. So does May, who doesn't look that different from Amy, her reflection. Oren and Aivlis both have a neutral expression. Perhaps this photo represents a *calm before the storm.* Leon can only assume that this photo was taken back when things were okay.

"Leon!" Ellia cries out, seeing Leon sitting on the stairs. He throws all caution aside. He doesn't care if she sees him broken like this. This is who he had to be behind closed doors. He wipes his tears, and the two hug.

"My grandfather drove me here…are you okay? What happened?"

Leon fights a few sobs and says, "He's dead…Ellia…he's dead. Both my dad and his dad. They're gone!"

"What? No, they're not! I saw him!"

Leon draws back from the hug. "You…saw him?"

"Yes. He's alive. They're taking him to the hospital."

"How do you know? How do you know he didn't just die?"

Ellia looks away, tears welling in her eyes. "Because…my grandfather had a few near-death experiences. And when they pronounced him dead, they wrapped him in that black shroud. Until they saw his arm move." Ellia holds Leon's arms tightly. "And your dad—I mean. Oren. He was rolled into an ambulance on a cot. So, he's not dead."

Smiles forming on both of their faces, Ellia adds, "You can still tell him, Leon. You can tell him the truth."

Leon pulls her up with him, standing on his feet. "What hospital are they going to?"

"Nietsie Hospital. It's not too far from here."

"How far of a walk is it?"

"You're not walking, silly. C'mon." Leon follows her outside, and she leads him to an old vehicle with her grandfather inside.

"Wait!" Leon shouts. "I forgot my reacher!" He rushes inside and upstairs to grab his phone. To his surprise, he has a text from Miles, asking, *"How's it going? Any luck with his family?"*

Leon hurries to the truck outside. To Leon's surprise, and even Ellia's, the elder man doesn't give Leon a look of disgust. Ellia gets in the front seat and waves Leon inside.

"Nietsie hospital, hm?" the grandfather says as Leon puts on his seatbelt.

The car ride is silent. They pass the demolished passenger side of Oren's truck. The truck has a dent nearly the size of the eighteen-wheeler that hit it. To Leon's amusement, he was mistaken to have thought Oren would have died from the impact. Naturally, being so accustomed to drivers sitting in the left side, it made Leon think that Oren was killed because that's where the vehicle was hit. Luckily for him, this happened on Planet Heart.

"I'm...um," the grandfather says, eyeing the wreckage. "I'm sorry to hear about your father...Néol."

"Thanks..." Leon says, as both he and Ellia are shocked to hear such kind words.

"I used to have a drinking problem myself..." the grandfather admits. "My liver nearly died from it. Thought I was powerful enough to hide in my own house and sin. But God sure proved me wrong..." the old man cackles. "I'm just as small as any other human out here. In this universe, everything we do, Néol...has a consequence. That goes for all of us. Remember that."

They arrive at the hospital, and Leon detaches his seatbelt. "You're right. Thanks Mr. Hactneir. I'll keep that in mind."

The grandfather grins. "Go on, you two."

Leon steps out of the truck and dashes for the door. Ellia follows until her grandfather calls her back. "Wait," he says.

Leon turns around to wait for Ellia. She and her grandfather talk for a bit, and then she runs back up to Leon.

"My grandfather says he's feeling sleepy. So, he's gonna head home."

"Oh, alright. Anything else?"

"I'll tell you the rest after—c'mon! You need to see your—I mean Néol's dad!"

The two enter the hospital, and Leon passes the line of people to shout *Yelltnarg* to the secretary who tells him *his father* is resting on the seventh floor. Ellia follows Leon to the elevators, but they're both occupied. He frequently presses the *up* button, but the indicator above tells him that the elevators are far toward the fifteenth floor. Ellia has trouble keeping up with Leon who charges for the staircase and up a few floors.

"You...you go ahead of me," Ellia says, panting as Leon shouts, "You sure?" From almost four floors above.

"Yes! Just go," Ellia says, catching her breath as she slowly walks up the stairs.

Leon passes the fifth, the sixth, and finally arrives at the seventh floor. He sees two male nurses wearing black scrubs rolling someone away on a cot.

"Hey," Leon shouts. "Is there someone named Oren Yelltnarg here?"

While rolling this person away, one nurse says, "I'm sorry, are you his son?"

Leon nods.

"We had to transfer him to emergency care. We're booked, and he wouldn't have made it if he were to wait here."

"Can you tell me where they're transferring him?"

"To *Co-op* City's Hospital."

The two nurses speedily wheel away the person on the cot to the elevator.

"Finally," Ellia says, exiting the staircase. "What's wrong?"

"They're moving him somewhere else. To Co-op Cities Hospital."

"Oh."

Leon shakes his head, walking back into the staircase and takes a seat. "I have no idea how we're gonna get there now."

Ellia says, "Can I see your phone?"

"Sure," Leon tosses it to her.

She dials in a number then says, "Hey. It's Ellia. I need your help. Can you pick Néol and me up from Nietsie hospital? I'll give you gas money. And then. No, not to go home. I need to go to the city. I'll tell you when you get here. Bye."

She hangs up the phone and throws it back to Leon.

"Who was that?" Leon asks.

"That was Jonas." Ellia starts walking down the staircase, and Leon follows.

Ellia adds, "But before they get here, we need to talk about you and Néol."

"What about us?"

"I like you the way you are. But the others? They know Néol really well. We have to get you to at least act like him for the time being. Otherwise, you'll keep standing out like a sore pinky."

"Good point. So. How do I start?"

Ellia stops walking as they arrive at the sixth floor. Her hands go to her hips while she thinks. "Um…stand still for me. No like, ugh. How would you stand if you were waiting in line?"

"Uh. Like this?" Leon says, just keeping his hands at his sides.

"Try putting your hands in your pockets."

"Like this?"

"Perfect…and now…try leaning against the wall." Leon tries not to laugh while doing this. But he starts to understand more of what Ellia's suggesting. To be Néol is to not care about who's in the room with him. To be standoffish where Leon would be open and embracing. She explains Néol's introversion through what she's observed over the years. And, through this knowledge, shares what she knows to Leon so that he, at least for now, can act even more like his reflection. Twenty minutes pass, and Jonas arrives in a big black van in front of the hospital. The windows are very tinted.

Jonas slams the car door behind him. "Alright. So, what's this story about you needing to go to the city?"

With a glower in his face, Leon walks over to Jonas with his hands in his hoodie's pockets. He clears his throat and says, "Ellia and I need to get to the city." He clears his throat again and thinks, *How is Néol's voice so deep? He makes it sound easy. Must be all the cigarettes.*

Jonas responds, "Why *you*? Gonna spread more of your bullcrap to your family?"

"Yeah," Leon says, looking away. "And are you gonna get in the way of that?"

Jonas swallows and stares right into Leon's eyes, trying to detect weakness.

"Well?" Leon says, his heart thumping as Ellia watches intently. The front passenger window rolls down, and Eden peeks through, as does Anjelica who is in the back.

"Everything okay, guys?" Eden asks.

"What's taking you three so long?" Anjelica asks.

Jonas shows his teeth. "Eden. Give Ellia your seat. Néol. You sit in the back."

Leon smirks the way Ellia told him Néol would and says, "No. Eden gets to sit up front. You'll be fine."

Jonas balls his fist and walks over to Néol, but Ellia gets in the middle. "Guys. Not out here."

Jonas blows hot air through his nose, then turns to the side. "I want thirty ASUs from *both* of you."

"What? No, Jonas!" Ellia shouts. "Ten from me, ten from L—Néol!"

"You heard her." Leon adds in thought, *I can't believe this is working!*

Jonas grumbles a few swears to himself and gets into his driver's seat. Leon and Ellia let out a big sigh of relief and enter the vehicle, sitting in the backseat next to Anjelica. Leon sits on the end where he can lean his head on the window.

Ellia leans close to Leon and whispers, *"Oh my gosh, I thought you two were gonna fight out there.* But Leon, keeping up his Néol persona, simply smirks. Ellia rolls her eyes at this but understands why. Leon is enjoying this…perhaps a little too much.

Ellia adds in another whisper, *"The city's about twenty minutes away, so at least we'll have some time to rest."*

Leon turns away dismissively. Ellia playfully pushes him, whispering, *"Okay, Néol…I get it."*

Leon chuckles, sees Jonas glaring at them from up front, and whispers, *"Haha, alright, alright. So. Twenty minutes. Not too bad."*

"Are you nervous?"

"A little. But. I'm kinda excited. If his family gets back together…then this will all work out. Maybe."

"*Well…I forgot to tell you. When he was younger, he told his mom that he didn't want them together.*" Leon wears a look of shock while Ellia continues, "*It's like I told you. He didn't think like other kids… But he said that he knew what people looked like when they were in love. So. It's fifty-fifty.*"

His look of shock fades and becomes determined once he turns to look out the window. "I'm gonna do my best."

Ellia smiles at this, reaches for his hand, and leans on his shoulder. Anjelica sees this and awes to herself. She grabs a book from her bag named *Dolfa Tihler* and continues reading from the middle.

Leon doesn't know where this next action comes from. Perhaps his heart. Or instinct. But. He leans over and kisses Ellia's forehead. This creates a warm feeling for the two, and they simply sit and enjoy each other's company for a few minutes.

Jonas punches Eden every time he sees a purple vehicle. Eden isn't allowed to strike back if he sees a purple vehicle because it would *endanger* the driver. How fair? They pass an environment that Ellia points out to Leon. A lake. And here they can see a few large birds swimming in ponds.

The water on Earth would be blue, but here it is a mixture of green and yellow. The water is as mucus as it is swampy and filled with all kinds of trash. Leon spots a bird with a plastic bag wrapped around its beak. A white garbage bag is caught on another's wings. Leon even sees a few fish that are lying with their sides up in the *water*. Can it even be called *water* at this point?

"*Hey,*" Leon whispers while Ellia lifts her head up. "*I never asked, but is there any reason why the sky is green and the clouds are yellow?*"

"*Pollution. Our country's been in a lot of debt…so we've been doing everything we can to get ahead. Burning fossil fuels is one way, but as you can see…it's killing everything… That's not even the source of it all.*"

Leon watches the sky in awe, and Ellia whispers, *"There are some areas here that you have to avoid. Because acid rain comes out and destroys the crops. It can also burn your skin."*

Leon rears his head. *"Really?"*

"But don't worry, where we're going won't have that. And if it helps, the pollution in this state is worse than most. One of the only clean lakes here is the lake you and I visit. Lake Ynomrah. At least I think so."

"I'd be shocked if it was just as bad everywhere else... Because then how would you fish or eat food?" Leon responds as Ellia yawns and leans her head on his shoulders again.

"Your yawns are contagious," Leon says, now yawning.

In a normal voice, Ellia says, "What can I say? I'm comfortable here." After this, she and Leon's eyes lock...they lean toward each other and...Ellia rears and holds her head. "Ow."

Leon draws his head back. "You good?" he asks as Néol would.

"Yeah...I..." And then she leans in and whispers, *"I heard a voice in my mind. Is that...is that what you feel when you first talked to—you know who?"*

"Yeah, but. It's not supposed to be painful. Unless...was she yelling?"

Ellia nods. *"Yeah, she was... I think it's because I had your name in my mind. She said why did I just think his name? She shouted that really loudly."*

Leon doesn't know what to add to that. He simply looks back out at the passing scenery.

Ellia bites her lip and kisses his cheek. Then while turning red, leans on his shoulder, saying, "I'm going to sleep."

Leon smiles. "Me too. You made me sleepy."

For the rest of the drive, Leon falls asleep with Ellia resting on his shoulder. Somehow, these two manage to stay asleep despite Jonas' reckless driving. Eden loses track of how many prayers he has said in the front seat. He feels like his seatbelt's done him no favors.

14

HALF
TRUTHS

☾　　☾　　☾

"**L**oveducks, we're here. Hello? Heart to Ellia and Leon?" Anjelica says, shutting her book.

Eden turns around. "Are they both still asleep? I knew Ellia was always a heavy sleeper, but I'm surprised with Néol. He never falls asleep!"

"They look so cute," Anjelica says. "I almost don't want to wake them up."

"Please do," Eden says adjusting his glasses, "because Ellia's snoring is quite obnoxious."

"Yes," Jonas adds. "*Please. Do.*" Jonas adds a few eye rolls, glowering and swearing a few times as he flicks his cigarette on the dashboard.

"Loveducks," Anjelica says once more, now poking Ellia in the ribs.

"Okay! Okay!" cries Ellia.

Leon somehow sleeps through this until Ellia starts jabbing his ribs with her fingers. "Alright! C'mon!" he shouts back, making Ellia, Eden, and Anjelica laugh.

"Alright, now get out," Jonas says grumpily.

In response, Leon smirks, then opens the door and steps out with Ellia right behind him, saying, "I'll be back, guys."

Leon stands in front of an even bigger hospital than the last. An alluring green and yellow sunset is above them. Leon looks up toward the yellow clouds masking the sun, and Ellia asks, "So. You ready?"

Leon nods. "Yup. And thanks for everything you told me about Néol and his family. I think I know just what to say."

Ellia stretches her arms out for a hug. "I know you'll do great. Tell him I said hi." Leon hugs her back and looks down at the ground. They release one another and Ellia adds, "And...I hope Oren's condition isn't too bad."

"Same. But. They moved him here to save him, right? So. There's gotta be good news."

"I'm gonna get Jonas and the others some ice cream at the mall in the meantime."

"Good idea. That'll cheer Jonas up. How will I let you know that I'm finished?"

"Good point," Ellia says, turning around to reach for the car door. She opens it and says, "Anj, can I borrow your reacher? It's for L—I mean...Néol to text me," Leon laughs at her slip up, and she hits him.

"Sure," Anjelica says, handing her a red phone shaped much like Leon's. Anjelica adds, "Are you trying to avoid calling him *love*?"

"Shaddup...And thanks..." Ellia says with reddening cheeks, slamming the car door. After she and Leon exchange numbers, she says, "Alright. Talk to you soon."

The two separate. Leon walks past the automatic sliding doors to a rather highly sophisticated interior. This hospital has tile floors, and the aesthetic is almost all glass. The setting sun's rays are shining down on him. He marches up toward the help desk which unfortunately has a line of people who are probably here for the same reason.

Farther ahead of this line are two elevators. A female doctor with blonde hair steps out from one of them. She whispers something to the secretary at the desk and then locks eyes with Leon.

"My goodness, you look so much better!" the doctor says, walking to Leon.

Leon looks around to see if she has mistaken him for someone else.

"No," the blonde doctor says, "I'm talking about you! You're Néol, aren't you?"

Leon shyly nods. "Did we meet somewhere?"

"We met here! I was the doctor who looked after you. I'm not surprised that you don't remember me, though."

"Oh…do you mean during my coma?"

"You remember! Yes. How've you been feeling since? How's your memory been doing?"

"It's good. My friends and family filled me in."

"I can only hope that everyone else here gets out as quickly as you did. It's like an epidemic. I swear. We *just* had a group of people—all in comatose states like yourself."

Wait. Are these other people Earthshine Patients? Former Knights? Ugh. One thing at a time, Leon. I'll leave them to Stefano.

"Doctor," Leon asks, "did you see my father here? He got into a car accident. I was told he was brought here."

"I'm sorry sweetie—" The doctor grabs Leon's arm and pulls him behind the secretary's desk. The people waiting in line grumble about Leon cutting in front of them, but the doctor says, "Néol, I'm sorry. What was your last name again? I'm sorry. I meet so many patients…"

"Yelltnarg," Leon says with a determined look.

"Nerak, can you look up where the Yelltnarg's are? He's here for his father."

Nerak the secretary nods. "Oh, are you with *them*? Your mother and sister are upstairs. I sent them up to the seventeenth floor."

"Seventeenth floor, got it! Thanks!" Leon says, running ahead to the elevator while the doctor shouts, "First room on your left! Be well!"

"Thanks, you too!" Leon runs to the elevator, ignoring the angry eyes of the people waiting in line. He presses the elevator button, and the one on the left opens for him. He presses the circular button that says *17*, and it glows. He crosses his arms, leaning on the wall, remembering how Néol would pose and act. He takes many deep breaths, hoping that all this turns out for the best so that he doesn't need to ask Miles for help.

He arrives at the seventeenth floor. He goes to the first room on his left and finds Néol's mother, who has one black eye and a swollen cheek, and *May,* who he nearly mistakes for his sister, Amy, sitting in a large waiting room.

"Néol?" May says with a voice less giddy than her reflection's.

"Hey," Leon says flatly to both of them.

Aivlis looks away and says, "I'm surprised that *you're* here. Especially after everything you've been through with him."

Leon looks at Aivlis' torn clothes and her red eyes. It looks like she's been crying. He looks away, saying as shortly as Néol would, "I had to see if he was alright."

"Well, we did too," May says. "And now that we know he's alive, we're getting food."

"Wait," Leon cries desperately, breaking his Néol persona as the two prepare to leave.

"What?" May asks.

"Give me, like, five minutes," Leon says, now being more like himself. "I just want to talk to him. A—and then you two."

"Néol, I'm hungry—"

"—Five minutes, May. I just need that from both of you."

May rolls her eyes and taps her feet. "Starting now, then. And if it's more than five minutes, you're buying my food."

Leon rushes to the secretary sitting at the front of this waiting room and thinks, *Jokes on you, I have no money.* He talks to the woman sitting at the large desk, and she points him just three rooms down the hallway. He wants to run but chooses to walk. He doesn't know what shape to expect his reflection's father to be in. With this in mind, he takes his time, pacing himself.

He finally arrives in the room, seeing a set of cots to the left of him. Unfortunately for Leon, Oren is silent as he is peacefully fast asleep. Fortunate for Leon because the man is breathing, but unfortunate because the two were supposed to have their talk. He supposes it's time to call Miles. He starts walking for the doorway, takes his phone out to call Miles when suddenly—

"I killed him."

Leon turns around to the straining voice to see Néol's father open his eyes.

"I killed him, Néol."

Leon swallows, and then walks back to Oren.

"Who?" Leon responds.

"The innocent freight truck driver...he... The airbag snapped his neck. He didn't stand a chance. But he had a family. He had. Two kids...like me..." Oren strains and looks to his right. "He was...lying right there...in that empty cot..."

Leon looks down to the side. Oren looks at Leon, shaking with tears welling in his bloodshot eyes. "I killed him…Néol…"

Oren shuts his eyes, and sobs start leaking from his mouth. He sobs so uncontrollably that it seems *he* doesn't even know where these emotions have come from—how they've come pouring out so strongly… Was this the result of what drinking had taken from him? The ability to feel?

Leon grits his teeth. He can't bear to watch. What should he do? Hug him? That's not what Néol would do. Maybe gently reassure him by placing a hand on his shoulder?

Leon is frozen. He's unsure of what he can do as Néol's father cries out for committing his most recent sin. What can Leon do? After all, he came all this way to speak to the man about why he should quit. It was to bring the family back together so he could go home. But if that's the case, how could May and Aivlis forgive Oren for what he did? He took someone's life. Someone's innocent life was taken because of his drunkenness. The very same thing that made Oren's family leave him in the first place. And that included Néol. He left for the same reason as they did but simply handled it differently. This broken man lying and crying in front of Leon is the source of why they all left.

"It's…it's a sign," Leon says as Oren looks at him, biting his lips to stop himself from crying out.

"What?...what's a sign?"

"It's a sign for you to stop, Oren. You're alive by the grace of God. Nothing more. You should've died. You could've left it all behind. But you didn't. And instead of dying, you've been given a choice." Leon points with his thumb to the door. "Your wife and daughter are out there, and they were about to leave. Like you could've left this E—Heart. But instead, you've got a chance to get rid of this once and for all."

And these next words make Leon think of his own family. "Imagine a world where you, your wife, son, and daughter could live in the same house in harmony. No fighting. No arguing. You guys working together to get one job done. To be a family. But you know what I saw after my coma? Nothing even close. You threw a bottle at my head. And Aiv—Mom has a black eye!"

To those last few words, Oren shuts his eyes.

"Look at me, Dad!" Leon shouts. "You can change how things go by giving up one thing. Just one thing."

Oren takes a deep breath. "I don't…know if I can. Néol, I've been in rehab *five* times. Five times! My old job offered it to me *for free* before they fired me. I quit on quitting."

"Why five times? What keeps happening?"

"There's this voice in my mind…" Oren says, looking at Leon as his jaw drops. "And every time it says *it* doesn't want a drink, suddenly *I* want one! Then I find myself at that liquor store buying the same thing I swore I'd let go of. It's an endless cycle!"

Leon looks away and thinks, *So it's true. It is because of my dad… My mom threatened to take my sister and me away from him… He tried quitting but fell back into it, and then his job threatened to fire him. It must've scared him so much that it made Oren unable to resist…*

"Fight it," Leon says firmly to Néol's father.

"You mean, you still want me to try?"

"That's why I'm here. And Mom and May are outside. I'm trying to talk them into giving you another shot."

Oren looks away. "May had it worse than you did when she was growing up. She begged me not to treat you the same way…but I suppose neglect is its own form of abuse… I can't blame her."

Leon says nothing.

Oren then looks at who he thinks is his son. "Néol. Even if they do refuse to come home, I will quit. You took the time to find me here. I will take this as a sign. I'll fight the voice in my mind…no matter what."

Leon nods, remembering his *five-minute* threat from May and tells Oren, "I'm gonna tell them what you said. When are they letting you go?"

"Tonight. They're just checking a few vitals, but somehow…nothing's broken," Oren says, looking at his arms.

"Nothing but that drunken spirit," Leon grumbles as he exits the room without saying goodbye. He knew this is what Néol would do.

Leon enters the waiting room, finding no one inside. Not even the secretary.

"C'mon May, are you that impatient?" Leon mutters, opening the door to see no one in the hallway. He enters the elevator, wishing it could fall to the first floor so that he could catch them in time. But still, no one's here. Not even in the hospital's lobby. He checks the parking lot and is grateful to find May entering the driver's seat of a rusting red sedan.

"May!" Leon shouts, calling her from nearly twenty yards away. He makes it over to her car, and she exits. Aivlis stays in the passenger seat.

"Go ahead," May says, crossing her arms, "tell me what you've told me a thousand times."

"I—" *Wait. Néol tried convincing her to stay? Of course. They were close. They suffered together.*

Leon tries to speak, but instead May cuts *him* off.

"Actually," May says with a smirk, "I wanna remind you of our last conversation before I moved. Mom and I said we were tired of him. And we invited you to come because we knew that if you stayed back with him, you two would fight. And that'd bring the cops, remember? And do you remember what you told us when we offered you your own apartment?"

Leon is silent. *I'm guessing I don't because* I *had amnesia...* he thinks in a mocking tone.

"You said," as May gets into Néol's character, crossing her arms like her brother would and imitates his gruff voice, "*No thanks. Think I've got my own plans.*"

Leon chuckles at this and May unfolds her arms and continues, "And I asked, *are you sure?* I gave you chance after chance. I told you I wouldn't go back and that you'd be alone. And you insisted that you'd be okay. So, my decision isn't changing. Maybe Mom's, but not mine. I like my independence."

Aivlis rolls down the passenger window and says, "Absolutely not. I'm never going back." She rolls the window back up.

May shrugs. "You heard her. Okay, Néol? I'm sorry."

Leon's speechless. May says goodbye and gets back into the driver's seat. They drive off, leaving him behind in silence.

Leon walks a long walk back to the hospital with his shoulders sunken. His chances of returning home? Even lower. Before calling Ellia, he scrolls down to Miles' name and calls him.

"*Hey, Leon. How're you? I was getting worried,*" Miles says.

"You win. I need your help."

"*Leave it to us,*" Miles says confidently. It's almost like he was expecting this call.

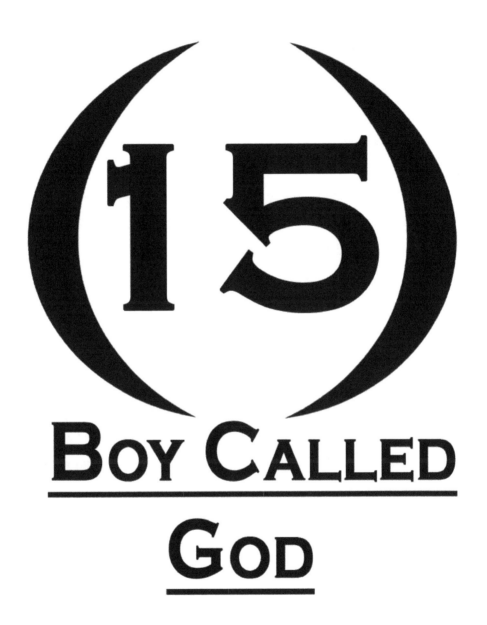

15

BOY CALLED

GOD

☾   ☾   ☾

After Leon's brief phone call with Miles, who thankfully didn't rub his failure in his face, Leon is picked up from the hospital by Jonas. During this car ride, Leon tells Ellia the bad news through a few whispers in Jonas' van.

Ellia tells Leon that her time around Jonas, Eden, and Anjelica wasn't any better. Jonas was nothing but rude to her the entire time. She thinks it was due to her rejecting his many flirtatious remarks. Throughout this drive, Jonas drives with the window down, chain smoking cigarettes, and the cold breeze chills Ellia, Eden, Anjelica, and Leon.

Like their ride to the city, Ellia leans on Leon. What Leon was not expecting was for her to bring him back a treat. She guessed that since Néol liked chocolate ice cream, Leon would enjoy vanilla. The smile she brings to Leon's face tells her that she was correct.

Leon doesn't want to be home alone with Oren because of the note they ended on. Plus, with Leon not feeling a real connection to the reflection of his father, he feels it would be awkward. So, he asks Ellia if he can stay over. Ellia has Leon wait outside her home and asks if *Néol* can spend the night since he doesn't feel comfortable at *his home*. Surprisingly, she doesn't need to plea to make this happen. Though, there is only one rule.

The grandfather tells Leon directly that he must sleep downstairs on the couch when it's time for bed. Leon and Ellia spend the entire night talking. And indeed, when it is time for bed, Leon weeps alone in frustration. He's worried that he might have risked his entire family's healthy dynamic just to save Néol's. For now, all Leon has is his ability to put his faith into Miles' plan, whatever that is.

☾　　☾　　☾

Planet Earth

January 2, 2010 (Saturday)

Colorado ∧ Aurorae

Leon's Residence ∧ Leon's Bedroom

8:36 a.m.

Knock. Knock. Knock.

"What?" Néol asks, glancing at his amulet's clock to see the time.

From outside, Nero, Leon's father says, "Who're you saying *what* to?"

Néol, in his black t-shirt and red boxers, rolls his eyes, leaps out of Leon's bed, and opens the door.

"Jeez, Leon," Nero says, fanning away Néol's smoky aroma. "You smell like cigarette smoke."

"What's up," Néol flatly says, ignoring Nero's remark.

Nero ignores this with a sigh. "You have the police here waiting for you. Something about your case with Allie. Know anything about it?"

"No?" Néol says, then thinks, *Unless, if this is Allure's little way of secretly wanting to meet with me…*

"Leon!" Silvia, Leon's mother shouts from downstairs. "They're asking for you, hurry up."

"I've got him, Silvia!" Nero shouts back then looks at Néol, adding, "Yeah, you'd better get ready. It doesn't sound good."

Nero shuts Leon's door, and Néol rubs his eyes. He puts his red hoodie on, his jacket, earrings, pants, and steps out from the bedroom. Then he slowly walks down the carpeted steps, hearing Leon's family chatter among themselves in worry. He knows this gossip is about who they think is Leon.

Néol opens the door and sees the officers. One short one with a full head of hair and one tall balding one.

Hmm. Not Nivmar or Milaw. What's going on here? Néol thinks.

"Leon Granttley?" the shorter officer asks.

"Yeah," Néol replies.

"We have a warrant for your arrest."

"What?"

The taller officer cuts the other off. "We have had reports of you visiting Allie Reincath's home. Did you forget about your restraining order?"

"You can ask any of the three inside," Néol says, widening the door to point at them. "I've been suspended from school and have been here the whole time."

The shorter officer steps forward, putting a hand near his gun holster. "We've received numerous reports about you *violating* the restraining order. We got a call about you standing in her front yard. Now, are we going to have to take you in by force?"

"Or will you comply?" the taller officer adds.

Néol blows air through his nose, cursing in his mind, wondering what's happening. He grumpily follows the officers' instructions, holding his arms up so that they can cuff him and follows them into their police car parked on the street. Néol spots an orange four-door car parked not too far behind them. What he doesn't see are the two people sitting in the orange car's driver's and passenger seats. Perhaps it's because their windows are so tinted.

The shorter officer gets into the driver's seat, and his partner opens the passenger door for Néol, and they start driving off. They make two left turns to start heading toward the police station.

"Pat," the short driving officer says. "You lost the bet yesterday, so *you* gotta read 'em his rights."

"No Rick, c'mon. You know you lost last time!"

Néol narrows his eyes, *What the hell is going on here? Who are these two idiots?*

Pat rolls his eyes and turns halfway around to Néol. "Alright...you have the right to remain—hey. Hold on... Who's that behind us? They've been behind us for a bit... I think they're tailing us..."

"Hmm. Run their plates," Rick says.

Pat looks at Néol and says, "You'd better make room back there. Because we've got company."

Néol glances at the passenger rearview mirror and sees the same orange car from before.

Meanwhile, in the orange sedan, Selim is in the driver's seat, and next to him is a young adult with brown skin, long platinum hair, moon shaped bangs passing his chin, and a teal button-up over purple armor. He has a ponytail running midway down his back, purple eyes, and a large body. He must at least be 6'3. In his hands is a teal pinwheel that is spinning very fast.

SEE THE PLATINUM-HAIRED MAN

"Selim," the platinum-haired man says in a British accent, "I thought you were taking us to an abandoned neighborhood."

"I was—" Selim says, slamming his foot on the brakes, "but it's probably been years since Stefano ever printed out updated maps..."

The platinum-haired fellow replies in a deep and throaty voice, compared to Selim's, "Two steps forward and one step back… We can't get him if we're in a—"

"—Ah, *Éphraim*," Selim chuckles. "This ain't your first time riding with me. You know I've got this."

"I wish I had a second seatbelt."

"Like you'd need it!"

After this remark, Selim does a complete U-turn, and the police car they were originally following does the same, driving behind Selim and Éphraim but with their sirens and lights on.

"Oh, well now we've made a scene," Éphraim says, worried.

"You know what to do," Selim says with a smirk.

Éphraim rolls down the windows and looks at the street posts in the neighborhood. He sees crows perched on them. Éphraim lifts his fingers up and down. There's nothing in his hands and yet—

"Nice one, Éph!" Selim shouts, watching sparks fly from at least twenty crows perched on the wires of the electric posts.

"There," Éphraim says, sighing in relief as these supposed birds fall and meet the ground, shattering as sounds of crushing metal comes from them.

It's just as Faviané said to Leon recently; *All that is living isn't real.*

"The less surveillance, the better," Selim adds, now making a sharp left onto a new road with a large sign saying, *Dead end.*

The cops follow Selim and Éphraim's orange car onto the short dirt road, where thankfully there are no houses or any signs of wildlife. Selim brakes, turns the wheel, and spins the car so that Éphraim's passenger side faces the approaching police car.

"Freeze!" the officer shouts from the car's megaphone.

Éphraim nods as he watches the police officers approach the vehicle with pistols out. Néol watches this curiously.

"Hands up!" Officer Rick says, stepping around the vehicle to get at Selim's side. Éphraim and Selim both have their hands up in the air. "Alright," he says to Officer Pat, "I've got a clear shot on 'em. Investigate them."

Éphraim shuts his eyes and suddenly—

"What is this! Hey! Get back here!" Rick shouts, trying to keep a grip on his pistol that wants to escape him. The gun's practically pulling him around like he's a fish clipped onto a fishing hook.

"Someone's got butterfingers," Pat chortles, not even looking at his struggling partner.

"No! Look over here! Something's—pulling. My gun!" Rick shouts back at his partner. Éphraim tries hiding a frown while Selim bursts out laughing at the strange phenomenon. Do they know something that these officers don't?

Pat rolls his eyes. "Rick, c'mon—" But then he makes eye contact with the floating pistol facing toward them both. He drops his gun and falls to his knees at the fearsome sight of the floating barrel staring him right in the eye.

"I think there's paranormal activity going on here..." Officer Pat says.

Éphraim rolls his window down. "Both of you, stay right where you are."

"What? You're doing this?" the officers ask in unison.

The officers break out in a sweat, staring at the gun facing in their direction. Somehow this gun is floating up and down. No suspected owner but the air, and perhaps the ashen-haired man. The two officers start shaking.

269

Officer Pat whispers to his partner, *"You didn't get through to HQ, did you?"*

"No. I told you already. The radios were down… I couldn't request for backup or anything."

Éphraim shuts his eyes, and the pistol independently shoots both officers in the head. Éphraim steps out of the orange car, giving a long sigh as Selim asks, "Is it over? Can I open my eyes?"

"Not yet. The worst part's almost over," Éphraim says as the bloody corpses of these two officers float in the air. Éphraim gives one long sigh as two holes—both of them being six feet deep—are dug beneath these two bodies. But not with one shovel. Nor with Éphraim's hands. The two corpses gently float into these holes, and the mound of dirt returns to the holes whence it came—erasing Néol's captors for good.

Éphraim shouts, "You can look now, Selim!"

"Finally!" Selim shouts back in relief, opening his eyes to watch Éphraim walk toward the police car. Néol is still sitting in the back seat, wondering what he just saw. He knows, though, that if this platinum-haired man is here to take him captive, he has no choice. He can only watch as Éphraim solemnly walks over to the backseat, opening the backdoor…without his hands.

"There are no strings," Éphraim says, "I promise."

Néol chuckles. "Would've fooled me. What kinda white magic is that, then?"

"Couldn't tell you."

"You seem pretty bummed all of a sudden. First time killing someone, I guess?" Néol adds with a smirk.

"I don't like taking lives if I don't need to," Éphraim replies as the cuffs around Néol's wrists literally snap off and fall onto his lap. "Come with me."

"Thanks for breaking me out," Néol says, massaging his wrists. "But I'm not interested—hey. What the—" Néol suddenly starts floating in the air.

"You don't have a choice—Néol Yelltnarg," Éphraim says firmly to Néol, who is shocked that his real name is known by this strange man.

"Yes," Éphraim adds as Néol floats even higher, now almost three stories above in the air, "I know exactly who you are—and *where* you come from."

"How am I floating like this?" Néol keeps his cool. He wants to demand to be put down, but falling from the height he's at would lead to his and Leon's death.

"I told you," Éphraim says, "there are *no* strings. And. No magic."

Néol is gently brought back onto his two feet. Éphraim turns his back, walking to the orange car which he expects Néol to follow him toward. Néol grits his teeth and tries sneaking up on Éphraim who doesn't even turn around to face him or his balled fist which seems to be frozen in the air.

"I'm out of your league, Néol. And I mean that respectfully." Suddenly, Néol is thrown onto his back, sliding backwards onto this dirt road.

"So obviously, you don't want to kill me." Néol slowly stands back up, dusting himself. "What do you want, then?"

"I told you. *Come with me.* We're going to talk in the car."

Néol grumbles a few swears about the mystery of this man's unique psychic abilities and the things he would do to Éphraim if he didn't have them…

"Uh, Éphraim?" Selim calls out with his arm hanging out of the window. "Don't forget to scrap the car?"

"Oh. Silly me," Éphraim says, facing the police car.

Scrap the car? What the hell is this guy? Néol wonders as suddenly—the police car is folded like origami. This of course is no shock to Selim, and now even Néol realizes that this platinum-haired man has two hands but can choose to never use them. Éphraim starts from the hood of the car, folding it part by part until this police car becomes a cube the size of his own fists. With his own mind, Éphraim lifts this tiny cube and sends it flying up toward the heavens, never to be seen again.

"I probably shouldn't have done that… I hope it doesn't fall and hit anyone."

Néol knows now, he truly has no choice to follow Éphraim. Éphraim returns to the passenger seat, and Néol unwillingly enters the back seat.

"Selim?" Néol says in shock, now seeing the driver.

"Heya, fellow Heartling. Long time no see," Selim replies with a smirk much like Néol's.

"Alright," Néol says. "What's going on here? I know I saw you before at the Heartshine Facility."

"Smart man," Selim says. "You've got good memory, unlike your reflection. You're right. I *did* sign up for the Heartshine Facility. Probably at the same time as you. Maybe for the same reason. I watched my mom cheat on my dad a lot, leading to a divorce…and that wasn't fun to watch. Got worse when they put me in the middle of it. Made me super *depressed*. The first couple days I went to the facility, I met with Festano Igor. He promised me *great* changes…saying that there was a better world ahead of me."

"No different so far," Néol replies.

Selim chuckles. "Then on another day, Festano showed me Planet Earth. Showed me everything better about this planet. Like how we can eat any food we'd like without getting sick. Or how the families we know on Heart suck compared to the ones here... And even how the people in Earth are the reason why we were miserable. I really believed 'em. And we had the whole switch planned out too. But then, for some reason, Festano stopped showing up to the facility. I thought my therapy sessions were comin' to an end."

Néol raises an eyebrow.

"But then," Selim continues, "*Festano* returned. I noticed a few changes in 'em—like how he just suddenly grew out a beard and changed his whole wardrobe. I figured maybe old people had phases like us teens. That day, he brought me to Earth and showed me a bit more. See, before when Festano brought me here, he *only* showed me things that I *wanted* to see."

Selim goes on, "But that day, he showed me another side. He showed me that the life of my reflection, Miles, wasn't as perfect as I thought it'd be. Miles struggled with voices in his mind. And he was bullied a lot. Yeah, he had two loving parents, unlike me, but their love was a two-edged sword. They chastised him with every chance they would get for his disorder. They'd tell him he was crazy and to get over it! His brother, Marvin, was no better. It made me feel really bad."

Néol blinks and looks away.

"And so," Selim says, looking outside, "I asked Festano if I could cancel the operation. I told 'em I'd rather stay in Heart than ruin someone's life. But the old man offered me somethin' *better*. To become Miles' friend, and to prevent others like my old self from switching over to Earth," Selim chuckles. "And right after I agreed, he revealed himself to be *Stefano Giro*. He told me that he was from Earth the whole time. Explains the sudden beard growth, right? And since then, Néol, I've been workin' with Miles."

Néol shakes his head. "And this is the part where you ask me to stop what I'm up to."

"I mean—be honest with yourself, man," Selim replies. "Do you really like it here that much? Are you bonding with his family the way you thought you would? Hm?"

Néol sighs and says nothing.

"C'mon," Selim says, smiling. "I spilled *my* guts, now you spill yours…"

"I never asked you to."

"Néol—I'm not gonna tell everyone."

"Hmph. Funnily enough… I've never told *anyone* why I wanted to switch."

"What? No one? Not even Ellia?"

"You heard me. And she barely knows anything about me as it is. Not even my parents know about this facility thing—or at least that I continued going. Let's just say I got good at faking it."

"I'm confused. So. You enrolled and then—"

Néol adjusts himself so that his feet are atop the seat and sets his back against the car door. "I enrolled in the Heartshine Facility when I was five. I didn't like my family and wanted some kind of escape. I got to know Festano like you and then was *also* promised this world."

Néol continues, "And you know. Up until I was fourteen, I was excited to come to this world. I thought to myself—*I could start all over with a new family*. No more fights. Arguing. Abuse. But I grew out of that as time passed. I fully accepted that my parents shouldn't be together and that my family is toxic for a reason. I started caring about other things. Instead of a new family, I sought a new start. What could I do if I had a chance to restart life with all the knowledge that I have now?" Néol opens his eyes and grins.

Selim and Éphraim both raise an eyebrow to these words.

Néol continues, "Then I finally came here. And I realized how *annoying* everyone here is. His parents are on you twenty-four seven. And with this court case on *Leon's* back, I really don't have much freedom. I sold his freedom just to get here. Maybe even my own soul."

"What did Festano have you do to come here?" Selim asks.

"Hate to interrupt," Éphraim says, "but Selim, we should start moving. Before those crows come looking for us."

"Right," Selim says, starting the car, driving them out of the dirt road. He, like Miles did with Leon, starts taking random routes around this suburban town.

Néol says, "You know about what happened to that Allie girl already. And then to get Leon to our world, I had to kill someone."

Selim swallows and looks over at Éphraim. "How'd you do it?" he asks nervously.

"Do what, kill the guy? It was on the day I brought Leon to Heart. Festano's plan is *always* to stage a coma. And to do that, he thought of staging a car accident but with a *real* victim. The Lunae Lux ordered that I'd deliver Leon to them after I dragged him through the Eleventh Dimension. Once he arrived on Planet Heart, they…let's just say they *made* two cars crash. They removed the corpses, put Leon inside one of the cars, and had *him* brought to the hospital."

"Wait…" Selim utters. "And then they said he had a coma?"

"Yup. When all they really did was drug him up on sleeping meds. Then. I heard him awaken after a few hours. After he awoke, my parents brought him back to my old house to live as me."

"But *you* never actually killed that person."

"Technically, no."

"Then why are you so proud to take the credit like you did?"

"Who said I was proud? No. I'm taking responsibility. If I had never enrolled, that person wouldn't have died."

Selim swallows. "Man… What Festano had me do was child's play compared to you…"

"From what you know," Néol replies quickly. "Festano bases his assignments on what he thinks the person can handle."

Éphraim turns to face Néol. "I hold no judgement toward you with why you enrolled at the Heartshine Facility. I'm sure with whatever you've gone through, it was enough to make you want to take action. And I respect you for trying to do something about your pain. Most people would sit and wait for things to get better."

"Glad you see it that way."

"Now," Éphraim continues, "think about the big picture here. It's not about what you did. It's what you'll do now."

"And what's there to do now? Go back to Heart? Bring Leon back? A little hard to go back to that dying world knowing that there's more out there."

"Sorry to cut you off, Éphraim," Selim says, "but Néol, who said you'd have to go back to that boring ol' world? We have you in here today, to ask if you'll join us: Me, Leon, Miles, Éphraim over here, and the rest of the Neo Knights. If you feel bad about what you did to those people, then this is how you can redeem yourself."

"I'm not looking for redemption."

Selim blurts, "Then what do you want?"

Éphraim interjects "No. It's not about what *he* wants. Néol. Look. You've been used by Festano. You always have been. He never cared about bringing you to a world of delight. He just wanted you to be a guinea pig for an even *bigger* experiment."

"I know I've been used. Figured that out after I got here. What I *didn't* know is that once you're switched to Planet Earth, they treat you like they never met you. And, wait. You two are telling me you wanna fight them? You want to fight the Lunae Lux?"

"What other choice do we have?" Éphraim replies.

"You two clearly haven't seen the monopoly that they have on both of these worlds. If not more."

"Well," Éphraim calmly replies, "the very man who reflects Festano is on our side. On certain times of the year, Stefano can read his mind. And sometimes it gives us an edge."

"Look Éphraim, I don't care what abilities you have. Even *you* can't take on Festano and his army."

"With you, we can," Selim says.

"Huh?" Néol says, raising an eyebrow.

"Yes," Selim adds, slowly driving down a straight road. "Because you would be the second reflection besides myself to join the cause."

"What are you trying to stop him from? Just this facility thing?"

Selim chortles. "I thought you knew all about 'em?"

"You're not helping yourself here," Néol calmly replies.

"Meh, you're no fun," Selim pouts.

Éphraim chimes in, "Festano's goal was never to stop at *switching* people around. Stefano says that it's Festano's way of building an audience. He wants to build trust with Heartlings who unlike *you*, Néol, believe there's a future here. That they have truly found happiness on this planet…thanks to the misery of their other. Because *with* that audience, he can start the next of his many projects."

Néol listens intently as Éphraim starts searching his pockets. The platinum-haired man finds a folded piece of paper and allows it to float over to Néol who thinks, *showoff.*

Here's what Néol sees:

Boy Named God

My goals are as infinite as the universe is. But my body is not. I'm running out of time to achieve many of these things as death knocks on my door.

<u>**The Promised City.**</u>
<u>**The Promised World.**</u>
<u>**My undying mind and body.**</u>

*But there is hope. So long as that child of mine is born—he can finish what I have left. Oh, **Boy Called God**, find me the answers I seek so that my son can be the* you *that* you *could never be.*

*The results of my research lie in **you**.*

—É.R.É.

Néol finishes reading, and the letter floats out of his hands and back toward Éphraim in the front.

Éphraim says, "Stefano had us go to his mansion to retrieve some things, and we found that. What do you make of it?"

"I don't get it. There's a lot of riddles."

"Neither do we," Selim replies.

Éphraim shakes his head. "And we'd rather not figure out *what* those things mean. There are talks of *gods* in there. A son being born from him. I don't want to imagine what else this man could create, Néol. Whatever ideas he has—I assume it's bigger than the patients in *both* facilities."

"Say I don't go with you guys—"

"—If you're not with us, then you're against us," Éphraim retorts.

"So, you're holding me hostage, is what you're saying."

"No," Éphraim says. "You'd be free to go. However, we would be forced to let Leon's earthly problems come to you."

"Hmph. So whitemail. Must've been you two that made up those police reports with Allie, then."

"Yes, that was us," Éphraim says, "and you'd given us no choice at that point."

"Why do you need me, then? You can just take Leon and go about your night."

"Because if you *and* Leon come with us—we'd have two hybrids."

Néol says, "You know that Festano hates the idea of hybrids, right? That said, it'd make me a big target for him just by being around Leon."

"Ha!" Selim blurts. "Haven't you seen what our man, Éphraim, can do here? *He's* your protection. And we have people in the Neo Knights who are trained in militarized combat. You'd be in good hands."

"What's your end goal after you stop Festano?"

"End goal?" Selim asks, now looking at Éphraim for an answer.

"Yeah," Néol says, "end goal. Clearly none of you have thought that far ahead. Tells me that this is gonna be a long battle, then."

"You mean war," Éphraim says, correcting him.

Selim chimes back in, "Well, I'm gonna be honest, Néol… I don't want things to go back to normal. How could I after knowing there're more worlds besides Heart? When this is all over—I wanna see 'em all."

"I agree with you there. I'm not gonna be on Heart when it dies. So. If it means making a home somewhere else, then so be it. No point in sticking with what I always knew."

Selim smiles. "Wait, so does that mean—"

Néol smirks. "Be warned, you two. Nothing's gonna be *normal* going forward. What *we* make is the new normal. I'll go with you guys to see just what that is. And if I get to stop Festano by doing that…then so be it…"

$$\mathbb{C} \qquad \mathbb{C} \qquad \mathbb{C}$$

Planet Heart
July 3, 2009 (Sunday)
Odaroloc /\ Eroaura
Ellia's Living Room
9:45 a.m.

Leon awakens on Ellia's couch. He rushes to the bathroom as quickly as he can to rub the crust from his eyes. He wants to hide the fact that he cried tears of frustration the night prior.

Once he wipes his eyes in the mirror, he stares at his reflection for a little…wishing it would show Néol like it did multiple before times in his life. But nothing. Solemnly, he leaves the bathroom to sit back on the couch where he sees Ellia's bright and shining face.

"Good morning," Ellia says, yawning.

"Morning. How'd you sleep?"

"Like an adult. It was amazing."

He takes a seat next to her, and she asks, "So. You called Miles yesterday, right?"

"Yeah, he said he'd help out. But if *I* couldn't do anything…I don't know what he could do."

"What will you do until then?" Ellia says, leaning her head on his shoulder.

"Well—"

Since you're up. We've gotta talk.

"What?" Leon says aloud with a smile on his face.

"Hm?" Ellia asks curiously as she leans off of him.

"I think Néol just contacted me…" Leon says, shaking.

Ellia looks away sadly and thinks, *I figured this would happen.* But she looks at Leon with a big smile and says, "I'm so happy for you…What's he saying?"

"I'll check."

You want to talk? Leon thinks. *About what?*

I know you reached out to Miles and Selim. Meet me at the Eleventh Dimension. Get to my place, and I'll tell you what to do next.

"Ellia—" Leon says giddily. "Néol. He's ready to switch back! I don't know what Miles did, but—it looks like he's coming home!"

"I'm *so*...happy for you..." Ellia says with a smile but with tears welling in her eyes. And now, Leon feels bad for rejoicing, knowing what it could mean for them both.

"No, Leon. Please don't look at me like that," Ellia says, looking away.

"I...I'm sorry. I didn't mean it like I was happy to leave you here. I want to take you with me."

"I just feel like you'll forget me when you leave..."

Leon pulls her in tightly. "No...Ellia, I could never forget you." She looks up at him, losing the fight against her tears as she cries into his arms.

"Ellia," Leon says with a smile, "you're the whole reason why I've made it this far. You believed me from the start. You have no idea how much you've done for me. So, no. I'm not gonna forget you. Now that I can go home and spread the truth—I'll be able to come back here someday. Somehow. And when that day comes, we can...be together."

"You'd want to be with me?"

"Of course! What did you think this was all about?"

"But...what about Allie, don't you like her too?"

"I did. But it's like you said. I didn't like her for who she was. How could I? I didn't know her romantically. And by the time I got to try and tell her what I felt...*all of this* happened. And maybe it was meant to. So that I could meet you." Ellia looks away, her smile almost as big as Leon's.

Leon adds, with an even bigger smile, "So, even when she knows the truth about who did what to her, *I'll* be the friend she needs. And. If you reach out to her—we can make that drawing a reality. You know, the one with all of us. Me, you, Néol, and Allie. We can all spend time together just like you dreamed. I know it's possible."

"Leon..."

Instinctively driven by a warmth and fuzziness inside, the pair's lips meet. The warmth radiating from their pounding hearts and racing thoughts make them blissfully unaware of Ellia's grandfather who clears his throat in the kitchen. Their eyes widen, their heads jerk from one another as they gaze at the grandfather who surprisingly has a smile on his face.

"No, by all means…continue," the grandfather says. "I get it. I was young once, too." The grandfather chortles as Ellia's face turns redder than a tomato as she runs over and playfully hits her grandfather's arms with her fists.

"Why didn't you say something earlier!" Ellia cries out as Leon and the grandfather share a laugh.

The grandfather serves the three of them breakfast. Leon is surprised to see that pancakes in this world taste the same. Though, Leon was skeptical at first with why the eggs were green. He reluctantly ate them to not insult the grandfather's cooking. The eggs did eventually make his stomach upset. Leon takes a shower and then prepares to leave. Ellia meets Leon one last time in her driveway.

"Well," Leon says, looking up at the green morning sky mixed with scarlet, "I guess this is it."

"Thank you for everything, Leon. I thought I knew what feelings were before, but…this is new to me."

"For you and me both. But look. I…" He looks away and whispers, "*I should be honest. The reacher won't have good signal on Earth. So, I don't know if I'll be able to talk with you as much as I'd like. I'm not even allowed to be on Planet Earth. And since I'm not…I could get in trouble with the Lunae Lux at any time.*"

"I'm praying you don't."

He speaks in a normal voice. "But if I do—I hope you don't think I'm ignoring you or that I forgot our promise."

"I was already planning your murder."

Leon blinks twice to this as she laughs.

"You're fine, Leon. I got to see the *you* that works hard for the things that you want. Seeing everything that you did just to get to Earth again shows me what you'd do just to see *me* again…"

Their hands instinctively hold one another's, and she adds, "I'll wait for you to come back. But if you take *too long,* I'm gonna come find you."

"Is that a threat or promise?"

"It's both." They share a laugh, and she continues, "But seriously. I know it could probably be a few weeks."

"Or months…" Leon says. "Hopefully not years…"

"And even if it is—I'll wait. What I feel here is worth waiting for."

Leon nods, and he kisses her forehead, then holds her close. "Goodbye, Ellia."

"No, not *goodbye.* Bye, *for now.*"

"Haha, alright. *Bye for now.*"

And she holds out her pinky for them to lock fingers once more. Their lips meet one last time. The sun above him shines brightly and after this final goodbye, Leon leaves her to watch him walk out the cul-de-sac.

I'll miss you, Leon, Ellia thinks with a few tears dripping down her cheek.

What? Allie replies in thought. *No! I could never miss him! No! These thoughts need to stay out of my head! Stay out of my head, Leon!*

Leon's steps are filled with pride and joy as he knows now that he can use the mirror to return home. This time, *without* the use of Planetshine. Because of Néol's willingness to cooperate, he can finally see his family. His best friend, Jason. His acquaintances, Jacaline, and Deen. Allie and all the others who doubted him so much. He thinks of all the ways possible for him to discreetly share the truth of the reflecting worlds with them, so that they can see what he sees.

Leon returns to Néol's home. The driveway is empty. To Leon's surprise, he sees a bunch of suitcases and duffel bags by the front door. The myriad of mess is still in the kitchen, living room, and the rest of the house. However, Leon counts at least seven bags near the door. Nosily, he opens one of the zippers and finds feminine clothing.

"Could these be…Néol's mother's?" he asks, holding up a shirt with white, black, and green stripes. "There's no way this would fit Oren… And I doubt May would wear this. Wow. I guess it did work. But then…*my family*…" Leon shakes his head then runs to the bathroom upstairs, realizing that time is of the essence.

"I should call Miles. He can probably tell me more about what happened…" Leon takes out his reacher and tries just that. He calls Miles three times but there is no answer. "Darn. Alright. I guess I'll do this on my own, then."

Leon faces Néol's bathroom mirror. He holds his amulet's compass toward it. The amulet confirms that he is facing east.

Hey, Néol, Leon thinks, *I'm gonna go to the Eleventh Dimension with your bathroom mirror.*

Fine by me, Néol immediately responds.

Leon steps in front of the bathroom mirror and slowly pushes his hand toward the surface. He expects it to feel like what any mirror would, if anyone were to push their hand to one.

A hard surface. But no longer. Now, with his new connection to Néol, his hand seeps through the mirror like it's water. But nothing from the mirror splashes onto his hands like one might expect. Instead, it swishes back and forth like a smooth pool of gel. Not one drop of water or any liquid is on Leon's hands. He climbs onto the bathroom counter and walks through the mirror—arriving at the Eleventh Dimension's bridge.

☾   ☾   ☾

The Eleventh Dimension
Odaroloc /\ Eroaura
July 3, 2009 (Friday)
Time in this dimension: 00:00
Time on Planet Heart: 10:20 a.m.

This Eleventh Dimension's bridge is shaped like an *S*. There are streams of color in this galaxy's sky that are green and blue, much like the Northern Lights. Or Southern Lights, as some would say on Heart. Leon looks around in awe and sees his reflection leaning against the gateway far ahead of him. Néol's eyes are shut, and he has a cigarette in his mouth.

"I can't believe it…this is *actually* happening…" Leon says, walking on the crystal bridge leading to Earth. After a walk that feels like an eternity, Leon finally makes it to Néol.

"So. You made it," Néol says, opening his eyes as he ashes the cigarette on his sleeve and throws it to the void below.

"Yeah, so how's this gonna work?"

"I spoke to Selim and this other guy. So, here's the plan. We won't be able to—"

"—*Leon?* Can you hurry up? I need to take a shower!" Amy shouts, her voice leaking from the gateway.

"Wait…" Leon says. "Do they…not know about us switching back?"

"Yeah, Leon," Néol says grumpily, "because I just *suddenly* explained to them where I came from. They know *nothing* about us."

"LEON!" Amy shouts once more. "I HAVE WORK IN TWENTY MINUTES!"

"You stay in here," Néol says. "I'll be right back."

"Dude…what is going on…" Leon says as he watches Néol sift back through the portal.

16

HOME IS WHERE
THE EARTH IS
HEART

C   C   C

<u>Planet Earth</u>
<u>January 2, 2010 (Saturday)</u>
<u>Colorado ∧ Aurorae</u>
<u>Leon's Residence ∧ Leon's Bathroom</u>
<u>10:35 p.m.</u>

Néol slips through the mirror and lands on Leon's tiled bathroom floor, crouching. A millisecond later, Leon slides through the mirror—his feet miss the bathroom counter, and he lands on top of Néol's back who, like a bull, bucks Leon to the side, making him fall back and hit the wall.

"What was that for!" Leon shouts, rubbing his behind, his back, and his head while getting up slowly.

"You?" Néol now whispers, "*You just landed on my back! And I told you to stay back!*"

"You did," Leon says, now getting in Néol's face, "but you forgot that this is my place!"

"*Yell a little louder, why don't you!*"

From the outside, Amy can only stand and look at the bathroom door with shock and confusion. "Leon! Is someone in there with you?"

289

"No!" Leon shouts back right away to Amy. "Can I have some privacy, please?"

"The paint is drying in Mom and Dad's bathroom! And I REALLY have to go!"

"Damn it!" Leon shouts, flushing the toilet to pretend that he's *actually* using the bathroom. Néol shakes his head.

Amy knocks and says, "If dad finds you smoking in the shower again, he's gonna be pissed!"

Leon glares at Néol. "In the shower, dude? Really?"

"I'm coming out," Néol shouts in his deeper voice, then whispers to Leon, "*You get back in that mirror now and wait. There's a lot to explain to you.*"

Leon grits his teeth and angrily whispers back, "*Do you have any idea what I went through to get back here?*"

"*I know* exactly *what you went through. Now—*"

The doorknob starts twisting, and the two reflections stare at it. The door swings open and Amy sees Leon standing on top of the sink while Néol is hiding inside the shower with the curtain closed.

"Leon…what are you doing?" Amy asks with her hands on her hips.

Néol thinks, *Yeah, Leon. Good plan. I get behind the shower curtain, and you get into the mirror.*

Shut up! I didn't think this through perfectly.

You're telling me.

Leon turns around and leaps down onto the ground. "I was exercising. Yeah!"

"By…climbing on the sink?" Amy asks, now squinting her eyes.

"I thought you had to go to the bathroom!" Leon shouts, now making his escape through the door.

Amy grabs his arm and sniffs him. "Hmm." Leon shrugs her off and she adds, "Well, *you* don't smell like a chain smoker for once. But it still smells like you smoked in here."

No. No. No. Leon thinks, *Think quickly, Leon—uh! I can't! Néol—we're caught!*

Amy pulls the shower curtain and sees Leon…or who she thinks is Leon…then she turns around to see Leon who's standing like a deer in headlights.

"How are you—" Amy pauses, now looking at Néol in the shower. "What…what is going on? What is going on?" While shaking, she backs out of the bathroom. "Wh—why do you two look so alike?" Amy adds as Néol steps out of the bathtub, shaking his head. Leon is at a loss for words. She looks at both reflections, gazing at every difference she can find.

Well, Leon, Néol thinks, *since you wanted to ignore me and do this your way, you can explain everything to her.*

"Where are Mom and Dad?" Leon asks in a gentle but shaky voice.

"Leon. Answer me. Please. Who is this?" she asks, her eyes cycling back and forth between the two.

"This is Néol," Leon responds, as gently as he can. "Now, listen. There's a lot to explain. But I need you to listen carefully and be calm."

"Oh, I'm far from calm! And I'm close to calling the cops on both of you since I have no idea which one of you is my real brother!"

"I am!" Leon and Néol both shout and then look at each other.

Why would you do that? Leon thinks.

Listen, Leon. At this point, we're both unpredictable to each other and to her. And we've got a bigger problem. If she calls the cops, we're through. And there goes anything with Miles and Selim.

"Why are you two just staring at each other?" Amy asks. "Okay. That's it. I'm letting the police solve this issue. I'm late for work!" Amy walks away, muttering angrily about how she has no time for drama.

Leon charges for Amy in the hallway, grabbing her arm. "Amy, please. Don't call them…"

"Let go of me, Leon," Amy says firmly.

"Please!"

"What's our father's middle name?"

"Justin! That's why he gave *me* that middle name," Leon exclaims.

"Hmph. I suppose you might've saved *yourself*. What about you?" she asks, glaring at Néol. "What's our mother's middle name?"

Leon thinks, *It's Layne.*

"Layne," Néol says out loud.

"Nevermind. You're both screwed."

I don't know why I went along with that, Néol thinks as he facepalms himself.

Amy makes her way to her bedroom where Leon expects the house phone to be. Néol charges out the bathroom, through the hallway past Leon, and to Amy, blocking the way into her bedroom.

"I can't let you go in there, Amy," Néol says.

Amy pushes Néol to the side. "I'm calling the cops on *both* of you."

Leon shouts, "NO!"

Amy storms into her room, grabs the house phone from her dresser, and dials *911*. She shuts and locks the door behind her as Leon and Néol wait outside. Leon paces back and forth while Néol crosses his arms.

"Now what?" Leon asks in a panicked tone.

"*Now what?*" Néol growls. "We wait for them to show up. Unless you wanna run back to Heart?"

"Wait. Sh. Listen," Leon says, putting his ear to Amy's door to hear her conversation.

"Hi, I'm in a weird situation. Someone who looks *exactly* like my brother is in my house. I don't know who is who. I don't trust either of the two since they both know personal information about myself and my family. But I'm late for work, and I just want this solved. Yes. That's the right address. Thanks." Amy opens her bedroom door, pushes past the two in the hallway, and walks into the bathroom.

"Amy," Leon cries out, "why'd you have to do that?"

"I don't have time to talk about it right now. Oh. And Mom and Dad will *love* hearing about this. Especially since they're celebrating Dad's promotion. I wonder how this will blow over," Amy says with a false smirk, leaving the two behind in the carpeted hallway. She slams and locks the bathroom door.

Néol shakes his head. "Follow me into your room. We need to talk, *now*."

Leon bitterly follows his reflection to his bedroom. As he follows Néol, he says mockingly under his breath, "Follow *you* to *my* bedroom. I just *love* the ring to that."

Néol shakes his head, opening the door to Leon's new room.

Immediately, Leon looks around. "What…did you do to my posters—"

"—Listen. The police are on the way. You probably already know this, but we're not supposed to be in contact. Festano forbids that. So, they might take us both to Hell."

"No, I'm not going there. I just got back!"

"When the cops get here, they might ask for *you*. I'm going to go first—"

The two reflections hear knocking on the front door.

"Great," Néol says, gritting his teeth. "Stay. Here."

Leon crosses his arms, looking around the room to all the new changes. He looks scornfully at the new posters of bands he would never listen to. The cigarette ash on his dresser. His closet now filled with Néol's clothes. Some clothes still have tags on them. He sits down angrily, and then a black cat leaps atop his lap. She meows, and her copper eyes lock right onto his.

"No way...are you...*Raven?*" Leon asks, now seeing the white crest on her chest. "You're the one who disappeared years ago!" China Jr. leaps up on his other leg, and he takes turns petting the purring cats.

SCAN FOR THE CATS

"At least *you two* are getting along..." Leon says under his breath.

Meanwhile, Néol charges down the stairs and glances through the windows to the side of the front door.

Néol thinks, *Leon. They didn't send the police. They sent the Lunae Lux.*

Leon's mouth gapes to this revelation. He slowly opens his bedroom door to listen to the conversation downstairs.

A male and female Lunae Lux soldier are standing outside Leon's front door. The male guard speaks first. "So. It seems you violated the first rule of your transfer."

SEE THE LUNAE LUX

The female guard says, "Allure Igor has summoned you to the Earthshine Facility. She will conduct your final judgement there."

Néol looks straight at the guards' masks. "Fine by me. Let's go."

"Not so fast," the male guard says, holding his gloved hand toward Néol. "Where's your reflection? She requested both of you."

Immediately Néol thinks, *Leon. Get in the mirror. They're both here for you, too.*

I can't! My sister's in the bathroom, remember?

Find any mirror, then! Stay on the bridge until I say the coast is clear. When you get on that bridge, DO NOT walk through the gateway ahead of you.

Leon panics. He puts both cats on the ground. They both innocently watch him nearly trip over his two feet as he rushes to his parents' bedroom. Once he pushes through their door, he runs straight for the bathroom. He climbs on the bathroom sink and slips through the mirror.

"He's not here," Néol says.

"You're not a good liar. I'm gonna look," the female guard says. "You stay with 'em." She marches into the house.

The female guard starts her search first in the kitchen. She searches thoroughly through all the kitchen cabinets. The pantry. The closets. The basement. Behind the living room couches. The garages. Even under Amy's purple car in the garage. Then she marches up the stairs, poking through the warm and misty bathroom that Amy left behind. She inspects the bathtub and even the cabinet beneath the sink. Then she starts looking through Leon's bedroom. The two cats scurry past her feet and hide somewhere downstairs. The guard knocks on Amy's door who opens it and shrieks at the sun and moon mask staring right into her soul.

"Step aside, I'm here for the other imposter." The guard pushes her to the side, glancing behind Amy's bed, behind her dresser, her closet, and under her bed.

"Excuse me?" Amy says, watching as this guard now marches into her parents' bedroom, still finding nothing.

Leon is hiding within his parents' bathroom mirror. He is waiting on the crystal bridge, and through this mirror portal, he can hear the female guard rummaging through his parents' room. The smell of the paint seeps in through the gateway.

He is trembling as he listens to the guard now angrily tip over Silvia's precious dresser. Now enraged at this, Amy shouts slurs and charges for the soldier. With one arm, the guard pushes Amy straight into the wall, and she falls to the ground. The female guard leaves her behind, hurrying down the stairs to approach Néol and her partner. Leon wonders what caused the loud boom.

"Nothing," the female guard says, looking at her partner.

Now the two of them glower at Néol, and the male says, "I'm sure you sent him a thought or two to warn him about our arrival. There's only one of two worlds he can hide in. So, he can't hide for long. Regardless, you're coming with us."

"Then let's get this over with," Néol says, walking ahead of them to the armored black van ahead. And just as soon as the two guards and Néol enter the black van, a white van enters Leon's driveway.

Leon, you're good to go now. However, your parents just got here. You're gonna have to explain this to them, alone. I'll keep you posted on whatever the hell's gonna happen next with me and Allure. Call Miles, and tell him about what's going on asap.

Within the Eleventh Dimension, Leon rushes through the portal and leaps out onto the floor tiles of his parents' bathroom. He gets outside to see Amy, who is sitting on the ground, dazing off, and looking up at the ceiling.

"AMY!" Leon shouts, now trying to pick her up, but she shoves him off.

"I'm sorry…" Amy says. "I didn't mean to push you. It's just that everything hurts…my head…my back hurts…"

"What happened to you? I heard a loud crash."

Amy wearily looks at Leon's face. "Are you...my real brother?"

"Yes... And the other guy was my—never mind that. What happened to you?"

"That...creepy masked officer...she shoved me into the wall."

After hearing this, Leon looks up and behind at the imprint in the white wall that is the shape of his sister. Dust from this new dent crumbles below onto her hair which he dusts off.

Leon looks down and trembles. "Amy. I don't have much time to explain this..." Suddenly, the front door opens, and Nero can be heard laughing with Silvia. Their voices trail off to the kitchen.

"Well," Amy says, "they're home... I guess *you* can explain this entire mess to them."

Leon swallows, *Great... I definitely got what I wanted. I wanted to tell everyone the truth...but not like this...*

"Amy," Leon says. "Do I need to call an ambulance for you?"

"No...but I could use some ice...and to just lie down... I think I should call out from work..."

Leon shakes his head. "I was trying to stop you from calling them. I knew they would do this." He gently helps lie her down so she's flat on her back instead of sitting up.

"I had no choice... I didn't know who was who. I just wanted us all to be safe. Who was that masked woman?"

"Well, it definitely wasn't the police. It was the Lunae—"

"—Hey—Amy—Leon!" Nero shouts from downstairs. "What in the hell happened to this kitchen?" Then Leon and Amy hear their parents yelling about the living room. Their angry voices come charging up the staircase.

Leon panics. He stands and backs away from Amy. He shuts his eyes for a moment and mutters, "What do I do…what do I do?"

Leon, Néol says in thought, *I'm about ten minutes from the facility. Did you call Miles yet?*

Crap. No.

Hurry. We're running out of time.

Leon grabs the reacher from his pocket, quickly dials Miles' number, but the phone goes straight to voicemail.

"C'mon, Miles!"

"Leon…Amy…" Nero says wide-eyed at the foot of his bedroom door. He looks at his two children. At Amy lying on the ground. Leon standing in panic. And then the mess of his room. What sets him off is the tipped over dresser. It happens so quickly. He charges straight for Leon, nearly stepping on his daughter, lifting Leon by the collar of his hoodie, tossing him onto the bed. Leon puts his hands up to protect his face, but Amy shouts, "No, dad!"

Nero's fist freezes, and he looks back at Amy. "No? Look at this house! Why were you two fighting? What happened here?"

"And whose black cat was running around in here?" Silvia asks, now entering her bedroom. "What is going on?"

Nero backs away from Leon, and the parents cross their arms.

Leon thinks, *How much time can I explain this all in? I can't tell them everything. I have to tell them what they can handle…just like Stefano did with me…*

Leon keeps his seat on the bed but adjusts himself comfortably. "I'm going to explain the last month to you all…"

"No, just explain the last—whatever—few hours!" Nero shouts back.

"You have to know everything, otherwise what I'll say won't make sense!"

"I'm listening," Nero firmly says, "and watch your tone."

Leon takes a deep breath. "Here goes nothing... I was kidnapped on my birthday. I was taken away by these strange, masked figures. The same kind of mask that you saw just now, Amy." To these words, Amy tilts her head in wonder.

Leon continues, "That masked person was a member of a secret organization within the Earthshine Facility. They kidnap patients and...bring them *somewhere else.* As for where that other place is, I can't explain. But. They do this because they send an imposter to live in their place." Leon starts speaking quicker and quicker as he continues, stammering at random points, "T-the *me* that you've been seeing for the last—I don't know, couple of weeks? That wasn't me. That was—someone who looks like me." *Screw it. I'm telling them everything!* "That person was my reflection!" Leon adds firmly as they each stare at him with a mixture of confusion and shock.

Leon balls his fist. "I was trapped in a world that reflects ours...and the guy that did everything to Allie—was *my reflection.* All the things that I did or said without understanding—it was because of *him.* He was the one behind the acts. But the one who put him up to it—is the reflection of Stefano Giro."

"Leon...slow down..." Nero says. "You're saying a lot at once. Reflecting world? What kind of fantasy are you on about now?"

Five minutes, Leon, Néol adds in thought. *I can see it here on their GPS.*

"Wait, I got it!" Leon shouts. "Dad—do you remember the newspaper you brought home that one day? Those disappearances? It was all because of the Earthshine Facility!" Leon looks at all three of their faces, expecting the same intrigue and open mindedness that Ellia showed him. But here, he receives the *same exact* treatment he left behind before his *switch*. It slowly lowers his morale.

Nero looks at his wife and then at Amy to see if they are keeping up with this fantasy.

Leon's voice cracks. "You don't remember? A long time ago before I got enrolled—you brought this newspaper home. And you almost didn't want me to go because of it. I was one of those disappearances! I'm telling the truth!"

Nero looks at Silvia again, then walks over to the wall to examine the hole above Amy. Nero crosses his arms and shakes his head. "And you're saying, Leon," Nero says, turning back around, "that this *masked person* did this?"

"Amy," Leon says. "Why don't you tell them? You said you saw it."

Amy wearily nods. "That part of his story's at least true…and she was really strong. I literally flew backwards off the ground."

Nero narrows his eyes. "So, you called the cops, and that person came…"

"No," Silvia says, standing between Leon, Nero, and Amy. "I'm not buying into any of this nonsense. We'll come back to the wall later. But Leon, I know those therapists weren't perfect. No one is. No human is perfectly good at solving problems for others. This elaborate story about another world is charming but also detrimental. The three of us worried that you were graduating prematurely and were even more shocked that Allure Igor made you a Knight… We thought, at first, it was best to let you make your *own* choice in being honest enough to admit what you did."

Leon stares. His heart cracks as his mother continues, "I have to be honest with you, Leon. I know you did it. You had to have. *There were photographs.* And believe me. It hurts that I, as your mother, have to say this against my own son... But it's about time I stopped coddling you and be honest with you…"

"Mom, I—"

"—Let your mother finish," Nero says firmly.

Leon grits his teeth, and Silvia adds, "And then to think. You got suspended from school. You stole from stores. Then with this Allie conspiracy, first you blamed The Voice. Then today it's now an imposter…I'm starting to wonder if these are signs of schizophrenia…not DID."

Amy interjects, "No, Mom, there really was another person here that looked like Leon. That part is also true."

Silvia looks at her daughter. "So, this so-called *reflecting* person is who pushed you into a wall? I'm guessing he put a mask on, too, then."

Amy replies, "The person who pushed me into the wall was a police officer."

"No, it wasn't a police officer…" Leon says, realizing that none of the three are keeping up with anything he has said.

Nero massages his temples. "I need to understand what happened here with the police. Why were they here? And why did they try to raid us?"

Two minutes, Leon, Néol thinks.

I've got one chance at this... Leon thinks.

"Amy," Leon says. "You can explain the rest to them after this. But. Dad. I can smell it on your breath. And Mom, even you too. The family of that *imposter* you're all in doubt of...his family was broken up because of *his* father's drinking habits. I was stuck there for almost a month. I tried to put his family back together by helping his dad quit drinking. I did it even knowing...that it would change you both... And here...I'm watching it happen again right in front of me."

Nero and Silvia look at each other in confusion. Nero says, "Leon, your mother and I are celebra—"

"—Celebrating your promotion? Oh, I know, Amy told me. And then this bottle of champagne will turn into one glass of wine on Fridays. Then Saturdays. Then Sundays. Then eventually, the whole week! And you'll be battling against a voice in *your* mind that will say, *I don't need the drink.* Trust me. I know."

Amy looks at Leon very curiously. And the parents look at one another.

"I'm going to call your therapist," Silvia says, while Leon clenches his teeth even harder. "Go to your room and wait for us to come back from the hospital with Amy. We'll discuss what to do next with you. You're not to leave your room again until you confess to *everything*, Leon. To the molestation of Allie Reincath. To the destruction you've caused in this house. To the police who tried searching for whatever... I'm sick of this fiction you've created. Go to your room."

Leon's reacher vibrates once. He pulls it out to see Miles' name. There's a text message that says, *Come outside! We're in your driveway!*

Leon gets up from the bed, brushing past his family. He can feel their angry eyes on him as he bolts straight down the staircase.

"LEON!" his father shouts, now charging after him. Leon pushes open the front door. He can see an orange sedan with tinted windows outside the driveway. He trusts his gut by assuming it's Miles. He takes one step out onto the porch as his father grabs him by his arm, shouting, "Your mother said to go in the room!"

"I—I—have to go!" Leon shouts, struggling to break free as he looks up at crows watching him from the streetlights. Suddenly, their heads spin around and around until loud snaps are heard. These crows fall to the ground as Leon tries pulling away from his father even more. Then comes his mother, charging down the stairs and past Nero, grabbing Leon's other arm.

"LEON! Please come inside!" Silvia shouts.

"I HAVE TO GO!" Leon cries out, but their combined forces are too strong. Éphraim, the platinum-haired man, can be seen rolling down his window in the passenger seat. One of his hands raises and imitates a pushing motion. When suddenly, Nero and Silvia fall back onto the ground. Leon is freed and is left standing.

"Leon! C'mon!" Éphraim shouts from his open window.

Leon takes one last look at his parents while running ahead. "I'm sorry, guys! I'll come back one day to explain it all—I'll show you *exactly* where I was talking about!"

"Leon…please don't go…" He can hear his mother whimper from the distance as both parents watch him run to the orange car. Nero holds her, and she weeps. Miles opens the door for him, and Leon jumps in. The orange car takes off.

"Seatbelt, please," Miles says, glaring at Leon who is sitting next to him in the rear passenger seat.

Leon clips the seatbelt on. "You guys, thank you so much...you came just in time..." he says, catching his breath.

"I'm sorry I didn't pick up the phone earlier..." Miles says. "I knew what your calls were about. I had a lot to juggle. Did Néol get to tell you anything?"

"Not really...we didn't have much time to talk..."

Leon looks forward to see Selim driving in the front, with Éphraim, to his right. Éphraim leans around, holds his hand out to Leon and says, "The pleasure is mine, Leon Granttley. My name is Éphraim Desruc."

The force of this car's sudden turn makes Leon fall onto Miles' side.

Miles narrows his eyes, saying, "And the reckless driver in the front is none other than my reflection—"

"—Selim Elé! It's nice to finally meet ya, Leon!"

"Nice to meet both of you," Leon says.

Miles gets Leon's focus. "Alright, so here's what's next. We're going to the Earthshine Facility. Néol's there. We've gotta think of a way to get him out *before* they take him into custody."

"Don't they already have him, though?" Leon asks.

"Yes, but Allure likes to have *one final* meet with Heartlings before sending them off to Hell. She calls this her final judgement. I've seen it happen before..."

Leon gulps.

Éphraim in the front speaks, "And if she has Néol, she'll be looking for you right after, if not already."

Leon blurts, "But what can we do if she's already started this *judgement*? Néol got there a few minutes ago."

"Simple!" Selim shouts. "Our boy, Éphraim over here, goes in— guns blazin'!"

"No, Selim," Miles says, correcting him. "This is a high-profile task. We have to do this as discreetly as possible."

"Meh," Selim replies, making another turn. "Well, think quickly because we're, like, two streets away."

Éphraim responds, "Well, Selim, it's not like you can go in either. It's against the rules. You also have to pretend you've never been there before."

"True. Miles?" Selim asks.

"I can't. I have to stay in contact with Stefano to find out our next move."

On their left is the great courtyard of the Earthshine Facility. They have a few more meters before they arrive at its entrance.

"I'll do it," Leon says firmly, looking at the Facility as they get closer to the entrance.

No one disagrees with this. Selim brakes and parks the car right in front of the courtyard's fenced gate. Éphraim lifts his fingers up and down like before. The crows perched on the street signs, the sidewalk, and even some roosting on parked vehicles snap and fall apart.

"Figures they'd have more crows here than anywhere else," Éphraim says.

"Alright, Leon," Miles says, "it's all you. Please don't get in trouble... You remember how to get to Allure's office, right?"

Leon disconnects his seatbelt. "How could I ever forget?" he says with a grin. "And you guys will be out here?"

"That we will, my new friend!" Selim says assuringly.

"I'll see you guys soon, then." Leon opens the door and charges for the building. He runs past the fountain, the automatic doors, passing all the familiar and not so familiar patients, the waiting room, then turns right to the nearest hallway, arriving at Allure's shut door, nervously knocking a few times.

Néol, Leon thinks, *I'm here.*

Sitting in front of Allure's desk, Néol grins. "You should get that."

Allure raises an eyebrow. "For all you know that could be one of my soldiers who are ready to take you away."

She gets up from her seat, glaring at Néol as she walks to the door to open it, finding Leon's grinning face. She grabs Leon's ear so harshly that she could tear it off at any moment. She swings Leon forward, he stumbles and grabs the bookshelf to regain his balance. A few books fall. Leon rubs his ear as Allure shouts, "SIT! No, you sit on the ground." Allure sits back behind her desk as Leon sits down. "No, not pretzel style, ON YOUR KNEES!"

Leon adjusts himself per her demand and grumbles a few things as Néol stares ahead at the angered therapist.

"You've got some nerve showing up... Unbelievable. Un. Be. LEIVABLE!" Allure shouts, throwing her clipboard to the side as papers fall and scatter.

"What was it all for? What was it all for, Néol? I'm asking you," Allure shouts quickly, tapping her long black fingernails on the desk.

"Things changed," Néol replies. And Leon looks at him curiously.

"What could have *possibly* changed? You had it all made for you. You wanted a family. You got one. You came to us when you were nothing but a sniffling, drooling crybaby—pleading for freedom from your drunken father! We gave you a plan to have something special and you threw it all in the trash by befriending this *thing*! Here in front of me, I'm facing not one but *two* disgraces." She stands and looks down at Leon, pointing her knife of a black fingernail at him. "And you! I warned you. All you had to do was live as your reflection. And what did you do?"

She glares at Néol and shouts while her spit mists on his face. "And all you ended up doing was feeling sorry for your poor little—" as she whispers, "*reflection.*" She sits back down while Néol wipes his face in disgust.

Allure shakes her head, massaging her forehead. "I have no time for this… I've never. *Never* experienced something so traitorous before. Sure, I've had Heartlings come back to me to ask to go back to Heart…but to work together? I mean, you understand why this is a problem, do you not? This would break the order! If anyone else from Heart sees this, it will all fall apart… And I cannot let you take this away." Allure grabs her sharp golden pen from her desk and aims it toward the two of them. "You hear me?!"

Néol shamelessly laughs.

"Say something! What do you have to say for yourself!"

Néol clears his throat. "Allure, your solution was temporary. Always was. And that's why I grew out of it. I lost interest because I knew that the only *true* thing I wanted…was something new. And you gave me that."

"And now you're throwing it away."

"Yeah. For something *I* want."

"When all you could've done was to just usurp your reflection's happiness. Your life could've been easier… What will you make of this in Hell?"

"I won't have any regrets. That's for sure. Because I'm not going to Hell."

Allure chortles. "Oh, so you think. Even though you'd considered Hell for Leon over here until my dear husband showed you it for yourself…"

Allure looks to Leon who appears shocked. She smiles a devilish smile that stretches more than any smile should. "Leon…are you certain you can trust your reflection? Did you think that he picked you living on Heart because he cared about you? No. This *other* of yours cares for nothing while you care for all. That is the truth of your existences."

Leon looks down and away as these seeds of doubt dig deep within his heart. He wants to ask Néol if this is all true, but what answer could come from Néol at this point? Anything going forward could just be *another* lie. *Another* story.

Allure grabs a pill bottle labeled *Nirpsa*, opens it, and drops three black tablets into her palm, dryly swallowing them. "Ugh…this is the same migraine that came when those two interns showed up… The one blessing and the one curse to my whole career. That's what you two are to me. You're cancers!"

Allure opens her drawer and presses a purple button inside. "I'll make sure you're both forgotten. Then no one will be inspired by your treachery," she says, as suddenly the door swings open.

Leon and Néol turn to see countless guards at the door, each with electrical batons in their hands. Every few seconds, electric bolts crackle from these rods.

"Guards…" Allure says. "One or two of you. Knock on the doors of all the other therapists. Call them and their patients out to see this."

Leon swallows, his and Néol's hearts pounding. The guards follow her orders, and the footsteps of many patients and therapists trample into the long hallway, standing around Allure's door. She walks outside and commands Néol and Leon to follow her. The patients all chatter among themselves curiously, some of them recognizing Leon but not his reflection.

"To all of you watching," Allure says, "these two are examples of what could happen, say, if you don't accept your disorder. The one here on the right, you might think looks *exactly like* the other. But in truth, our patient over here, Leon Granttley, scoured the internet…looking for someone who he could place the blame on for what he did to the one he cared for the most."

"No!" Leon shouts defiantly as one of the guards silences him, pointing the rod at his chin.

"Yes…" Allure replies with a big smile, pointing to Néol. "This lookalike is an imposter that he hired to be his scapegoat. Well, if any of you patients—more specifically, Bishops—are looking to blame someone for your misdeeds or disorder…look no further. This will not be tolerated at the Earthshine Facility. For this crime against our policy and to any who repeat this, you will be punished! Now. Take them away," Allure says to the herd of Lunae Lux soldiers who approach Leon and Néol. When suddenly, the soldiers are sent straight upward—their backs hit and stick to the ceiling. They drop each of their guns to the ground.

"I can't move!" one of the guards cries out as the others fight what feels like reversed gravity.

Allure looks up to the frozen guards. "What? What happened to you all? Is Faviané here or something? No…she shouldn't be here, yet…" She and the other patients and therapists in the hallway look around in confusion.

"YOU!" Allure says, her eyes stabbing straight at Éphraim in the sea of faces. He winks and runs away with Leon and Néol who both chase behind him. "BOTH OF YOU! GET BACK HERE!" she yells.

The guards glued to the ceiling suddenly fall onto their stomachs. They groan from the pain. Allure pushes aside a few patients and fellow therapists, rushing for her desk to grab her reacher, screaming into the microphone, "We have a code white! I need all feet on deck for a pursuit!" She slams the phone on her desk and starts giggling. "I suppose *all* is not lost…now that I know that the *Boy Called God* project has finally shown itself…"

Meanwhile, Leon and Néol are both outside, following closely behind Éphraim who shouts, "The car's just ahead!"

Selim pulls forward with the orange sedan, Miles opens the back door for Leon and Néol to jump in. Éphraim opens his front passenger door, of course without his hands. Once all the doors shut, the orange car takes off.

"Seatbelts everyone!" Miles shouts. "We've gotta move!" Leon, Néol, Selim, and Éphraim clip their seatbelts in.

"That was too close…" Leon says, catching his breath.

"You're telling me," Néol replies, gasping as well.

"Éphraim…" Leon asks. "What was that?"

Éphraim chuckles. "What was *what*?"

"You know, with the soldiers getting knocked off their feet?"

"I don't know what you're talking about."

"Huh?" Leon says, tilting his head.

"Hey uh—guys?" Selim asks, driving swiftly. "We've got company."

"What?" Miles says, turning round to see three black vans driving behind them.

"I'll break off our license plate. Then they can't track us," Éphraim says, using his mind to snap the screws attached to the license plate, folding it like origami, then letting it fall on the road.

"Okay," Selim says, "so here's the new plan—"

"—No, Selim," Miles says quickly, "you drive, I'll explain!" He looks at both Leon and Néol and says, "We're on high alert. Stefano knows we are. And—"

"—I'm sorry about this, guys!" Selim says, swiftly turning the wheel to the right as everyone in the car sways in the same direction.

"Everyone duck your heads!" Éphraim shouts. "They've pulled out machine guns!"

"They have *what*?" Leon says, as Néol grabs his hood, pulling him down.

Éphraim rolls down the window, glancing at the multiplying black vehicles that surround their orange car. "Selim!" Éphraim shouts, his voice competing with the rushing wind. "Drive like you normally would! I'll take care of the coming bullets!"

"Does *driving normally* still mean speed?"

"Yes!" Éphraim shouts back.

Selim merges right onto a four-lane highway, apologizing to everyone again for the bumpy ride. From behind, Lunae Lux guards lean out the windows of their black vans, firing more than twenty bullets toward the orange car's tires. Éphraim leans out the window with one hand held out, stops their bullets right where they are, then with the flick of his wrist, sends these bullets flying toward the guards' tires. One of the three stricken vans spins out of control, crashing into a civilian's car in the next lane.

Éphraim bites his lower lip. "I really wish they didn't do this out here in public…"

Selim presses even harder on the accelerator, the car now flying past 110 miles per hour. The second black van behind them speeds forward, now parallel with theirs. They inch closer and closer until the black from their vehicle scrapes off onto the right side of this orange car's paint.

"What was that?" Leon asks, responding to the harsh bump.

Éphraim ignores Leon. He glances around to see at least four rows of innocent drivers on the highway. He sees a family in one minivan. He shakes his head, snaps his fingers, and one by one, their tires all pop. It sounds like firecrackers are going off as they each brake out of panic and fall behind. Éphraim pops the tires of *all* the civilians nearby, getting them to brake and slow down. This allows Selim some extra room to drive. The remaining two black vehicles persevere, catching up to Selim and the others.

Now, with all the innocent passersby out of the way, Éphraim lifts both hands, sending this second van full of Lunae Lux members flipping over a few times.

"Nice one, Éphraim!" Selim shouts. "Still got that last one behind us, though!"

"I know," Éphraim says. "Oh no. Is that a—" Éphraim watches as one of these daring Lunae Lux soldiers in the van behind aims a long gun out the window.

"*A sniper rifle?*" Éphraim shouts. "These guys are insane!"

"Anything I should do?" Selim asks, a little worried.

Éphraim watches the soldier's trigger finger, while asking, "How far are we from the graveyard?"

"Fifteen minutes!"

"Alright. Speed up!"

"One hundred and twenty miles per hour? Let's do it!" Selim roars.

Éphraim holds his hand out the vehicle, waiting for the guard to fire the long bullet he expects any sniper rifle to fire. But to their left is a new black van, this one more compact and militarized than the rest. It slams into the left side of the orange sedan. The impact makes them sway back and forth. Selim struggles to straighten the car's wheels. The door of this new black van opens, and out comes a Lunae Lux member with two sickle blades. He leaps onto the roof of the orange car, stabbing the blades onto the roof, using his hanging body to block Selim's eyes.

"Dude, c'mon I can't see!" Selim whines loudly, trying to look past the hanging soldier. The new compact van veers a few feet away from the orange car.

Éphraim grits his teeth, he faces forward to the suicidal guard whose body seems to be glued to the glass. Éphraim makes a pushing motion, and suddenly the guard goes flying off into the air, miles ahead.

Leon leans upward to curiously turn around when suddenly all the glass behind him shatters. The shards of glass are no less than a centimeter away from his face. He shuts his eyes as each shard ceases like they're frozen in ice. This goes for the giant sniper bullet that was flying toward him too.

"Stay. Down. Leon!" Éphraim shouts. "If I didn't stop that, you'd be dead!"

"Sorry!" Leon shouts, bending back down.

Idiot, Néol thinks. *Almost got us killed for nothing.*

Éphraim lets out a loud grunt. He sways his hand backward, sending this same giant bullet and shards of glass flying toward the tires of the vehicle behind them. This black van loses balance, tipping and flipping over as smoke rises to the skies. Éphraim then snaps both of his fingers, and the van to their left has all four of its tires pop. The vehicle rolls and rolls until a fiery explosion overtakes it.

"Dude, seriously?" Selim says, looking back to see two Lunae Lux members on sporty motorcycles. Their bikes have two wheels in the front and back. Despite Selim pushing 120 miles per hour, these cyclists catch up with green fire bursting out from their mufflers.

"I've got eyes on the platinum-haired one," one cyclist says, now moving to the right of the orange car.

"Copy that. Moving to the driver's side," the other cyclist says. And the two cyclists pull out guns with hooks at the ends.

"That does it," Éphraim says, lifting both of his hands up into the air. Suddenly, both motorcyclists on the left and right float high above. Éphraim claps both of his hands together—and the two cyclists (including their bikes) slam into each other. Éphraim separates his hands, and the two now dead cyclists and their bikes are sent flying in opposite directions.

"Phew…" Selim says. "Finally… WAIT!"

And just like that, Éphraim sees exactly what Selim sees. There may be no cars on the highway, but there *is* a spike trap—a wall of spikes laid out specifically for their orange car's tires.

Éphraim loudly grunts this time—raising both of his hands to the roof of the car while the entire vehicle floats in the air—averting the trap full of spikes. He gently lowers his hands to his lap as the car follows this same slow descension to the ground.

"I think…I think we're safe now," Selim says as he and Éphraim take a deep breath. Leon, Néol, and Miles each raise their heads.

"What…was that?" Leon asks.

"That was the Lunae Lux at the most desperate I've seen them," Éphraim says, panting a bit. "This should tell you all how valuable a hybrid is."

"No kidding," Leon replies. "I…I've never seen Allure that angry."

"I have," Néol replies, "when I had second thoughts about coming here."

"Is where we're going safe?" Leon asks. "Miles?"

"Yeah," Miles says. "Sorry. I'm just still trying to process the last few hours. Haven't slept a lot."

"I know that feeling," Leon says, angrily looking at Néol whose fist is holding up his face.

Miles continues, "A few days ago when you called me, Leon, I talked to Selim." Miles explains exactly what occurred between the police, Selim, Éphraim, and Néol the other day.

"Néol here," Miles says, "decided to join the cause."

"Wait, really?" Leon asks, now facing his reflection.

Néol nods. "When you originally got to Earth, that's what I was gonna tell you. But you were stubborn."

"Yeah because—okay, moving on. Continue Miles."

Miles laughs. "Well, then came the next tough part. Getting you two in the same place at the same time. Leon, when you called me earlier—"

"—Which time?" Leon asks, narrowing his eyes. "I called many times."

Miles rolls his eyes. "I don't know. Just keep up. Anyway. When you called, Stefano heard the Lunae Lux were on their way to your home on Earth. So, he thought of a last-minute strategy. To sacrifice himself…"

"What? Why?"

"He's putting his faith in us hybrids. I tried talking him out of it, but when his mind is set on something…"

"That's stupid!" Leon shouts. "We're just two normal people."

"Festano is very threatened by hybrids," Miles says. "He completely hates the idea of two reflections working together. He doesn't know about Selim and me, so to him, you both would be the first. And he'll wipe out any that he can find so that others won't get inspired. So, Stefano is using himself as a decoy. He's going to allow himself to get caught, and through that he will give Festano everything he wants. That way, he'll care even less about the two of you. I... personally think it won't work, though."

Leon shakes his head. "So where are we going now, then?"

"Ciler Graveyard," Miles responds. "The two of you will go out and meet him there."

Selim butts in, "And when the cops go in to get him, Éphraim will go in and save you both!"

17

THE UNSEEN

BLOT

☾　　☾　　☾

S elim parks the car, and he, Éphraim, Miles, Selim, Néol, and Leon step out onto a dark, foggy, marshy, and grassy area.

"Gross…" Selim says, the muddy water splashing on his shoes and pants.

Éphraim looks at an upward gravel driveway ahead of him. While pointing to it, he looks at Leon and Néol, saying, "Just up there is where Stefano should be. I couldn't tell you *where* within the graveyard. But I'm sure he'll find you."

Miles stretches. "Agreed. He's expecting you. Most likely he'll stay hidden until the time is right."

"Alright…but just to make sure," Leon says, looking around, "you guys are sure we won't be followed?" He starts looking around the nearby trees for crows.

"I can't guarantee that," Miles responds, "but if you do run into trouble in there, Éphraim *will* come and get you."

Leon takes a deep breath, and Néol says, "Let's go," as he walks up the gravel driveway. "The sooner we get this done, the better."

"Good luck, guys," Miles says, while he, Selim, and Éphraim wave to them. Leon follows Néol up the gravel hill, and they both enter the gravesite barred by a tall black fence.

"Finally…" Selim says. "Alright, well I'm gonna take a much-needed nap in the car."

"Selim," Miles says. "Is that fair to Éphraim who has to keep watch? Especially after he just fought off a—"

"—It's quite alright, Miles," Éphraim says, smiling.

Selim blows a raspberry to Miles and then enters the car, sits on the driver's seat, reclining. Miles's phone starts to vibrate. He rolls his eyes to Selim then picks his phone up,

"Hey, what's up, Toni?"

"Miles! There's an Amber alert for an ORANGE car without a license plate! Penny told me they have A LOT of cops and even MORE Lunae Lux guards looking around for Leon and Néol! What's going on over there on Earth?"

"We…we had a little situation with Leon and Néol. We'll have to explain later."

"You're at Ciler Graveyard, aren't you? Penny says they're on their way there now! I think Festano must have read Stefano's mind! You have to get them and get out!"

"What? Oh no!" Miles hangs up as Éphraim looks at him with concern.

"I take it you have bad news," Éphraim says, when suddenly he sees crows in mass fly atop tree branches around them, then a few on the ground beside them, and another murder which flies into the gravesite.

"Horrible news…" Miles replies. "Festano knows about what we're doing…and worse…there's an Amber alert out for this car…Éphraim, what do we do?"

You'll die, that's what you'll do, one voice in Miles' mind says.

Yes. Let it all fade to nothing. This fight you lose.

"Whoa," Selim says, cracking open the driver's door. "What's all this I'm hearing in your mind, Miles?"

"We have to find the nearest mirror and leave," Éphraim says firmly.

"But—Leon and Néol!" Miles shouts. "Oh no! And my car…"

"I'm sorry, Miles," Éphraim replies. "It has to be this way."

Meanwhile, Leon and Néol wander within the graveyard in silence. Néol doesn't seems bothered by the quietness. Leon would call this awkward, while Néol would see it as something soothing. Their paths are lit by tall light-posts that flicker on and off.

"Wait," Leon says, looking at a worn-out sign hanging above a set of graves. "I wanna look at this."

Néol's heart beats quickly as he says, "Leon, we've gotta meet—"

"—I just wanna look at these."

Néol sighs. He pulls a cigarette out of his pocket and lights it.

Leon wanders closer to this sign, and it reads:

To Those of The Earthshine Facility.

"Wow. We have our own section?" Leon wanders by the tombstones and notices hanging signs that say certain years on them. The word *numerous* does an injustice to how many graves there truly are in this section dedicated to patients such as Leon.

Leon and Néol don't have enough time in the day to read all of the years, but the furthest back that they can see is the year 2004.

"How many people from the Earthshine Facility died?" Leon wonders, looking around for the year 2009. "Scott…" Leon reads on one tombstone. Shock steals his breath, "Scott Aivlove…" Leon remembers that this was *The Screaming Man* from his facility.

The tomb reads:

Scott Aivlove
October 8, 1965—December 11, 2009
A beloved family member of the Earthshine Facility

"I can't believe he died on the night of the switch, too." Leon wanders to the tombstone next to it, and it reads:

Obi Blake
January 10, 1989—December 11, 2009
A beloved family member of the Earthshine Facility

"Wait, that's weird…" Leon says aloud. "I thought you also switched with me… Did you *also* die that night?" Leon looks at the next grave to the right which says:

Lisa Miller
April 14, 1999—December 11, 2009
A beloved family member of the Earthshine Facility

"I'm pretty sure I remember hearing your name that night, too…" Leon cycles over to the *next* grave, and what shocks him is the fact that it says this:

Leon Granttley
December 11, 1992—December 11, 2009
A beloved family member of the Earthshine Facility.

Leon reads this in his mind as he says it out loud, while Néol hears him and wanders closer to his reflection.

"Néol?" Leon calls with gaping eyes. He takes a deep breath and asks, "Why does this say what it does?"

Néol takes one last puff on his cigarette, then throws it down to the muddy ground. "You won't like the answer. But it was in case you died. During the switch or even in Heart. This would allow the facility a quick scapegoat to avoid more lawsuits."

"So, you knew this?"

"You wouldn't have asked me if you didn't think I knew."

"Don't be a smart ass! How am I supposed to trust you when you are capable of all of this? You knew I could've died! You knew all these things could've happened!"

"I guess we'll never know, now, will we?" Néol says with a smirk.

"You two have to keep it down," an elder voice says, approaching the two who turn to see Stefano Giro.

"Stefano!" Leon shouts as Néol slaps Leon in the back of the head.

"What did the man just say?" Néol asks, shaking his head. Leon tries shoving him back but misses.

Stefano sighs, "Come with me, you two. Hurry. We're very, very short on time. And I *have to* show you something."

Stefano leads them past a trail of graves. They pass more hanging signs with years on them. They pass a series of them for the year 2005 and continue walking.

"Stefano," Leon asks, "is it really true? Are you really giving yourself up?"

"Yes."

"Why though? The rest of the Neo Knights need you. Néol and I are just two people."

Stefano leads them past the sign that says *2004*, and he says, "It's not just about me, Leon…or even just you two. This is about me making my next move."

"By martyring yourself?"

"Don't forget about the very first Reflection Principle. If *I* die, then so will Festano. He doesn't want that. Instead, he will put me in Hell with the risk of death in mind. Principle 3.2 states that he would use my misery against me to build himself even higher. However, there's *something* in this graveyard that told me that Hell is *exactly* where I must go."

"Oh?" Leon replies as Néol pulls out another cigarette. They each pass the year 2003.

"Yes. Some fifteen years ago, my reflection mentioned that he wanted children. He told it to me and his wife, *Allure*—"

"—Allure's his wife?" Leon blurts.

"You didn't catch onto that?" Néol says crassly.

"No, because *I* didn't work for them. I'm sorry, what were you saying, Stefano?"

"Yes…Allure Igor is Festano's wife…and her reflection is *my* wife. Laurel Giro. One glaring difference is that she and I did not want children. We had our reasons…but we wanted to travel the world and spread the Earthshine Facility's philosophies. The healthy ones that weren't perverted by Festano…anyhow. Festano, on the other hand, was someone who was desperate for a child. He would moan about how the mind and body would rot and how it killed him knowing that his goals could never be completed."

"I saw a note about that from Éphraim," Néol says.

Stefano nods. "You should tell Leon more about that later. Because Festano mentions something in there about a *Boy named God*. And quite frankly, since the title is dramatic like he is, I have a suspicion that it's connected to the boy that Allure gave birth to. And his name is *Aron Aeternum Igor*."

The boy's name brings goosebumps to both Stefano and Leon. Stefano leads them past a hanging sign saying *2000*, then asks, "If Aron is the boy that Festano so desperately wanted to have, then why kill my wife and daughter? Wouldn't he lose the very things he wanted? Marriage and fatherhood?"

Leon and Néol don't respond to this.

Stefano stops and now enters a row of graves and then stops and stands in front of one. "For years I thought to myself that Festano was cruel and cold beyond reason. I saw these two graves next to me and thought to myself, *Festano—how dare you kill my wife and daughter!* But then I realized…Allure Igor works at the Earthshine Facility and handles most of his operations…so again I asked, what would he gain by killing my wife?"

He stands to the side, revealing a tombstone which says:

Laurel Giro

July 19, 1975—March 2, 2000

"Forever in my heart, always in my memory."

"This is the supposed tomb of my wife," Stefano says solemnly, "or at least I thought that years ago. How I mourned the loss of someone still living and breathing. But thankfully, one day I was daring enough to venture out to Earth and saw Allure. Never did I think that woman's vile presence would give me hope. So, then I thought even deeper and wondered…could this, too, be fake?" And Stefano steps to the side again to reveal another tomb which says:

Nora Munretéa Giro

June 17, 2004—January 1, 2006

My beloved who I will love for all time.

"Okay…" Leon says with a hand to his chin. "But I don't get it. Why make graves and lie about their deaths?"

Stefano says, "Bearing Principle 3.2 in mind, I think it was to steal my hope. I think he wanted my pride and joy to be taken from me. He hoped it would immobilize me and that it would stop me from moving forward in life. But he was wrong. I formed the Neo Knights and rebelled against him. And the fruits of my labor are standing right in front of me."

Stefano takes a deep breath. "I trust you both, Miles, Selim, Éphraim, and a set few others with the internal matters of the Neo Knights. You all have learned enough from me to sustain yourselves. All the new members of the Neo Knights have all the mentors they could possibly need to adjust to Heart. I made sure of that. And now, we have not just one but *two* hybrids."

Leon looks away, remembering some of his distrust for his reflection.

Stefano adds, "With this all known…I will willingly go to Hell to find them. If they're not there—then I lose. But if I find them, we all win. Sadly, I couldn't let either of you two know my findings since there are no means of contact down there. However, I trust that someday all those in Hell will be freed. That mission I leave to you both and the rest of the Neo Knights."

"I see…" Leon looks down. "So that's why you wanted us to meet here."

Néol tosses his cigarette and stomps it out.

"Yes," Stefano says. "I figured if I were to go out that this would be my second to last move."

"Don't say that," Leon says. "You're not dying."

An all too familiar voice creeps into their ears. "No, he's certainly not dying, but where he's going, he'll wish he had," Detective Nivmar says, with his partner Milaw next to him.

Stefano mutters, "Boys, put your hands up and slowly get on your knees. The easier we make this for them, the better it will be."

"Hold on," Leon says. "*We?*"

"Yeah," Néol replies, looking around for Éphraim. "I don't remember that being a part of the agreement."

Detective Nivmar and Officer Milaw grab their pistols and point them at the three. Leon and Néol slowly but unwillingly get to their knees and raise their hands, just like Stefano.

Nivmar says, "Néol…Leon. Whoever was in that orange car up and left you both behind. That little stunt you all pulled at the facility caused a whole lot of trouble. I'm not even gonna mention what happened on the highway. Allure assured us she'll have her revenge on you." Nivmar eyes Stefano up and down and adds, "And then there's you. Do you have any idea how long we've been looking for you, Giro? You know how happy your reflection will be to *finally* have you?"

"I'm sure he'll be *very* pleased," Stefano replies. "The chase, is over. But on my terms."

Nivmar pats Stefano's shoulder. "You're telling me. I'm just surprised that you gave yourself up. I was hoping for a flashier showdown. Oh, well. Might've happened if you were young like these ones over here."

Milaw chimes in, grabbing handcuffs from her sides. "I don't care about how this ends. I just want *this* all to end…just so we can go back to our own world."

"You know as well as I do that that's up to Festano," Nivmar replies to her.

"Of course. Because why would a nightmare die young?" Milaw says.

"Speak for yourself," Nivmar replies.

Leon and Néol keep looking around for the platinum-haired man, but no matter what direction they look in, he doesn't show. And if Éphraim doesn't, then it is even less likely that Miles or Selim will.

Milaw approaches Leon and tells him to spread his arms. She checks his pockets, grabbing his reacher to the ground to smash it. Leon looks away with a broken heart. She does the same with Stefano's reacher once his turn comes. Néol doesn't have a reacher. She still checks his pockets, only finding a wallet. Luckily for him, he is allowed to keep it. After this, the three are handcuffed and are walked out of the cemetery and back to the driveway to see that the orange car is still parked out front.

Gleefully, Leon thinks, *We're saved!*

No, Néol thinks. *It's like Nivmar said. They left.*

No...They wouldn't do that...no. They're still in there.

"Milaw," Nivmar says, "you checked the trunk too, right?"

"Yep," Milaw replies.

Leon's heart drops.

Officer Milaw reluctantly wraps blindfolds around the three hostages' eyes. And now. They see nothing. Then, she jabs earplugs into their ears. The three feel a slight prick in their arms. Their bodies slowly lose energy. But before they can fully fall asleep, the three are crammed into the back of a police car.

"Hey, Milaw," they hear Detective Nivmar say. "I'm gonna have another car brought here. I've got some questions for Stefano."

"Sure, whatever," Milaw says.

Leon and Néol hear the car door open, a bit of shuffling, and taunts from Nivmar to Stefano. Stefano is taken away, the door slams, and Milaw starts driving.

Where they are going, none of the three can know. They each fall asleep...

An unknown amount of time passes.

Leon awakens on the shoulders of someone tall. He's being held up like luggage. His arms are still cuffed. His sight is still blotted. The air is freezing cold—then is suddenly blazing hot.

"Where…am I?" Leon asks, his shivers now fading and morphing to sweats. He tries moving his restrained arms. He notices his earplugs have been removed.

"Oh, you're finally awake," a soft voice says.

This isn't Nivmar's voice at all. Nor is it Milaw's. And what Leon is being held atop feels hard. Could he be atop this female soldier's shoulder armor?

"Now that you're awake, you can walk," the mysterious voice says. "But remember. Don't try to run away this time."

"When did I try—okay. I won't," Leon says, then thinks, *Néol, are you near me?*

Yeah. I'm up. I don't know where we are, either. I can only assume that Stefano's with us.

Where are we?

I just said I don't know where we are.

What's going on? Why was I asleep?

Officer Milaw didn't check the dosage of that tranquilizer. So, you were asleep for a longer time than me. After that, you tried fighting back and got tased.

I don't remember any of that…

Yeah, because you were knocked out.

Stefano clears his throat.

Okay, Leon thinks, *So Stefano's here, too. I'm just gonna assume that he's walking, too.*

Leon is set down onto his feet by this soldier. The female guard grabs his wrist and pushes him forward.

"Walk straight," she commands. "I'll guide you so you won't fall off."

Fall off? Just where are we? Leon swallows.

Suddenly it is blistering cold once more. Leon feels a hard surface beneath his feet. Like metal, almost. Or stone. He feels a cool wind rushing against him like before. He can feel crystals of snow touching his neck. He starts shivering. He wishes to have brought a thick winter coat. But just as soon as he wishes that, the temperature changes once more. It's now blazing hot.

"Where are we that the weather keeps switching?" Leon asks aloud.

"You're at your new home," the female guard responds. "That's all I'm telling you. Keep walking."

Néol, Leon thinks, *do* you *know where we are?*

I might. But I could be wrong, too. I can't see, remember?

Figured I'd ask since you worked with Festano.

You wanna play this game now? Alright, you be passive aggressive, and I'll be aggressive.

Oh yeah? Well, if I could see you right now—

—You'd what, fight me again? Try it. Because we all know that went well the last time.

"That does it!" Leon shouts, trying to swing his feet to the right and left. But his kicks strike no one but Stefano who cries out, "Ouch, what was that for?"

"Sorry," Leon says aloud. "I was *trying* to kick Néol." Néol loudly cackles at Leon's failure.

"You two need to—" But Stefano stops himself, realizing what kind of punishment he could receive for giving this newly formed hybrid advice.

Stefano instead thinks, *I suppose Leon is still angry with Néol over everything that has happened...if the two don't make up, then the bond will shatter...then neither of them will be able to switch without Planetshine.*

"Look at you," Néol chortles, "kicking the very person that tried to help you. That's so like you. So selfish. Self-righteous. Full of pride."

"Oh yeah? Mr. I-want-a-new-family-so-bad-that-he-molested-someone-just-to-get-it! Oh yeah, and I'm the bad guy. You're just full of envy!"

"Poor idiot doesn't even know what he's talking about."

"What do you mean! You ruined my life by doing what you did to Allie! And you ruined hers, too!"

"Come and do something about it then."

"I would—" Leon starts swinging his feet around again, while somehow being mindful of where Stefano could be, "—if I could just fricking find you!"

All Néol can do is laugh at Leon while Stefano shakes his head at the chaos Festano has caused.

Stefano thinks, *I wonder...could Leon be this angry because of Néol's calmness at this matter? So be it. I'll have to take the risk...*

Stefano stops walking, and the female guard shoves a gun to the right side of his back.

"Keep. Moving. Stefano," the soldier says firmly.

"You two," Stefano says, disregarding the guards warning. "Listen to me carefully. You must put your differences aside—"

"—I said shut up!" A loud bang sounds, Stefano cries out, falling to the ground.

"No!" Leon shouts. Even Néol is shocked to hear gunfire.

As Stefano falls to the ground, only the female guard can see this, but he's feverishly rolling on the spot she shot him in. Surprisingly, there's less blood than an outsider would have imagined.

But what the guard knows is that these bullets are actually tiny moons with teeth. Once they leave the barrel of this pistol, they chomp away at whatever they can. In this unfortunate case, Stefano's back. Like a bee sting, these microscopic beastly moons eat away at his flesh.

These are what the bullets look like:

Despite this, somehow…Stefano fights the pain to say, "Put…your…differences aside…Leon...Né—AH! You—GAH!"

As he cries out, the soldier shouts, "I'll intensify it if you keep talking!"

Stefano perseveres and yells, "You might not forgive him today! Maybe not tomorrow! But you must *sometime* if you want to save these worlds! Everything happening here is bigger than us! The universe is at stake—Néol! Have it in you to—" And the female soldier switches the gauge on her gun from *3* to *5*. And Stefano yelps, turning to the side with drool rolling out of his mouth. His eyes roll backwards.

"Stefano?" Leon whimpers, hearing no movement from the old man's body.

"Oh no…" the female guard whimpers. "What did I just—" And then she gets a call on her radio. "*We just saw what you did out there. Who gave you authorization to use the thorn gun on him?*"

"I'm sorry! I—he was giving advice to—"

"*—Do you realize you could've killed our leader?! Get inside! Put those two in a cell, and—*"

Stefano coughs a few times, then turns his head, looking around. He remembers he can't see with his blindfold. The female guard gulps, presses a button on her gun which says *retract,* and the tiny moon that ate past the fabric of Stefano's shirt and into his flesh, flies right back into the gun like a magnet.

"He's up now," the soldier says to the radio, taking a great sigh of relief.

"*Good, but you just went from* Grunt *to Trainee, Ammé.*"

"Great. Now all the others know my name. Now my family's screwed. GREAT! ALRIGHT, YOU! GET UP! GET UP NOW!" Ammé shouts, now clumsily yet roughly grabbing the old man's arms to help him stand. "WALK!"

"I suppose it pays to be the reflection of your adversary, hm, Ammé?" Stefano says out loud, fighting a smile.

"Be. Quiet," Ammé replies, clenching her jaw.

"I've said what I needed to," Stefano replies, wishing he could rub his fresh back wound. He can feel a bit of blood leaking.

Ammé escorts the three of them across what they each assume to be a bridge.

18

A HYBRID'S

VALUE

C   C   C

D eleantur Estates is a large luxurious apartment complex that Miles hinted about to Leon once when the idea of the Neo Knights was first introduced to him. This development is completely private and uncharted in Odaroloc's map. It is fenced and requires an access code to drive inside. Only Stefano and the Neo Knights know how to find this location. Not even the crows know where it is.

Miles and Selim share a two-bedroom apartment. Toni and Tenny also have a two-bedroom apartment to themselves. So do Caleb and Scudero. Ellen is by herself, just like Aepis, and Ombretta.

The typical hangout spot for this group is Toni's apartment. There is a giant *island* or center countertop in the middle of her giant kitchen, surrounded by ten barstools. Currently, six of those seats are filled by Caleb, Ellen, Toni, Tenny, and Scudero who are each awaiting Miles' arrival.

Toni's door bursts open, and Caleb shouts, "Jeez, Miles! Knock first?"

"Shoes, please!" Toni shouts at him, pointing at her welcome mat.

"Miles," Ellen joins in, looking at his darkened eyelids. "I thought you promised us that you'd sleep more."

"I *have* been sleeping," Miles replies while taking off his shoes.

"For more than four hours?" Ellen asks.

"...No..."

"MILES!" Everyone shouts at him, even Scudero who is normally quiet.

"I'm sorry, okay? It's been *one month* since they've been gone! I'm worried! I have no idea if they're in Hell or not. I can't stop thinking about that day. I need this riddle solved!" Miles shouts, reaching into his pocket for an envelope.

"Let me see this darn riddle you keep talking about," Caleb says.

"Here," Miles says, passing everyone a sheet of paper from the envelope. "I printed one out for everyone."

"Aww...so you admit that you need our help," Caleb chortles, nudging Scudero who joins in with a few chuckles.

"This is serious, guys..." Miles says solemnly.

"Caleb, Scudero, be more understanding," Ellen says, now getting up to rub Miles' shoulders. "Take a seat, Miles."

"Sweetie," Toni says, excusing Miles for barging in without hugging her, "are you sure that this is your only lead?"

"Yes," Miles says. "Selim and Éphraim scoured Stefano's mansion, and this was the only thing they could find. Said that it caught their attention because it had Néol's name in it."

"Excuse me, Toni?" Tenny says, rapidly tapping her shoulder before Toni can reply to Miles. "Can I go hug Alvin?"

"Yes, Tenny, sweetie. You can hug your teddy bear."

Tenny leaps for joy and then rushes to the leather couch to hug Alvin, the bear.

Toni says what she was going to. "I see... Well, have Selim and Éphraim been any help? They discovered this code, after all."

Miles says, "Selim got annoyed with it, but Éphraim said that he'd give it a shot if everyone here couldn't solve it."

335

"Ohh, I see!" Caleb shouts. "So it's up to me. Challenge accepted. Okay. Ellen, why don't you grab Miles a glass of his elixir, while Scudero and I race to see who can finish first?"

Ellen crosses her arms. "One. You can get it yourself. Two. I'm taking part in this, too."

"Then it's no longer a challenge. It's a race," Caleb replies, grinning as he stands up. "Toni, which drawer had the paper and pencils again?"

"The one by the stove. If pencils were forks and spoons, you'd remember."

"You're not wrong," Caleb says, grabbing a few sheets of paper and pencils for everyone at the counter. They all read the paper that Miles handed to them. It says:

A Be Hemline Noel Shh Tot
N39.754060 -26647017S

"Uh. Miles?" Caleb says, holding the paper close and far away from himself, as if it should change.

"I think I'll address the elephant in the room," Scudero says, and everyone watches him in shock for speaking loudly once more. "This looks like gibberish…"

"Yeah! Where's the real riddle?" Caleb asks.

"That *is* the real riddle," Miles says coldly, "and I'm getting some warm milk."

"You know where it is," Toni says.

"Alright…Miles," Caleb says. "You drink your elixir while I'll be the first to solve this."

While everyone tries their hand at solving this puzzle, Tenny retrieves a teal and yellow comforter decorated with smiling suns and moons from his bedroom and takes a nap on the couch.

Nearly forty-five minutes pass. Everyone's one sheet of paper full of scribbles turns to two sheets. Then three sheets. Ellen is the only one who stops at just two sheets.

"You know who'd be good at this?" Scudero says. "Evardo."

"I tried him," Miles says, trying not to sound angry. "I tried Penny, too. I don't want to tell too many other people about this."

"Makes sense," Scudero says, looking down, then thinks to himself, *Otherwise other Neo Knights will figure out that Stefano's been taken.*

"I give up," Caleb says, slamming his pencil down.

"Thought you'd be the *first* to finish," Ellen says mockingly, covering her reddening face as she laughs at Caleb.

"Nah, I don't care anymore. This is way too tough. Glad I didn't gamble dinner over this," Caleb pouts.

Toni stands up, fidgeting with her lighter. "Today might be the day, everyone."

"No, Toni!" Ellen shouts, "Please! Not the blue flame!"

"This fricking thing's making me lose my mind. I give up. I have to."

"That says a lot," Scudero chimes in. "You're the one who always helps me with Sudoku."

"And *me* with crossword puzzles," Ellen adds.

Toni doesn't respond. She takes a deep breath, then shoves the lighter into her pocket, silently staring out her windows with crossed arms as they all sigh in relief.

"Well," Miles says, "thanks anyway for trying everyone…" He starts anxiously playing with his curls.

"Miles—" Ellen utters.

But Miles guesses her next sentence and replies, "It's my fault. All three of us. I told them both they'd be backed up by Éphraim. I wasn't expecting things to go this horribly… Leon and Néol both trusted me, and I screwed it up!" He slams his fists on the countertop.

"Miles," Toni replies without turning around. "Do us a favor and ignore those voices. It's *not* your fault, okay? We will find them."

"How?"

Knock. Knock. Knock.

"Oh great," Caleb says. "That must be *him*."

"Aepis?" Ellen asks, looking at her violet amulet's clock. "But he said he'd be here later."

Caleb walks to the door. "When does he ever keep his word?" He unlocks the door and opens it for Aepis who knocks Caleb's red cap to the ground.

"Oh. Let me get that for you," Aepis says, walking past the red cap.

Caleb growls, "Dude, I thought you said you'd get it!"

"I would, but I never keep my word," he winks.

Aepis gives Toni a long hug from behind and asks, "What troubles you, my dear Toni?"

"Miles' stupid riddle."

"*Riddle?*" Aepis asks. "Hmm. Did you try giving it to Lovyam?"

"Éphraim did," Miles says, "and Lovyam got a little nosey. He asked him what it was for and wouldn't try it until Éphraim told him. So that's a thing now."

"So, what you're telling me is that Lovyam knows that Stefano's been taken?" Aepis asks.

"No…" Miles replies, looking away.

"Tsk tsk. He'll figure it out soon, then," Aepis says, raising an eyebrow. "Let me see the riddle and what everyone did to try and solve it."

Ellen gathers all the papers, hands them to Aepis, and then he looks at the original riddle that Miles gave the group.

"Well?" Miles asks.

Aepis blinks and looks at Miles. "The only person here who figured out a part of it is Scudero."

"I did?!" Scudero exclaims loudly, probably louder than anyone's ever heard him yell before.

"Yes," Aepis confirms. "These numbers are coordinates. Scudero, you were smart to separate the numbers and the letters—" Aepis feels a vibration in his pocket. "—Ugh. I'm needed elsewhere. Good luck, you all," Aepis says, running for the door.

"Well, that was quick," Caleb says.

"Thanks for trying, everyone," Miles says, rubbing his eyes. "I'm gonna bring this to Selim and Éphraim and see what they can do." He finishes this sentence with a long yawn.

This time around, Toni walks her way to Miles and gives him a long goodbye hug. He doesn't let go. He could fall asleep in her arms at any moment with the amount of stress and fatigue eating him alive. Caleb and all the others say their goodbyes to him and wish him luck.

Miles and Selim's apartment is just a few doors away from Toni's down a long-carpeted hallway. He unlocks his door to see Éphraim's and Selim's shoes inside by the door. To Miles' left is the living room. To his right is a hallway leading to one bathroom and two bedroom doors. And straight in front of him is his kitchen.

Miles forgets to take his shoes off as Selim peers over from the kitchen, shouting, "There you are!" Miles meets both Selim and Éphraim in the kitchen. A bunch of shopping bags are on the counter. Éphraim has items such as eggs, milk, sugar, along with many other groceries floating into their designated places. Selim leans on the counter and asks, "How'd it go?"

"Clearly not good…sorry. I didn't mean that," Miles says.

"It's alright," Selim replies. "Éphraim and I were talking about it earlier."

Éphraim looks away from the two as the fridge door shuts with all their groceries now put away. "I'm sorry again, Miles."

"Éphraim—you really don't have to apologize. This whole thing was my plan. But you know," Miles grabs the envelope from his pocket, "Scudero and Aepis had an idea. They suggested to separate the numbers from the words."

"Sounds better than anything I did," Selim says, then looks at Éphraim. "Why don't you give it a shot? You're the only one who hasn't tried yet."

"Might as well," Éphraim replies.

"And in the meantime, Miles!" Selim exclaims. "I'm gonna make you some Chrenf toast. My treat."

Miles lets out a smile. "And with—"

"—Yes, and with your precious warm milk. But don't drink it all! I need some for my *Captain Munch*."

No promises, Miles thinks.

"I heard that!" Selim shouts back at Miles as the two share a laugh.

Miles hands Éphraim the letter and then he walks to a small desk in the living room.

Éphraim sets the riddle in front of him. He puts his hand to his chin, thinking, *Selim and I found this on the center of Stefano's desk. There was no reference to what it could mean or directions on how to decode it. Nothing but our own knowledge. I know Stefano well—and if there's anything I know about him, it's that he'll never directly give you any answer. Not unless you've worked for it. So, using everything that he's given us...what can we say is useful about this code? Aepis says to separate the numbers, but what then do we get?*

Éphraim stares at the code for a bit. He reaches for the printer's paper tray beneath him and grabs six pieces of paper. Then with his mind, he makes seven pencils float over to him, and they each start writing different interpretations of this code.

The original code is:

A Be Hemline Noel Shh Tot

N39.754060 -26647017S

After approximately fifteen minutes, Éphraim's mind sets each of the papers side by side so that he can compare them. Éphraim scans all the codes and then shouts, "GUYS!"

Selim first comes running into the living room with a frying pan in hand, Miles slumps shortly after him.

"What is it?" Selim says, looking back and forth, wielding the frying pan like a weapon. "Is it the Lunae Lux?"

Éphraim chuckles. "No, no. But I *did* just realize something."

Miles' eyes light up to these words.

Éphraim stands up, and the papers each stack up then float into Selim's hands.

"I want you both to read through all of those."

Miles leans close to Selim as he scans each of them. Here's what the codes say:

1. *A Be Noel Hemline Tot Shh*
2. *A Hemline Be Noel Shh Tot*
3. *A Be Noel Shh Hemline Tot*
4. *Noel Shh Tot A Be Hemline*
5. *Hemline Noel Shh Tot A Be*
6. *Noel Shh A Be Hemline Tot*
7. *Neol A Shh Be Tot Hemline*

Selim looks at Éphraim in confusion. "I don't get it. None of these make any sense."

"Precisely…" Éphraim says, his hand to his chin as he paces back and forth. "And perhaps they're not supposed to."

Miles tilts his head.

"I think," Éphraim adds, "and I could be crazy…but I think that the coordinates on the paper lead to *where* we're supposed to decipher that code."

"Where does it lead to?" Miles says. "You mean we'd have to *literally* go there?"

Éphraim pulls out his cellphone with two screens, opens its internet browser, and types in *Elgoog*, Planet Heart's search engine. He searches the coordinates given from those numbers, and they bring nothing.

"I'll be right back. Stay right here," Éphraim says, leaving the two behind as they look at each other.

Éphraim wanders to their hallway and then into the bathroom. With the use of the bathroom mirror, which is facing toward the east, he steps off into the Eleventh Dimension, onto the bridge, and wanders *near* the gateway.

"Alright," Éphraim says. "Earth's signal should be able to reach me at this distance."

"Éph?" Selim asks, stepping through the mirror with Miles behind him. "What's this all about?"

Éphraim types the same coordinates onto *Google*, a search engine founded on Earth, and then says, "Guys, those coordinates are Earth based."

"What?" Miles shouts.

"Yes!" Éphraim says. "Those papers I handed you guys. I tried moving those *words* in every place I could think of. But no matter what, they wouldn't make sense. I'm sure you guys saw the same thing, too."

Miles and Selim nod in agreement.

Éphraim continues, "So, I thought—maybe it's not the words we're supposed to unscramble..."

Miles and Selim both say, "But the letters!" Then they look at each other and high-five.

"Exactly...think of the second Reflection Principle," Éphraim continues. "It says that if we come to a new dimension, we wouldn't be able to read words or numbers for fifteen days. Well...if we keep trying to read this riddle here in Heart, we'll never be able to read it, right? Of course not. Because this isn't the dimension it  originated in... But where these coordinates lead. Maybe Stefano wrote us a code in a phrase that even he couldn't read."

Miles crosses his arms. "Oh...maybe he did that to prevent Festano from reading his mind."

Selim nods. "Makes sense! Whatever he wants us to know is *so secret* that he couldn't risk Festano knowing!"

Miles holds his head. "It's the most basic principle, yet I didn't think of that..."

Éphraim smiles. "There, there, Miles. If it weren't for you asking the others for help, I would've been just as lost. Thank Scudero and Aepis, really."

Éphraim nods confidently, facing the gateway behind him. "We've got our answer, you two. Let's get something to eat, then head off to those coordinates."

Miles says, "I think we should keep this from Toni and the others. Especially Ellen. She'll worry."

Selim nods in agreement. "True. They'd probably get the mercenaries to get involved."

The three return to their apartment, having breakfast for dinner which helps cheer Miles up even more. But as much as they each enjoy their servings of Chrenf toast, bacon, and eggs, along with their choice of beverages, they're anxious to leave and see just what this code means and what it can do to save Leon and Néol. They know that without their orange car to hide them, or even travel more speedily, they're wide open to any crows that want to stalk them. However, the good news is that even with the Amber alert out for their old orange car, none of the Lunae Lux that pursued them lived long enough to see any of their faces. Only Leon and Néol were considered wanted. Éphraim's face remains a mystery, however his unique hair color does not.

They decide to leave the estates at around 2a.m. They figured if they traveled this early, they could avoid any or all suspicion from any nearby crows. Éphraim drives them all to an abandoned farm area in Odaroloc, Nomarch. He does this in his own black van with heavily tinted windows. With the use of a mirror, they then switch to that location's reflection, Monarch, Colorado. This area, too, is an abandoned farmland covered in some snow.

☾　　☾　　☾

The mirror brings the three to a series of abandoned red farmhouses with wood that looks like it was bleached. These snow-filled structures stand at least three stories tall. All that is around this abandoned farmhouse is tall amber grass and snow that covers the remains.

Miles scans up and down the dark and barren area. "No electric poles, not a single soul in sight. I can't blame whoever chose to leave here."

"I'm thankful for there not being crows around, though," Éphraim says. "Maybe this is why Stefano picked this area, right Selim?"

"Huh? Oh, sorry. I was lost looking at the view over there," he says, pointing to a snowy mountain far in the horizon.

"Alright," Éphraim says, cracking his knuckles, "let's get started with this barn. The coordinates led us exactly here, after all."

Miles trenches through some of the snow and pulls the barn's main sliding door to open it. Sadly, it won't budge.

"Nothing…" Miles says, scrunching his lips.

"Keep pullin'," Selim instructs.

Miles and Selim together pull on the door, and it slides open, exposing a dank and dusty room filled with bundles of smelly hay.

"Sure could use an air filter," Selim says.

Éphraim sneezes into his elbow. "I should've packed dust masks."

"You're blessed," Selim says.

Èphraim thanks Selim, then glances up to the ceiling to see the barn's skeletal structure. Miles pouts, "Nothing… Let's check the next barn."

Èphraim pats Miles' shoulder. "Don't give up yet. Let's try digging through the hay. Remember. We were led here for a reason."

Selim's face turned sour. "But Èphraim…"

"Don't say it, Selim…" Èphraim says as he and Miles both facepalm. "Hay is for—"

Èphraim shakes his head. "Honestly… I'm surprised that even that joke is the same on Heart."

"It's not," Selim says with a pout. "I stole this joke from the Earthlings. Had to steal what I could since people on Heart don't know how to laugh," Selim adds with a sigh. "I'll dig at the west end over here," he says as he grabs a flashlight from his pocket to shine in the corner of the room.

Èphraim nods. "Then I'll take the east. Miles, you'll handle the center, won't you?"

"Sure thing," Miles says with a nod, looking through a hole in the ceiling. "Stefano… What are you trying to tell us?"

Selim scornfully spreads his hands through the straw that smells like manure. "We won't know till we look," he says as the three of them rummage through it.

Throughout this, Èphraim and Selim sneeze a couple of times.

"You're blessed…again. If you sneeze once more, you're on your own," Selim says as they both wipe their noses.

Miles finishes digging through his portion of the straw and leaves the barn in frustration. Èphraim and Selim continue scraping through their remaining piles. "Nothing…" Miles says, walking outside. "Even that shack was empty." He retrieves his orange moon amulet from his pocket for the time. "That's one hour we won't get back."

Miles takes a walk farther away from the barn and thinks. *The coordinates brought us here... Now why would Stefano bring us to a place that's completely empty? It couldn't have been a coincidence... The letter at the mansion... Was it a mistake for Selim and Éphraim to look there?* Miles ponders.

"Miles! Miles!" Selim blurts as his other's eyes enliven. "We found something!"

A rush of adrenaline shocks Miles as he runs his way back to meet the two in the center of the barn.

Éphraim's arms are crossed. He steps to the side to reveal a shaft. "This was beneath all the straw on my side... It was just a cover up."

Miles grins. "Well? What're you waiting for? Open it up!" He balls his fists in excitement, nearly bursting out from his boots.

Éphraim nods with a smile. "We were waiting for you," he says, bending downward to pull the knob upward.

Selim tilts his head to the side. "Eh?"

"A mirror..." Miles crosses his arms. "Why here?"

Selim bends his knees and leans down to the large mirror in the hole.

"No, Selim," Éphraim says with his right open palm toward him. "Step aside. You'll throw out your back by doing that."

"Oh, fine," Selim says, backing away.

Éphraim holds his right palm toward the mirror and curves his hand upward until his fingers firmly point to the ceiling. The dark mirror with its golden frame floats upward into Miles' open hands.

"It's here for a reason," Éphraim says as his mind shuts the shaft's lid. "The three of us can transfer between Earth and Heart as we please... So I doubt it's here for that."

"But what for, then?" Selim asks with a hooked eyebrow.

Éphraim softly shrugs. "Set it in each direction, and let's find out."

Miles turns to the center wall ahead. "There…" He runs forward and sets the mirror against the wall. "Let's go," he says, running through the portal.

The rippled surface bounces like jelly. The other two trail behind Miles until they meet on the ethereal bridge of the Eleventh Dimension.

"Nothing…" Miles says, staring dead ahead to the rainbow road sloping off into nothingness.

"Five-year-old me would've loved to slide off that," Selim says.

Èphraim gently pushes past Selim. "Strange… I've never seen a severed road within this space before…"

"Neither have I," Miles replies.

Selim chuckles, grabbing the jade amulet from his back pocket. He checks the compass rose. "We're facing north. So maybe…this just means that anything northward is useless."

Miles turns around. "What?"

Selim waves goodbye then dashes through the polished surface.

Èphraim tugs at Miles' arm. "He may be on to something."

The two follow behind in Selim's footsteps. As they exit, they find Selim pacing back and forth with his jade amulet in hand.

"Ah, perfect timin'," he says. "One of you…be a doll and set the mirror…" He wanders to the direction of west. "Right…over here."

Èphraim faces the mirror. "Hmm… On the west?"

Selim nods. "Yessir."

Èphraim lifts the mirror and dashes over to the left side of the room. "Good thing our left and rights mean the same thing," Èphraim says.

"Some reflections aren't as lucky as us, right Miles?" Selim says as his face lights up.

Miles chuckles. "I hope you're going somewhere with this," he says with a raised eyebrow.

"Trust me," Selim says with a wide grin. Èphraim poises himself to run into the mirror. However, Selim's arm interrupts him.

"Ah—ah. Allow me," Selim says, charging through the portal.

"By all means," Éphraim replies. "Miles? Care to go first?"

Miles nods, then runs to the mirror. Before the tip of Miles' boot gets close to the gateway, Selim barges back through. "Don't bother, this one's just like the first. So, let's try the east!"

Miles lightly chuckles. "Alrighty then…" He lifts the mirror toward the east side of the hay-filled barn.

Selim bites his lower lip. "Alright… Let's see if anything changed…" he says, charging through.

Miles waves Èphraim forward. The two follow behind into the mirror to find Selim frozen in front of a gigantic doorway.

A triumphant smirk overtakes Selim's face. "Boys…I think I figured it out," Selim says, returning his amulet to his back pocket. He turns around to face the others. "For whatever reason, the other paths facing north and west didn't have a destination… *east* though…takes us into a different sector of the dimension."

Selim turns around, his arms crossed. "I think whatever the good doctor wanted us to see is up ahead." He points his thumb to the plateau of sand sitting below the ethereal path.

Èphraim snaps his fingers. "Ah, I understand. So, the coordinates that led us here—"

Miles finishes, "—Led to a dimension where the letters can be unscrambled."

Selim nods. "I'm placing all my bets on there being a dead end at the end of that path…just like what happened with the north and west…if we're lucky, at least." Selim takes a few steps ahead.

"Hold on, Selim," Miles says, steeping forward. "We're going to a different region of the Eleventh Dimension at this point. No one's ever been that far."

"Well, clearly Stefano has in order to leave us this message."

"Right, but—"

Èphraim steps ahead of Miles. "I think what Miles is trying to say…is that it might be dangerous up ahead. This place might be abandoned, but we can't afford to take any risks."

Selim balls his fist and narrows his eyes. "But—"

Èphraim continues, "I'll go up ahead to unscramble the message. You two head back to the Estates. Remember. The Lunae Lux aren't looking for you. Toni confirmed it."

Miles grabs the envelope and hands it to Èphraim. "Well…you *are* the only one who can defend yourself."

"Wait!" Selim yells. "It takes fifteen days for messages to become readable in an unknown dimension, remember? You're gonna need food and stuff to survive."

Èphraim rests his hands behind his back. "Well…if you two are going back home, why don't you loop back and bring a few days' worth of food? I don't mind staying on the *poor man's diet* for a few weeks. No need to give me anything fancy."

The two turn to face the archway, and Èphraim grins with his teeth showing. "Be safe, guys."

Miles and Selim gleefully run ahead. "See ya in fifteen days, Èphraim!" Selim yells.

Éphraim waves and sees the two run back into the portal. Then, he walks farther down this crystal path. It takes him about ten hours to follow this long road to his destination. He arrives at a dead end with a circular crystal platform. In the center is a soft chair colored like a rainbow crystal, facing in his direction. His eyebrows rise at the sight.

"It's almost like this chair was set here for me…" He takes a seat on the chair and says, "it fits me perfectly…and it's comfortable. And it has a recliner… Stefano, how?"

Éphraim grabs his phone, then uses a *voice-to-text* message in their group chat, saying, "*I finally made it. Safe and sound.*" He has to text them using this feature because he can't read the letters he would need to text them in this dimension.

Éphraim knows the rules which Stefano taught him well. He can't leave this dimension. Not even once if he wants to decipher the code.

Even though he was humble with asking for nothing but simple food like dry cereal, ham sandwiches, and such, Miles and Selim collaborated and cooked him healthy and nutritious meals such as grilled salmon, vegetables, and lots of water. They packed an abundance of food for him, stuffing his bag full so that he could never run out. They even packed him a comfy sleeping bag so that he wouldn't need to sleep on the hard crystal ground.

He waits at this location patiently for fifteen days. During which, a few strange voices appear in his mind. He ignores them and continues enjoying his solitude.

And on the final day, he does nothing but stare at the code until he watches the letters from the riddle be guided to their rightful spots by tiny white strings of light. Éphraim smiles in amazement at the decoding message.

A Be Hemline Noel Shh Tot

Becomes:

Hell is beneath the moon.

"Beneath the moon?" Èphraim says, shaking with the paper still in hand. "Hell is beneath the moon…"

He sits on the floor and crosses his legs into a pretzel formation. Èphraim lays the paper in front of him and ponders in deep thought. He grabs his phone and calls Miles. The phone's signal, however, is terrible. He walks all the way to the crystal gate near Earth and then tries calling again.

"Hey! Did you figure it out?" Miles asks.

"Miles," Éphraim says in a hurry, "I need you to grab that brochure from the Earthshine Facility."

"Uh. Selim, you heard that, right? Can you get it? Thanks. He's getting it. Everything okay?"

"Yes! I just… I think I figured out *exactly* where not only Hell is, but Leon and Néol!"

"Oh! Selim! Hurry!"

Éphraim hears Selim shout that he's got the brochure. "Okay," Éphraim says, "read it for me. I'll explain after."

Here's what Miles reads out loud:

Nuova

Under cynosure for our grand elixir, the fleeting promise of our master lies in assemblage.

Crave home and salvation.

Under the moon we are under the man who sees all.

The demesne prowess keeps us brooded from our loved ones; they seek to only deceive us.

But the man in the mirror is my friend; to stare is fugacious. We must bring a forbearance to those who wish for help but fail to seek it.

Accept the cure, and under Luna, all will be cast to the sea.

On the horizon will be your dwelling.

The jaded demons will fade, denouement ends, and under the moon you will find truth in yourself.

☾.-ƎE-.☽

"And there're some weird symbols at the end..." Miles says. "So? What's it mean?"

"Hell...Hell is beneath the Facility."

"What?" Miles and Selim shout. "The Earthshine Facility doesn't have a basement."

"Ah. But the Heartshine Facility does..."

19

TWO SIDES
ONE STORY

Colorado /\ Aurorae

Month & Day: Unknown

(Two years ago)

Year: 2007

A Prison of The Mind

Time: Unrecalled

L eon's eyes were sealed shut. They call what he saw *inner darkness*. He has been here many times. This was back when Néol was not yet known to Leon, back when he was just *the devil*.

This was when Néol—or—Leon was made into Allie's offender. These were the days of when Leon was a Pawn.

Focus, Leon, an all too familiar voice demanded—hoping that Leon did not fall prey to the collage of—oh. He can hardly remember. The voice in his mind was trying to get him to shut his eyes and escape the cries of madness from the three television screens ahead of him.

A bead of sweat rolled past Leon's cheek and rolled down his neck. He wanted to wipe it away like he wished to wipe his dried tears, but alas—his hands—wrists were restrained to his chair. Leon tilted his head to the side— a stream of drool slid down his chin and neck.

He jumped awake and caught himself in front of the three twisted TV screens that glared at him. Leon recalled that none of the three were angled evenly. These TVs hung crookedly on the wall. One of the screens had a series of cracks from the center—resembling an almost spiral-like spider web.

All three screens switched on. A face—THE face of the founder of Leon and so many others' misery appeared onto the screens. Or at least. Just his head? Leon's weary eyes locked onto Festano's as his did the same. He forgot that this was nothing more than a visual sequence.

C'mon, The Voice in Leon's mind said. *Ignore what they're saying to you.*

Leon tilted his head to the side. He almost fell asleep again.

"Huh," Leon drunkenly uttered.

One screen played a bunch of strange things that were narrated by a weird female robotic-like voice. The face of Festano bounced all over the screen in a strange psychedelic manner. It was almost as if someone copied his face and sloppily pasted it all over the screen.

One monitor said, "This message being played is being registered in your subconscious mind… Every time you hear his voice. Every time you breathe. Think. Feel. Hear. Fear… Every time you look into the mirror. Your mind. Will. Trigger these thoughts. The man in the mirror is your. FRIEND. SAY IT. Say the words for me, Pawn."

If you repeat anything that this voice says, you'll lose your mind! The Voice in Leon's mind shouted.

"The man…" Leon muttered, "…in…the…mirror…"

Suddenly on another monitor, copies of the Lunae Lux's sigil are shown along with many other bizarre things. The robotic voice continued, "We are playing a message… Absorb all of this… Your subconscious mind will trigger…the unconscious mind…absorb our message. Absorb our message. Ab—absorb. You. You. You know these words. Repeat—repeat after us. Accept the cure, and under Luna—under Luna—under Luna—all will be cast to the sea. On the horizon—" This hypnotic trance is ceased by a screaming male voice in his mind.

The Voice shouted, *You idiot! NO! Don't say anything else!*

Two Lunae Lux soldiers appeared on another screen. One male, one female. They danced in front of a bunch of floating cartoon-like suns and moons with irritated faces. These celestial beings had hatred written on their faces. Yet, regardless of the anger on the angry suns' and moons' faces, they started to dance with the two Lunae Lux soldiers.

It made no sense to Leon. Why would such ugly and angry creatures dance like this? The guards swung their arms, their hips, all that one could imagine. All that was missing was music. Normal music. Instead, all he heard were offbeat drums and a woman shouting random gibberish about a wallet and whom one should praise.

Leon started losing track of what chaos was in front of him until one soldier walked on his hands. He shook his head. "Right…yeah. The Voice in my head. He doesn't want me to listen. Wait. There is no voice. There is no voice! Right." Leon looks down at his restrained arms "How long have I been tied up like this? What day is it? When can I go back to my cell…Dr. Igor? Let me out! I'm ready to talk!" he lied as he glared at the red light in the top corner of the room. "Hey!" Leon shouted at what he thought was a camera. "Please let me out!"

There was a guard that watched Leon on his computer monitor. He pressed a button on his keyboard, and instantly the screen changed and showed him another patient who was watching the same disturbing things Leon just saw. This patient was an old man who nodded in and out of consciousness. His name was Scott.

The door behind this surveilling guard opened.

"You're relieved. Go on lunch," Thorne said to the guard that sat in the computer chair. "I'm going to be in here for a bit with the master."

The male soldier nodded. He stood up and moved the chair out of the way so that Thorne could look at the computer. Outside was Festano who had his arms crossed.

"Hurry now," Festano said to the male soldier who scurried away. Festano walked into the security footage room and said to Thorne, "You'd think these soldiers were playing pinball on these computers again with how slow he moved."

Thorne said nothing.

Festano stepped forward, pulled the chair to the front of the monitor, sat down, and said, "So, what did you call me here for?"

"The results of your labor, lord."

Thorne pressed a button on the keyboard to unmute the sound from the computer screen. The sound played and showed Scott sitting in the chair reciting the same poem that Leon nearly did.

Scott, the screaming man, cried out, "I admit it! I did it! I stole the medicine for my wife! I even robbed the bank that same day for her medical bills! She needs it! She needs it right now! I admit that I took it, okay?"

"Yes?" Festano looked at Thorne very angrily. "I'm very aware that our *Black Mirror* program can shatter the mind. I thought you brought me here to show me something new."

Thorne cleared his throat. "I did." Then he pressed a button which switched to show a different room. Now the footage showed Leon who was tied by his arms and was shouting at the camera.

"PLEASE!" Leon yelled. "Let me out! I didn't molest her! I didn't molest Allie! I wasn't there that day! Please!"

Festano gritted his teeth and shot up from his seat. "What are you showing me here? A hole in the system? How does he still not believe he did it?"

Thorne paused the footage. "He's been a part of the program for about two months now. I thought you'd be happy. You wanted me to show you a rebellious patient if we found one. And he's the first to ever say anything of the sort..."

"Nonsense! Why would I ever ask for that!" Festano said, as he stormed for the doorway. "Why on Heart would I do that, Thorne? Hm? Answer me!"

"I'm…not sure… But I have Faviané as a witness to when you—"

"—I would not finish that sentence."

"My apologies...sir."

"On the day of his switch, I want that one sent to Hell. Whoever that boy was, you drag him there by his ankles if you must. Once one resists, then they *all* resist! They all must conform to this *reality*. Am I understood, Thorne?"

"Yes. I will take care of that right away, Lord Festano."

And to those words, the old man held his head and cried out in pain. Festano fell to his knees. Thorne ran to him and laid him on his back.

"Lord Festano!"

"Ow…What was that?" the old man said and looked around the room in confusion.

"Sir?"

"Thorne? Why, if it isn't *Alvin Thorne!*" Festano cried out as he reached his arms out to hug the large man that held him up.

"Sir?..." Thorne asked in confusion as he helped Festano back to his feet.

The old man released him, backed away, and dusted himself off.

"Right, my apologies," Festano said, messing his hair up.

"So, what were we up to?" Festano asked. "Are we in the Earthshine Facility?"

"Yes… We were…looking at the computer. I called you to show you our first rebellious patient, and then you were angry. You told me to drag him to Hell, which I was about arrange."

The old man's eyes widened. "I…said that? Quick. Show me what you just showed me."

Thorne hesitantly but obediently led his master back to the computer to show him the same thing as before: Leon strapped to his chair by his arms and legs. And still he cried out.

"PLEASE!" Leon shouted. "I didn't…do it…I didn't hurt her…"

However, this time Festano had a wide smile on his face.

"Splendid!" Festano shouted.

"What?"

"And you said I told you to take him to Hell? I forbid it. And if I ever say such a thing again…ignore me. It's just my temper."

"…Alright…"

"Thorne," Festano said and looked up at the tall masked man. "We've had countless patients fall for our lies. Why do you think our Black Mirror program has succeeded up until now?"

"Our scientists concluded that the Black Mirror program has a high success rate with patients who have OCDs or phobias. As for regular Pawns like Leon who are *told* they have a disorder, their minds normally cave after just a few hours. They get so tired of the torture that they admit they have a disorder. And then, naturally, they admit to whatever crime we fabricated."

The old man's eyes were filled with life. Tears rose in them as he listened.

"Sir?"

"This boy…his reflection is Néol Yelltnarg…isn't it?"

"That is correct."

"It's just as I wanted. Néol enrolled *because* he was envious. And Leon is *rebelling*. They are just what we needed."

"It took a while to find, too," Thorne added, now with more pep in his deep voice. "We broke many patients in this search. So, I took your advice with not prying *too* deeply. After all, they're already tiny shells of what they once were."

Festano didn't say a word. He just stood and stared at the monitor.

Thorne filled the silence and said, "From my observation, Lord Festano, I've noticed that young children and adults are the *most* fragile. The psyche of a child is young and underdeveloped. They bear so little within them to resist such torture. As for the adults. They have *too much that* they've earned and endured in life to lose. The middle ground, as you see in front of you, is what bore the best results. Leon Granttley is a teenager within that perfect middle ground. He's been accused of something involving his identity, and best of all, he resists the idea of him touching that girl. Thus, making him the perfect candidate for you."

"You've done well, Thorne. Remember what I said. You will *not* send him to Hell. And in the future when he becomes a Knight, I declare it an official order that we never send him there. The most we are to do is imprison him in *The World Betwixt*. Am I understood?"

"Yes, Lord Festano. I will take care of it."

☾　　　☾　　　☾

From the moment Leon, Néol, and Stefano were blindfolded at Ciler Graveyard, their journey going forward has been a literal blur. Or rather, a literal blot.

From what their feet can feel, Leon, Néol, and Stefano are walked across a large bridge, up a flight of stairs, and past a gigantic gate which nearly deafens their eardrums once it slams, sending vibrations throughout their bodies.

After this, Ammé, their now demoted escort, leads them into an elevator which goes at least sixty floors beneath ground. It is here that these three use the sounds of the echoing groans, wails, and cries from all around to tell them one thing:

They are in prison.

This is confirmed by the sounds of the other prisoners' chains and the frequent slamming and opening of cell doors. Did they finally arrive in Hell? Intense fumes rule the air. But before the three can focus or identify the scents, Stefano is shoved to another guard who takes him elsewhere.

Leon and Néol are brought into a cell where they both strike their heads upon walking in. Ammé, the grunt-now-trainee says, "Forgot to say…watch your heads. This cell division has smaller ceilings."

Are you kidding me? Leon thinks. *So, we have to crouch while being in here?*

Looks like it, Néol replies.

Leon holds in all the anger that he can as the cell door shuts. "Wait!" Leon cries out. "Can we at least get our blindfolds removed? Or our handcuffs?"

"No," the female soldier says, slamming the cell door shut as the two reflections hear her footsteps trail away.

"NO!" Leon cries out, following the sound of her footsteps. He grabs hold of the cell bars. "Where are we going after this? AMMÉ!" he shouts again, but sadly, nothing. This cramped cell is their new home.

Every prisoner, including the newcomers Leon and Néol, wishes that they lost their sense of smell. The putrid scent of urine, vomit, and feces pervades the air. The smells of coppery blood, rotting cheese, and sulfur is strong here. It is as if each of the rancid scents is competing to see which can smell the worst.

Within no more than what feels like five minutes, their nostrils burn. They get a headache which they want to pass out from. They stretch their hands out to wander around like the blind boys they are to see how much room they can work with. Sadly for them, not much at all. To them, it feels like this cell is the size of a private bathroom with just a few inches added to it. And what's more, they must navigate through this tiny space, blindfolded and handcuffed. They find one toilet in the corner of the cell. The *only* benefit of their blindfolds is that they don't have to watch each other perform their *duties*.

Leon spends the first of these long hours pacing around. Then randomly humming songs to himself. On occasion, when the wailing prisoners around him are quiet, he rests.

Néol on the other hand spends a few of these days working out with simple push-ups and sit-ups. This doesn't last for long. With each workout he loses more and more energy. And sadly, either the Lunae Lux Wardens forget to bring food or just do not care to. That being the case, the two reflections start feeling more and more hungry. They and the other prisoners around cry out for food, but to their dismay, no one comes. Néol starts becoming paler, sweating even. And spends most of this time huddled in the corner trying to sleep when he can.

What feels like a week passes, and suddenly, something comes sliding underneath the cell door.

"Food—" Leon cries out, his hunger-headache pounding.

"I—I can smell that from h-here," Néol says, shivering. "I hate to d-disappoint you, but that ain't f-food."

Leon lifts the musty styrofoam tray with holes in it and feels some small *things* crawl on him. He throws the tray at the revolting feeling and cries out, now sensing something in his sleeves. Did the *rice* from Oren's kitchen follow him?

He shouts in anger, slamming himself against the wall as he hopes this will squish *whatever* crawled inside his sleeve.

"T-told you," Néol says.

Frustrated, Leon takes a seat at the corner of the wall, hiding and choking back tears. The two reflections drift in and out of consciousness for what feels like a week more. No visitors. No guards. The two hardly even talk. They don't have the energy to. The two reflections at first refused to lie flat on the ground because of its stickiness and its smell. But their pride breaks quickly as they can no longer sleep with their backs facing the wall.

What feels like a few more weeks pass.

Desperate for food, Leon feels around him for the first and only tray of food he and Néol received. Unlike before, *it* feels fuzzy…*it* feels like it was once bread. He sniffs it. He takes a small bite and swallows—only to throw up seconds later. Néol cringes at the sound of splashing and the smell to follow.

"Fungus…ugh…" Leon mutters "Why…"

"F—f—figures…" Néol replies bitterly, now fighting off a few shivers.

"What's wrong with you? It's not cold?"

"N—n-n-othing."

I hate these damn nicotine withdrawals, Néol growls in thought. And Leon raises his eyebrows to this leaked information from Néol.

Leon leans beside the wall once more and says, "No bed. No blankets…no nothing. I…really did have it good on Heart. I had it so good… I had it so good, and I didn't even know it." He shuts his eyes, sobbing a bit, thinking of how he will never see his family, friends, or even Ellia again. He wishes he could start his stay all over at the Heartshine Facility. Or maybe even the moment Miles lectured him for his reckless behavior.

Néol says and thinks nothing to Leon's thoughts of regret. He shuts his eyes, as does Leon, and the two fall asleep.

Leon opens his eyes, and suddenly he can see.

"*Where am I?*" Leon asks aloud, his voice echoing. He looks beneath him and sees lush grass. He looks to his right side and sees a driveway.

"*I know this spot.*" He turns around and sees the cream-colored siding of a house. Then he looks up and sees a young boy falling out of a window, face first.

"*That's me!*" Leon shouts, jumping away from the young boy who, to his relief, lands on his stomach.

In the blink of an eye, everything flashes white. Leon can see nothing but whiteness. The bright white light fades.

Now he's sitting on a chair in a therapist's office. He sees Stefano sit down behind the desk. But now, Leon is a young boy. He looks at his arms, hands, and legs which are much smaller.

"*What's…happening to me?*" Leon asks aloud but in his old childlike voice.

Stefano takes a bite from his vanilla frosted doughnut and asks, "Leon, would you say you regret having a voice in your mind?"

With no control over his new younger body, Leon shouts, "*Yes! He's mean to me!*"

Suddenly, Leon awakens.

All he sees is darkness. It must be because of his blindfold. He shakes his head, saying aloud, "I was dreaming…"

Another few days pass by.

"I never even got to tell them goodbye…" Leon mutters, suddenly cackling to himself. "Even when I told them everything—they mocked me…"

"T-this a—again?" Néol utters, shivering.

"I can't stop. Thinking about it. I have nothing else to think about. There's nothing else to do in here…"

Néol's reply is him shutting his eyes. Leon yawns and shuts his eyes as well. The two reflections again fall deep into slumber.

Leon opens his eyes again to now see himself in a blue hoodie approaching a ranch house—a one story home. However, this time he is not in the body of his younger self. Instead, he is actually watching his younger self stand in front of this mysterious home.

"Allie's...house? Why am I...here?" Leon asks aloud as he watches the younger him knock on the door to this place. He sees an old woman wearing green suddenly open the door.

"Huh?" Leon says aloud. *"Allie's...grandmother?"*

He cannot hear what the younger him is saying in this *memory*. Whatever he says makes the grandmother walk away with a smile on her face.

Suddenly, Allie comes to the door. This memory must have taken place two years ago when he was fifteen years old. Leon knows this for sure since there is no memory of him and Allie ever having a full conversation without screams and shouts at one another. Not after what *he* did to her... But here, Young Leon walks in the house after her.

"That was weird..." Leon says to himself, looking at his cuff-less hand. *"Why don't I remember this?"* Leon looks up and sees streaks of red on a pitch-black sky.

"Where is this? Am I on Heart? Is this real?"

Leon looks all around him to where he expects to see houses and a road. But strangely enough, there is nothing in these other areas but darkness accented by grey fog. The only thing Leon is allowed to see is this ranch home. Creeped out, Leon looks down at himself. He sees that he is wearing black ripped jeans. He finds a chain on the side of these jeans. He looks at his arms and sees a black overcoat over his...red hoodie?

"Why am I wearing Néol's clothes?"

He touches his itching ears, feeling studded earrings. He looks at his rough hands. He reaches beneath his red hood to find Néol's more jagged amulet. Then...he nervously rubs beneath his chin to find a scar.

"Why am I in his body?" *h*e blares, his voice echoing throughout this empty realm.

SEE NÉOL'S AMULET

Finally, the door to this one-story house opens and the younger Leon walks out. He waves goodbye to Allie. Young Leon tries to give her a hug, but it looks like she rejects him, while smirking.

"I'm so confused…" Leon says, watching his younger self walk away toward the darkness. And now—the world around him shifts. In the blink of an eye, everything turns to darkness.

"Hello?" Leon cries out, his voice echoing even more in the black abyss.

A bright flash shows, and suddenly—Leon is in front of his own home. Not Néol's home on Heart, but his own on Earth. But it is not complete. He looks up at the sky to see this same darkness with gray fog running around. Hints of scarlet appear in the sky. A bright moon also appears in the sky from thin air. Streaks of blue appear—making a stunning mixture of blue and red. The moon is so bright that it could have replaced the sun.

Leon looks at his arms and sees now that he is wearing his own clothes. His blue hoodie. His black hole-less jeans. No earrings. No scar. He is back in his normal body. He watches as this younger version of Néol is knocking on the front door of his house on Earth.

"Néol?" Leon shouts out loud, covering his mouth. But this younger Néol does not seem phased. In fact, even though Leon practically screamed his reflection's name, Néol appears to not care—or perhaps, he does not know that Leon is here.

Leon tilts his head curiously. He swallows and walks toward Néol. Still. Néol does not care for the sound of his reflection's footsteps. Néol leans for the doorknob, twists, and steps through. Leon grits his teeth and tries to grab Néol's arm but sifts right through. Leon can't believe his eyes.

"*I couldn't touch him... What is this?...*" Leon asks, looking at his hands. Suddenly the wind around him starts to hiss and whoosh. Leon looks around to see the sky shifting—like a time-lapse film showing the day as it swiftly turns to evening.

Leon tries opening his own front door, but sadly, even though he can see the doorknob in front of him, he cannot grab it. The only solid thing around him, is the ground. He shakes his head, walking back out onto his driveway. He takes a seat on the black pavement.

Leon says, "*Everything that ever went wrong with my life all came from that one day with Allie. If I could go back and change everything—*" Suddenly a shadow approaches Leon. He looks up to see the mysterious figure in front of him.

"*Allie?*" Leon blurts, rolling onto his back. But she, too, is unfazed. She walks through him to his front door with her camera in hand.

"*Wait,*" Leon says, looking at a red car in his driveway, "*I remember this car...this was the car that Dad left home to trade in that day. He traded it in for that white van. I think he brought Mom and my sister with him to pick it up... And then I remember a tow truck coming for this red car later on. Where was I then? I told everyone I was at the facility...but was that true?*"

Allie opens the door and Leon takes his only chance to get into his own home and follows her inside.

"Happy birthday, Leon," Allie says to the boy wearing red in front of her.

"*Okay. So that's Néol,*" Leon says. "*Now I'm really confused...where was I on this day? Why don't I remember anything?*"

Allie plays with her hair and says, "I'm surprised you don't want to spend your birthday with your family."

The boy in red smirks and says in his younger voice, "Well, it's like I told you. I wanted to tell you what I felt…"

"Right…" Allie says, looking away. "Leon. Can we sit somewhere and talk?"

Pretending to be Leon, Néol nods. He leads her to the living room, and Leon follows.

Suddenly—Leon awakens to darkness. He cannot see, but he feels a hand on his shoulder. He's back in the smelly and cramped prison cell.

"W-what are you doing?" Néol asks, shaking Leon whose back is against the cell wall.

"Sleeping," Leon says. "And you?" Leon moves his legs around and accidentally kicks Néol's. "Sorry—wh—why are you standing right in front of me?"

"I want to know w-what you're doing."

"I just said. I was sleeping. I know you can't see that my eyes were shut, but I was."

"Stay out of my mind." And with those cold words, Néol trots back to his corner of the cell.

"What…are you talking about?" Leon asks out loud. "Stay out of your head? I'm not in your—" His eyes gape. Leon wasn't just dreaming. He wasn't reading Néol's mind. *He was watching Néol's past.* And by no control of his own, either.

Is hunger, the lack of sleep, the headaches, and the lack of nicotine making Néol malfunction to the point to where he's sharing even *dreams* with Leon? Seeing how guarded Néol regularly is, Leon knows that without these rare circumstances, he will never dive this deeply into Néol's mind ever again.

Without a single word or thought, Leon shuts his eyes again—praying that he can resume *exactly* where he left off in that strange nightmare that he would call, Néol's memory.

But sadly, Leon arrives in a different memory. In this flashback, he is sleeping in bed. He is again younger here but even younger than how he saw himself earlier. He must have been at least eight years old. He can tell by the way his room is organized. The only thing he had at this point in his life was a dresser. There were no posters on his wall. It was a simpler time. Leon watches as his past self sits forward in bed, flares his nostrils, and asks, "What's that smell?"

Leon and his younger self hear a cat's yowl, followed by miniature meows belonging to kittens.

The Present Leon's eyes start to sting. "*I remember this…this is when China gave birth to China Jr. and Raven…*" A tear rolls down Present Leon's cheek.

Past Leon shouts, "Mommy! Daddy! Two kittens!" The younger Leon cries out again, "Two kittens! China's a mommy!"

"*Why am I watching this now, though?*" Present Leon asks, watching his younger self run out the bedroom and straight to his parents' room.

"*Ha. I remember this. Dad gave me a laundry basket for the two kittens. We had to run all the way to the basement for it.*"

Present Leon watches the door slowly crack open. He is shocked to see a boy wearing a red t-shirt creep into the room on his tiptoes.

"*You…*" Present Leon mutters, watching as the young boy in red scoops the wet black kitten into his hands and runs straight out of the room. A few seconds later, Leon and his father come running in with a laundry basket.

"Where did the black cat go?" Young Leon asks in a sad voice, looking all over the cat treehouse.

"Maybe you just imagined it, Leon," Past Nero says. "It wouldn't be the first time."

After the memory, Leon awakens in the cell again, now with tears streaming down under his blindfold. Leon thinks, *That cat back at my place... If that was Raven, then how much did Néol take from me? But...he was a kid...he barely had a family...can I blame him? No! I'm not giving him any sympathy until I see what he did to Allie for myself! If I see no look of remorse—no hesitation—I will never trust him! Never!*

Across from Leon, Néol is snoring loudly. Leon clenches his jaw. He takes a long shaky breath and shuts his eyes so that he can enter the same memory that Néol interrupted earlier.

Leon opens his eyes this time but now boldly as he stands in front of his yard on Planet Earth. The front door is wide open just like how Allie left it. He charges inside to see Allie say *exactly* what she said earlier.

"Right..." Allie says, looking away. "Leon. Can we sit somewhere and talk?"

Younger Néol nods, as he pretends to be Leon. He leads her to the living room, and this time, Leon follows.

"*Mom and Dad aren't home,*" Leon says out loud, "*and clearly, I wasn't with them either. Otherwise, they would've been able to help me with my alibi. How did Néol get me out of the house?*"

Leon stands and watches as Néol and Allie sit on the living room sofa. Next to them are two glasses with fizzing water. The fizziness in the glass closest to Néol looks calmer.

The younger Néol smirks. "But first, I want to celebrate with these glasses of sparkling water."

Allie giggles. "Aw. You wanna be a grown up so badly that you brought us mock champagne."

"Something like that," Néol says, turning away.

Leon grits his teeth. *"Is that how you drugged her? You bastard!"* Leon shouts. *"ALLIE! Don't!"*

"Cheers," Néol says before they both finish their glasses and set them back on the center table.

"So," Allie says. "What was it you wanted to tell me?"

"I like you a lot, Allie," Néol says.

Leon is shaking with rage as he watches lie after lie pour from Néol's mouth.

"I know you do," Allie says. "Jason and the others told me. I'm glad I got to hear it from you. But Leon, aren't you worried?"

"About?" Néol replies.

"You have another voice in your mind. You don't have control over it, yet—what if it makes you do something you regret?"

Past Néol's smile cracks from his mouth. He tries to hide it as quickly as possible. Allie sees this.

"Something I regret? Never. That's why I communicate with him. I'll be stronger than I ever was... And I'd like you to be a part of that journey."

Allie smiles to this…but…her hands start to shake, more than Leon's as he watches this.

"Allie?" Leon cries out as Allie's eyes start to lose focus. Her eyes flutter like they want to shut.

Allie blurts, "Where's the bathroom again—"

"—Once you leave the living room, make two rights," Néol says quickly.

"Thanks!" Allie says, almost tripping over her two feet as she runs for the bathroom. Leon stares at Néol in disbelief, gazes at the empty glasses, then runs after Allie to the bathroom. Leon stands from afar as Néol follows as well.

Allie shuts the bathroom door behind her. "What's…happening…to…me…?" Allie asks, barely holding herself up with her arms as she stares at herself in the mirror. "Leon?" she cries out. "Was there something in that water? Maybe…" She retches. "Do you guys have a—" she hiccups, "— a bad water filter?"

Néol pushes open the bathroom door. "No. But I'll help you upstairs."

"*No, Néol…*" Leon says aloud. "*Please don't.*"

"What?" Allie asks as Néol catches her by her two lifeless arms. Her entire body follows in losing control as Néol lifts her up the stairs. Leon rushes through and past them both up the stairs.

"*Where is he taking her? Oh no! To my room! Because that's where he—no, no, no…*"

"L—Leon…" Allie whimpers as Néol continues up the carpeted stairs. Leon looks at Néol's face and is shocked to see a blank expression. The top half of Néol's face is completely covered in darkness. Leon can't see what his eyes should reveal. But he *does* watch as Néol lifts Allie into his bedroom.

"*I can't watch this…*" Leon says, falling to his knees. "*I can't watch what you're gonna do to her…*" He covers his eyes.

"*Oh, no, no,*" Present Néol says, grabbing Leon by his blue hood and bringing him up to his feet. "*You come digging into* my *memories, you're gonna watch.*"

"*You want me to watch you molest her?*" Leon shouts back. "*What is wrong with you!*"

Néol releases Leon's hood and leans against the wall. "*You made it this far. You might as well.*"

"*Don't be surprised if I kill us both in trying to get revenge on you.*"

Néol smirks, pointing to the younger Néol who is frozen in place with Allie in his arms. In a matter of seconds, the memory takes life and motion once more. And now Young Néol starts walking toward Leon's bed. Tears roll down Allie's cheeks as she stares up at Néol while he sets her on top of the bed.

"Leon…whatever you're about to do…" Allie pleads, "don't…" She shuts her eyes after these words.

The younger Néol walks out of the room and runs down the stairs. Present Leon tries to follow him, but the Present Néol grabs Leon's arm and says, "*He's coming back.*"

"*Huh?*"

"*You think I'd know, wouldn't you?*" Néol says with a smirk. "*This is* my *memory after all.*"

Just like the Present Néol said, Past Néol (the fifteen-year-old version of him) runs upstairs with a high-tech camera in hand. Not just any camera—this is Allie's personal camera which she uses for her hobbies. The one she promised to preserve all her memories with. The good and bad.

Past Néol sets the camera on the carpeted floor. Then, he grabs a red lighter from his pocket, starts the flame, and holds his right hand over the ember.

"*What the… Why do that?*" Leon asks Present Néol who says nothing in return.

Now, Past Néol's hand is red and burning. He grabs Allie's neck.

"*No!*" Leon cries out, trying to stretch forward, but now his body is frozen.

Present Néol says, "*Sometimes, Leon, you need to learn to just watch and see what happens before you react.*"

"*I'm doing what I would've done!*" Leon shouts angrily, now not being able to do anything at all.

"*My memory. My rules,*" Present Néol says.

Past Néol ignites the flame and holds his hands to the fire to do the same as earlier. This time, though, he doesn't grab her neck. Instead, he reaches for her arms. Her legs. Her wrists.

"*What?*" Leon says, stupefied.

Present Néol grins as Past Néol pulls her shirt upward...but stops once he sees her bellybutton. This time, Past Néol grunts as this flame burns his hands once more. He leaves a handprint on her stomach. This one brighter and redder than the others. Finally, he unzips her pants. And to this, Leon does the only thing he can do and shuts his eyes. His eyes open to the several flashes that come from Allie's camera.

"There," Past Néol says. "You've got all the proof you need to say he molested you."

"*What?*" Leon says, his body now free to look toward Present Néol, as suddenly the environment starts to quake. The floor starts to form cracks. The ceiling. Everything starts to crack, and white light pokes through—covering all.

Leon opens his eyes to the same blackness of his blindfold. But he knows he's awake, now. He can smell the same putrid environment from before—the dank smells, the cold and sticky ground... But, what he didn't have before was this *revelation*.

"Néol, what did I just see?"

"...I met with Allie on June eleventh, 2007, as you saw in my memory. The Heartshine Facility scheduled me with my first task as a *Pupa*."

"Hold on," Leon says. "If we're six months apart—then this really did happen on my birthday!"

"Indeed. And it was also *my* birthday."

"I wasn't even a Pawn yet. And that part of the dream where I was watching myself visit her grandmother... What was that?"

"That was *me* watching you, years ago. I saw what you wanted and intercepted it ahead of time. Just like when I took *Shadow*."

Leon grits his teeth. "We'll get back to *Raven*, later. Back to Allie. Where was I that day?"

"They drugged you at the facility. Wiped your memory clean. That's truly why you don't remember anything."

"That's the part that never made any sense to me," Leon says. "I wasn't a Pawn, yet the only thing I remembered about that day was *being* at the facility. So that's what happened. They brought me there. Drugged me—"

"—And then had me take over."

"But I don't understand...you didn't even molest her! You just—you burned your hands and grabbed her at random spots!" Leon gasps. "At every spot that the police saw in those photos! You took those? No wonder! I kept asking how she could take them if she was asleep!"

"Festano wanted it to be done. But the way I saw it...I just needed Allie to *think* she was molested. That way she'd blame you. And I knew how society would treat you afterwards."

Leon starts fuming with rage.

Néol adds, "Festano needed you people from Earth to be blamed with something irredeemable. And DID was the easiest to bring to the world's attention. And that all started from you blaming the *devil in your head* after jumping out the window. That's what made people watch you more."

Leon doesn't say a word.

"And then when Allie came to, she had all the proof she needed to think that you sexually assaulted her."

"And every time people asked me about her—I'd say I didn't do it!" Leon says.

"And that's what we needed you to say. That was the most common phrase said by anyone with your disorder. As you know, people like you wouldn't own up to something like that. And who would be best to cure the said disorder?"

"The Earthshine Facility... It was you all along...those are the only words going around in my mind right now. I read your reports from the Heartshine Facility. Why did you beat all those people up? Why do all these bad things to people and then not do something worse with Allie? It makes no sense!"

Néol smirks. "Why didn't I molest Allie, you ask?"

"Yes!"

"Because I *wanted* to hurt all those people."

"Because you wanted to..." Tears leak underneath Leon's blindfold. "Néol...who are you? How am I supposed to trust you? You're so unpredictable..."

"I never asked you to trust me. And I'm not gonna ask you to, either."

"...Toni...Miles...and all the other Neo Knights...they all fell for this same type of lie...they all believe they *really* have mental disorders..."

"Indeed, Leon. And they've long adjusted to their flaws and found many ways of coping. Because those labels are what validate them, removing it would remove a huge chunk of who they are. And *you*, Leon, are the exception."

"Why me?"

"You're certainly no chosen one," Néol chuckles, "really and truly—the more I thought about you going to Hell, and even becoming a *Sitio*, the more I realized I'd be at risk of losing my own life. So, during your days of being a Pawn, I interfered with their hypnosis process."

"You what?"

CRASH. BOOM.

The entire building starts to shake very roughly. The rumbling goes on for at least fifteen seconds. An alarm starts to go off. Leon, Néol, and all the rest of the prisoners lose their balance against this quake.

"*Attention Lunae Lux staff—all feet on deck. Supporting Tower A has been breached and has crashed into the main building. There is an intruder on the premises. I repeat…*"

"Something crashed into us?" Leon asks, trying to massage his wrists. Leon and Néol then hear their cell doors swing open.

"You two!" a male soldier blares. "Outside! You're all being moved!"

"We can't see, remember?" Néol replies.

"Smartass—I oughta—"

Suddenly, a deep and all too familiar voice says, "Negative. These two are to come with me."

That sounds like Thorne, Néol thinks.

Oh no, Leon thinks in response.

"Up and at 'em, you two," Thorne says. "Yes, walk your way over here, even with your blindfolds. I don't care if you can't see. Make your way to me, and I'll guide you to Festano."

SEE THORNE

"To Festano?" Leon says with fear.

"HURRY UP!"

Leon and Néol both swiftly stand and rush over to Thorne who says, "You two lost a lot of weight. I take it the food was appetizing."

Leon and Néol say nothing to this. From what they can hear now that they're outside of the cells, there is a lot of chaos. They can hear a lot of the prisoners crying and scrambling around. But from what it sounds like, only Leon and Néol are outside of their cells.

"WE HEARD WHAT YOU SAID, THORNE! LET US OUT TOO!" one prisoner cries.

"WHY THEM! WHAT ABOUT US!" another shouts.

Thorne shoves both reflections forward. "Keep walking. The elevator doors are already open. Walk inside and wait for me."

Leon and Néol blindly walk into the elevator. How long has it been since they've last been in here? Thorne steps inside, and his weight makes a huge difference. The three can feel the elevator shift a bit after he steps on. They hear him press a button, and the elevator rises for what feels like two hundred floors.

Thorne leans against the wall. "Festano wants to see you both... Why, I couldn't tell you. But I know better now than to question the good leader."

Leon shudders and thinks, *It's probably to send us to Hell. It's time for us to receive our punishment.*

They arrive at the desired floor, and Thorne pushes them forward out of the elevator. "Wait. I almost forgot," Thorne says, untying the blindfold around their eyes.

Bright purple and green lights blind both Leon and Néol whose eyes have not seen light in the longest time. Surprisingly, Thorne gives them a few minutes to let their eyes adjust. When Leon and Néol are finally able to see again, they see a humungous door with two colossal sun-shaped doorknobs in front of him. They both spin around rapidly, and the large doors open, revealing a purple mist that leaks out.

"Go on," Thorne says. "He's expecting you."

Leon swallows, looks at his reflection's bonier face, and the two of them walk toward the consuming purple fog.

20
TWO MINDS
ONE SERIES

☾　　☾　　☾

L eon and Néol pass the purple fog and arrive at a large oval office; probably larger than the president's office on Planet Earth. There are four bookshelves in the four corners of this expansive office. Leon notices a book title on a bookshelf close to him which says *How to Win and Manipulate Your Yriends*. Another books title says *38 Rules to Manipulate* and another book that says *Dolfa Tihler*. There are two large bird cages in two corners of the room. At the moment, only Festano can see what's inside of the cages.

"You were supposed to be sent to Hell." These are Festano's first words after gazing upon Leon's worried face.

"What?" Leon utters, remembering that Allure said that Néol specifically asked to *not* have him sent there.

"But sir," Thorne says, "two years ago, you told me *not* to send him there. And you also asked me to bring them here to speak with you just an hour ago."

"In the middle of a panic like this? Someone just infiltrated our castle! Thorne, YOU should be directing troops to find the perpetrator! Not escorting these two wretches to me!"

"Lord *Festano*—you asked me to bring them here."

The old man screams out loud and starts to hold his head. Leon, Néol, and Thorne watch in confusion as the man stands up from his chair, bumps into one large bird cage beside him, alerting a strange creature within. The creature on the left is as pale as the moon, the other is as dark as a sunspot. These are the same types of beings that Leon saw in the limo with Allure. But these are lengthier and perhaps more well fed than the others. They even have enormous ear gauges.

"Sir?" Thorne asks, rushing toward his master as Leon and Néol stand and stare in confusion.

Festano falls to his knees, screaming out loud, "*REYLT!* I LOVED YOU!" And then he collapses.

Thorne picks his master up and shakes him. Festano's eyes slowly open, and he says in a much lighter voice, "Alvin...where am I? Where is Reylt?"

"Reylt, sir? You're...you're in your office. I'm...I'm calling an elite nurse—"

"—No," Festano says as Thorne helps him back up to his feet. "I'm fine—Ah! And I see you've brought them here! Leon and Néol!"

Both reflections stare in confusion. They wonder why Festano is greeting them like a long-lost friend. The tempered old man takes a seat and ruffles his hair once more.

"Lord Festano," Thorne says, walking back behind Leon and Néol. "I'm going to have Stefano delivered to you. Perhaps his misery can fuel you."

"Good idea! It'll be good to see him again," the old man says enthusiastically. Leon and Néol raise their eyebrows to his comment.

Thorne makes a call on his radio while Festano does nothing but take turns staring at both Leon and Néol. The two reflections turn around to see Noire show up through the thick purple smog. Leon and Néol look behind them and see Stefano Giro who is wearing nothing but dirty blue scrubs with a Neo Knights symbol on it.

SCAN FOR NOIRE

"There ya go!" Noire says, dashing forward and putting his foot in front of Stefano, tripping him so he falls on the ground. Noire kicks him and leaves Stefano behind him. The old man grunts, wearily getting himself back up.

"No! Stay down!" Noire says, kicking Stefano in the ribs. Everyone hears a few bones crack.

"Festano," Leon blurts, "why do this? Why put everyone through all this pain?"

Festano grins, staring right into Leon's soul and says, "*One* would say I'm seeking...peace."

Noire snickers. "C'mon old man," he says, dragging Stefano closer to the desk by his arms. Noire rips the scrubs off of Stefano's body, leaving him practically naked and defenseless.

"Where's the peace in this?" Leon blurts as a shivering Néol thinks, *You're gonna get our punishment worsened.*

Festano clears his throat, but still his voice does not sound as deep and gruff as it did when Leon and Néol first entered the room. "I can truly tell you that there *is* no peace where you're looking, Leon." the old man says, frowning for some reason.

Suddenly, the man holds his head and screams out, startling Thorne, Noire, and everyone else in the room.

Leon ignores the man's shouts and asks, "What about those creatures in the back?"

"Oh," says Festano, but now in a gruff voice, turning around to both the pale and dark creatures. "My mind never stopped breeding them...so I did what my hands could and brought my thoughts to life..."

"Leon," Stefano croaks from below, "you're not going to get anything from Festano. I've reasoned this same thing with him for years. There's no getting through to him."

"What...are...you...doing... Stop this..." Festano growls out loud, holding his head again.

Leon, Thorne, Noire, Néol, and even Stefano look at Festano in confusion as he mumbles angrily to himself.

"Go back..." Festano says, shaking his head, his voice sounding stern. "I said, enough! This is *my* question to answer. Leon...before I have you brought to Hell, I will have you know this. These worlds are cursed. They rely on each other to exist. When one world suffers, the other thrives and vice versa. I for one detest that dynamic. Imagine something bad happening to you and *not* shaking your fists to the sky—cursing God or the devil. Or whatever it is you believe... What if the true essence of your misery comes from your reflection? What if you could blame everything that ever went wrong on one source? Would you not attempt to seize control of that scale? If you could obtain that balance? The ability to control your life? The worlds?"

Leon doesn't reply and Festano continues.

"It doesn't matter whether or not you see it. But what *I* want. Is *that* scale. I want to seize that scale and bring true freedom to everyone within Heart. To give my dying planet a chance and its people the ability to truly enjoy life…among…many other things… And so, Leon, when you ask— where's the *peace* in all this—you must subtract yourself from this equation. Because the truth is, there will never be peace for you. Not again. You've had *your* freedom. You've had your fun. Those stories ended with your reflection's unhappiness."

Happiness, Leon thinks. *I hope what you got here is just that, Néol.*

Will you shut up, already, Néol replies in thought while shuddering.

Festano continues, "That said, Thorne and Noire, take these three away to—"

Suddenly Faviané bursts through the purple fog. "Lord Festano!"

"Stop calling me that!" the old man cries out again, holding his head, swinging it back and forth as tears shine in his eyes. Again, everyone in the room watches in shock and confusion.

"Lord…Festano?" Faviané asks again, tilting her head.

"Y—yes. Sorry, what were you going to say?" he asks in a softer voice.

"I…I investigated the source of Tower A's collapse. Everyone was wrong. It *wasn't* because of my connections to the spirits. It was an actual infiltrator."

Noire chimes in, "But Ané, didn't they say there were random objects and stuff moving and flying around?"

"Yes, Noire. But I wasn't present in this world when the tower fell. I was dealing with the police on Earth with Allure. So that is ruled out."

Festano stands up and holds his chin.

Faviané continues, "Also…the *Sitios* on the main floor have been freed. They're roaming around as we speak."

"Faviané," Festano says gently, "are you positive that these spirits didn't run amok while you weren't here?"

"Yes, lord, I'm positive. If they move off my command, *I'm* directly affected…not the people or the environment. This is very deliberate. I don't know where these intruders are, but they're *certainly* here."

"Has the footage proven this?"

"Our cameras were destroyed."

Festano scratches his chin. "Hmph…AGH!" The old man cries out once more and holds his head, stumbling and knocking over a cup full of pens and pencils from his desk.

"Sir!" Thorne, Faviané, and Noire chorus in concerned tones.

"I'm fine! I'm fine!" Festano shouts in a gruff voice, then thinks, *This tower falling wouldn't happen to be your doing, would it, Stefano?*

No. I didn't call anyone here, Stefano replies.

Lies, Stefano. It must've been you. We're nowhere that people would guess about.

I didn't, I swear to you.

Well, good. Because regardless of who comes…you're staying with me…

I've had enough! a voice from within Festano's mind shouts. The sudden appearance of this *other* voice shocks even Stefano. ***Go back to where you came from!***

Festano cries out in pain once more. His fists are tightly balled. He straightens himself up. "As I was saying… Have these two brought back to their cells for now." Festano reaches atop the chair for his gray scarf, then calmly wraps it around his neck.

The boys tremble in front of him.

"Sir, what do we do with *him?*" asks Noire, the one in the bright red grinning mask, while staring at the barely conscious therapist lying on the floor.

"Are you sure this is how you want it?" Thorne asks his superior who is lighting the pipe that once sat on his desk. His dark green peacoat all buttoned, Festano glowers toward his masked subjects, Thorne and Noire. The words *Don't challenge my judgement* are smeared on his frowning face.

"R-right away, then," Noire blurts as he nudges Thorne who is paralyzed from confusion and fear. The two guards then dart off through the doorway, pressing toward the hazy amethyst mist.

Faviané turns her mask toward Néol. But something suddenly throws her into the wall, and the books in the shelves topple all around her. "Not me!" she blurts, while looking back toward Néol.

Suddenly, something causes Néol and the chair to flip over to the side. Néol wearily lifts himself upward then briefly massages his right wrist.

"You were nowhere near me…" Néol intones, then dusts himself off.

"Thank you," Faviané says with relief as she turns to Leon while backing away from the bookshelves. A book with its spine facing upward sits atop her boot. She reaches down to remove the book named *Finding Your Better Half* and then throws it onto Festano's desk. Faviané gazes at Leon who covers his face from her crescent mask.

Something throws Leon toward the left bookshelf. His handcuffed hands barely save him from the impact of the crash, but the force roughly drives him outside the doorway.

"What is this?" Leon cries.

Néol slowly focuses on the doorway to the fading sound of his other's voice. "Your guess is as good as mine."

Festano slowly inhales once he lights his pipe. "I'd catch up with him if I were you. He'll need you more than you'll know." Festano grins at Néol from the corner of his eye. Néol looks downward at Stefano who gradually nods in approval.

"Right," Néol simpers as he chases after Leon and Faviané who are farther ahead in the mist.

Leon turns to his side to see that nothing but the wind is forcing him out the foggy doorway. All he can do is feel the enigmatic wintry force roughly move him about like a doll. As Leon is pushed away from the emptying office, he can only wonder what he is leaving behind...

Festano's gigantic doors close from behind Leon and Néol. And Thorne is behind them both. "Well, well, well..." Thorne says, glaring ahead to the man with ashen hair standing in front of the elevator, pointing a uniquely colored spear in Thorne's direction. "It's the *Boy called God.* I never thought *you'd* come here."

"I'm not here for you," Éphraim says, looking at Leon and Néol who stare back in shock. Both boys see two Lunae Lux soldiers laid to rest behind Éphraim.

Thorne bends his knees and equips two spiked golden brass knuckles. "So, *you* must be the intruder. Where are the others you brought with you, then?"

"Oh. They're around here somewhere," Éphraim says, smirking. "They've *probably* found Hell by now."

Thorne growls. Leon and Néol are suddenly lifted off their feet and float toward Éphraim's side. Their handcuff links are snapped, falling to the ground. Relieved, they rub their wrists.

"You two," Éphraim says, "stand to the side. This is gonna get ugly."

"Thorne!" Faviané shouts on the radio clipped to his belt. *"We need your help gathering these sitios! There're too many out here! At least seventy!"*

Thorne grunts, "You're kidding me…"

Éphraim tightens his grip on his spear. "It looks like you have somewhere you need to be."

"Are you responsible for this?" Thorne asks.

"Perhaps."

"Mark my words. I will have your blood. And when I do—

"

"—THORNE!" Faviané blares on the radio.

"I'm coming, Ané!" Thorne shouts to the radio, running backwards to Festano's office, not taking his eyes off the three for a second until he vanishes through the purple smog.

The spear in Éphraim's hand slowly evaporates into thin air. Leon and Néol watch this weapon fade with curious looks. Éphraim lets out a sigh of relief and turns for the elevator behind him. "Are you two alright?"

"Are we alright?" Leon shouts. "I'm so happy you're here!"

Néol's response is a smirk. He lets out a few shivers.

Éphraim presses the circular button, opening the elevator doors, and before the three step inside—they find two armed Grunt soldiers with guns.

"Freeze!" the two Lunae Lux guards shout, guns pointing at Éphraim. They fire almost right on sight, and Éphraim's mind reflects these bullets, sending them straight back into the necks of these now deceased soldiers. They both fall to the ground, dropping their weapons.

"How did you—" Leon asks as Néol yanks him by his arm into the elevator.

"Thanks, Néol," Éphraim says. "We've got no time for questions." He then presses a circular button that Leon squints toward.

"Uh…" Leon utters, staring at the three hundred elevator buttons. "Why can't I read anything…are we not on Heart?

"Remind me to explain later. Like I said, we've got no time now. We've got to get out of here."

Suddenly, the three hear Noire's laughter through the elevator's speakers. Noire cackles, *"Thorne might've let you all go, but you ain't getting that lucky with me! You're dying here!"*

The sound of a cable snapping outside alerts the three of them.

"No, they didn't…" Éphraim mutters, as now the entire platform starts falling so swiftly that they're free-falling. The three of them bend their knees.

"Are we falling?" Leon cries out. Néol grits his teeth, enviously watching Éphraim to see what special next moves his powers will pull.

Éphraim looks up and all around him. He looks at the doors, and with his mind, pries the two doors open. Éphraim watches as they fall at least twenty—forty—fifty floors below.

"Step to the side, you two! But not too close to the wall!" Éphraim shouts.

The two follow his command. Éphraim stretches his arms out. Suddenly, the elevator's four walls protrude outward. The stretched outsides of the elevator's walls graze the environment around. But sadly, this only slightly slows the speed of their fall.

Éphraim lifts his hands upward to pop the elevator's roof out of place and tosses it to the side. Éphraim climbs to the top where the elevator roof was. Outside of this elevator, he sees cables moving up and down. They're the cables that belong to the elevators, enabling them to move. With his mind, he snaps their cords at a certain length and commands the long thick wires over to himself. The elevator farther away falls to the depths below. Éphraim hopes to himself that no one was in there.

Éphraim shouts, "I've got a rope! I'm gonna grab on, and then one of you grab onto my leg!"

Both reflections nod.

Éphraim grabs the thick wire, and Néol grabs Éphraim's leg, holding on tightly. Éphraim climbs up the rope a bit more, and Leon follows the pattern by grappling onto Néol's leg. Éphraim swings, with the two beneath him hanging on with all the little strength they have left.

"Alright," Éphraim says. "Now that we've lost momentum…we can get to a new floor. You two see that glowing entrance over there?"

The two reflections look up and over to an elevator doorway, one that a Lunae Lux employee *would* have entered after their safe elevator ride.

"I see it," Néol replies.

Leon cries out, slipping down from Néol's calf, down to his shoe, "Guys, I can't hang on… My arms are so weak…"

"C'mon, Leon, seriously?" Néol shouts. "You want Ellia to see you like this?"

"Hey! Don't you start! We're here because of you!"

"If you don't shut the hell up, I'm gonna kick my shoe off so you fall!"

"GUYS!" Éphraim shouts. "We don't have time for that! Do you want to get out or not?"

They're both silent.

"Settle it later," Éphraim adds. "Leon, you can let go of Néol's shoe. I'm going to lift you over to the doorway. Néol, you can go next."

"How are you doing this?" Leon asks.

"Doing *what*?" Éphraim chuckles.

Leon shakes his head. "So, I should let go?" Leon says, looking to the dark abyss beneath him.

"Yes."

Leon counts to three, and then all his fingers release Néol's shoe at once. He doesn't fall downward. Not at all. Éphraim kept his word. Leon is mystified as he floats all the way over to the glowing doorway.

"Wow…" Leon says in awe.

"Your turn, Néol," Éphraim says.

Néol is quicker to release Éphraim's leg than Leon. Néol is floated over to the doorway next to Leon who dismissively turns away. Éphraim, now being last, floats over to the doorway to meet them both.

Ahead of them is a hallway which they walk within. There is a series of large windows showing them a blue sky with clouds all around. Leon wonders where they are. Néol, on the other hand, does not.

The steel wall and the windows ahead of these three breaks off like cardboard and falls below into the blue abyss. Éphraim did this with just his mind. The cool wind from the outside whooshes their hair and clothes. The wintry weather chills Leon and Néol, and they shiver in place.

They each look down and see a dark skinny tower that is leaning into the even *bigger* tower that they're currently in. They have to be at least two hundred stories up. Perhaps even more. By looking at the blue clouds all around, one could assume they're in the sky.

"Éphraim…" Néol says. "Did you knock this tower down?"

Éphraim's reply is a smirk. "Alright, you two. We're going to slide down this tower. It's our quickest and safest escape."

"What?" Leon exclaims.

"Yes," Éphraim says firmly. "They took down the elevators. And the staircases are most certainly off limits. Don't worry. I'll carry you two like before. C'mon!"

Without another word, Éphraim jumps down the sloped tower and slides down as smoothly and swiftly as a bullet train. The sky suddenly flashes white, blinding the two reflections for a split second. Now the sky is completely red. The air is warmer, ceasing Leon's and Néol's shivers.

"Are we just supposed to jump down after him?" Leon asks, uncovering his eyes after being blinded from the white flash.

Néol shrugs when suddenly the two float into the air and are brought all the way over to Éphraim's sides.

"I was going to say, hang on…" Éphraim chuckles. "But that'd be pointless. So, just tell me if you see anything behind us!" Éphraim takes a long deep breath—and suddenly a gust of wind pushes Éphraim down swiftly—traveling at least seventy miles per hour, with Leon and Néol both floating behind him at a slightly slower speed.

How are we both floating behind him like this? Leon thinks.

Néol thinks, *It's like he thinks it and whatever he wants happens.*

And the two follow Éphraim, floating in the air behind him like gnats as the wind blows their hair, their cheeks, and clothing.

"The tower I knocked over is at least one hundred and fifty floors high!" Éphraim shouts, competing with the wind. "So we've got a bit to go!"

Leon and Néol take in the sights of the red sky around them. Now that they're farther down the smoking tower, they see a humungous castle held up by seven—formerly eight—tall towers with gold spears for roofs. They seem to look a lot like the spikes on Thorne's shoulders.

The three slide through plumes of black smoke. Éphraim sees a tall wave of green and scarlet fire ahead of them. He forms an X with his arms. Then he swiftly chops the air, putting his arms back to his sides. And just like that, the flames are extinguished. Leon and Néol weren't even given a chance to worry.

Leon and Néol look behind them, seeing the Gothic-styled main tower they came from. Out of all these other towers, it is the widest in girth and tallest in height. The top of this main spire is so high that it pierces through even the peach-colored clouds above. They slide farther down and see a colossal sun-shaped gateway. This entryway is even bigger than the one they saw leading to Festano's office. That must have been the door they passed before going to prison. The one that slammed so loudly that it almost deafened them.

Éphraim notices something scratch the ground by his feet.

"What was that?" Éphraim asks, slightly turning to the side.

"Éphraim!" Leon shouts, they're firing at us!"

Back at the main tower is Thorne looking through a window alongside soldiers who have guns aimed at Leon, Néol, and Éphraim.

"READY? WATER!" Thorne commands, and each of his soldiers fires storms of bullets toward Leon and Néol who cover their faces. But this storm of bullets stop right where they are.

Leon and Néol both lower their arms, staring at the bullets as they're suspended in midair. Éphraim lets out one big roar and these bullets are sent flying back to the barrels they came from. Insanely enough, this is all being done as they're sliding down the leaning tower.

The bullets shatter some of the windows of the main spire, fatally striking all the guards who fired toward the three. Thorne slams his fist on the wall. "This isn't good. Festano's gonna be angry. They know where we are. And I can't find these other intruders he mentioned… I need more men!"

Leon, Néol, and Éphraim can see a courtyard just ahead of them. They see some of those strange eyeless creatures from earlier lurking about. Leon and Néol look at Éphraim for assurance.

"Don't worry!" Éphraim says. "You both are in good hands. Now, brace yourself. I'm gonna jump and land on the courtyard ahead. Can you two handle a bit of running?"

"I'll try!" Leon says.

"You'd *better* try," Néol retorts. "And you better not let those things catch you, either."

Shut up! Leon shouts in thought.

Éphraim smirks and then takes one great leap, Leon and Néol following behind him as if they're attached by some invisible belt. Éphraim lands perfectly on the ground, gently setting Leon and Néol back to their feet.

"There's a bridge just ahead! You two run ahead of me!" Éphraim shouts, running backwards, not taking his sight off of the main tower for a second. Some of the creatures try chasing him. Without lifting a finger, Éphraim sends all seven of these creatures flying onto their backs. He runs forward, leaving them behind to catch up to Leon and Néol. Surprisingly, he doesn't see a single soldier.

Just like Éphraim said, there's a long crystal and stone bridge ahead of the trio. It stretches far off beyond where any of them, except Éphraim, can see. Leon and Néol start running as fast as they can go—Éphraim catches up to them and passes them. He gives them no time to look around or catch their breath as he escorts them out of this strange world by stepping through a gateway. This gateway looks exactly like the ones they would find in the Eleventh Dimension.

They run through one portal, then follow Éphraim as he charges through another. Suddenly, they're in a strange room with four mirrors. Éphraim allows them no time to see what's around. As far as he's concerned, the Lunae Lux could appear behind them at any second.

They rush through a hot and smelly hallway with many cells and windows. Leon and Néol follow Éphraim who charges into a circular room with a towering ladder. Éphraim climbs this as quickly as possible, still with Leon and Néol following behind him.

Once they arrive at the peak of this ladder, they arrive at the area that the three know as—The Heartshine Facility. Éphraim runs them outside into the facility's courtyard and toward a teal two-door sports car honking out in the front. Éphraim spots a couple of crows flying above, cawing and glaring at the vehicle. Within seconds, the crows all fall to the ground, circuits sparking from each of them. Black feathers are raining down, surrounding the teal vehicle. Panting, Éphraim's mind opens the two doors to this teal car, and the three squeeze inside.

"We did it…we made it…" Éphraim sighs in relief.

"Yeah, ya did!" shouts Selim in the driver's seat, starting the car as they speed off, tires squealing on the ground.

"I'm so glad…" Miles replies from the front seat. "I was worried we lost you." Miles looks back at both Leon and Néol, sad to see how much skinnier they are.

Leon and Néol let out a few pants. Miles chortles while Selim asks, "Uh. Why're *you two* panting? Éphraim looks like *he* did all the heavy liftin'."

Everyone but Néol shares a laugh, and Leon blurts, "Wait. Éphraim, didn't you say there were others in that world?"

Éphraim chortles, "Oh. My apologies. I was just bluffing. I figured saying that to Thorne would take their focus off of us."

Néol asks in shock, "You broke in there. All by yourself?"

"That's Éphraim for ya," Selim says. "Too modest for his own good. But he did. And he had us wait out here for you. Took no more than three hours."

"How did you even find us?" Leon asks.

"I'll explain…" Miles says in a low tone, then turns to look behind at Leon and Néol. "First…I want you both to know that we didn't want to abandon you. It wasn't a part of the plan. You see, I found out from Toni that there was an Amber alert for that orange car…and I panicked."

Selim chimes in, "We knew that Éphraim could break all of us out if we were caught. But we would still have to come back and work with other Neo Knights. We did the math and thought—it's better to have two fugitives instead of five."

Éphraim speaks, "And so we did everything we could. We studied this strange riddle that Stefano left behind—our only clue—and then…here we are."

Miles blurts, "But I promise you both, we were originally going to have Éphraim go into the graveyard to find you. But without a car to run away in, we knew we'd be in trouble."

"It's fine…" Leon says, looking out the window. "To be honest, I did think you forgot about us…and there just came a point where they stopped feeding us. I thought we were gonna die in there." Leon turns to Éphraim and says, "So, that loud crash," Leon says. "That…that was actually you?"

Éphraim doesn't say a word. His response is grabbing his teal pinwheel from his pocket. He uses his mind to play with the rotors.

Leon narrows his eyes. "Éphraim?"

Miles and Selim chuckle in response.

Miles thinks, *Éphraim always does this when people ask him about his powers.*

Selim replies in thought, *I know! It never gets old.*

Leon sighs. "So, you crashed the tower into the castle? And then you scaled it to find us? Hey, Éphraim! I'm talking to you!"

"I think he hears you, Leon," Néol says, chuckling.

398

Leon rolls his eyes. "Fine. Well. Thanks for knocking the tower over. I guess. And for saving us."

"You're absolutely welcome, Leon."

"Oh, now you talk? Alright then, I'll just ask—what are you?"

"Human. Like you," he says with a smile and shut eyes.

Leon falls back onto the seat. "Clearly you don't want to share the big secret behind your powers. But anyway, I mean it. Thanks for not forgetting about us."

Selim rolls down the window. "The only thing you should thank us for is giving you guys a place to shower! You stink!"

"Selim," Miles says, "I know they smell, but we don't want anyone to see us...that's why we got the windows tinted?"

"Ugh, fine," Selim says, bitterly rolling the windows back up.

"How long were we gone?" Leon asks.

Miles looks at Selim, then takes a breath and says, "You've been gone for a whole month. Today is *August 7th*."

Immediately, Leon panics. "Oh crap! What about my family? Ellia? Allie? My friends?"

Miles turns around and looks at Leon. "Your family's taken it pretty hard since you disappeared. Your father was about to head to the Earthshine Facility one day to start a storm. We had to flatten his tires so he wouldn't go. He replaced the tires himself and tried driving. So Éphraim literally had your dad's car keys float away from him to creep him out of going."

"It was too funny!" Selim chimes in. "He thought it was a bad omen."

Éphraim and Miles glare at Selim for not reading Leon's saddened expression properly. Leon looks away and sighs.

Éphraim then turns to Néol, still spinning the teal pinwheel with his mind. "And I know you're not one to ask, but your family is also doing well. None of them have really asked about where you've been. They assume that you've been taking care of yourself."

"It's better that way," Néol says. "Thanks."

"And…" Leon asks. "Where were we? You said you'd explain once we left."

Éphraim replies, "We were in a world between Earth and Heart."

Leon puts his hand to his chin. "It looked like Jupiter…and then Neptune at other points. The sky kept changing."

Éphraim shakes his head. "It was neither of the two. But in terms of colors—I suppose they are very similar. You probably noticed that the climate was warm when the sky was red, but then after the great white flash it would switch to a blue sky, bringing wintry weather. That is the strange and bizarre pattern of that world."

Leon says, "I'm gonna ask you more about that when I'm more awake…I'm sorry…I'm really," he yawns, "sleepy."

"Can't blame you," Éphraim says. "Well, rest up. We've got maybe one hour's left of a drive, right Selim?"

Selim nods in agreement.

"Say…" Leon sleepily asks. "Where are we going?"

"Your new home," Miles replies.

Home… Leon thinks, his eyes fluttering as he drifts off. *I wonder…will I actually be safe there?*

☾   ☾   ☾

<u>Planet Heart</u>

<u>August 7, 2009 (Friday)</u>

<u>Odaroloc ∧ Nepsa</u>

<u>Deleantur Estates</u>

<u>10:15 p.m.</u>

Father nature is booming. A thunderstorm rages, raining mercilessly and producing constant thunder. Rain bullets toward the ground—making for a smooth ambience for people like Leon to sleep through. Leon awakens again—but atop a bed. A real bed.

Leon opens his eyes and slowly sits up. "That was the best rest I took in a while…" He looks around him to see a twin bed, much like his own, to the right of him. Néol is sitting atop it with his back against the headrest.

Miles pushes open the bedroom door and says, "Oh. You're awake."

"Yeah… Where am I?"

"Welcome to *Deleantur Estates*. This is the place I told you about…the one Stefano bought for everyone."

Leon looks down, remembering that Stefano is still back at that citadel. "Stefano," Leon says, "why did he—"

Miles looks away. "We talked about this, Leon. He made a sacrifice. He did it for us all."

Leon looks away. "Right. He wants us to find Hell and save everyone there." He lets out a sigh.

Miles clears his throat and continues as if Leon never interrupted him. "The bed you're on is yours. And to your right, is Néol's."

"Miles," Leon says, "what's next? We find Hell, we save Stefano, then what? Are we really stuck here? On Heart?"

"Until this is all resolved, I suppose we are," Miles says, leaning his back on the dresser behind him. "And—you went to Festano's lair, you saw his army for yourself. You saw what we're really up against…" Miles looks Leon firmly in the eye. "If you want to run back home once again, they're who you'll have to answer to."

Leon lets out a deep sigh. *I don't want to just go home. I want to tell them the truth… I want to tell them everything. The longer I wait, the longer they'll be hurt.*

Néol looks at Leon as he thinks this.

Leon continues in thought, *And one day I will.*

Miles narrows his eyes then glances at Néol. "What's he thinking over there, Néol?"

Néol snickers. "Oh just something about wanting to go home like usual."

"Gee, thanks for selling me out," Leon says, turning away from the two of them.

Miles chuckles. "Now that you two are back, we have to keep you being locked up a secret. Other Neo Knights will be angry if they find out that *only* you two were saved," Miles sighs.

Éphraim knocks and then enters. "Oh. I didn't know you two would still be up," he says as he stretches and looks at Leon and Néol. "Well, you two, it's been a pleasure. I'm going to get some *eye-shut* after that little venture. I'm starting to get a bit of a headache. But. It's good seeing you two again. We bought *plenty* of groceries while preparing for your return. So, there's a *lot* of food. We'll be making breakfast in the morning for you, too."

Leon smiles. Néol grins and then looks away.

"But you both need to shower before you do anything else," Selim says, holding his nose.

"Selim," Miles says, "they're exhausted. Let them rest."

"Oh, fine. But you guys are gonna wash your own sheets, then. I'm pretty beat, too."

"Any questions?" Miles asks, looking at the two reflections.

Leon sighs. "No...I guess...we just have to wait and see what happens."

Miles and Selim walk to the doorway. Miles says, "Well. More like pray for the Lunae Lux not to find us is *really* what we should do."

"Goodnight," Selim and Miles both say, shutting off the light.

After about ten minutes, Leon hears rustling from Néol's bed. Néol steps out of the bedroom and finds Selim and Éphraim at the door, both have their shoes on for some strange reason.

"Perfect timing," Néol says. "If I'm gonna be staying here, one of you has to go and get me cigarettes."

Éphraim chuckles. "Sure, what kind, Néol?"

"*Oroblam Blues*. Mild. Thanks. And a red lighter, too." Néol grabs a wallet from his pocket and hands Éphraim thirty ASUs.

Néol walks back to his and Leon's room, and calmly lies in bed. About thirty minutes later, Selim returns using the light from the hallway to see into the dark bedroom and tosses both the lighter and cigarette box to Néol. While under the covers, Leon groggily opens one eye. He hears the rustling of the plastic that is wrapped around the cigarette box.

Of course he's opening it now, Leon thinks. *Wait a second. No, he isn't...he is* not *gonna light that in here.*

"Yes I am," Néol says aloud.

"Néol! Seriously? Inside?" Leon shouts, kicking the blanket off of him.

403

"I have the window open."

"No, dude!" Leon shouts, slapping the lit cigarette out of his hand. Its blazing end lands on the end of the curtain.

"You'd better pick that up!" Néol shouts back, shoving Leon down to the bed.

Meanwhile, Selim and Éphraim are both watching this fight from inside their van. It appears they have surveillance cameras that are showing them this quarrel through a computer screen.

"YES!" Selim shouts. "Hasn't even been a whole day and those two are fighting again. Miles owes me pineapple juice."

Éphraim yawns. "I suppose you woke me up for a good reason then… I'll go put out the fire."

"Wait!" Selim shouts, staring at the footage on his screen. "They're putting it out! *Together!*"

Éphraim smiles. "Hmm. I suppose it'll take a while…but perhaps *someday* they'll be like you and Miles."

"Eh. Maybe not. These two are like fire and ice. But who knows. Maybe they can make that work for them."

"True enough," Éphraim says, rubbing his forehead while slightly grunting.

"You okay?" Selim asks.

"Yeah. I'm alright. Just a tiny headache is all. Let's head back inside. I think we can say for sure that no one's followed us."

"Yeah, good call."

The two exit Éphraim's black van, cross the large crow-less parking lot filled with cars, enter the apartment complex, ride the elevator all the way back up to the eighteenth floor, and enter their apartment. Selim and Éphraim wish one another a goodnight then split off. Selim returns to his and Miles's bedroom, while Éphraim lies back on the living room sofa. He lies there for a few hours. But for some reason…he hears something in his mind…

…He followed power…

…He followed power…

…He followed power…

…He followed power…

…He followed power…

…He followed power…

…You will pay…

"What the…" Éphraim mutters, sitting up in the dark living room. "Why am I hearing voices? It sounded…like they were buzzing in my ears…" He shakes his head, massaging his aching forehead. "I'm tired. Sleepy from…all the traveling." He lies back down, feeling for something in his sides.

"I knew something was wrong. I forgot my pinwheel in the van. Won't be able to sleep without it…"

Éphraim gets up and grabs the doorknob when suddenly all the lights shut off.

"What?"

Shrill screams can be heard echoing in the apartment hallways. Miles bursts out of his bedroom door with his phone in hand, and he says, "Yes, I can hear you, Toni. What's happening? What? Slow down!" Toni's voice is drowned out by the screaming in her apartment.

405

Toni shouts on the phone, *Meet me at my apartment! Hurry!* Then the call ends.

Éphraim watches him, concerned. "Everything okay? What's going on?"

"Éphraim—we *were* followed…"

Éphraim nods, then tries flicking the light switch again, but Miles says, "They cut our power." Miles starts shaking.

And now…

It's time for you all to meet your end…

Miles holds his head. "No, no, no, not now! They just made it back. They just made it back!"

Éphraim tightly grabs Miles' shoulders. "Hey. Stay with me, Miles. Be strong. Round Selim and the others up. Make as *little* noise as possible. I'll go outside and see what's happening." Éphraim grabs his boots and steps out the door.

Miles looks left and right around him, using his reacher as a source of light. He opens the door and shouts, "Wait, Éphraim! Don't forget your spear!" He slams the door.

Éphraim gently opens the door to whisper, "*Miles…I can summon Doubtly Fruitful anywhere…remember?*"

"Sorry. I'm not thinking clearly…"

"*It'll be okay, Miles. As long as I'm here. Everything will be fine.*"

"Forgetting is not a sin, it is a virtue."

-(°.-ƎE-.)-

To be continued in:

PLANET EARTH /\ PLANET HEART
[DATA LOG]

[IF YOU LOOK UP THESE DATES, YOU'LL FIND THAT THEY CORRESPOND TO THE MOON'S ACTUAL POSITION]

[Chapter 1: Forgotten Names & Faces]

December 9, 2009 (Wednesday) /\ June 9, 2009 (Tuesday)

[Chapter 2: The Voice In My Mind]

December 10, 2009 (Thursday) /\ June 10, 2009 (Wednesday)

[Chapter 3: Marks of The Chosen]

December 10, 2009 (Thursday) /\ June 10, 2009 (Wednesday)

[Chapter 4: A Forgotten Moonlit Night]

December 10, 2009 (Thursday) /\ June 10, 2009 (Wednesday)

December 11, 2009 (Friday) /\ June 11, 2009 (Thursday)

[Chapter 5: Man In The Mirror]

December 11, 2009 (Friday) /\ June 11, 2009 (Thursday)

[Chapter 6: A Second Birthday]

December 12, 2009 (Saturday) /\ June 12, 2009 (Friday)

[Chapter 7: Into The Mirror]

Day 1-December 13, 2009 (Sunday) ∧ June 13, 2009 (Saturday)

Day 2-December 14, 2009 (Monday) ∧ June 14, 2009 (Sunday)

Day 3-December 15, 2009 (Tuesday) ∧ June 15, 2009 (Monday)

Day 4-December 16, 2009 (Wednesday) ∧ June 16, 2009 (Tuesday)

Day 5-December 17, 2009 (Thursday) ∧ June 17, 2009 (Wednesday)

Day 6-December 18, 2009 (Friday) ∧ June 18, 2009 (Thursday)

Day 7-December 19, 2009 (Saturday) ∧ June 19, 2009 (Friday)

Day 8-December 20, 2009 (Sunday) ∧ June 20, 2009 (Saturday)

Day 9-December 21, 2009 (Monday) ∧ June 21, 2009 (Sunday)

Day 10-December 22, 2009 (Tuesday) ∧ June 22, 2009 (Monday)

Day 11-December 23, 2009 (Wednesday) ∧ June 23, 2009 (Tuesday)

Day 12-December 24, 2009 (Thursday) ∧ June 24, 2009 (Wednesday)

Day 13-December 25, 2009 (Friday) ∧ June 25, 2009 (Thursday)

Day 14-December 26, 2009 (Saturday) ∧ June 26, 2009 (Friday)

Day 15-December 27, 2009 (Sunday) ∧ June 27, 2009 (Saturday)

[Chapter 8: Fluid Bodies & Faces]

December 28, 2009 (Monday) ∧ June 28, 2009) (Sunday)

[Chapter 9: Black Feathers Flock Together]

December 29, 2009 (Tuesday) ∧ June 29, 2009 (Monday)

[Chapter 10: Another Side]

December 30, 2009 (Wednesday) ∧ June 30, 2009 (Tuesday)

[Chapter 11: Meeting Ground]

December 31, 2009 (Thursday) ∧ July 1, 2009 (Wednesday)

[Chapter 12: The Child Who Smiled]

December 31, 2009 (Thursday) ∧ July 1, 2009 (Wednesday)

[Chapter 13: Mirrored Siblings]

January 1, 2010 (Sunday) ∧ July 2, 2009 (Thursday)

409

[Chapter 14: Half Truths]

January 1, 2010 (Sunday) ∧ July 2, 2009 (Thursday)

[Chapter 15: Boy Called God]

January 2, 2010 (Saturday) ∧ July 3, 2009 (Friday)

[Chapter 16: Home Is Where the Earth Is]

January 2, 2010 (Saturday) ∧ July 3, 2009 (Friday)

[Chapter 17: The Unseen Blot]

January 2, 2010 (Saturday) ∧ July 3, 2009 (Friday)

[Chapter 18: A Hybrid's Value]

January 22, 2010 (Friday) ∧ July 23, 2009 (Thursday)

[Chapter 19: Two Sides | One Story]

?????????????????????????????????

[Chapter 20: Two Minds | One Series]

February 6, 2010, (Saturday) ∧ August 7, 2009 (Friday)

STAFF ROLL

Allie S. Reincath ∧ Ellia K. Hactneir
Laurel L. Giro ∧ Allure E. Igor
Leon J. Granttley ∧ Néol N. Yelltnarg

Amy A. Granttley ∧ May A.Yelltnarg
Jason K. Garcia ∧ Jonas B. Aicrag
Deen J. Schutz ∧ Eden È. Zutsch
Jacaline A. Rivas ∧ Anjelica M. Savir

Miles S. C. Lee ∧ Selim N. G. Elé
Ombretta K. Erembol ∧ Rettabom A. A. Lobmere

Etay Lerrence ∧ Yate Ecnerrel
Hades Miranda ∧ Sadeh Adnarim
Alecia Flowers ∧ Caelia Srewolf

Wilma Monica ∧ Milaw Acinom
Noire
Thorne
Faviané
Elder Laither

Obi Blake ∧ Iob Ekalb
Scott Aivlove ∧ Totcs Evoliva
Lisa Miller ∧ Asil Rellim

Nero F. Granttley ∧ Oren S. Yelltnarg
Silvia P. Granttley ∧ Aivlis L. Yelltnarg

Stefano S. Giro ∧ Festano V. Igor

Ellen Hilroy ∧ Nelle Yorlih
Caleb Samee ∧ Belac Esame
Toni M. Perreco ∧ Iont E. Ocerrep
Tenny G. ∧ Yennt Y.
Aepis O. Cordelia ∧ Sepia A. Ailedroc
Rob Scudero ∧ Orb Oreducs
Èphraim L. Desruc
Nora M. Giro ∧ Aron A. Igor

Master QR Code

ALL CHARACTERS

ALL REFLECTION PRINCIPLES

Pronunciation Guide

- Faviané is pronounced: Fay-vee-awn-aye
- Laither is pronounced: Lay-ther
- Iont is pronounced: I-ownt
- Aepis is pronounced: I-piz
- Éphraim is pronounced: Ay-fra-ham
- Lovyam is pronounced: Law-vee-am

Ratings help our stories reach new eyes.

When you finish, I would love nothing more than to hear what you've thought of the story.

Your thoughts (good or bad) will only make the series stronger. When you finish *The Other Side*, please be sure to leave us a rating and review!

About The Author(s)

<u>Justin Jay Gladstone</u> was born in New York within the Bronx. He left for Pennsylvania when he was eight years old. He has been writing stories for as long as he can remember. He is the active writer for *The Other Side*.

He develops relationships for the protagonists in the series as well as characters from Planet Earth. His work is more affiliated with everything that is more immediate.

Nitsuj Yaj Enotsdalg is the co-author and director of the series. For the past fourteen years, he has focused on the over-arching scope of the series, as well as each of the antagonists and characters from Planet Heart. He has written more than eight books that take place after this one. He has also published each of the rules to *Equilibrium & Chaos*.

Lightning Source UK Ltd.
Milton Keynes UK
UKHW010710180223
417179UK00001B/123